DRAGON FANG

Also by Joseph P. Cody

THE TIGER'S FURY

HUBOT - Human Robot

METANOIA - Total Conversion

PHANTOM TEAM

WILD VIOLETS - Growing Up
In The 1940s And 50s

DRAGON FANG

JOSEPH P. CODY

A Thriller

Autotech Industries

St. Paul, Minnesota

This book is written, printed, and bound in the United States of America

First Edition: December 2008

ISBN-13: 978-0-9791167-3-5
ISBN-10: 0-9791167-3-2

A Publication of:

Autotech Industries
688 – 11th Avenue NW
St. Paul, Minnesota 55112

Note: Autotech Industries is a publisher; it does not sell books. This and other books by Joseph P. Cody may be purchased from Amazon.com or any book store.

To my family for their forbearance through the many hours of writing.

— 1 —

July 6, NSA, Fort Mead, Maryland

"Beep, beep . . . beep." The cadence of the three beeps indicated a priority signal intercept had arrived. Greg Daley was unaware of anything happening in the room except for what he saw on his monitor. In a hushed triumphant voice he said, "He's got it!" Phase one of operation *fishhook* had been completed.

Daley worked for the National Security Agency as a signals analyst for North Africa with emphasis on Libya. The message intercept that held such interest to Daley was an airline reservation being made by a CIA operative, one Amir Massof, to fly from Tripoli to Cairo. It announced the successful completion of a clandestine operation in Tripoli that resulted in a copy of the Chinese document, *mirage*, being transferred to Massof from a Chinese national who was in that city as part of a military delegation. The intelligence agencies of the United States government were certain they had obtained the ultra-secret protocol without the Chinese knowing it.

Through the past week Daley had spent many stressful hours working with an agent in the CIA as operation *fishhook* was put together. Daley became involved to set up message formats, names, and key works in the massive NSA computers so the transfer of the sensitive document would be known through the agency's signals intercept capability.

Phase two of the operation involved getting the document to CIA headquarters in Langley, Virginia. Continued monitoring of electronic traffic would track the man carrying the document as he made his way to Langley. Daley quickly sent a message to his counterpart at the CIA, Yousuf Hamoud, as well as his division head. Hamoud had been extremely difficult at times, though Daley had to admire his fluent knowledge of proper Arabic as well as many dialects from Libya to Iran while he struggled with Arabic as a second language.

As the plane made its way to Cairo all communications by the pilot, phone calls made by passengers, and other communications, radio, telephone, Internet, everything, in that part of the world would be screened to be sure there was no attempt to impede Mr. Massof's travels. The NSA made these intercepts routinely, but today there would be special attention by the analysts for any suspicious traffic.

Since the time of the hand over of *mirage* could not be know in advance, provisions were made to make reservations for connecting flights while Massof was en route to Cairo. These flights would terminate at Dulles Airport outside Washington, D.C. Within a half hour the itinerary was set. Other signals analysts at the NSA would soon get into the act tracking Massof as he left Cairo destined for Shipole Airport near Amsterdam, and from there to Dulles. In Cairo, he would use another identity, and still another in Amsterdam. Daley was the only person in the NSA who knew these names. In the CIA only Hamoud's direct supervisor knew them. The other people working operation *fishhook* knew enough of the operation to do their part and no more. There had been leaks of information on sensitive operations lately, and no chances were being taken on this one.

As soon as Massof's travel plans were set, Yousuf Hamoud alerted the stations in the two intermediate cities that phase two of operation *fishhook* had commenced. Field agents would maintain discrete surveillance of the courier as he changed planes in their respective cities.

As Hamoud ate that last of his half-eaten sandwich left from lunch he slipped a pill into his mouth with the last bite, and washed it down with a gulp of cold coffee. Predictably, seven minutes after taking the pill he got severe stomach cramps and headed to the men's room where he threw up. A few minutes later he arrived back at his workstation looking like a ghost. He said the sandwich he bought on the way to work must have been tainted, and he was worthless for the rest of the day. Reluctantly, his supervisor let him go home. Hamoud promised to return as soon as he was able, though he knew he would be replaced for the remainder of the operation. As Hamoud walked past a water cooler in the hall he put a second pill in his mouth and took a few swallows of water. The antidote would take effect in eight to twelve minutes.

Ten miles from the CIA compound Hamoud pulled into a parking lot by a jogging trail. Using the untraceable cell phone his handler had paced at his disposal he pressed the first preprogrammed speed dial number. "Yes," the person on the other end answered with a heavy Asian accent.

"We have acquired a bottle of rare wine as you requested." Both parties of the phone call knew not to mention *mirage*, and to use code words lest their conversation be flagged by the NSA. "It will arrive at Dulles from Shipole on KLM Flight 974 tomorrow. Our mutual acquaintance will send it over with a friend but failed to mention the friend's name." This meant that Hamoud did not know the identity Massof would be using on the connecting flights. As he spoke, he noticed he was beginning to feel human again. They weren't kidding. Those pills would do the job.

"Yes, that is good so far. You must get the friend's name!" was the terse reply.

"Hey. Stop pushing. I got you what I could. I had to take one of those horrid pills to get out in time to get you this much. You wanted the earliest possible alert. Well, you got it. If I had stayed around a few more hours I might have gotten more!"

"Watch the way you talk to me!" This was an admonishment not to say too much. "This is not enough. This is vital! We must have more information!" the voice spat back in vicious demand.

Hamoud was taken aback. "Back off. I got you this much. And, I did get you *the list* awhile back, didn't I? I've done a good job for you. I don't own the place! Anyway, from here on it's out of my hands." They both knew that when Hamoud returned the next day he would not be on this operation any more. They didn't change personnel any more than necessary on important projects to prevent someone from doing exactly what he was doing.

There was a pause on the other end of the phone followed by, "Are you positive this is the man with the item?"

What was certain to Hamoud was not to his handler. "This was my project until I got sick today. I was in on all of the planning. The big bosses know they are getting something important. Once the plane gets on the ground Customs will be all over it, if you get my meaning." This meant there would be a phalanx of CIA agents around the courier until they got him safely to headquarters at Langley." To add emphases he added, "This is the guy, and he has it. You can count on that."

"This had better be right. If you get any more information, call the other number. There will always be someone to answer the phone."

Hamoud hung up the phone and pulled out of the parking area. As he drove to his apartment, he hardly noticed where he was going. Here he was, in it again. He hated it and loved it at the same time—working both sides. He nearly made his big score with Iraq a few years back while working for the CIA in Saudi Arabia. If it hadn't been for that tank commander he would have made enough to retire. That operation had fallen apart so badly he had been forced to drop out of sight to keep from being chewed up in the aftermath. Almost daily he ran through those events in his mind. Sooner or later he'd figure it out.

He was glad to be in the U.S. with its "anything goes" lifestyle. When he approached the CIA to come to work for them again, they wanted to put him back in the Middle East. He convinced them that he had been compromised on the Iraqi operation. He would be walking around with a target on his back if he were to return to that part of the world. This he knew to be an understatement if anything. What he had somehow forgotten to tell the CIA was that he had made a deal with the Chinese to go in as a mole before making reapplication to Langley. In the past the CIA would have looked upon him as a bad bet because of his history. Poor CIA. Life can be so difficult at times. After that nasty September 11, 2001, thing they were in a bind for the language skills he possessed. He was snapped up.

The list he'd obtained for his handler advanced him a long way toward his goal of early retirement while still among the living. It was valuable and he knew it, so he held out for, and received, a good chunk of cash. It was a list of the CIA operatives in the Pacific Rim, especially China. When the project to get *mirage* made the connection with the man going to Libya he was called in because of his skills in the Arabic language and culture. This started him working with operatives in China, which gave him access to the list.

The owner of the voice on the other end of Hamoud's phone call, Allen Wu, arrived at the Chinese embassy in Washington twenty minutes later. Along the way his BlackBerry alerted him that he had a message. After passing through security he went immediately to his work area. The text message was from yet another operative confirming the information he had gotten from Hamoud. Here again, the courier's name was not known. He had to go with what he had so went to the communications section and placed a secure call to China.

In Beijing the call was transferred to the Zhongnanhai compound. Zhongnanhai was the two-hundred-fifty acre fortified enclave where

China's ruling elite resided. It was walking distance from Tiananmen Square. Sang Dingfei, director of the Chinese Secret Intelligence Service, CSIS, took the call in the early morning.

Only seven men knew the content of *mirage*. These were Chairman Kang Jyan, China's supreme leader, and six members of the Politburo, including Dingfei, who shared Jyan's view of the future of China. Seven copies of the document had been used at the meeting where the plan was discussed and approved. Normally such a sensitive subject would not have been committed to writing. But, this one was involved enough that each man needed to study it in detail.

After the plan of action was agreed upon Dingfei was ordered to destroy all but the Chairman's copy. This he had done in the presence of a witness. As was the ironclad policy, Dingfei carefully checked the document number, and the copy number as they were being burned. Through the use of the operative list Dingfei had received from his informer in the CIA, he was able to determine that in spite of the precautions, a copy of *mirage* was being ferreted out of the country. As with any document, it required someone to type it, reviews made, followed by revisions, more typing, and finally copies made and distributed. In the process a copy disappeared. The search for the one responsible for this security breach would likely take some time. Unquestionably, the hunt would end in a bloody accounting.

Dingfei had lost the trail of the missing document until the name was found in a communications intercept from Tripoli. He quickly narrowed the search to a Chinese engineer there on a military assignment. That man mysteriously died before Dingfei's agents could get to him and make him talk. They might have lost the trail again if it had not been for their informant in the CIA.

As Dingfei entered Jyan's quarters, he was struck as always by the lack of lavishness he saw. To be sure, they were comfortable with every amenity, and sized for the entertaining he did both professionally and socially. Yet, there was no more than needed.

"Sir, I am sorry to disturb you, but there is an urgent matter that has come up and the solution requires your approval."

The Chairman was in a robe and slippers making coffee. In his late sixties he looked the part of an aging Chinese warrior, which in fact he was. He came from one of the top ruling families, but as the third son he was not seen as a likely leader. His training was in military operations and martial arts. In his twisted path to power, he used these skills to

eliminate opponents with remorseless treachery. In the process he became a hardened man with no vestige of happiness in his life. He was
fond of Dingfei who he had hand picked for the job. This didn't mean he
wouldn't have his head cut off at the slightest infraction.

The two of them had discussed the possibility that *mirage* had been
compromised on a previous occasion. This was so vital that Dingfei had
been assigned to handle its recovery or destruction personally.

"Yes, you have information on *mirage*, I presume."

Looking a little uncomfortable Dingfei replied, "Yes sir, I do. We
have learned an operative of the CIA is on his way to deliver it to the
Americans in Washington, D.C."

"Can this operative be intercepted and eliminated?"

"Unfortunately, that does not seem possible. We know he will be on
KLM Flight 974 from Amsterdam to Dulles Airport between Baltimore
and Washington. We do not know his identity." Dingfei paused being
reticent to proceed with the logic of the situation. Then he continued to
make his case. "Profiling the likely courier and eliminating anyone who
fits the description would not be completely sure. Even the extreme
measure of killing everyone in the Shipole terminal waiting to get on the
plane by a suicide attack would not suffice. We must eliminate everyone
who actually gets on that plane, which means destroying the plane in
flight. Since we do not have the assets in place to do that in any conven-
tional way, I see no alternative other than invoking Dragon Fang to stop
the plane."

The Chairman's eyes flashed. "That was only meant to be used once!
What if they learn of it?"

Dingfei had expected no less of a response. "If the plane is not destroyed we will have no further use for Dragon Fang. It is an enigma.
However, our source in the CIA will be able to learn if they suspect how
the plane was destroyed. If they fail to discover it, we will be free to use
it again."

Jyan leaned back in his comfortable stuffed chair. "And if they do
discover China was behind it we will be made an international pariah
rather than the devil United States." Jyan pondered the situation. He had
not gotten where he was without taking risks, many much greater than
this. Perhaps, it would not be too bad a thing for China to be an outcast
for a decade or so at this point. His country was becoming westernized at
an alarming rate.

He looked at Dingfei for a long minute before he replied. "I agree we must ensure *mirage* does not fall into Western hands. Is your information actionable?

"Yes, sir. It is good. Our operative at the CIA has been above ninety percent. In addition, the flight number and date have been corroborated by our agent in the NSA. He has been very good, though relatively new. We give it ninety-eight percent probably of being true."

In intelligence gathering each agent was rated on the accuracy of his information. If only absolutely certain facts were acceptable little would be learned. It was axiomatic that no data would be used to instigate action unless it was confirmed by at least one other source. Two well placed sources with good track records made this information nearly certain.

Jyan nodded. "You may invoke Dragon Fang if there is no other way." With that, he flicked his index finger and Yang knew the meeting was over.

Mirage, like similar plans in international chess, was born of necessity. This one was caused by a major breakthrough in something called nanotechnology. Chairman Kang Jyan had a good grasp of what it would mean to world politics but only a fuzzy idea of the technology itself. If it met only a tenth of what was promised, the plans he had made would be justified. In fact, few people in the world knew the exact details of the breakthrough. Three genius scientists managed to get together and pool their training, experience, and brainpower. They discovered a way to make things one molecule at a time, which was the real meaning of nanotechnology. This would make desk top computers possible with millions of times more computing power than now existed, and super computers of unimagined power.

Computers were only one application. Small machines could be made that were injected into a person's blood. The size of a bacterium, they would swim around in the bodily fluids checking microorganisms. When they met one known to cause disease, they would destroy it. Microscopic machines, nano machines, could work synergistically to build anything from a ball point pen to gem quality diamonds to cell phones to an automobile, all one molecule at a time.

There was one huge drawback with the nano breakthrough. To make the basic tools and building blocks needed to realize the myriad products required a factory, called a foundry in this technology, of unprecedented proportions and expense. It was decided among all of the industrialized nations on the planet that they would pool their resources and build one such foundry. The search for a site was stalemated since there could not be found a place on which all agreed. Finally international politics forced a solution—Taiwan.

Taiwan was selected because it was a small country that could not force its will on any of the other members. Second, it had a thriving semiconductor industry, and its associated infrastructure already. Third, it had a market economy and a democratic government. Finally and most importantly, it was a way of bringing China into the project. By making China a full member of the consortium, China would have a vested interest in seeing the project succeed. It would, as well, keep Taiwan forever as a state independent of China.

Chairman Jyan saw the situation from a different prospective. Even though China was making Herculean efforts to modernize, he knew China's economy was not strong enough to invest the capital needed to compete with other nations to actually realize products from the building blocks the foundry would produce. In fact, China's research and development expenditures were the lowest of any industrialized country. Any excess revenues China produced were poured into building up its military forces to regain the hegemony of its ancient sphere of influence and beyond. He also knew in his heart, not without confirmation from intercepted messages, that a primary reason for Taiwan as the location of the foundry was to specifically keep China from ever claiming its offshore province. China's diplomats had bargained hard to mitigate or remove the latter problem, but to no avail. There had been recent progress behind the scenes on getting the currency of Taiwan changed from the Taiwan dollar to the Taiwan yuan as part of the treaty. But it was doubtful that this concession would have any real effect if the treaty went forward.

There was another reason the chairman did not want the nano treaty to succeed. China had made breakthroughs in the area of using variations of DNA molecules to make many of the same products that nanotechnology promised. It was the other way of doing things—adapt a system that already existed rather than starting over. DNA made something one molecule at a time, too, but in a different way. After all, the DNA molecule not only contained all of the information needed to make the body of the creature it described, but given the right environment, it also had the motivating force to make it happen.

If China could advance its technology, and at the same time delay the advances in nanotechnology, they would be ahead in the race to control the world. For the first time in history that prize was now possible.

Communist Russia tried and collapsed. The United States tried, and at last count was failing. Islam was on the march again, but behind the curve. It was China's time.

Great fanfare was planned for the signing of the international nanotechnology treaty in Washington. This would occur a few weeks from now. All of the signatures but one would be affixed in Washington. The last signature, that of China, would be affixed to it in San Jose, California, the center of Silicon Valley. This was a small quid pro quo that China insisted upon as a symbolic gesture showing that the center of microelectronic technology would now shift to the Far East.

Apparently the U.S. had learned that *mirage* contained information about the treaty, and automatically assumed it gave China's bottom line bargaining position. With this information they would know how far they could push China. In this, they were wrong. Not only were they wrong about the contents of *mirage*, what they specifically did not realize was that they had pushed the Dragon much too far already.

With Massof safely on his way from Cairo to Amsterdam Greg Daley turned over his part of the mission to an understudy for North African signals analysis. In his twenties, Daley had developed a good career path in the National Security Agency. His natural intelligence along with a generally laid back personality permitted him to work productively for one of the most invasive agencies anywhere. His successful dogging of those strange messages from the desert of Libya while he was still a trainee that had uncovered the totally unknown chemical weapons program in Iraq had gotten him noticed. As his family continued to grow he had incentive to parley that into a good resume, which at the NSA meant rapid advancement.

He was aware his employer could learn anything they wanted to know about anyone on earth. This of course included its own employees. That they knew his financial affairs up to the minute, he took for granted. He even commented to his wife at times that they probably knew the brand of underwear he wore. He had not expected that there was an ever present threat to their operations from moles, operatives from other governments or even other agencies within the U.S. government. If the NSA had such extensive data gathering prowess, how was this possible? At first it seemed ridiculous. But after a few years, he began to realize that in an organization that employed at least a hundred-thousand official

NSA employees, and nearly as many as employees of other major aerospace and software companies, there were not enough resources to eliminate the problem. It was one thing to have the data available, quite another to analyze it and draw conclusions about the trust worthiness of each employee on a weekly or monthly basis.

A relatively little noticed event a few weeks before had left Daley stunned. A man who had been in the group of inductees with him had been killed while crossing a street by what was reported as a hit-and-run drunken driver. He and Daley had become friends as they went through the barrage of tests and evaluations together. During their training period they were in many of the same classes. After that they ran into each other from time to time and would chat over a cup of coffee. On their last meeting they had lunch together. Daley's friend had mentioned in hushed tones that he knew of a mole in the CIA and planned to go to Internal Affairs with his information after he found one more piece of evidence. The next day Daley learned of the accident.

The implications of this were obvious to Daley. There had to be someone else in the NSA who knew about the mole in the CIA, and this person was necessarily a mole himself. Daley's friend was of Chinese extraction and as such had been a signals analyst for China. He assumed that meant the NSA mole was in the Far East division.

Mainly, it left Daley with the certain feeling that nobody could be trusted in this business. He conducted his affairs as openly as possible. He hoped this would project the image that he never had special information that could be hidden if he were to disappear. But, it was the nature of the business to uncover secrets. At times he put together some pretty radical implications from intercepts he ran across. Until he had enough information to put his ideas into a credible report he said nothing to anybody. But, he had to store the pieces of information in computer files as he was putting together his reports. These could be accessed by anyone with clearance, and wrong conclusions could be reached.

As Daley left the building this day he felt rung out. Things had gone as planned, and he was pleased with the results. But, the stress of watching for the unexpected had taken its toll, and he looked forward to the evening with his family.

— 2 —

Seven hours after Flight 974 took off from Amsterdam, a nondescript light blue panel van drove east on Interstate Highway I-495 on Long Island, New York. The driver was Roger Ling, a commodities broker of twenty-eight who had arrived in the New York area ten years before. Having been raised in Shanghai, the New York area suited him fine. Though he was fluent in Mandarin, there was only a hint of it in his otherwise New Yorker accent. The man in the back of the van, Fred Wengie, had arrived in the U.S. two years before from the rural areas not far from Beijing.

Ling asked, "How's the cell phone coming back there? I'm only ten minutes from our prime deployment location."

Wengie was carefully checking the connections to a stolen cell phone he had in pieces on the special workbench behind the front seats. All of the equipment immediately around him was proper to his profession of communications specialist. His English was acceptable, but he spoke in his more comfortable native tongue as the tension mounted. "Nearly there. Don't push me or I will make a mistake." A few minutes later he said, "There, time for a trial call." He typed commands on the laptop computer near the bench. The phone wire from the back of the computer was connected to the cell phone. A second cable from the phone connected to the standard vehicle cell phone antenna on the van. The computer dialed the information number of the local library. As soon as there was an answer he severed the connection. "Communications check completed. Now all you have to do is get us to the deployment location without being stopped by the police."

Wengie was apprehensive about what was to come. When he was approached several months before to do work for his homeland he knew that if he refused there would be repercussions for his relatives back in

China. This he did not want, especially because he hoped to get permission to bring his mother and brother to the U.S., too. Until now the work had been easy, nothing more than training on the computer he had been given.

Suddenly, Wengie was brought back to the job at hand by having to brace himself as the van swung sharply around. They were in a deserted parking lot in the rear of a two story building with no windows in the back. The van stopped, and with a jerk started backing, then stopped again.

The July sun was less than an hour from setting and everyone who worked in the building associated with the parking lot had gone home. The whole New York area was under a large high pressure system which was good news for Wengie. His task this evening would be easier with no clouds to worry about, though it would offer them more risk of being caught.

Leaving the engine running, Ling was out of his seat instantly. Squeezing past Wengie, he went to the rear of the van. The equipment there was not at all proper to Wengie's profession. It included complicated and precise optical instruments. The van was equipped with a standard looking air intake scoop on the roof near the rear. Its purpose was far more sinister. As Ling turned a wheel the air scoop rose eight inches and turned to the rear. After a few adjustments a keying device snapped into place. This aligned the optical path of the instruments with a mirror in the air scoop.

The instruments consisted of a large telescope with a heavy tubular device beside it mounted coaxially with the telescope. The telescope had an infrared eyepiece that could be interchanged with a normal one by pressing a lever. The portentous looking device attached to the telescope was an infrared laser. The laser was not intense enough to do damage, but more than adequate to illuminate a target with coded pulses. The homing device on a certain projectile was equipped with a sensor programmed to guide itself to a collision course with the item the laser illuminated.

As power supplies were turned on, the van's engine automatically increased in speed to operate its oversized alternator for power. Wengie took his place in a low seat behind the telescope. By means of a joy stick, he rotated the air scoop and changed the angle of the mirror to aim the sighting path of both the telescope and the laser until a radio tower several miles away was in the crosshairs of the eyepiece. Switching to the infrared mode of the telescope, he briefly pressed the laser button. He saw the reflection from the tower. "Laser's up," Wengie commented, followed by, "twenty minutes to expected intercept point."

Sitting on a box with a small tray across his legs, Ling was intent on the laptop computer screen as Wengie turned on two scanner radios. Both were set to scan a small number of air traffic controller frequencies. As each stopped at a radio transmission Wengie listened until he heard the flight number. If it was not 974 he pressed the button for it to continue scanning.

As Ling booted up a special program, he nudged Wengie. "Hey Fred, take a look at the graphics on this program. Somebody went to a mess of trouble to make it look fancy." The first screen showed a coiled up dragon with satellites going around it like the pictorial of an atom with the dragon as the nucleus and the satellites as electrons. A banner across the bottom displayed DRAGON FANG. Next appeared a screen with the earth and several nearly polar orbits around it and two satellites in each orbit. Having little knowledge of technical matters, Ling drew no further inference from the display. Now on a bar across the bottom of the screen appeared the following: "Enter coordinates of intercept point."

Ling took a slip of paper out of his pocket with numbers received earlier in the day. He entered 72° 34' W, 40° 41' N. The program responded with "Intercept point located six kilometers off Westhampton Beach, Long Island, New York, USA, in Atlantic Ocean. Is target moving or stationary?"

Ling clicked in the moving block. It responded, "Airborne, or sea?"

Moving the cursor he clicked in the airborne block.

The next prompt from the computer was, "Fang presently in strike window, optimum strike position in 18 minutes, leave striking window in 27 minutes. Do you wish to initiate strike sequence? Yes, No."

Ling clicked on "Yes."

A band of text immediately appeared in the center of the screen. "Telephone connection software and hardware available. Initiating telephone chain call for strike authentication. Approximate time 2.5 minutes. Please wait." Immediately Ling heard the tones of a phone being dialed. These signals were sent to the cell phone Wengie had altered.

A new screen appeared. At the top were the words "Authentication connection being established with Dragon Fang." Below it was a graphic of the earth with communications satellites around it. The connection to the local phone system was depicted with the sound of the oscillator making the ringing sound on the line. Immediately the phone on the other end was "picked up" in Hoboken, New Jersey, by a computer followed by

a five second series of tones like a fax being sent. This was followed by
more dial tones and the oscillator. The display showed a link to a phone
in Manhattan, and then following a similar sequence to a satellite, then to
another satellite, followed by a down link to Madrid, Spain. These connections occurred in seconds. The process was repeated by another
phone call to the other side of Madrid. In the graphics a dot changed
from gray to white as each step in the process was completed. On the
other side of Madrid there was a pickup sound again. This was followed
by yet another call. This one ended across the Mediterranean in Tripoli,
Libya.

Fred broke into Roger's concentration, "That's it. Flight 974 contacted Nantucket. He's coming on down the highway in the sky, Jet
Route J62. J62 goes from the VORTAC at Nantucket to the one at Rob-
binsville, New Jersey, and passes five or six kilometers off shore from
us. That's a common route from Northern Europe to Dulles. Let's see,
we're about two-hundred kilometers from the Nantucket VORTAC so I
should be able to pick him up visually in ten to twelve minutes."

Wengie waited a bit and switched the telescope to low power and infrared to locate the plane. Had the sky been cloudy, Wengie would have
extended a highly accurate directional radio antenna to locate the aircraft.
The anti-collision beacon on the target plane would have then been used
to aim the laser. There was no reason to extend the directional antenna
now and draw more attention to themselves than necessary.

When Ling looked back at his computer screen he saw only a message,
"Connection made, authentication processing." A few seconds later another
line of characters appeared, "Authentication complete. Illuminate target."

Ling shook his head as he said, "This is an awfully complicated process to launch a missile at an airplane."

Wengie was scanning the sky at low power where he expected Flight
974 to be. "They don't trust anybody, so it has to be complicated. There,
I think that's it. Yeah, I'm sure, a KLM A340. No other planes in sight.
About twenty kilometers away, coming toward us."

"How can you be sure it's the right plane? They all look alike."

Wengie replied without taking his eye away from the instrument.
"Not to me. I have training equipment in my apartment, sort of like a
computer game. It shows me views of airplanes at all angles and lighting
conditions. With this I practice identifying the airplane type and the airline from the shape and markings. There's also a gadget that I put on my

head like a helmet with small TV sets in it. It works much like this tele-scope so I practice aiming the laser."

After a pause he continued, "There it is. No doubt at all. That's Flight 974 coming right down the old road. No moving around. I don't want the van to move at the wrong time."

After about a minute Ling said, "According to the computer, we should have intercept in thirty-five seconds, with estimated four seconds error either way."

"Okay. Still now. Let's see if they know what they're talking about. Near the end of the time, count down the seconds for me."

After a pause, "Now it's seven, six, five, four, three. . . ."

Wengie pulled his eye away from the eyepiece. "Wow! That was bright!" The interior of the van lit up from the light reflected off the building and through the windshield.

Back at the eyepiece, Wengie put it on low power as he watched a ball of flame expand with debris flying in all directions. Wengie swal-lowed, "When I got a hit in the trainer it never looked like this. It went 'Bong' to say I had scored." In disbelief he trailed on, "It was just a computer game. This is real . . . . I don't feel so good."

Parts of what moments before had been an airplane with two-hundred, thirty-six people on it were still falling to the sea when Ling snapped, "Fred! Move! You know the drill. Get to it!" As he spoke, Ling discon-nected the two scanners and moved them to the front.

Mechanically Wengie flew into a practiced sequence of actions. He flipped off the power switches and uncoupled the air scoop housing from the optics. Following this he set sheets of cardboard into place behind the telescope and laser to give the appearance of boxes piled in the van to anyone who opened the rear doors. Seconds later, both men were in the front seats with Ling driving. He guided the van toward the street and turned left. Cars were pulled over with people standing beside them. Some were pointing and talking excitedly. As rehearsed, Wengie pointed in the direction of the explosion and talked to Ling as if trying to convince him to stop. There was now a large dark smudge in the sky where Flight 974 had met its doom.

––––––––––––––

Wengie wouldn't know about it, but Ling was well aware that this was nearly the same spot where outbound TWA Flight 800 went down.

The system that destroyed that flight was the prototype of this one. It was a kinetic missile from earth orbit. At one time it would have been referred to as a smart rock. Striking the airplane caused the projectile to lose its heat shield so it began to burn on the remainder of its journey to the sea. The immense speed of the weapon made it difficult for an observer to tell if the trail of fire it left in its wake were going up to or down from the plane. Some observers would interpret it as an exhaust plume from a missile launched from a boat homing on the plane since that was the most logical explanation. It was understood that some people would rightly perceive the explosion occurring first. The net effect was several contradictory accounts which left the authorities free to publish any explanation of the event they thought would satisfy the public while leaving the true events, known or suspected, hidden.

Yousuf Hamoud's replacement at the CIA put down the telephone receiver staring ahead in disbelief. "Chief," he said with a crack in his voice, "Chief, it's too much to believe, I mean, what I just heard." He swiveled his chair around to look to his right into the office of his supervisor who was normally called chief.

The supervisor looked out with a puzzled look. "So, spit it out. What did you hear? Try me, I can believe nearly anything," he said with a hint of amusement in his voice. He was thinking it was something like the guy had learned his wife was pregnant. They had been trying long enough.

"Chief, we lost *mirage*. Flight 974 disintegrated a few minutes ago over the Atlantic off Long Island. From the report it didn't crash, it disintegrated in a ball of fire."

A coworker came in, "A minute ago they announced on the TV in the break room that a plane exploded off Long Island. It wouldn't be . . . oh no. It was!" The expressions on the faces of those on duty told the whole story.

The chief was on the phone in an instant with the duty officer. "Call back everyone you can find. We have to move fast before the trail gets cold." In a raised voice he said to his open office door, "Give a call to that group in the NSA and have them work the signals. Especially get that guy that worked this thing in Libya."

"Yeah, you mean Daley at NSA. I've worked with him, seems pretty sharp."

— 3 —

Long Island, New York

On Interstate 495 Roger Ling and Fred Wengie headed back to the city moving along at traffic speed. Wengie had changed the scanner radios to police frequencies and was trying to concentrate on intercepts from two radios at once. This was difficult because the airline explosion produced a lot of traffic.

Ling looked at Wengie as he adjusted the volume on one of the radios. "Relax, Fred, we're okay. All the cops are back there talking to people who saw an explosion in the sky. We're twenty miles from there already. We only have another forty-five miles until we're safely in the garage so we can let things blow over."

"Sure, sure. As long as I don't hear anything about a blue van I'll be happy."

One of the radios stopped at a signal, " . . . van is sought in connection with the aircraft explosion. Boy in Westhampton reported seeing it leave a deserted parking lot seconds after the explosion. Occupants may have witnessed the incident. Stop and question."

Wengie looked up, his eyes about to bulge out. "Someone saw us! They will find us."

"Cool it!" Ling snapped. "They only think we might have seen something. They don't think we did anything. Anyway with any luck we'll be in the garage before any cop sees us."

Officer Cid O'Donnel heard the bulletin about the light blue van as he was driving eastbound on I-495. He looked in his rear view mirror as well as in front as far as he could see. Mostly he scanned the traffic in the westbound lane. As he went around a slight curve he saw a blue van a half-dozen cars in front of him as well as one on the other side of the median. He hit his lights and siren and accelerated into the left lane.

Drivers pulled out of his way as best they could. Even though it was about sunset the traffic was heavy. As he came up on the van in front of him he nailed the license plate and called it in. He didn't think this was the guy, since it was going in the wrong direction. Coming to a crossover he hit his brakes hard nearly getting rear ended by a following car. Squealing his tires he came up to speed in the opposite direction half on the left shoulder and half in the traffic lane. The traffic in the west-bound lane was not so heavy, being headed toward the city. Accelerating to ninety miles an hour he expected to overtake the blue van in a few minutes.

Wengie was in a state, "That patrol car in the other lane hit his lights as soon as we were close enough for him to spot us. He'll turn around and come up on us from behind. Drive faster!"

"No. That would be worse. There's a sign for an exit in two miles we'll get off the interstate and lay low until it gets dark." Ling took the exit ramp and slowed to a stoplight. He looked both ways—lights and businesses to the left, residential to the right. He went right.

"You should have gone the other way. There would have been more places to hide the van."

A quarter mile later Ling took a left on to a residential street and stopped by the curb on the right where he could see back to the freeway exit.

O'Donnel was now traveling with the setting sun off to his right front. At times trees shielded it, and it was hard to see wearing his dark glasses. The rest of the time he needed the glasses. He knew this van fit the description in the dispatch, but there was no urgency other than to inquire as to whether the occupants had seen anything. He knew the van driver would have seen him hit his lights so if there were any reason why the driver did not want to be stopped he'd exit as soon as he could. Decision time. O'Donnel took the exit. He looked left and right. An honest citizen would likely go home to the right, a criminal might go that way too, on the logic of being contrary to the expected. He turned right.

"That state patrol car took our exit and he's coming our way," Ling said as he slowly pulled away from the curb. He could feel his palms start to sweat. "Fred, get down out of sight. No, go in the back. He would have seen a van with two occupants. We have to look different." In a flash the realization came on him. There was only one chance. They had to disappear in plain sight. The street he was on curved to the right. The houses were upper middle-class, mostly with double attached garages, many with triple garages. He drove slowly. There, that looked about right. A house with a triple garage and no lights on. There were toys on the grass beside the drive, and a large SUV furthest to the right. He pulled in beside the SUV thirty feet from the street.

"Fred, get out and put those toys on the driveway behind our van and the other vehicle. Tip over that tricycle half way to the street, but be sure there is room for me to get around the stuff to the left as I back to the street."

Wengie snapped the latch on the side door, and, looking too much like a burglar, did as he was told. Ling could only shake his head as he watched through the side mirror—he should have done it himself.

With Wengie back in the van Ling said, "Now sit quietly where you can watch the street to the right out of the rear windows. I'll slouch down and watch to the left.

———————————

As O'Donnel drove into the residential neighborhood, he was having second thoughts about finding the van. There was no particular reason for it to have taken that exit, to say nothing of turning right. As he made his way through the curving streets he became aware of how hopeless this was. Better to get back on the interstate and do my job, he thought. Up ahead he saw a van on the tarmac in front of a garage. The set sun behind the house cast deepening shadows over the scene. The van appeared to be a darker blue than the one on the freeway, and from appearances it had been there for some time. He started to drive away, but then stopped and typed the plate number into the computer swung out over the passenger seat. It came back READY COMMUNICATIONS, INC., QUEENS, NY. Probably been home for hours and took the family out for dinner, he thought as he drove away. Yet, something nagged at him.

———————————

"Hey," Wengie whispered with stress in his voice, "there's a cop car coming down the street."

"Stay cool," Ling whispered as he reached under the seat for the .45 automatic he kept there. Watching his side mirror he saw the state trooper's car slowly creep into view. It looked like it was speeding up when the brake lights came on and it stopped. He could see movement in the front seat. He's checking the plates, Ling thought. Time stood still until finally the brake lights went out and the car drove off down the street.

Ten minutes later Ling backed out into the street and getting back on the main drag decided to go in the direction away from the freeway.

With a cup of coffee in one hand, Greg Daley walked to his workstation. He had already put in a long day, and being called back made him feel tired before he started. He had heard the news of the plane going down from his neighbor as he was playing with the kids in his back yard. He knew there wasn't much he could do that wouldn't have waited until morning, but he had to try. Since the hand over of the *mirage* document the day before he had sifted communications from Libya, and Tripoli in particular, looking for anything that might mean someone had seen or even knew about the transaction. So, he started where he left off and ran all his flag words with no results. He tried a secondary pass of the intercepts for the last twenty-four hours where he studied message structure. The NSA computers would throw out messages like those from air traffic controllers or transactions from one bank to another. These by design would have similar structures for their category. What he was looking for was someone sending too many emails, or too many similar phone calls, even though they did not have any flag words.

As he expected, there were a lot of hits. On a whim he narrowed the search to the hour before the plane went down. This was a manageable list considering how tired he was. He was about to discard one when he hesitated. There was a pair of messages, one coming into Tripoli and one going out twenty seconds later. These were short machine messages, like a one line fax intended to be sent automatically similar to a meeting reminder. They came from different phones on opposite sides of the city, and were even in different languages. What flagged them was the structure at the end of message code. The programmer who put together the message formats had tried hard to make the messages appear completely unconnected, but had left parts of his own touch in both. This was not unlike a master at reading Morse code identifying the sender by the way he handled the key.

The actual message content was different in the two messages so it did not appear to be the retransmission of the same message. On any other occasion, these messages would never have been connected, and Daley was not at all sure they were connected now. Sipping his coffee he could feel the rush of the chase.

At times Daley marveled at how deeply imbedded in the human psyche was the desire to catch something. He supposed it was built in through countless generations to give primitive hunters a survival advantage. This was among the most abstract of all enterprises but still it was there. He imagined that mathematicians could even feel this as they sought the next higher unknown prime number or a similar esoteric goal.

He back traced the message that came into Tripoli and found it originated in Madrid. Scanning the intercepts into that city he found what he was looking for. Twenty-five seconds before this message was sent out to Tripoli a message with the same telltale signature came into a phone on the opposite side of town. He was hitting wrong keys in his feverish effort to instruct the computers to find where that message came from. Yes, from New York. Now, find another message in the greater New York area with that marker. His hands were shaking a little as he okayed the supervisory program's request to put more main frame computer power on to the task. New York was an area saturated in communications, and the NSA was scooping up all local land line messages as well as those to and from satellites and cell phones.

The NSA measured its computer capacity in acres. At various times, of which this was one, Daley wondered what part of an acre of computers he was monopolizing. He expected his phone to ring any minute with someone in the computer services division demanding to know what was so all fired important that he had authorized an emergency assignment of compute power.

The New York area would have a colossal number of calls to sift through. Having a gut feeling about this, a feeling that had served him well many times, Daley narrowed the search to the east half of Long Island. Hopefully, he would locate the origin on the chain of calls. To his great amazement his screen was blank except for two items in the thirty minutes before the message had gone from Manhattan to Madrid. One was to the information number at the public library in Eastport. The other was to an office in Hoboken, New Jersey. Both calls were made from Westhampton, Long Island on a cell phone belonging to one Katie Meyer. The call to Hoboken was traced to the phone that sent the call from Manhattan to Madrid.

Immediately Daley went to work on the call that left Tripoli and found it went to Mumbai, India. Following the same system it left another phone from Mumbai and went to Beijing. Bingo! A Chinese connection. Pulling up on his screen what was known about the destruction of Flight 974 he saw that Westhampton was nearly the closest point of land to the flight path of the plane at the time it disintegrated.

Again typing too fast and making mistakes, he put together a report of what he had found. After the spell checker did the best it could he printed it and walked over to the office of the shift supervisor.

"I have a possible link to China of the shoot down of 974."

Looking skeptical but with a start of a smile in the corners of his eyes he motioned him to a chair in front of his desk and said, "Let's hear it."

As Daley told the story the man across from him began to look very serious. Message structure was a proven way to connect otherwise completely unrelated messages, and this appeared to be a fine piece of work in its application. Many times what the message said was less important than who was talking to whom. In time, they would find out what information was being transmitted, but for now it was important to know that someone in the Chinese capital had been contacted through an extremely sophisticated chain of calls from virtually the point of the disaster minutes before it happened.

The authentication message could have been sent directly using a one time pad to encrypt it. That would surely have gotten it flagged. You don't use a sophisticated code to send a message wishing your friend happy birthday. It was understood that embassies, military commanders, and such would send encoded messages, but not someone using a cell phone.

Within an hour Kati Meyer had been located. Authorities found that she had lost her cell phone on the midtown subway earlier in the day. In fact, she suspected it had been stolen. Also, she had been at a church in the Bronx helping to direct a play as part of a summer program for teens at the time of the calls. Her alibi was squeaky tight. So, they knew who was behind the destruction of the plane, they suspected why it had been done, but not how.

The next morning, CIA headquarters

Lance Kenyon, the DNI (Director of National Intelligence) sat alone in his office on the top floor of the Langley headquarters building. It was a little after six a.m. his usual time to be at the office. Morale among the troops, including his own, was as low as anyone could remember. The day before they practically had the champaign uncorked in the celebration for obtaining *mirage*. Now, not only did they not have the key document, but the Chinese were still one step ahead of them. From the State Department's point of view, the loss of the document meant the negotiators would have to work harder at the nanotechnology bargaining table. However, the extreme steps the Chinese had taken to keep *mirage* out of their hands implied there was more at stake than simply cutting the best deal. More importantly was how they destroyed Flight 974, and how they knew the document was on that plane.

He suspected a mole. There had to be one and whoever it was would destroy the agency and Kenyon's career with it if he wasn't stopped. Everyone who had knowledge of operation *fishhook* had been screened as their lives and habits were scrubbed one way and then the other. There was a limit to how far you could go, though. If no one were allowed to go home, or have a life, there would be no employees. It was hard enough to get good people. More and more people were beginning to look at the federal government as the enemy. At the very least, fewer and fewer trusted it.

The phone rang and he belatedly picked it up. "Yes," was his only greeting.

"Sir, this is ShuHo Zeng, it is important I speak to you immediately. There has been a strange development with *mirage*."

Kenyon was about to say, "Development, does that mean bad or worse?" But, he stopped himself and said, "Good, come right up. I have time before I brief the president again." He shook his head thinking he was losing it. Why did he have to include the word "again" at the end of the sentence?

In his fifteen months as DNI, Kenyon had gotten to know many of the division chiefs. Zeng, U.S. born full blood Chinese, was the head of the Far East division. He knew the language and customs of China well and was a solid man. In what seemed like a minute there was a knock on the door. Zeng entered looking like he had not been home all night.

"Good morning, ShuHo. You look like you've had a long night of it. Pour yourself a cup of coffee and have a doughnut if you like." The coffee maker was on the credenza behind Kenyon.

Zeng laid his red folder on the side of Kenyon's desk as he nodded. "It has been too long a night. This thing has us really stumped." He sipped the coffee and took big bites of the jelly bun he had chosen. "This is terrible nutrition," he said indicating the gob of fat and carbohydrates in his hand, "but, I haven't eaten all night and it tastes wonderful."

Kenyon watched with amusement without saying anything for the twenty seconds it took for the confection to disappear. With the food gone, and the cup empty Zeng refilled it and said, "When we started after *mirage,* as a long shot gamble I alerted a deep cover agent we have had in China for seven years and never used. Nobody knows about this one, who we presently call Topaz Wind. Only I know his true identity, and it will stay that way. Too many of our agents have been compromised in recent weeks."

Kenyon nodded thinking how Zeng had taken the news as one by one most of his agents in China had been deported, or worse, imprisoned.

"Late last night," Zeng continued, "we received this message." He opened the red folder, took out a sheet of paper, and handed it to Kenyon. It read:

> *Have info on how* mirage *works and its purpose. You want? Code Tan.*

"I've spent most of the night," Zeng continued, "verifying how the message came to me, checking every step. I believe it is authentic."

Kenyon read the single line over and over. Leaning forward he said, "We don't want to know how it . . . no. What are we talking about here? Is this the same *mirage*? What does it mean how it works? We're talking about treaty negotiations, not a machine. And, of course we want it. Why would he ask?"

Zeng finished his second cup of coffee. "To answer your last question first, if we have him send what he has to us it may compromise him and get him imprisoned. At the very least, we won't be able to use him again for many months. As for your first question, maybe everyone was thinking too narrowly and made wrong assumptions."

"Okay. Yes, we want it if we can get it. If we had it, we'd know if our assumptions were wrong. Getting it out may be easier said than done, am I right? What does 'Code Tan' mean?"

Zeng, obviously tired, was thinking through the situation trying not to let anything slip to a bureaucrat. "Yes, it will be hard to get, especially because Code Tan means there is a lot of information in electronic form. Our individual," he was careful not to use the word "man" as even the gender of the deep cover agent might give away too much, "may have a lengthy manual, detailed drawings, a computer program, or all of the above probably on a computer disc. It cannot be sent out the way that short message was."

Turning to refill his own cup Kenyon said, "I suppose I'm better off not knowing how the short message came out."

Rubbing his hand over his face Zeng responded, "Indeed you are. You really don't want to know."

What Zeng was saying was true. With so many of their assets compromised he had instigated a plan in his division that was risky. They knew their trained agents were compromised, how was unclear. So, it forced them to search for ordinary people going to China on legitimate business. Those chosen would either have a small message planted on their luggage or other personal effects without them knowing it. Or, they were recruited to do one simple thing like carry in an innocuous book, like a travel guide, and then told to leave it in a hotel lobby, or similar place. The Chinese knew they were doing it. They simply did not have enough resources to follow every American.

"Well, take all reasonable steps to get what your guy has. By the way, this was good work. Get some sleep."

— 4 —

Friday, July 8, Taylors Falls, Minnesota

It had been one of the rainiest Julys in recent memory in the upper Midwest. The runoff made the streams and rivers flow at flood stage, and in some cases considerably above. The St. Croix River forming the border between Minnesota and Wisconsin was no exception. Water flowing through the narrow crevasse of bedrock at Interstate Park located at Taylors Falls pounded and lashed at the rocks as it roiled down the chute on its way to its meeting with the Mississippi River fifty miles downstream. The falls were more properly a stretch of intense rapids with no single place where the water actually fell off a precipice. The geometry of the rocks was custom made for kayaks and those people with the daring to test themselves against the force of tons of water ricocheting off crags of rock creating under water whirlpools and freak eddies.

Darin Harris stood on a ledge of rock waiting for a little blue and white kayak, pointed at both ends, to appear at the head of the rapids far to his left under the highway bridge. His long-time friend Ed Breckon was taking his third shot at it today. Typically, he turned over at least once in the sixty seconds it took to shoot the rapids. It amazed Harris how these guys totally under water, hanging out of what was now the bottom of the small craft, managed to right themselves with a stroke of the paddle. All the players in this odd game against the water wore helmets, rubber gloves, and abrasion resistant shirts.

Breckon's goal was to make the run once during the high water without overturning. Darin watched Ed as he made a good showing of himself for the first half of the run. At that point the whole kayak was drawn under by a strong undertow behind a huge submerged rock. Breckon was up to his shoulders and on the verge of going over when the bow popped out. By dragging the left paddle in the water he pivoted in the direction he was falling and stabilized himself. A second later he was in a cascade rushing over the next rock that plunged the bow deep into a pool dug out by eons of running water on the lee side of the boulder. This pivoted him completely around and laid him flat on the water going backwards. He righted himself and skillfully guided the craft through the last of the cataracts either extending his paddle as a rudder, or giving a quick stroke on one side or the other to keep the agile craft on course. In seconds he was in calmer water on the far side of the river at the bottom of the rapids.

Harris ran down along the trail to where Breckon would come ashore. He saw Breckon fighting hard as he came across the main channel and then paddled near the shore where there was the least current. Breckon's destination was a quay where the Taylors Falls Queen, an excursion paddle boat, landed to pick up and discharge passengers. He was grinning as Harris grabbed the bow. Harris took the paddle and Breckon untied the tarp string around his waist that kept water from filling the kayak. He grabbed the gunwale on either side of the small cockpit and lifted himself out into the knee deep water.

Breckon, in his late twenties, had a solid build and exercised to keep trim. He was an even six feet tall and one hundred-eighty pounds. Black hair and blue eyes set off well balanced facial features above a square jaw. He was soaked from head to foot, but the bright sun of the eighty-five degree day made that of little concern. "I think I can count laying over on the side as tipping a lot and not overturning," he said laughing.

Harris shook his head, "You're nuts. In case you haven't noticed, nobody else is trying it. If something happened to you there's no help. If it were the weekend, there'd at least be more people around."

"Yeah, I know. I like it this way. Glad we decided to take the day off, though, supposed to rain tomorrow."

"I hope you're not going to try again."

They lifted the small craft and turned it over to let the water run out, raising first the bow and then the stern several times. "No, I've had it. How about your giving it a try?"

"Not a chance. That water's too vicious. Don't you think you've been pushing it a little hard? What are you trying to prove?"

Harris knew what was eating Breckon, the same thing that had been bothering him for the last several years. He had grown tired of bringing it up while Breckon was getting feistier each time it was mentioned. It was naturally a terrible thing being taken against his will to Iraq and used as a slave. That he was responsible for so many men getting killed as he made his burst for freedom was regrettable, but absolutely nobody even came close to faulting him for it. For one thing, Breckon had saved Harris's life when he blasted the last two to their final reward with that AK-47. Didn't that count for anything? Since then Breckon had changed jobs, dropped his girlfriend, and taken up martial arts with a vengeance. When he finally began to tire of the karate, self defense classes Harris had hoped he was coming out of it. Then, last summer he had taken up whitewater kayaking. Generally that was a safe enough thing to do if a person used a little common sense. Breckon was showing less and less of that as he looked for increasingly dangerous rapids.

They tied the kayak to the roof rack on Breckon's car. "You can get into dry clothes while I drive the car over to the picnic area. We'll have lunch. You have to be hungry after that."

As Harris drove he broached the sensitive topic. "You have to snap out of it, you know. Enough time's gone by. You can't go back and fix anything. And, call Cindy, will you. She's crazy about you, and I think the reverse is true, too, if you'd give it a chance."

"You're into my personal life again. That's off limits."

"So, I'm off limits. Come on, tell me you'll give her a call. I doubt she's seeing anybody else." Harris was grinning as he glanced at Breckon. "Come on, come on, promise?"

"Okay, but only to make you happy. She's not interested in me any more, and this'll prove it. Let's talk about something else."

They talked about the trip they had planned to the Montana mountains in August. Breckon had a bundle of sticks in the trunk of his car that he collected while on walks. Pulling into a parking spot Harris said, "Grab the wood and I'll take the bag of food. We'll cremate a wiener on a stick."

Harris and Breckon had been friends since they first met in grade school. Harris, an outgoing person, had more of an artistic bent than Breckon. In that way, they complemented each other. Harris's flair expressed itself in writing, drawing, and photography. With these skills he managed to survive as a freelance writer and photographer. Harris was a little less than six feet, had dark brown hair and blue eyes. He had a rather long face with pronounced cheek bones. He was easy to like and he got along well with everyone.

As Breckon put the fire together he continued talking about the trip. "This year it's going to happen. How many years has it been since the last time we made it? Something always comes up." The closest real mountains to Minneapolis were the Absoroka range in Montana and Wyoming. On them was the high plateau of the Bear Tooth Wilderness. The previous trip they had gone up the north side. There they parked at a trailhead at six-thousand feet and walked up four-thousand feet carrying their packs. That was a tough climb and it was hard to stay close to water without having to melt snow.

Harris was sizzling a couple of hot dogs on a stick. "You know, I was looking at maps of that area and if we drove up that switchback on the way from Red Lodge to Yellowstone Park, we'd start a lot higher up. We should look at that."

Breckon wolfed down hot dogs as fast as they could get them hot and black. "There's probably two months' worth of carcinogens on each one of these crusty black dogs, but wow, they're good. I didn't realize I was so hungry. But about the trip, I supposed there'd be more people starting on the south side because it's easier, but we could get farther in and leave the pilgrims behind. When we get back to town let's study the maps."

The Sunday afternoon was perfect as Ed and Cindy strolled in Como Park in St. Paul. They walked arm-in-arm in lock step. "This is nice," Ed said. "I'm glad I called you."

"It's not that hard you know. You pick up the receiver and punch a few buttons. Why did you call, if I may ask, not that I'm complaining?"

"Darin was on my case the other day. That's a pretty lame excuse, isn't it?"

"Yeah. You sure know how to make a girl feel good. But, let's not talk about that. How are you doing?"

"Not too good. I'm still stuck back in Iraq. It doesn't make any sense, you know, all the killing. And, why was I the one to survive. Sometimes I think the others were the lucky ones."

They walked in silence first watching Frisbee throwers and then a volleyball game. "Here's a park bench in the shade," Ed said. "Let's sit and watch the world go by."

Cindy looked at him intently for a minute, then said, "I know it was hard. I've been thinking about it too. Let me mention this to you. Have you ever heard of divine providence?"

"Yeah, guess so. Go on."

"It goes something like this. God is good and only makes what is good. So, how do we account for evil in the world?"

"Man has free will, is rotten to the core, and does evil things. How does this fit with God being only good?"

"God permits evil. He doesn't will it. Divine providence helps us understand what that means. When a person does something immoral, evil, God would not permit that evil if He did not cause a good to come from that very evil. That's divine providence as simply as it can be stated. In most instances, we won't have any idea of what the good is until we're in eternity, so don't spend a lot of time trying to figure it out. This in no way exonerates, or otherwise lets the perpetrators of evil off the hook. They have to pay for their deeds in this life or the next because they have free will so could have decided not to do them.

"You were in a situation where evil was going to happen no matter what you did. If you honestly ask God to forgive you for any fault there was in your actions that's the best you can do. God is not an ogre. He does forgive."

Ed thought awhile and then smiled at Cindy. "That's sure another way of looking at it. Where you getting this stuff?"

"Oh, I've been asking around, talking to people I know. Think about it, will you?"

"Yeah. I will. Now to a more pressing matter. Let's find something to eat. Any ideas?"

Monday, Roseville, Minnesota

Breckon slapped his magnetic card at the six inch square box on the wall near the main entrance of Control Engineering, Ltd. It made a meek beep as if it had fallen-and-couldn't-get-up. At the same time the door clicked to say it had unlocked for five seconds so he could enter. It was six-thirty, a half-hour before the door automatically unlocked to start the business day. Breckon rubbed his left shoulder as he walked down the hall to his cubical. He hardly noticed hitting that rock under water on his second run on Friday. The bruise was getting increasingly uncomfortable. He was used to it, though. At the height of his martial arts craze, something he only occasionally worked at these days, he was sore and stiff most of the time.

His job was agreeable to him. An above average electrical engineer, he was assigned projects with enough variety to make life interesting, yet not so demanding that he had to live at the job. This was what nearly killed him at his last place of employment. Currently he was lead engineer for the electrical control systems of a large combination office and residential building in Nanjing, China.

Foreign travel was definitely not something Breckon wanted to do. He made it a condition of his employment at Control Systems that he would not be sent out as an installation and start-up supervisor. This requirement was acceptable to the company because the company had a good service department to handle that. The man on site for this job, Stefan Lassitor, was quite good and he and Breckon worked well together. Breckon had to admit it would be something of a hoot to go to China for a week or so. It was the lure of the Orient, and a communist country all in one. But, he always maintained that he wasn't going so nobody got any wrong ideas.

Shortly after eight, Charlie Gunther, Breckon's supervisor, called him into his office. Gunther was easy to work for except for wild ideas at times. He would listen to arguments against them, though, so Breckon and he had a congenial relationship. When Gunther saw Breckon he shook his head. "We've run into a tough one here. The second in command for the general contractor in Nanjing called our Number One on Friday and it really hit the fan. You sure picked a good day to take off." Gunther usually called the president of Control Engineering "Number One." "Stefan also called me, said he couldn't get you."

"Yeah. I suppose so. I was not in my apartment most of the time on Friday. That's what days off are for. What can I say? It's summer, and in this patch of God's good earth that doesn't last long. I hate to ask, but what's unraveling now?"

"As I can gather, and I hope I'm understanding this correctly, there's a misconception about the computerized elevator controls and how the whole system is supposed to operate." Breckon had used Control System's proprietary software that ran successfully in a dozen installations. The customer demanded the source code and signed a disclaimer that if they changed anything they were completely liable. Gunther continued, "Stefan is trying to get it sorted out, but he's one against about a dozen of them. You know what's coming, you're smart enough, and I'm sorry about it." Gunther paused to let what he said register. "You have to go over there for a few days and help him out. You know every line of code and can sort out what they did to it."

Breckon sat for a long moment. It was a good thing this was an emergency so he wouldn't have time to think about it. "Okay, I'll go for a week, no longer. I can fix anything they've screwed up in that amount of time. And, I want a couple of days on company expenses to get rested up after the horrid trip over there—I've heard people talk about it. And, if I'm going to go through all of that, I want time to look around. I know once I hit the site I'll be lucky to see daylight for the rest of the time I'm there."

Gunther looked relieved. "Good. Very good. Today is Monday. I'll tell Number One to pass along that you'll be on site a week from today. They can easily work around the elevator controls that long." Gunther looked a little sheepish, "We had your passport as you agreed at the start of the project in case an emergency like this came up. We took the liberty to send in a visa application Friday. We FedEx'd it to CIBT (Center for International Business and Travel) in Chicago with the rush fee and will have it back on Wednesday. You leave Thursday morning."

"What if I had said no?" Breckon asked rubbing his chin thoughtfully.

Gunther smiled, "You didn't."

Breckon rose to leave when Gunther motioned him to stay. "A couple of other things. You can fly United from Minneapolis to Chicago, and then to Beijing. From there you take Air China to Nanjing. Or, you can go Northwest from Minneapolis to Japan, and then to Shanghai. You spend a short night in a hotel in Shanghai. From there you go by bus, about seven hours, to Nanjing. Your choice."

"What's the bus ride like?"

"From what I hear, small seats, and rough roads. The upside is you get to see the local scenery."

Though he knew it would not be the same, Breckon could not help thinking about his trip to Iraq. The faster the better was all he could come up with. "Guess I'll opt for United to Beijing."

"Okay, we'll lay you on for that. One other thing. We had to send a second master control panel for the air conditioning over there, as you know. We want the first one back so we can stick it up our subcontractor's nose for all the wiring mistakes he made. Please see to sending it back while you're there. Lassitor's buried with other stuff and never seems to get to it."

"Yeah, Fine," Breckon was not looking happy as he stood up rubbing his shoulder.

Gunther had half a grin as he said. "I see your left wing is drooping a little today. You into that sock and punch stuff again?

Breckon perked up as he said, "No. I was floating down the river in my kayak minding my own business when this belligerent rock jumped out and whacked me on the shoulder. There oughta be a law."

Rolling his eyes, Gunther replied, "Right."

After Breckon left his office Gunther thought he's send an email to Lassitor to be sure there was a driver at the airport holding up a sign with Breckon's name on it to take him to the hotel. It was the least he could do since he had not expected Breckon to agree to the trip so easily.

CIA Langley, Virginia

Sam Li was one of ShuHo Zeng's best up-and-coming lieutenants. Zeng put him in charge of the details of getting out of China whatever Topaz Wind had. "Sam, it has to move fast. That's a recipe for disaster in this business. I know that. It's just that there are no alternatives. Search the visa applications for business travelers to China like we've been doing. When you come up with likely candidates, let me know. I want to be informed every step of the way. We can't afford to lose this one, nor compromise Topaz Wind. We really could use a win about now."

The next day Zeng and Li were examining visa applications. "Boy, slim pickins," quipped Zeng, sounding doubly absurd as he tried to imitate a southern accent with an Asian accent. "Only two for Nanjing in the next week that fit the profile." There was precedent for the way they selected the couriers. They had to be traveling alone, employed by a U.S. company doing business in China, and be professional people. Normally they did a background check to be sure they were who they appeared to be. The woman, Terra Finwick, they had used before. She was a project manager for a Minneapolis based food processing company presently building a plant over there.

"If it wasn't for the rush visa order for the guy there'd only be one. The woman's been there several times. She always gets the visa for two entries and goes from Minneapolis to Tokyo and then Shanghai. The guy's a first-timer."

Zeng read the short bio on each of them. "What's the chance they'll cooperate? We'll need them both. The woman arrives first and will bring the alert message that the computer will be coming in." With the unknown nature of the information to be received from Topaz Wind, but knowing it would be in electronic form, they planned to send a laptop computer into the country. It contained a sophisticated program that took information from a disk and mingled it with normal business programs and files. After that was accomplished the special program was deleted and the hard drive on the laptop was defragmented to eliminate all trace of what had been done. The computer would then be taken back to the U.S. by yet another traveler. If the computer were sent in by normal means, like the diplomatic pouch, it would get to a U.S. embassy safely enough. But, the Chinese carefully tracked everything and everyone that left the embassy, something they could not allow.

"I don't think we'll have a problem with Ms. Finwick. Her last assignment was to leave a magazine in a taxi. It was easy and went off without a hitch. We upgraded her hotel room to a luxury suite. She loves the first class treatment. She'll do it. The man, this Ed Breckon, is another story. Usually guys are less impressed with things like better accommodations, and this mission could appear risky to him."

The look in Zeng's eyes became hard, "He'll have to do it. Figure out a way. How good are our agents in Minneapolis?"

"They've done this several times."

"Make the case to them that they have to succeed."

Later that day, CIA office, Joint Terrorism Task Force, Minneapolis

"Oh no! Look at this," Mel Winger said as he walked from the laser printer to Burl Carson's desk. "I can't believe those knot heads in Washington would even consider this."

Carson watched Winger sit down as he shook his head. "Alright, are you going to let me in on it?"

"Believe me you're going to wish you were left out. They want us to recruit Ed Breckon to carry a CIA laptop computer into China. He's headed there later this week."

Carson leaned back in his swivel chair rubbing his eyes with the heels of his hands. "Look at the bright side. He almost started a regional war in the Middle East on his last foreign trip. Maybe he'll start World War III this time, and we'll all be a cloud of radioactive ions a week from now, and you'll be free of this month's mortgage payment." He chuckled at the thought of it. "This is obviously coming from a different department, and the departments don't talk to each other. You gonna tell 'em it ain't such a good idea?"

"Yeah. I have to say something, but you can count on them saying 'there's no other way.'" Winger hit a speed dial combination on his phone and asked for an extension.

"Sam Li speaking."

"Sam, this is Mel Winger in Minneapolis. Been reading your email about the recruiting. The woman's no problem, we've used her before. But, this Breckon, we know him. Believe me, do we know him. This is not a good idea. I don't know what the plan is, but you will *not* be happy with the results."

"Are you telling me you can't handle it?" Li spit out in a characteristic Asian accent. "Do I have to fly someone in from Chicago to do a simple job like that? He's the man, there's no other way!"

Winger smiled for a second. "Oh, we'll do it, no problem there. But, know this. He was involved in something in the Middle East a few years ago. Nothing that was totally proven, mind you, but he screwed things up so bad that the president of the United States, to say nothing of the president of Iraq, wanted his head on a stick. I'm not sure you want to do this."

"A two-bit electrical engineer from a nothing company? What? It must be on the Fortune Five Million list? He's going to screw up international politics? Forget it! Get the job done!"

Winger held the telephone receiver in front of his face looking at it since the volume was definitely higher than when the conversation started. Putting it gently back against his ear he said, "Okay. We'll do it."

Carson was grinning as Winger hung up the phone. "There was no winning that one. I could hear it way over here. They must really have their tails in a knot. Wonder what's going on. You know, this might not be so bad. Maybe we can even the score for the way Breckon treated us. I still can't use my right shoulder completely even after two surgeries." After a pause he continued, "How should we do it? We could intercept his luggage after he checks here in Minneapolis and plant the computer."

"I suppose we could. But, if something goes wrong we won't be able to ask him about it. No. We'll give it to him and make him take it. I can't wait to push him around a little."

They began work on how they would approach Breckon. They agreed it would be best to do it as he arrived at the airport so he wouldn't have time to undo anything. Being part of the world's largest intelligence gathering community had its advantages. They checked airline records for the local international airport for the last three years, and determined each time Breckon traveled and how long he had been gone. After that they checked the parking ramp records to see when his car had been parked there. It is not generally known that airport security orbited through all of the parking ramps at least once a day and recorded the license plate number of each vehicle and where it was parked.

Carson put together the data and came over to Winger's desk. "Looks like if he plans to be gone ten days or less he drives his car to the airport. He'll be gone eight days, so he'll park at the airport. That's good. We pick him up coming in and talk to him right after he parks the car."

"Sounds like a plan," replied Winger. "All we need now is the computer from Langley."

Langley, Virginia, later the same day

Sam Li loaded the special software on the laptop computer and got it on an over night flight to Minneapolis. Now he prepared an email to be encoded and sent to the embassy in Shanghai. They still had a few low level operatives in China who could pass on messages and similar minor activities. The mole had compromised mainly their operatives that were in sensitive positions having access to classified information.

Li instructed the CIA contingent in the embassy to recover the computer in Breckon's suitcase. Normally Li would have had one of his baggage handlers "steal" it. Theft of items like computers and cameras from checked baggage was almost certain. All airports fought that problem. They were short in the baggage handler category of assets at present so it would have to be a taxi driver. Li would send a photo of Breckon to the embassy and they could send someone to the airport to collect him. Not wanting to make their man stand out for scrutiny, he would not hold up a sign with Breckon's name on it. Instead he'd casually walk up beside Breckon and say he was hired by Breckon's boss, Charlie Gunther of Control Engineering. They had learned other information about the building project in Nanjing and Breckon's part in it. Much of this information was obtained by the NSA through interception of Breckon's emails to and from the site. The operative could lay as much detail as needed on Breckon to convince him he was there to be of service.

— 5 —

"What do you know," Breckon said to himself as he found a parking space on the fifth level of the parking ramp closest to the main terminal. "Must be my lucky day." Since he found a space below the top level it also meant there was a roof over his car in case of a hail storm. He could have taken a taxi. But, with so many of the taxi drivers being foreigners he didn't like to use them. They could hardly speak English and only knew the longest possible route to the airport. If he tried to direct them differently they'd get confused and make the wrong turn. And, from his experience, the more or less American drivers tended to be surly and rude.

He got out, locked the doors on his car, and lifted his suitcase from the trunk. He had not noticed the large van following him up the helical ramp to level five. It parked four spaces away in the direction Breckon would walk to the terminal. Breckon extended the handle on his large suitcase and started pulling it along on its wheels with his smaller computer bag resting on top of it. As he reached the van two men stepped out in front of him.

A chill went down his back as memories of what had happened in the apartment parking lot those years ago raced through his mind. "Mr. Breckon," said the smaller of the two men, "we are with the CIA and we need to talk to you for a few minutes."

It hit him in a flash. "You! You're the same two guys that were at plant two!"

"Yes, we had hoped you wouldn't remember. But, please, we are here today on a totally unrelated matter. It is most important that we speak with you. It'll only take a few minutes."

"So, what already?" Breckon could feel the hair on the back of his neck bristling. "You're blocking my way. I have a plane to catch."

"Yes, we know that," Winger continued. "We have something to show you, will you please get into the back of the van with us?"

"No! From the trick you tried on me I know I can't trust you. Open the door, you both get in, I'll stand out here and look." Breckon had it in his mind to take off running.

Carson said, "Fine if that's what you want. But, don't take off running. We can make sure your visa gets screwed up, and your passport is questionable. When you get to China you could spend a month in the pokey. Oh, and don't say you decided not to go on the trip, either. We'll arrange for the police to find a kilo of cocaine in your apartment with your finger prints all over it. We're not kidding. We need your help." It gave Winger a measure of satisfaction to be able to abuse Breckon this way. This man had physically beaten them both. And, to add insult to injury, they had spent months, mostly on their own time, trying to expose him. In the end they found nothing more incriminating than his propensity to fight back when pushed into a corner, a trait shared by about fifty percent of the males in the U.S.

"Yeah, that's what I figured," Breckon responded. "At first you wanted to talk to me, then had to show me something, now it's I have to help you. And, since you trashed my apartment last time, you know I'll believe you're as rotten as you say you are. Is that it?"

Winger had the sliding door on the side of the van open and was sitting behind the driver's seat. "Hey, that's not fair. We told you we didn't do your apartment. But, we are under the gun and one way or the other you have to help us. You see, the CIA in Washington checked all the visa applications and yours came up. There weren't any others we could use. Anyway it's simple. You won't even notice anything out of the ordinary."

Breckon let out a long breath. "So, get on with it. Make me laugh."

Picking up the bag with the computer in it and opening the zipper Winger said. "Here's a common laptop computer. All you have to do is bury it in among your clothes in your large bag that you will check as luggage and that's that. When you get to your hotel it will be gone."

Breckon laughed, "It'll be stolen before it even gets on the plane in Chicago. That's a dumb plan."

"No it won't. We have ways to assure that will not happen."

Breckon thought a minute. "What if it's a bomb? What if you guys aren't CIA at all? I'm taking a 'parcel' from a stranger."

Carson, who was standing beside Breckon said, "You sure checked our IDs at our last meeting. And, we know you also called headquarters to verify who we were after we left."

Breckon shook his head. "Show me that it works. Come on. Show me or no deal, no matter what you do to me."

Winger frowned and shrugged his shoulders. "Fine. Here." He gave the computer to Carson who opened it and set it on the floor of the van as he crouched beside the van in the open side door. He was no keyboard whiz. Breckon watched as he punched in the password using one finger on each hand, W-E-L-C-O-M-E-M-A-T. Well, Breckon thought, they had to use something. The computer finished booting up and had the same Microsoft Office suite as was on his computer. It even had the same Computer Aided Design (CAD) program he had.

Breckon thought there could hardly be enough explosive in a fully operating computer to bring down a Boeing 777. He was starting to hate this trip even more than he had before. "Okay, give me the stupid computer. What's in it for me?" Breckon proceeded to open the zipper on his suitcase and stuffed the laptop, none too gently, in among his clothes.

"We'll think of something," Winger replied. "We always compensate citizens for serving their country."

Breckon was walking away as he said over his shoulder, "Don't blame me if something goes wrong."

Carson turned to Winger and in a low voice said, "Why do I have this sinking feeling that something will. Why did his name, of all people, have to come up?"

Breckon arrived at the airport more than two hours early in hopes of getting on the flight to Chicago an hour before his scheduled flight because there was only twenty-five minutes to make his connection to China if he took his scheduled flight. He knew *he* could make the connection but would his luggage? The hour earlier flight was canceled, so he took off at ten a.m. as scheduled. Arriving at Chicago at eleven-thirty, he had thirty-five minutes before his flight to China left at twelve-oh-five.

The nose of the big Boeing 777 was pointed at the large window when he arrived at the check-in gate. It reminded him of a moose looking in the window of a small cabin. When finally he was in his window seat, fourth from the back on the right side of the plane, he saw the luggage wagons pulled up in rows, and one by one the aluminum containers were loaded. He wondered if his suitcase had made it as the last of the containers were hoisted up and rolled into the belly of the plane. He saw an airport pickup drive up. The driver got out, lifted a black suitcase from the back, and walked over to one of the baggage handlers. He was carrying Breckon's suitcase! An inclined conveyor belt was in place that went up into the rear of the cargo hold. Late arriving bags were loaded with this.

The pickup driver pointed to the case and the handler nodded. When the pickup had gone the handler walked over to his buddy whose arms were as large as most men's legs, and they exchanged a few comments. The second one grabbed Breckon's bag and gave it a mighty heave so it flew over to the conveyor bouncing and rolling when it landed. Breckon could imagine the handler had been told to treat it gently. It was then thrown on the conveyor and inched its way up into the hold. Well Breckon thought, at least it was aboard, not that the computer inside would ever work again.

The plane took off on time and away they went, next stop Beijing, fourteen hours later. The 777 had a small viewing screen in the back of each seat that showed movies. There were three movies that they rotated through as many times as needed to fill the time. Or, one could watch the progress of the flight on several screens. One was close in for the local terrain and cities. Another showed the whole hemisphere with the track the plane had already traveled and the destination. Included was the part of the earth that was in daylight and the part covered by night. It was two a.m. at their destination, and they would chase the sun on this flight. Having left shortly after noon, the flight would arrive in Beijing at two-thirty p.m. It would be the next day due to crossing the International Date Line.

They flew nearly north and passed over Duluth, Minnesota, then Winnipeg, and then over thousands of miles of totally uninhabited wilderness of Northern Canada. It occurred to Breckon that the people who said there would soon be standing room only on earth due to the exploding population should fly over Canada. They flew for hours and not a road, not a sign of any habitation until finally they were over the north coast of Alaska. Sure enough, there was the North Slope oil field with its local roads, buildings, above ground pipes and, of course, oil wells. The size of the entire operation reminded Breckon of a postage stamp on the side of a barn, because the space it occupied was so minute compared to the incredibly vast wasteland.

The plane inched along at six-hundred miles per hour with an outside temperature falling to seventy below zero at times. The seat back displays also showed the effective ground speed that changed as they alternately encountered head and tail winds. Finally they went across the Bering Straight and then were over Siberia. More hours and thousands of miles of wasteland. Over northern Canada there were always lots of lakes, which in late July, were covered with ice except where it had melted around the edges. Siberia was arid with no sign of a lake. Finally they were headed down the coast of China. More and more habitation appeared as they approached Beijing.

On their approach to the airport flying over the outskirts of the capital city, Breckon was filled with a dark feeling. The sky was overcast and all they passed over were large apartment complexes like he had seen in pictures of Russia. There were plenty of paved roads, but no cars, only buses and trucks. On the ground taxing up to their gate Breckon was struck with the lack of activity. O'Hare in Chicago had been a beehive of movement with seemingly every square inch used for something. There were few planes here, and most of the tarmac was empty space.

When they deplaned they were given forms that United should have had, but didn't. Three-hundred-fifty people were filling out these silly things on suitcases, books, walls, you name it. It was rather outrageous after having just wasted fourteen hours doing nothing. From there Breckon walked with the cattle procession for what seemed a mile and eventually arrived at the immigration and naturalization hall. Along the way Breckon noticed how the Chinese were trying to make a world class airport out of this, and how far they had to go.

The process of checking passports was very efficient. This was because to get an entry visa you had to send your passport to a visa processing company, like CIBT. The passport had to have two unused facing pages so the visa could be pasted to one page and the stamps and initials on the facing page. The official simply entered the visa number into his computer. When it came up with the information that matched the passport number, that was it. Stamp, initial and away you go.

Next was customs. Breckon had been dreading this ever since he knew he was making the trip. He collected his bag and followed the new herd to the next hall. To his surprise he walked right through. The only parcels they were inspecting were things that were not suitcases, that is, boxes, crates, and similar items. This was so unexpected as to leave him thinking he had taken a wrong turn and the police were about to pounce on him for trying to evade customs. But, right in front of him were the doors to the street with taxicabs coming and going.

On the plane he had been unable to sleep and now he was tired. By his body's clock it was two a.m. This left him feeling like he had not slept for days. His flight from Beijing to Nanjing was on Air China leaving at six p.m. local. After waiting in wrong lines several times he finally got to the check-in desk so he could get rid of his large suitcase. After considerable confusion he learned he could not check in until ninety minutes before the flight.

The main hall of the terminal was crowded so he spent most of the next two and a half hours sitting on the floor up against a wall. He did find a glassed in counter where he changed two-hundred dollars to RMB with his credit card and bought a candy bar and bottle of soda at a shop along the concourse. (RMB stood for Renminbi meaning "People's Currency." One U.S. dollar equaled something less than seven RMB.)

Finally, it was eighty minutes before his flight so he checked in. With his large bag checked it was easier to get around. Breckon found the direction to go for his gate number and started off. He came to the line for the normal check of boarding pass and picture ID, followed by the metal detectors and x-ray for the carry-on baggage. He handed his boarding pass and passport to the small Chinese man who was in complete uniform. The man said something in Chinese that Breckon of course did not understand. Breckon could only look helpless and say, "I do not understand." To this the man kept repeating the same phrase, louder and louder as he several times thrust his hand and outstretched finger in the air. Breckon looked in the direction he was pointing and saw only overhead girders. Finally the man physically pushed Breckon to the side as he directed his attention to the next passenger in line. Breckon reached over and grabbed his passport and boarding pass and went back the way he had come.

Standing in bewilderment thirty feet behind the gate Breckon watched the other passengers. They all seemed to be handing "Mr. Rude" a small slip of paper in addition to the other documents. People were streaming past him on both sides. He retreated still further. Looking around he finally focused on a counter with a series of stations with clerks behind each. It looked like an airline check-in, but with no particular airline logo evident. Or, it could be for foreign currency exchange. That didn't figure because where he got his RMB it was fronted with bulletproof glass. Whatever it was the lines of clients moved fast. It was a short simple transaction. As he was about to direct his attention elsewhere he spotted it. A simple sign in Chinese and English "Airport Tax." All the people paid something and took a little slip of paper and then made their way to the security check.

Breckon got in one of the lines. When his turn came he laid his passport and boarding pass on the counter. The passport was pushed back at him. Looking at the boarding pass the clerk laid an official looking slip of paper next to the boarding pass. It had a large "50" on it so Breckon handed her a fifty RMB note. This must be the ticket, literally, Breckon thought.

He tried the security check again being sure to get in a different line than before. It worked. The rest of the security check went without incident. Breckon walked over to the wall of the large corridor to stop and verify that he still had everything. He thought of how that guy must have known at least a few English words, and that he was deliberately being difficult. This experience had done nothing to allay Breckon's sense of foreboding. As he started on once again he reminded himself that no matter how things appeared with people rushing about, this was still a totalitarian communist regime.

He found his gate on the same level as the tarmac. Watching the flow of things he saw they were loading buses to take the passengers to the planes. Breckon had seen this at a few U.S. airports, too. There were alpha/numeric displays about two feet high by four feet long above each gate. Displayed in red were the gate number, and under it the current time. To the right of this was the airline and flight number followed by the scheduled departure time. Under the flight number was the destination city. No Chinese characters were used.

The time dragged on and to keep himself alert he watched and listened as each flight was called over the PA system, first in Chinese, and then in English. Suddenly it occurred to him that flights leaving after his were being called and loaded. Upon checking at the desk he found one attendant who spoke English and was told there was a slight delay for Air China Flight 1503, his flight. Six o'clock came and went and still nothing. By seven o'clock the waiting area was mostly empty, except for passengers on Flight 1503. Suddenly, most of the people lined up and were given what looked like a meal in a Styrofoam box. He got in line and taking a cue from those in front of him showed his boarding pass and received a box, a half liter bottle of water, and chop sticks. Great. His first experience with pre-industrial eating. There was no choice but to ignore the warnings about getting sick from the food. He had to take the chance. He was hungrier than he imagined and it tasted good.

At eight o'clock Breckon was beyond caring whether he lived or died. He didn't want to die making a fool out of himself—just quietly pass away so the night clean-up crew could find his corpse and do whatever they did. He assumed they would be practiced in the drill.

He was shaken out of his semi-lucid musings by an announcement in Mandarin and the place sprang into life with a surge of humanity headed for the up escalator that wasn't running. By the time it came in English he was practically alone and at the back of the pack. The announcement said there was a new gate assignment for his flight. Grabbing his carry-on bag it occurred to him how similar all people behave in certain circumstances. This was the same response he would have expected at any American airport.

All through the afternoon Breckon had observed small crowds of people standing in front of TV monitors with somber looks. He had watched the monitors from time to time, too. The concern did not seem to be a natural disaster or anything like that, but something to do with international politics. After learning the flight was further delayed, Breckon took a renewed interest in the TV crowds as a new apprehension settled over him. What if the U.S. had done something to make the Chinese particularly angry, like a spy plane coming down in the middle of the country? Since his flight to Nanjing was strictly a domestic flight, there were no other western looking passengers to be seen. If this crowd, already irritated by the delay, wanted to vent its rage on the West, he would be the obvious target.

At eight-thirty they finally boarded the plane. Breckon was in a middle seat. He noticed he could count on one hand the number of women on the plane. He hung his chin on his chest resting his eyes when the man to his right said in perfect English with only the slightest accent, "Are you all right?"

Breckon looked up, turned his head, and saw a Chinese man with a concerned smile. He was taller than average for the race, but not so as to call attention to himself. Breckon replied, "It's been a long day. I left home over twenty-five hours ago and have had no sleep since. It's been stressful and tiring figuring everything out. That bed in the Sheraton Hotel in Nanjing is calling to me. Do you know why we have had such a long delay?"

"Mainly it is heavy fog from what they have said. This is your first time to China?"

Managing a thin smile Breckon replied, "Yes it is. I'm sure it shows."

The man in his early thirties turned out to be a sales representative for a large U.S. manufacturer of industrial air conditioning and heat exchanger equipment. As they chatted Breckon asked, "What is the meaning of the groups of people standing so solemnly staring at the TV monitors in the terminal?"

The man had an amused look on his face that Breckon, in his sleep deprived state, thought was close to condescending. "I would guess," he began, "that what happens in this part of the world isn't terribly important in the U.S. On the other hand, if you've been busy you might have missed it. There are negotiations going on with China, Taiwan, the United States, and the European Community on switching the currency of Taiwan from the Taiwan dollar to the Taiwan yuan with the provision that it would equalize with the Chinese yuan over an unspecified period of time. If that happened, it will be tacit agreement around the world that Taiwan is part of China. The decision was supposed to be announced in Geneva, Switzerland earlier today and has been delayed from hour to hour."

Breckon said he had heard mention of this at home and his seat companion continued. "I would guess the Americans assume the time to equalize will be set in the distant future, while the Chinese people have been led to believe it will happen quickly. That's probably why it'd be seen as a major victory here, and much less significant in the U.S."

At that moment, the flight attendant announced they were to deplane. Breckon's neighbor said the flight had been delayed further, and it would be more comfortable waiting in the terminal. To this Breckon could most heartily agree. Chalk one up for the Chinese. He knew no U.S. airline would be as considerate from the cases where passengers were kept bottled up on airplanes for six and eight hours prior to taking off.

Time dragged on into the night. Breckon began to think about how odd it was that the only topic on anybody's mind here was the Taiwan currency negotiations, and nothing about the nanotechnology treaty. He had assumed the nano treaty would be a big story all over the world. As he had gotten on the plane before, there were complimentary newspapers, one pile in Chinese the other in English. He now started looking through the English language paper he had taken. His eyes stung from lack of sleep as he flipped through the paper reading headlines. There was nothing about the nano treaty, but a large front page article about the Taiwan currency negotiations. It was as if those in power knew that the former would not happen while the latter would.

From time to time it seemed like they were about ready to go and a line would quickly form at the gate, only to be disbanded a few minutes later. The terminal was all but deserted except for those waiting for Flight 1503, and nearly all of these were watching the monitors. At ten minutes after ten the flight attendant at last approached the podium and began speaking. The crowds watching the TV's turned almost as a body and said something emphatic. The young lady stopped speaking. Breckon assumed they had said the equivalent of "shut up." Seconds later the crowd exploded in a roar of glee leaving no mistake that the agreement had been reached in favor of China. Five minutes later they were allowed to board the plane.

Again, nothing happened. Breckon didn't want to pester his seat mate who had been so kind as to speak to him, but he finally asked about the continuing delay. "We can't leave until all the passengers are on board. It seems a good number of them are off celebrating."

Breckon could understand that this was, after all, not a free society the way Americans think of freedom. If you said you were going to be on the plane, you were expected to be there.

During this delay, a local TV camera crew came on to the plane to interview the more distinguished looking passengers. As they panned the passengers from the front of the cabin Breckon imagined he would be on the local TV show the next morning. Shortly before eleven all passengers were either on board or had made what arrangements were necessary to miss the flight and they pushed back from the gate. The "monkey act" by the flight attendants demonstrating the use of the oxygen masks and emergency exit procedures was identical to that in the U.S. Of course it was. The U.S. invented all this right down to the Boeing 737 on which they would be flying.

At the end of the runway they waited some more—twenty-five minutes more. Breckon could see out the window as the plane in front of them took off. He saw no planes land but still they waited ten minutes. He assumed the air traffic control was antiquated to have to leave such a large gap between planes. The fog didn't seem to be so heavy. When at last they took off and were at altitude Breckon moved to an unoccupied aisle seat and managed to sleep for fifteen minutes. Tired as he was, the pain of his fatigue kept him awake most of the time.

At last they were at the gate in what he hoped was Nanjing. After deplaning they walked what seemed like another mile. During the ten minutes he waited for his bag to appear on the carousel, like any American carousel, he could only think about how he was beyond tired, beyond fatigue. Every part of him hurt until he wanted to tear something apart. When at last his bag appeared he grabbed it and headed in the direction the rest of the travelers were going, to what he could only expect was the door to the street and taxis.

— 6 —

Early Morning, July 15, Nanjing Airport

Unnoticed by Breckon as he walked toward the doors of the terminal of the Nanjing Airport, the man who talked to him on the plane was always a discreet number of steps behind, and always watching him. In fact, he had been observing him since he was sitting in the terminal in Beijing. His name was Richard Yang, a full blood Chinese born in the U.S. to Chinese immigrants. He spent over half of his time in China. He lived in Sacramento, California, with his wife and two children.

Three years before, the CIA had recruited Yang. Having refused to do anything that would jeopardize his life and career, he had finally agreed to be an observer, a watcher. He was paid rather well to simply watch and report on the mood of the people, political events, and occasionally individual people. Upon each return to the U.S., he would discuss what he saw and heard with his CIA handler. He had planned to fly from Beijing to Nanjing a day later, but was asked to change his plans so he could observe a certain man whose picture had been sent to him. He didn't even know the man's name. That he sat beside him on the plane was a shear coincidence, as far as he knew.

It was now nearly two a.m. Late as it was, Breckon saw a surprising number of people in the lobby of the airport who had come to pick up a family member or a business colleague. There were even people holding up signs written in Chinese characters. At first the tug on Breckon's sleeve went unnoticed as though it was someone brushing against him. Than a harder tug made him turn to his left. An Asian man said in good English, "Hello, you are Ed Breckon, are you not?"

Breckon was taken by surprise and said, "Stop pulling on me. Who are you?"

"I am Muan Yingqu. Charles Gunther from Control Engineering arranged for me to come and find you at the airport. He thought you might appreciate this after your long trip. Here let me take your bag for you," he said as he put his hand on the extended handle of the large bag Breckon was trailing behind him with his left hand.

Breckon, in his sleep deprived stupor responded, "Nobody said anything about this to me. I can manage my bag nicely. Why are you doing this? I was told to take a taxi to the hotel."

Jiang Wong was employed as a driver by the prime contractor on the project that involved Breckon. He had been given one hundred RMB by Stefan Lassitor to take the company van and pick up Breckon from the airport. That was good money for a two-hour job. The plane would arrive at 7:50 p.m. and he expected to be back home before ten. Much to his annoyance, he had forgotten to call the airport and check on the flight to see if it was on time. He had stood around the lobby for nearly seven hours until finally he found a place to sit down and promptly fell asleep. The commotion of people meeting their parties after such a long wait finally stirred him. Popping awake he jumped up and forced himself to the front of the crowd in the lobby. Waving his sign he said in as loud a voice as he could get away with, "Ed Breckon, Ed Breckon."

Breckon glanced over at the commotion and saw the sign with his name on it. He stopped abruptly. What was happening? As he stopped, a man walking behind him bumped into him and said something in Chinese that did not sound at all pleasant. This added to Breckon's aggravation. Meanwhile the man at his side seemed to be pulling ever harder at the handle on his large bag. Breckon looked to his left and snapped, "Stop it!"

Seeing Breckon as the only Caucasian in the crowd, and assuming he must be his quarry, the man with the sign came over and started to speak. "Herro, you be Ed Breckon? I be Jiang Wong. Stefan Rassitor send me with company van to drive you. You come," he said as he grabbed Breckon's right arm, almost causing the strap of his computer bag to slip off his shoulder. Breckon stepped back with a firm grip on both bags all the while trying to figure out what this was all about. His anger was rising.

"Back off!" Breckon barked. A few people stopped, turned, and looked. Yingqu was not a fully trained CIA agent. He was a local that had been recruited and trained to do simple errands for a fee. In time, if he continued to do well he would get more important assignments. He could see the second man was about to foil his mission to recover the computer. In addition, he had moved his taxi up close to the terminal when he knew Flight 1503 had landed. It would be towed away if he were gone much longer. In an instant he wrenched the large bag from Breckon's hand and started running to the left. He turned his head and yelled at Breckon to follow him quickly. But, in his excited state he said it in Mandarin.

Pent up stress and fatigue of having to stoically endure one indignity after another for over thirty hours left pools of unused adrenaline in Breckon's system. Unable to understand what the man said, and seeing his face contorted by his having turned his head nearly around as he spoke, Breckon thought he was taunting him. He wrenched his right arm free of the second man, and starting running so quickly he nearly fell on the polished floor, but was close behind the man in a dozen steps. He clipped the running man's left foot so as he brought it forward it hit the back of his right calf sending him sprawling on the floor. Instantly the man was up, but Breckon was ahead of him and smashed a foot to his locked right knee. It emitted a loud crunch as it folded beneath the man. As the man fell Breckon chopped the side of his left hand down on his collar bone breaking it with a sharp snap.

The second man was now beside Breckon saying, "You do bad thing!" He grabbed Breckon's right arm again. Breckon, by this time only marginally sane, jerked his right arm back and the computer bag hanging over his shoulder with it. At the same time he swung his left fist across his body and connected with the man's stomach in a thrust that left the man doubled over in pain. Instantly Breckon grabbed his large bag and exited the door to the street.

Outside on the sidewalk he saw taxis lined up by the curb with a man in a fancy suit about twenty feet to his right assigning cabs. Breckon reached into his pocket and pulled out three one-hundred RMB notes. Quickly approaching the man, bucking the short line, he held out the notes to him and said. "Please, next taxi to go to Sheraton Hotel."

The man, unaware of the commotion inside the terminal, was about to act indignant and then reached for the notes. Breckon pulled them back as he said, "Taxi first."

Motioning to the next cab he spoke to the driver. They went back and fourth a couple of times in Chinese as Breckon watched. Breckon was growing impatient, thinking the place would explode any minute. Finally the driver smiled, nodded his head enthusiastically and said, "Ah, Sheraton, Sheraton."

Breckon opened the door, threw in his large bag, even as the driver reached for it to put it in the trunk. Breckon simply said, "Go. Now we go."

The driver nodded enthusiastically again. "Go," and went around to the driver's side, got in and off they went. Breckon looked back and seeing more people coming out of the terminal could only imagine what he had gotten himself into.

Breckon noticed the driver was enclosed in a clear Plexiglas compartment. It seemed this must be to permit a passenger in the front seat as well as the back seat, without fear of interference of the passengers with the driver. Breckon reached over the front seat and dropped two one hundred RMB notes on the passenger side as he said, "Go fast to hotel. Very tired. Want to sleep."

A hand appeared from what seemed like no where and snatched the notes. "Fast, very tired." With that he put the pedal to the metal as Breckon began to wonder if it had been such a good idea. After hours of boredom waiting in the night for a fare, the young driver seized on the opportunity to push the limits. They sped through the blackest night Breckon could remember. The four lane divided highway had few exits and the median was built up so one seldom saw on-coming cars. The few vehicles headed in the same direction were passed in a blink. The speedometer was nudging one hundred-seventy kilometers per hour as Breckon tried unsuccessfully to do mental arithmetic to convert that to miles per hour.

The ride was something out of the Twilight Zone. Granted, it was the wee hours of the morning, but there were no lights to be seen along the expressway. Besides the danger of being killed in a car accident, he was beginning to wonder where they were going. He had no idea the airport was so far out of town. Maybe he was being taken to a secret interrogation station where he would be questioned and beaten for what he had done at the airport. After his crass disregard for China's laws, to say nothing of common human decency, they would teach this foreigner a lesson.

Back at the airport, Muan Yingqu was the center of attention with his broken bones. Wong managed to get to the door and out to the street where he heaved what little was in his stomach over the curb. He caught sight of Breckon getting into a taxi so knew he did not have to wait around for him. After sitting in a darkened corner for several minutes to get his breath he managed to get to the company van and drove back to the city.

Richard Yang had always assumed that when he was told to shadow a single individual that his target was an agent for someone. He had expected to eventually see a clandestine transfer of classified documents or something equally shadowy. He had a good imagination, and it delighted him to think of what he might see one day. On other assignments it had been hard keeping the target in sight because they were so smooth at blending in and being inconspicuous. This man was just the opposite. Even in Beijing he sat eating candy bars and drinking soda in full view of others who had nothing. Granted, this was accepted as normal in the U.S., but here it was considered highly rude. The business with the airport tax in Beijing was a classic, almost over played, as he thought of it. He did everything to appear as an unconscious, fumbling foreigner. To think I talked to him on the plane out of sympathy. Boy, he must have thought I'm a novice, Yang thought. Well, I am. But, my "act" was just as convincing as his.

What Yang witnessed in the airport lobby left even his imagination wanting. The two men, one after the other, approached their target. Words were exchanged but Yang had not made them out over the din in the lobby. Immediately one man grabbed the agent's suitcase and ran with it while the other held the agent's arm. It was so unexpected he had stood riveted to the floor. He remembered thinking *his* agent would never recover his travel bag filled with secrets. The total professionalism with which the agent broke free and overtook the thief was astonishing. Yang's teeth grated as he heard the crunch and snap of breaking bones. It was beyond what he'd even seen in a movie, and it was real life. He, Yang, was five meters away! He had been trained to carefully recount the sequence of events in his mind so he could accurately relate them later. This he was doing as he casually took out a cigarette and lit it.

An airport medic had arrived to help the man with the broken bones. Man, that guy was lethal, even without a weapon! Walking out the door to the sidewalk, he saw the second man retching over the curb. This man was close enough to touch. Yang felt a chill in his spine. The night was filled with danger and intrigue. It made him alive. His fingers even tingled a bit. He could hardly believe something big had gone down and he was right in the middle of it, coolly doing his job.

As he looked about there was no sign of the agent—not surprising. After the show of ineptness earlier in the day he would now become a chameleon, nobody would see him again. He heard the police captain call for a roadblock on the expressway to the city north the beltway of.

After a protracted eternity, Breckon began to see a few more buildings along the road. Most were the Russian style high rise apartment complexes without a single light on. Either the power was turned off at bed time, or there was severe discipline associated with unwarranted power use. Their speed had also dropped dramatically and Breckon started to breathe again. It seemed logical because the driver would know his speed might be monitored as they neared the city.

When Breckon gave the cab driver the two one-hundred RMB notes, unknowingly he was exercising the first imperative of escape and evasion—travel faster and further in your first moments of freedom than your enemy imagines you can. When a net is set up to trap you, you must already be outside the net. It was thirty kilometers from the airport to the city beltway. At one seventy km per hour, one-hundred-five mph, it took them eleven minutes to cover this distance. From the time the incident happened it took several minutes for the police to arrive at the scene, to ascertain what happened, who was suspected of doing it, and get a description of the man. Several additional minutes were expended getting a roadblock set up at the Round-The-City Highway. The roadblock required several cars and signs to slow the traffic to avoid accidents. The police acted with trained efficiency. The first car was stopped thirty seconds after the driver and Breckon passed the interchange.

Finally, the driver turned right on a main thoroughfare. The traffic lights had large seven segment numeric displays beside them that counted down until the light changed color. A person approaching an intersection with a green light knew how long it would be until it turned yellow, and if waiting for a red light to change a driver knew how long he had to wait. After what seemed like miles, actually only one, they pulled up to a large hotel. It was the Hilton.

"We here. You sleep good," said the driver. Breckon tried to no avail to explain they were at the wrong hotel. He could not leave his luggage in the car and go in to get someone who spoke English to explain the problem. There were four Chinese men standing between the cab and the hotel who might have thought Breckon was trying to get out of paying the cab fare. They looked like toughs and their facial expressions and body language were definitely threatening. The taxi meter said one-hundred, eighty-two RMB so Breckon gave him two-hundred, gathered up his belongings, and walked into the hotel past the glaring bystanders.

Even though the desk clerk spoke English, Breckon was too tired to try to explain what had happened, and get to the right hotel. He took a room at the Hilton telling the desk clerk to wake him up at 11:30. He'd get to the right hotel after a few hours sleep, and do it in the daylight.

Smoking his second cigarette, Richard Yang continued to act like he was waiting for someone to pick him up. From time to time he'd pretend to place a call in his cell phone, and act a little impatient. An hour after it all started he overheard the police call off the roadblock. The entire expressway had been combed from the belt road to the airport with nothing to show for it. Good luck, Yang sneered. He's way too good for you.

Later the same day

Check out time at the Hilton was noon and Breckon beat that by five minutes. He had expected the cab ride would be only a block or two, assuming all the major hotels would be in the same area. He was surprised at the nearly three mile drive down East Zhongshan Road which had a name change to Hanzhong Road before they came to the Sheraton Nanjing Kingsley Hotel and Towers. The street was packed with anything that had wheels: cars, buses, trucks, mopeds, and other conveyances he had never seen before. He arrived at the front desk at twelve-twenty to check in agreeing, with no fuss, to pay for the previous night's stay since the room was "held for late arrival." There was relief apparent in the clerk's expression at his easy acceptance of the charge. He was handed several messages, all in envelopes, along with his magnetic key card.

In his room, Breckon opened his suitcase for the first time. At the Hilton he had only slipped off his shoes before falling into bed. Of all the luck! The computer was still there! Stupid CIA couldn't get anything right, he thought. Now what do I do? Come to think of it, the airplane didn't explode either, so it must really be a computer.

He ordered a meal from room service and took a shower. To his annoyance he discovered he had forgotten to pack his electric shaver. The disposable blade razor provided by the hotel would have to do to scrape off his rapidly growing beard. Never having used a blade before, it left his skin raw. The food arrived about the time he had finished putting on clean clothes. After finishing a peaceful meal he knew, like it or not, it was time to open the messages. The first one was a fax from the president of Control Systems berating him for not calling in when he got to the hotel. Since he was supposed to arrive no later than 8:30 p.m., the big guy had expected a call. In case there were any messages from the client at the work site he would be able to assure everyone that help had arrived. Breckon mused that the man had given no thought to the possibility that he might be dead or in some dark dungeon being beaten for information.

The second envelope he opened was from Stefan. It was hand written and had obviously been hand delivered. He also was irate and somewhat confused, allowing as the report from Jiang Wong was hard to understand. It ended with: "Why did you attack my driver, and where did you go? Call me at the site if you ever show up!"

Finally, there was a message from Charlie Gunther who expressed real concern that something might have happened to him. The time difference made it hard to communicate except by emails and there was a lot being lost along the way. Charlie also asked Breckon to contact him.

Breckon's computer was not set up to send emails from China so he left a message on Charlie's phone. It was either one or three a.m. in Minneapolis. Breckon could never keep it straight. He explained about the many delays and then ending up at the wrong hotel saying nothing about the incident at the airport. The events of the early morning were worrying Breckon more and more as he started to feel human again. What was that all about? He was not even sure what had happened being in such a daze at the time. After thinking about it for awhile he lay back on his bed to relax and was soon asleep again.

When Breckon awoke, it was dark in his room. Disoriented he tried to place where he was. Sitting up it came to him, the hotel in Nanjing. Turning on a light he saw it was seven-thirty. Good, time to eat again. He decided to put his computer in his bag and lock the bag. At the same time he left the CIA computer in plain view hoping someone would steal it. Oh, please steal it. Anyone will do, house keeping, CIA, Chinese police. Anybody.

After consulting the guide on the table in his room, he went down to the floor above the main lobby. It was hardly a lobby, more like a marble football field. Looking from the balcony down at the front desk, he marveled at the grandness of it. Not that Days Inn and such motels were bad, he simply was not accustomed to this. The first restaurant he encountered was Aroma's. The menu was international and that suited him. He would be adventurous later.

July 16, CIA Headquarters, Langley, Virginia

ShuHo Zing paced the floor in his office reading and rereading the message in his hand. It was five o'clock Sunday afternoon, already five a.m. Monday in Nanjing considering daylight savings time in Virginia and none in China. ShuHo made it a policy not to come into work on Sunday, reserving that time to be with his family. There were exceptions, of course. International emergencies did happen on Sunday the same as on any other day. The duty officer had called him as instructed because a message from Topaz Wind had arrived. He had no choice but to attend to this immediately, especially since he could not think of a reason for such a message unless there was trouble. And trouble enough there appeared to be.

The message was brief and even though encoded when received was cryptic enough in plain text.

Negative computer. Must give direct. Set up meet. One more contact.

ShuHo was thinking how rushed his man must have been to make such a glaring mistake in the message. The error was in the first two words. They were ambiguous. In this business something like that could get a person killed. There was also the all too likely possibility that wrong actions would be taken and ruin the operation. He began to write out the possible explanations for the two words. Either he could not get out to get the computer from the dead drop, or the computer was not there, or the software did not work, the computer was no longer suitable, or finally he was watched too closely to pass the computer out. The rest of the message seemed clear enough. He'd have to directly hand over something, probably a computer disk. The meeting had to be set up and not changed because there could only be one more message to him, then he was out of action for the foreseeable future.

As of yesterday at this time Zing had no information from Muan Yingqu, though he had expected something from him. Of course, Yingqu would not make contact if he still had the computer. If caught with the computer it would probably mean his life. This would give credence to the possibility that the computer was not at the dead drop. A direct hand over at a meeting was the worst. Each operative would know the other so if one were compromised, he could be made to reveal the identity of the other. Even if all seemed to go well, the future work of both would be highly suspect. The thought of loosing Topaz Wind was hard to swallow. On the other hand, Yingqu was a low level operative and he could be dropped for further work. Too bad, though. He was coming along nicely. Still had rough edges, but was properly motivated. He needed the money and appeared to have no loyalties other than that.

As with all operatives, it had cost the CIA a lot to get Yingqu this far. After a few simple assignments that had no intelligence value at all he was carefully watched to see if he boasted to anyone or had contacts with the Chinese intelligence organizations. He appeared to be disciplined and clean.

ShuHo's concentration was broken as Sam Li knocked and walked in. "How's it going boss? Sunday afternoon's a tough time to come in."

ShuHo trying to be sympathetic said, "I know. But, there appears to be a problem with Topaz Wind." Sam was the only other person who knew any details of Topaz Wind, and even he did not know the man's real name and where he worked. "Here's the message. Let me know what you think. I don't want to prejudice your opinion by what I think."

Sam read the dispatch several times and said, "It looks like the computer is not an option and he must hand over the material directly." Sam knew all too well the implications of that option. "From what I understand about the pressure to undo our loss of *mirage* when the plane went down, I'd say we have to do it, even though it will compromise Topaz Wind."

ShuHo took off his glasses and laid them on his desk rubbing his eyes. "The only one we have in Nanjing that could take delivery is Muan Yingqu, and we can't reach him."

Smiling, Sam said, "Maybe he's celebrating. If he did get the computer to the dead drop, we owe him a month's salary. What about the watcher, Richard Yang? Maybe he knows something."

"Okay, alert Shanghai and have them contact Yang. Tell them he was observing the insertion of goods into country. Find out if he knows if it was passed to the agent. Get Jaoi Bin to make a safe call, he's good at that. Yang should be at the Jingling Hotel."

Sam let out a slow breath. "I'll do it at once, but we both know that's a long shot. We'd better start making other plans.

— 7 —

7:00 a.m., Monday, July 17, Nanjing, China

Richard Yang usually stayed at the Jingling Hotel when he was in Nanjing. It was like a home away from home. He knew many of the clerks at the front desk as well as much of the wait staff in the main restaurant. He was getting dressed when his phone rang. Picking it up he said, "Yes."

"Good morning, is this Richard?"

"Yes it is." Yang thought he recognized the voice.

"Well, this is Jaoi. I'm in kind of a rush so don't run on like you usually do. I need a little information."

"Okay." Yang knew this meant he was to give only short answers since this was by no means a secure call.

"Did you meet your colleague at the airport Friday?"

Yang paused a minute. Colleague meant target. Here there was a misunderstanding. Jaoi was referring to the target to receive the computer, whereas Yang assumed he meant the man he was following, Breckon. The plane finally got in Saturday morning, though it should have gotten in the evening before. And, he started following his target on Friday so he answered, "Yes."

"Good. More importantly, would you happen to know if he has the sample Freon dryer for the sales meeting tomorrow?"

This was easy, sample meant any deliverable like a camera, drawing, book, anything that was the object of the trip. He longed to tell what he had seen. But, from what had happened, he was absolutely sure his man still had the secret goods. He answered. "Yes. He does."

"Are you sure?" Bin knew how unlikely it would have been to see the actual hand off.

"Oh yes, absolutely sure."

"Ah, well good, that's good. Now another thing, and then I must be off to a meeting. You know how he likes to go some place we don't know until he gets rested up after traveling. Can you call around and see if you can find where he's staying?"

"I know where he is." Yang couldn't help stretching the truth a little. After all, on the plane the man had mentioned the hotel where he was staying.

"You do?"

Yang thought the voice sounded a little incredulous, and wanted to say more, but held to short answers. "Yes."

There was a short pause before the voice continued. "I know how you hate to run errands, but could you get a note to him? I'd really appreciate it."

This was against all the rules. Yang had been assured this would never happen. Even this call was pushing the agreement. But, he was getting that thrill again. The money would be good, too, as signified by "really appreciate it." He repeatedly ran the fingers of his free hand through his hair as he thought.

"How about it?"

"Okay."

"Fine. I'll fax you the message. Deliver it today."

"I will."

With that the line went dead. Yang sat down realizing he was over his head. What had he gotten himself into? Nothing at all, really. All he had to do was walk into the Sheraton Hotel, go to the elevators, and slip the message under his door. Oh, oh. How do I get his room number? It's a sure bet that Mr. Super Spy would know how to get mine. I'm just a . . . well, nothing. So, I leave an envelope at the front desk with a fifty RMB note and ask them to deliver it. But, I don't know the name he's registered under. No, wait. One of his assailants at the airport had that sign with Ed Breckon on it. Yang had only seen it for a few seconds, but there had been long sessions of intense training teaching him to recall things he had seen. He remembered that the man he was watching did respond to it. It was worth a try.

Rationalizing further, he thought that if the agent were registered under another name or said the Sheraton Hotel to throw him off, either were likely possibilities as he thought of it, he'd report back that the agent had moved. The guys in the CIA had to realize an agent like this would never stay in one place for long.

Yang had the morning off with his first customer call at 2:00 p.m. He spent two hours doing a little shopping and then returned to his room. When he arrived back he found a sealed envelope had been slid under his door. There were no marks on the outside other than his room number. Holding it up to the light he could make out nothing of what was inside. An irrational curiosity settled on his mind. What was it all about? What did super spies say to one another? Of course, it was probably in code so if he did open it he wouldn't know any more than he did now. But maybe not. It was in a standard hotel envelope, the same kind that were in the table drawer in his room, so if he opened it he could simply replace the envelope.

Wait a minute. It had his room number on it. He couldn't pass it along like that. He had to change the envelope or he could be identified. Something in his training was missing. What to do? It was obvious, he had to open the envelope. He had plain white envelopes in his brief case. Sure. That's what he'd be expected to do. He slit open the envelope and removed the folded paper handling it with tissues from the bathroom so as not to leave fingerprints. He should have quickly slipped it in the white envelope, sealed it, and be done with it. But . . . that curiosity. Slipping it into the white envelope he left the flap unsealed, put it on the table and checked some notes for his afternoon sales call. By the time he was about to leave for an early lunch the desire to know had broken down his otherwise good common sense that told him to leave it alone. He pulled it out of the envelope and unfolded it being careful not to leave any prints. In plain text it read:

Be at the intersection of Pailou and Lasa Roads at 1910 hours on Tuesday. On west side of intersection lean against small tree between two cross walks.

Yang knew where that was! It was up the hill from the corner where the Sheraton Hotel was located and Lasa Road ran along the southwest side of the block where Wutaishan Gym stood. That was a sports complex with a soccer field, tennis courts, indoor swimming pool, a moderate sized auditorium for athletic contests and similar facilities.

Shrugging his shoulders Yang tossed it off with a bit of a let down. So, Mr. Breckon, a.k.a. Mr. Super Spy, was to be at a certain place at a certain time to see something or meet someone. Probably not a meet. He had been told that was avoided if at all possible. So, the life of a super spy was not always exciting. In the meantime Mr. Super Spy would probably sit in his hotel room watching television. It occurred to Yang, that it didn't seem exciting at all. Then a terrible thought hit him. What if he would be shot as he leaned against the tree? Someone knew precisely where he would be at a certain time. The voice of the man who called this morning was that of Jaoi Bin, or so he had assumed. Now he wasn't so sure.

On the elevator down to the lobby of the Jingling Hotel, Yang made a decision. He was paid to be a watcher. So, he'd station himself a short distance away and observe what happened. It would also let him know that Breckon showed. That way, he would have proof that the message had been delivered correctly.

When he reached the Sheraton he approached from across the busy intersection and walked on the sidewalk in front of the hotel. The huge pillars that supported the two story high portico had a four foot high wall between them with plants on top. This insured the arriving guests were shielded from the sidewalk traffic. This also meant he was unobserved by anyone associated with the hotel. Seeing a teenage boy hanging about he approached him. He offered him fifty RMB to take the envelope, on which Yang had printed in block letters Ed Breckon, and ask at the desk if such a man were registered there. If so, he was to ask the staff to deliver the envelope to the man's room. If not, he was to return it. In either case, the youth was promised a second note of equal value upon his return.

Yang casually watched over the wall between the leaves of the plants. The boy sped on his mission and Yang could see through the glassed in hotel front as the youth approached the front desk. He saw him talk to the clerk and hand over the envelope. Upon his return, and a report of a successful mission, the young man was rewarded as promised. Yang continued on down the block to the Kentucky Fried Chicken franchise, went in, and ordered a meal.

Breckon arrived back at his room at 6:50 p.m. after his first day on the job. As he had guessed, the problem with the elevators at the job site was mostly political. Not bothering to read the details of how the elevator system was to work the Chinese programmer had taken it on himself to mess around with it so it would operate according to his assumptions. In the process he made the system inoperable. With face to save on the part of the programmer a dispute had arisen.

On older elevators when someone pressed the button to get an elevator the controls knew where the requestor was and an elevator stopped at that floor. Only when the person got on to the car did he press a button for his destination floor. This was not an efficient use of the elevators. The system Breckon's company had been installing used a better approach. The elevator system knew which floor the request came from and hence where the rider was. The rider put in the destination floor at the time of the request rather than when he got into the car. This way the computer program could assign the car that could most efficiently handle the request.

It was apparent from the start how the program had been altered. He didn't bother to correct the errors, but simply deleted the corrupted program and reloaded the original one. This certainly could have been done without his being there. After that he spent most of the day explaining through an interpreter how the system was supposed to operate.

Dealing with these people should have been easier, Breckon thought. He had begun to suspect that the interpreter was trying to make Breckon, and the rest of the American delegation, look like the foolish ones. Since Breckon's company had no one who spoke Chinese that they could trust, he couldn't prove it.

At last in the relative safety of his room he was frustrated and hungry. Spotting the envelope that had been slipped under his door didn't improve his outlook, nor the fact that the CIA's computer was still on the table where he left it. He put his wallet and the envelope in the room safe and showered. After that he went down for dinner. Lassitor would join him for dinner on Wednesday so until then he was on his own. Aroma's it was again. Why not? It was a good restaurant and he thought he had to try the Australian kangaroo that was on the menu.

Returning to his room after dinner Breckon saw the CIA computer was still there. Out of frustration he opened it again and let it boot up. On Sunday he had spent an hour looking through what he could find on it. It had taken him a few minutes to remember the password that the CIA guy had used at the Minneapolis airport, but finally it had come back to him—welcomemat. Everything seemed normal including letters, emails, spread sheets, and drawings, as well as the programs to make these documents.

Today he was looking through the deeply nested directories and sub-directories on the C drive when he saw one he had not noticed before called "Confucius." To his surprise, it was an exe file, that is, an executable file. So, he double clicked on it. A window opened up that filled half of the screen with the following:

THOUGHT FOR TODAY
Confucius say: When you have faults, do not fear to abandon them.
Dragon say: When you have faults, do not fear to fix them.

THOUGHT FOR TOMORROW
Confucius say: Gentlemen trust in justice, the vulgar trust in favor.
Dragon say: Gentlemen trust in justice, the vulgar trust in intrigue.

In the upper right corner of the window was the words "TODAY'S DATE" with the day of the week and the correct date under it. It would seem the "thoughts" changed each day. The slight variation on the Confucian saying seemed odd, like it was planned to confuse someone.

Finally, Breckon gave up on the computer and turned it off. Like a dark cloud on a pleasant summer day, he remembered the envelope and decided he had to open the darned thing. It was probably from the president of his company with an unreasonable demand. Couldn't he leave me alone so I can do the job he pays me for, Breckon thought? When he read the message he instantly knew it was from that cursed bunch at the CIA. Oh, screw them. He had enough to worry about. And what's more, he don't know where anything was in this town. How exasperating. He supposed they wanted him to give the computer to someone.

As he thought about it, giving the computer to someone didn't make sense. They were too secretive for that. Maybe at the meeting someone would give him a note about what to do with the computer. Why wouldn't they have simply put that note in this envelope, though? It would have saved a lot of fooling around. What if he were to ignore the meeting and didn't show? Those bastards would tamper with his visa or something worse and he'd wind up in a Chinese jail. He had no doubt that they'd be foul enough to do it. Here he was, minding his own business, taking a one week trip to a foreign country, and he found himself up to his ears in something, and he didn't even know what it was.

Leaning back in one of the easy chairs and putting his feet up on the other, the incident at the airport forced itself into his consciousness. Ever since it happened he tried to keep it out of his mind, not always success-fully. He had come to believe that that fracas just had to have something to do with the CIA computer. But, the CIA guys in Minneapolis had spe-cifically said the computer would disappear without him being any the wiser. Yet, there it was on the table. He unconsciously glanced in that direction in case it had magically disappeared since he turned it off. Nope.

So, what was the meaning of what had happened at the airport? One of the problems was he had been so tired he couldn't remember most of it clearly. Was it something about the Chinese people versus Americans? From what he saw on the job today, these were not pleasant people. There appeared to be no love for Americans as his work with the elevator controls showed. Even the driver for the company claimed to be an inno-cent victim of Breckon's irrational behavior. When Breckon asked him to explain why the other man grabbed his suitcase and headed for the door with it while Wong held his arm, the answer made no sense. After several futile attempts he gave up. Here again Breckon felt he couldn't trust the interpreter. He was looking forward to the time when that big 777 got out of Chinese air space—with him on it. He was counting down the days and the hours.

Drawn back to his problem, Breckon once again tried to connect the airport incident, the computer, and the note. Anything Breckon could think of did not put him at ease. One possibility was that the CIA had planted something else on him and the computer was a decoy. Having failed to get it at the airport they, whoever *they* were and whatever *it* was, were trying again. And, what about that stupid computer? If he really were supposed to bring the computer to the meeting, they would have said something in the note, however indirectly, like he should bring the "package" or something.

Breckon needed to get out for a few minutes to clear his head. On the sidewalk and walking west from the hotel, he marveled at all the people out at nearly nine o'clock. It was uncomfortably warm and humid. The lights from the commercial establishments as well as streetlights made most of the sidewalk well lit.

After fifteen minutes he turned around and started back. He went into a store next to the Hotel. It was roughly equivalent to a superette in the U.S. The only difference he could see was the narrow aisles, but then the people on average were smaller. There were canned food items with gruesome pictures on the labels. He was just as glad he didn't understand the Chinese characters. He bought candy bars, U.S. name brands, and a couple of one liter jugs of water. The check-out counter had a laser scanner to read the bar codes like any store in the U.S. Still unable to figure out the currency, he laid some on the counter, and the clerk picked out what was needed, and gave a few coins in change. He had done this before. They seemed to be honest people in that respect.

Back in his room Breckon studied a map of the city he had purchased on Sunday. To his surprise he found the meeting place was only a block from the hotel. Of course, the blocks in this part of Nanjing were a quarter mile on a side. It was across the main street that ran in front of the hotel and up a hill. He had walked up that way Sunday afternoon. He smiled at the thought of one of the strange street scenes he had encountered. Across the street, on the hill was a car parked along the curb. It was jacked up with three wheels off the road and these three tires removed. The car's owner was getting a new set of tires. The one rear tire on the road was holding the car from rolling backward. There was no block behind the single wheel, only the emergency brake held it.

Another thing Breckon came to understand was there was no weekend. It seemed like everyone had time off, but not all at the same time. Street repair projects, building construction, and commerce seemed to go on seven days a week. Breckon assumed this was to prevent people from having common time off for religious services, for family reunions, or political meetings. It was, after all, a totalitarian society.

Tuesday, Nanjing, China

Breckon was back at his hotel room at the Sheraton a little before six p.m. He decided he had to go to the meeting, though he was genuinely afraid. He ate a candy bar, and then another as he paced the floor of his room. It had occurred to him during the day that he could be kidnapped for the incident at the airport and this was a way to do it in a place where no one would recognize him or care. On his Sunday walk he became very much aware that once out of the hotel he was one Caucasian in a sea of Chinese.

Breckon checked his watch and it was six-fifty, time to go. His stomach was in knots and his hands shook a little. The terrible feeling of the stress he had encountered in Iraq bore down on him. He had hoped he would never experience that again. And, here he was in another foreign country, with potential unseen enemies on all sides. In Iraq at least he knew who his enemies were, namely everyone.

He left all of his identification in the room safe except copies of his passport, the page with his picture on it, and the page with his visa. He went down to the street level and out into the night. He had taken his faded blue denim jacket and decided to put it on even thought it was seventy-five degrees. People were everywhere. He had to wait for the traffic light before he could cross Hanzhong Road. Though it should not have, this irritated him. Once across the street he walked briskly up the west side of Pailou Road heading north. There were a few streetlights, but not enough to suit him. He had to control himself so as not to look at his watch every minute. Half way to his destination he glanced at it and saw he had to slacken his pace because he was ahead of schedule.

As he approached the street intersection, he knew he was a couple of minutes early. Lasa Road came down the hill from the northwest on the left. When it met Pailou Road it turned thirty degrees and headed east forming a three-corner intersection. There were a few trees between the sidewalk and the street on his side. Yes, there was a six-inch tree between the white hashed patterns painted on the street to mark the crosswalks on Pailau, and on Lasa Road. Since Pailou curved gently, there was about twenty feet between the start of the two crosswalks. Breckon casually walked up to the tree and leaned against it. People passed all around him. The change of traffic lights caused a small stampede as people crossed. Everyone seemed to have a single minded purpose and largely ignored Breckon except for casual glances. "A foreigner lost in the heart of China," was how he read their thoughts.

Trying not to seem too jumpy and alert, Breckon continued to look in all directions as traffic roared past him on the street, and pedestrians swept past him on the sidewalk. He glance at his watch, it was now nearly thirteen after seven. He had decided to wait five more minutes and then leave. With a start he became aware of a small man standing beside him on his right. The man watched the street light as if waiting for it to change so he could cross even though he was not standing at the crosswalk. Without turning his head he said, "The dragon say: Gentlemen trust in Justice."

The whole thing caught Breckon by surprise. He glanced and saw the thinning hair on top of the man's head, and as an instinctive reaction said, "What?"

The man repeated the phrase with tension in his voice.

Breckon scrambled to remember the rest. "The vulgar trust in favor . . . . No, no, intrigue, trust in intrigue."

The man gave a quick look at Breckon and said, "You are not very good." He hardly had the words out of his mouth when there was a shout from up Lasa Road to the left. A couple of men were dashing down the sidewalk pushing people out of the way as they ran. The small man grabbed Breckon's right wrist and thrust something into his hand as he said, "Protect it with your life." Startled, Breckon mechanically clutched the package and covered it with his coat. Immediately, the man darted out into the intersection against the light and not in the crosswalk. He deftly stepped out of the path of a small car and then a three wheeled power tricycle. At the center of the street he looked back at the commotion on the sidewalk where the pushers were shouting at him. He turned to continue crossing the lanes of traffic coming the opposite way. But as he took his first step a bus hit him. This threw him back in Breckon's direction so he fell into the middle of the opposite lane of traffic. Before he reached the pavement he connected with the bumper of a shinny black car rushing down the hill. He rolled back to the center of the intersection and lay there unmoving. Tires squealed as cars tried to avoid the man as well as other vehicles.

Breckon quickly stepped back as a car momentarily came over the curb. A woman and her child were struck slightly throwing them back. In a matter of seconds everything was stopped. There were a dozen crashed vehicles and people screaming and moaning. Forgetting the item Breckon clutched in his hand he watched as the two men that had pushed their way down the sidewalk ran out and stooped over the small man. They paid no attention to the other people nor the wellbeing of the man as they roughly turned him over. They rummaged through his pockets, loosened his belt, and pulled down his pants turning down his underwear as well as feeling up under his shirt.

A sensation in his hand brought Breckon's attention to what he was holding. The dead man had given it to him moments before he had dashed into the street. He froze as he realized those men were looking for what he was carrying. Why had the man dashed into the street *after* he had passed off the valuable commodity?

The pedestrians were curious but kept their distance not wanting to be associated with the incident as police sirens could now be heard coming down Lasa Road from the left. Several people had gathered in front of

Breckon so he carefully shoved the package behind his belt and closed two snaps of his jacket. The men, not finding what they were after on the body, stood up and looked intently at the accumulated onlookers. Luckily, a woman between Breckon and the men in the intersection took that instant to stand on tiptoes to get a better look. Since Breckon was a few steps down the hill, she mostly shielded him. He took that opportunity to turn and start walking back to the hotel. Walking casually took an extreme act of his will as he feared either those men or the police would accost him at any second. Half way to the hotel he heard running steps behind him. He fought the urge to run knowing there was no place to run to. After a bit the steps seemed to go off to the left. He glanced that way to see two teenagers running across the street, probably rushing to be the first to tell friends and neighbors about the accident.

— 8 —

Richard Yang arrived at his planned station on Lasa Road on the opposite side of the intersection from where Breckon was to wait. He traversed up and down the inclined sidewalk several times until he felt he had the best position to see the small tree between the crosswalks. Having arrived before seven, he knew he had a while to wait and used the time it to watch the vehicles pass in front of the meeting place. Only when a large truck or a bus passed was it out of view for a second. A little before seven-ten he saw Breckon appear. He was certain it was him, having had many hours to observe him on his trip from Beijing to Nanjing. Yang waited several minutes wondering if something was happening, and he was not well enough trained to see it. Breckon moved from one side of the tree to the other as he looked at his watch. No. It seemed it had not happened yet.

All the people were simply walking past Breckon, a few giving him the once-over. After a bus passed there was a small man standing near his man. Thus alerted, Yang made a mental inventory of the new man's features, age, size, clothing, and similar details as he had been taught. Two trucks going in the same direction, one in each traffic lane, came through the intersection at that moment so Breckon was out of sight for a few seconds.

Suddenly, a commotion across the street from Yang diverted his attention. Two men ran down the sidewalk shouting and pushing people out of the way. He quickly returned his attention on Breckon to see if this was part of what was to happen. To his shock, the small man rushed from Breckon's side out into traffic. Yang watched in disbelief as the man was hit first by a bus and then by a car. The squealing of tires, the crashes, the cries of pain were all barely registering in Yang's brain. When it had all stopped he could see the fallen man beside a car that had skidded sideways into a small truck. He thought about helping, but knew he was not to get involved. The running men were instantly on the scene leaning over the fallen man. They'd help, Yang thought. Once again, Yang could not believe what he saw. The men cared nothing about the injured man as they practically undressed him in their rush to find something. From the limpness of the man, it seemed he was unconscious, or more likely, dead. Yang didn't move a muscle as the men stood up and looked around at the gathered crowd. Wondering what Breckon would do about this, he glanced to that side of the intersection. Breckon had vanished.

The sound of approaching sirens caused Yang to turn and walk away from the scene. Reviewing in his mind what he had seen he pieced together that the running men were after something that the small man had, or thought he had. The small man clearly did not want to be caught or he would not have taken that fatal plunge into the street. It seemed he would not have stopped by Breckon if the two of them had not had something in common. No one else had stopped by him. But, he had not seen anything exchanged. If something did change hands it was cleverly done. Yang forgot that the passage of the trucks had kept them from his view for enough time for a hand off. The commotion across the street at the same time confused that part of the action in his mind. Yang was still left with the contradiction that the small man would not have dashed into the street if he no longer had whatever the running men wanted. He could have run down the sidewalk if he had only intended to lead his pursuers away from Breckon. But, he had to admit that causing the accident gave Breckon an overwhelming opportunity to escape.

As he walked away another possibility occurred to him. The Chinese authorities may have discovered the dead man was a spy. He passed off what he had and chose to kill himself rather than be interrogated. Yang had heard stories about what that was like.

———————————

Back in his room, Breckon pulled the package out from behind his belt and fell into an easy chair. Putting his feet up on the bed he closed his eyes and tried to relax. All he could hear was his heart pounding in his ears. Would his life ever settle down? Was he doomed to live out his days being thrown from one insane catastrophe to another? Other people don't live like this. Why me, God! He ran his palms over his face. His emotional state was as bad as his spiritual state, neither was in any way stable. His heart hurt for the man he had seen killed. He was certain he could not have lived after the pounding inflicted by the bus and the car. He still vividly saw the body rolling limply across the pavement, uncontrolled limbs flailing. A scene from his experience in Iraq flashed through his mind. It was of the last man he had killed. The second after Breckon shot him the lower wing of the big biplane had caught him in mid-stride and caused him to fold over the wing, dead. As he slipped off he tumbled in the sand, limbs flailing.

Breckon sprang out of the chair and shook his head violently. Rushing to the bathroom, he splashed cold water on his face. No! That wasn't going to happen again! He leaned forward, palms of his hands on the vanity with elbows locked, his head hanging limply. He closed his eyes as he felt a deep sense of foreboding. He knew he was in something way over his head. He could be dead at any minute. Everything was hidden. Death would catch him unawares—if he were lucky. Not only was he neck deep in a CIA operation being used as a piece of fodder, but he was in one of the most oppressive societies in the world. These people thought nothing of driving tanks through Tiananmen Square squashing thousands of their own citizens. A hated American would certainly be treated no better.

After a time he picked up the package he had been given at such cost. Untying the string holding the brown paper wrapping in place, he was half expecting it to explode in his face. What he saw did not surprise him since the size was right. It was a CD-ROM. It had the label of the manufacturer with nothing written on it to identify its contents. What horrors lie hidden in the micro-bits of protein that formed the ones and zeros in this innocuous looking disk?

He was tired but not sleepy. For thirty minutes he exercised in his room doing everything he could without exercise equipment, and then showered. Feeling a little better he began to assess his situation. Looking at the CD in the plastic jewel case lying on the table, he could hardly bring himself to touch it. A human life had been forfeited to bring it to him. What could possibly be so important? He tried to shrug off the thought that it was all done for political expediency, that the small man had died so a bureaucrat back in Washington would not be embarrassed or lose his job.

He had to get rid of the disk, and that CIA computer that kept clinging to him. If he were being watched, and after the incident at the airport it was likely, it was certain his room had been searched. Therefore, they knew about the CIA computer. He'd dump that the next day. Grabbing his computer bag he took stuff out of it until he could get both his and the CIA's computer into it.

Now, the disk. This they did not know he had so time was important. How could he get it out of China? He thought of taking it to the job in the morning and putting it in the air conditioning control panel he would be sending back to the states. That plan he rejected. In the event the crate was opened for inspection, and it likely would be, the CD would be discovered. He opened the clear plastic case and, with a permanent black marker he wrote "Vacation Pictures" on it, and slipped it in a paper sleeve from his computer bag. There was a FedEx office not far from the hotel. If he could send it by FedEx, paying in cash, it would likely get out. While back in the office at Control Systems he had received several overnight envelopes from Nanjing that way. If the ones he had received had been opened, it had been cleverly done. With so much traffic of this kind, he thought it was unlikely anyone would bother.

Who could he send it to that was not at his company? The first person that came to mind was the last person he wanted to get involved. It was Cindy Thomas. Now that he thought of her, he realized how much he missed her. It seemed like his present predicament was a continuation of his abnormal life, and she was a part of it. Since she was at a different employer now, too, still in purchasing, he'd send it to her at work. He had called her and said he was going to China. There was apprehension in her voice when she learned of the trip. It was as if she expected something would go wrong. At least, getting an envelope from China would not surprise her. He took the elevator down and made his way to the FedEx office.

7:15 a.m., Wednesday, Jingling Hotel, Nanjing, China

The phone rang while Richard Yang brushed his teeth. He let it ring and finished what he was doing. It continued to ring. He was still holding his towel as he walked out of the bathroom. He pondered his situation as he looked at the ringing phone. Finally, he picked up the receiver.

"Good morning, is this Richard," said a cheerful male voice. Yang recognized it as the same voice of two mornings before.

Pausing a few seconds he said, "Who is this!"

"Well, this is Jaoi, of course. Is this Richard?" The voice had lost much of its initial pleasantness.

"I don't know what is going on, but I saw a man killed last night at the meeting. I want out!"

There was an audible nasal sound almost like a sneer. "Now Richard!" The pleasantness was all gone now. "Yes, our lead man lost a big contract, but how you do exaggerate! This is a big expanding market. There will be other opportunities."

Yang interrupted. "I don't like the way this company does business, I quit!" With that he slammed down the receiver. A minute later the phone started ringing again which did not particularly surprise Yang. This was one job it would probably be hard to quit. He let the phone ring until eventually it stopped.

As he ate breakfast and prepared for another day, Yang thought about what had happened from the startling events at the airport to the man being killed in the intersection. He had an analytical mind and something was not making sense. In hindsight, the incident at the airport was clumsy. There were security cameras everywhere and guards scattered around. The operative had to know that. It was like he simply got mad and started knocking people around. In any case, why was Breckon still at large? The police certainly could have identified him from the airport cameras and located him at the Sheraton Hotel. Of course, they might be watching him and his room to see who he met before they picked him up. In that case it was likely they read the message Yang had delivered to Breckon's room and knew about the meeting. Maybe they did, and got to the meeting a few seconds late. That must have been the meaning of the men running down the sidewalk along Lasa Road. From their actions, the running men clearly thought the dead man had gotten something from Breckon. Their response after having searched him showed he had received nothing so it had to be the other way. Breckon had gotten something from the dead man.

All of this still left unanswered the question of the men at the airport who tried to steal the suitcase from Breckon in full view of the security cameras. What made them think they would get away with it? That didn't add up, either. Unless it was totally unrelated and was part of the growing underworld problem in China. Various people at the airport could be in on the take. It could be that way, but Yang didn't really believe it.

An hour ago Yang was fed up with the whole spook business, and now he was planning again. For one thing, he had forgotten about the money he was getting from the CIA. It had been useful at first, but now he had begun to depend on it. He enjoyed living in Sacramento, California, but the cost of living was high. His wife worked part time and he had two kids in grade school. It was amazing how much money the school activities took, to say nothing of the brand name clothes that were the rage at any particular time. The fact that the brands changed all too often had always seemed like a conspiracy to him. The bottom line was, he wanted his job back. He *needed* his job back.

What if he tracked down the man with the broken knee? He might learn something useful from him. Thinking about the terrible crunch he heard when the knee broke he imagined the man might still be in a hospital. Being a good salesman Yang was a good talker. He was sure the man would not recognize him from the airport so he decided to find him and see what he could learn.

Later that afternoon

Posing as a friend of the man with the broken knee, Yang located where the man had been taken. It had taken several calls but at last he was sure he had his man. The man was in one of the best hospitals in Nanjing. That was something of a surprise. But in today's China one never knew who had the money and influence. It did lend a little credibility to his theory that it was a mob related matter. They took care of their own.

When Yang arrived at the hospital, he was asked several questions that he managed to deftly handle with answers he made up as he spoke. He learned the man was in a room with two beds. He slowly walked down the hall where he had been directed. As he casually walked into the room he saw an old man asleep in the bed nearest the door. He was certain this was not his man. This left the occupant in the bed behind the pulled out curtain. Yang quietly sat down on a chair near the sleeping man. He tried to appear as if he were waiting for the old man to wake up, yet not wanting to disturb his sleep. His plan was to act restless after a time, casually look behind the curtain, and ask when the sleeping man might wake up. This he hoped would lead to a conversation that might reveal something.

Immediately he became aware that there was someone with the man behind the curtain. They spoke in hushed voices so Yang caught only snatches of their conversation. Suddenly the conversation seemed to change and the level of the voices increased.

" . . . Yeah, they had to replace the whole knee, so now I'm partly a robot." The man chuckled a little. "Can you believe it, I started to walk on it the day after they put it in."

"Does it hurt?"

"Not much. But, I'm taking quite a few pills. Some of them are painkillers. If there are no complications the doctor says I'll be walking normally in a month with no pain. The broken collar bone is causing more problems. This cast is uncomfortable and the bones hurt when I move in certain ways."

"That's unbelievable about your knee. Where do they find mechanical knees? I never heard of that."

"The U.S. Where else? The doctor said I got a good deal because this facility is trying to establish itself as a hospital of excellence in joint replacement. This is the ninth one this doctor has done. We all have our opinions of the Americans, but they make the best artificial joints. They replace a quarter million knees a year over there." Dropping the level of his voice again he continued, "Still in all, I plan to find the guy that did this to me, and then it'll be pay back time."

There was a pause and the voices became lower still. Yang leaned closer to the curtain so he could still follow the conversation.

"Be careful what you do. The MSS (Ministry of State Security) will decide what is to happen to the American, Breckon."

At the sound of Breckon's name Yang stiffened. There was no doubt who and what they were talking about.

"They may let him go so they can tail him in America. The whole incident at the airport was strange, right under the cameras. How he escaped the roadblock going into the city has everyone baffled. He must have had help. The funny thing is he never gave that second laptop computer to anyone, just left it setting in his room."

"Well, that makes sense," the other man said. "I was supposed to steal it from him before he got to his hotel. That's what the CIA was paying me for, and what I would have done had he not broken me up! Now he doesn't know what to do with it."

"Keep your voice down. We got into his room and downloaded the complete hard drive from both of his computers. We went though every program and file. Nothing there of any significance. Maybe I shouldn't tell you this, but you've paid your dues. He may have met with a man from a highly classified program last evening. They stood beside one another for a few seconds and then the other man rushed out into a street and got himself killed. We thought Breckon had given something to him, but the dead man had nothing."

"It's obvious, he gave something to Breckon."

"We've checked his room a couple of times but have found nothing. He's watched on the job as much as possible, but the guy moves around a lot. Oh, there is something I was asked to talk to you about. At the meeting last night we got a few good photos off the street surveillance camera of the crowd that gathered when the man was killed in the street. We matched a face with one from the security tape at the airport. This man was a few meters away from Breckon when you grabbed his bag. Here's his picture. Do you recognize him?"

Yang knew they were talking about him, and they even had his photo. His face became a shade whiter.

"No. Sorry. I don't. He may have been there, but there were a surprising number of people waiting for the arrival of that late flight."

"Now, it's time for you to call the CIA and report in," the second man continued. "You can say you were heavily sedated until now. This is what you tell them about the airport incident."

Yang had heard enough. Slowly getting up, he made every effort not to touch the curtain. He reached over and pinched the sleeping man's finger. The man snorted and moved in the bed masking the sounds of Yang's clothing as he made his way out the door. Walking down the hallway it was difficult not to break into a run and draw attention to himself. Turning the corner to the elevators, he glanced back. No one had come out of the room. An elevator door opened going up. He stepped in. The door opened two floors up. A women entered, and he got out. Quickly opening the door to the stairwell he walked down to the ground floor and out. He hailed a taxi at the hospital's main entrance and was safe, if only for the present.

In the cab, Yang began systematically recounting all he could remember of the conversation. The men on the other side of the curtain were MSS, and the guy Breckon took down was a double agent also working for the CIA. The MSS took care of counter espionage in China. It had a reputation that instilled fear in anyone. They had no rules other than to catch and punish spies.

Worst of all, they had a picture of Yang. This indicated an important operation for them to have done so much work on it. Imagine, finding his face in images of both places. Yet, they weren't perfect. They obviously did not see him have the meeting notice delivered to Breckon. He felt good about that. At least he had done something right.

This led him to wonder who Breckon really was. The guy behind the curtain confirmed what Yang had thought. Smashing somebody to pieces in a crowed terminal under cameras was not professional at all. The man Yang talked to on the plane appeared hardly lucid from lack of sleep. Maybe he got to the end of his rope and lashed out. It occurred to him that maybe Breckon, like himself, was a bit player, as it were. And, he had gotten dragged in beyond his depth. Enough about Breckon, though. Yang had bigger problems figuring out how to salvage his job with the CIA.

9:15 p.m., Tuesday, CIA Headquarters, Langley, Virginia

It was several hours later that ShuHo Zeng and Sam Li were together in Zeng's office. For the past hour they had tried to piece together what had happened in Nanjing. They learned that Muan Yingqu was in a hospital with broken bones under heavy sedation. This probably meant he was drugged into talking to the Chinese counter espionage agents. They also learned from the embassy in Shanghai that their deep cover agent, Topaz Wind, was killed at the meeting, an enormous loss for them.

The same communiqué revealed that Richard Yang had gone under ground. Yang had been the one to pass the meeting time and place to Yingqu. But, the notice could not have gone to Yingqu because at the time he was sedated in a hospital. Yang obviously made a mistake and sent the wrong man to meet Topaz Wind. Yang's harsh statement about seeing someone killed and his refusal to cooperate any further meant he had witnessed the meeting.

The problem caused by their shortage of resources had forced the CIA to use Yang with his lack of training. He had read the message, something he should not have done. So he watched the meeting from a discrete distance. This was logical since he was employed to watch. His lack of discipline gave them a little help. They were certain that Topaz Wind had gone to the meet, though they did not know if he handed off anything, or to whom.

Their discussions were interrupted by a buzz from ShuHo's computer. He leaned over and accepted a message on his monitor. It was a further dispatch from Shanghai. "It seems Muan Yingqu finally checked in with his handler." He printed the message and gave a copy to Li.

Muan Yingqu was attacked at the airport by Edmund Breckon, the man he went there to meet. Flight 1503 had been delayed until the early hours of Saturday. As the passengers emerged from the baggage claim area a disturbance broke out. In the melee Yingqu's knee was broken. He is recovering from a total replacement of his right knee and has been under heavy sedation. This confirmed the earlier dispatch. Doctors say he will be able to walk in two weeks. As a result of his injuries, he was not able to complete his assignment. He does not know what happened to Breckon or the parcel.

After a long pause, Li said, "In the confusion at the airport and the disappearance of Yingqu, there may have been a mix-up about who was the agent and who was the courier. What if Yang thought Breckon was the agent and he was sent to the meeting?"

ShuHo rubbed his face. "That's pretty thin. Yang was tailing Breckon all the way from Beijing. He surely knew he was the courier."

"Why? He was told only to watch Breckon. He wasn't told why he was there. Under normal circumstances he would have ended his surveillance when Breckon got in the taxi with Yingqu as the driver. Meanwhile, who did Topaz Wind meet if not Breckon? And, did he pass on the information before he died?"

"Richard Yang could give us a description of the man he thinks is the agent. He isn't scheduled to come back to the U.S. for a month though, and he'll be hard to find in China. He's running scared."

Two hours later, 11:15 a.m., Wednesday, Nanjing

Breckon was on the work site resolving problems with the intercom system in the executive suites. Having things pretty well untangled in the control room he made an excuse to go to the twenty-ninth floor to check some wiring. When he arrived he saw a small crew putting up light fixtures in partially completed offices. Going to the other end of the floor he found the electrical panels. In a dark area on the side of an electrical enclosure he set down the CIA's laptop computer. The night before he had erased all but a few innocuous looking letters and emails. With it booted up he gave it a hard bump on the back of a chair to crash the hard drive. After that, he carefully wiped off all fingerprints. Now, making sure there was dust on it, he left it in the shadows so someone would eventually find it. Being sure he wasn't watched, he took the stairs down two floors and then the elevator to the basement where he had been working.

Breckon took these precautions to get rid of the CIA's laptop because he wanted to be able to say it had been stolen. He was sure he wasn't through with those monkeys back in Minneapolis. They would be on his case about what happened to it since whoever was supposed to steal it had failed.

— 9 —

8:10 a.m., Saturday, Nanjing Airport

Breckon's flight for Beijing left at ten and he had plenty of time. He found that here, too, he could not check his bag until ninety minutes before the flight left. He purchased his airport tax coupon feeling like a seasoned China traveler now. Walking through the terminal, he found it was a modern facility complete with metal sculpture filling an atrium two floors high. He was no art critic, but it looked like a reasonable job as far as modern art went. The only thing odd about the airport was its size. It served a metropolitan area the size of Minneapolis and St. Paul, about three-million, yet was on the size of an airport serving a city of one tenth the population. The Chinese were doing everything a western country did, just not nearly as much per capita.

He boarded the plane at nine-thirty-five. It was about sixty percent full. At nine-fifty the door closed. They pushed back from the gate and were on their way. Apparently everyone who had prior reservations had arrived. In this society there was no possibility of passengers running to catch the plane at the last minute due to changed plans. It was the small things like this that intrigued Breckon. At first glance much seemed like the West, but underneath it was completely different. These people were not free.

They arrived at the gate at Beijing at the scheduled time of eleven fifty. Breckon had a four and a half hour layover until his flight to Chicago. Waiting in airports was not his favorite pastime but there was no alternative. He watched the people and they watched him. He tried to catch anyone taking a particular interest in him. After all that had happened, Breckon felt at any minute something would prevent him from boarding his plane.

Time slowly ground away the day. At a little after three o'clock he got in line at the United Airlines counter to check his large bag and get his boarding pass. During his time in Nanjing he had grown accustomed to seeing only slim people. In front of the United counters were mostly Americans. Fully half of the people were quite a bit over weight, and many others could have afforded to lose twenty pounds.

It was easier now with his large bag checked. The displays behind the counters showed his flight, 850, to be on time. Flight 851, the same flight that brought Breckon to Beijing, had arrived a short time before. It was the same airplane that spent half of its time in the air repeating the trip between Chicago and Beijing several times a week. Breckon had noticed with amusement that due to the time zones and the International Date Line he was due to take off at four-thirty-five p.m. Saturday and arrive in Chicago at four-thirty p.m. the same day after being in the air twelve hours and fifty-five minutes. All of that would suit him fine if he could just be on that plane.

Breckon was at the boarding gate an hour before Flight 850 was scheduled to leave. He thought he had seen a couple of men, both Asian, watching him. But, they were probably booked on this flight, too. Eventually certain people began to look familiar after having been in the near proximity for several hours. Breckon took a seat and closed his eyes as he tried to relax and rest a little. Suddenly he sensed there was someone near him as he looked up. Standing so they were nearly touching him were the two men.

The one on the left said, "Mr. Breckon we wish to speak to you."

The other one said, "Come with us."

Breckon had expected something like this might happen, and at the same time secretly denied that it would. When it did happen it took him completely off guard. They had shown no identification and Breckon didn't have the presence of mind to ask. As he walked away with them, his heart was pounding. The fact that they had waited until scant minutes before they would start boarding the plane was galling. He knew this would not be a short meeting and he felt himself growing angry, though he knew he had to control his temper at all costs.

There was the type of unmarked door along the concourse that one sees all the time in public places that don't warrant more than a disinterested glance. He was led to it and they entered. Inside was a rather spacious office and lounge area that was obviously a rest area for airport security personnel and other officials. Breckon was taken to an office with a desk and chairs. The first man sat down behind the desk. With a point of the finger Breckon was shown which chair he was to occupy.

They sat in silence for what seemed like an eternity to Breckon. Obviously a psyching-up period to make Breckon uncomfortable. At last the man behind the desk asked, "Do you know why you were called in here?"

A crazy thought struck Breckon—might as well give it a try. "Well, yes, I suppose I do. It has to do with my trying to go through the security check without an airport tax coupon when I arrived last week. The man seemed to get quite angry as he shouted something at me several times. I don't understand your language so I didn't know what he was saying. But, you have to believe me, it was an honest mistake. I didn't know what he wanted. I had no intention on disrupting the process, or cheating you out of the airport tax. Believe me, I was very tired, I never sleep on airplanes, boy I envy those people who can . . . . "

"Stop!" the man behind the desk shouted. "I do not know what your are talking about."

As soon as the man took a breath Breckon started again. "The airport tax! It took me fifteen minutes to figure out what that hollering man wanted. He had pointed at the ceiling which was not helpful. But finally I get it worked out and purchased the tax coupon. Boy, you guys sure are touchy. It was an honest mis . . . . "

"Stop!" the man behind the desk slapped his hand on the desk. "That, whatever you are talking about, is not why you are here! Put your bag up here," he said pointing to the top of the desk.

Breckon cautiously did as he was told. The man on Breckon's left grabbed it, opened the zipper, and took the laptop out along with all the other contents. He opened every pocket and pouch. He got up, taking Breckon's computer and CDs with him. He squeezed past Breckon, who made no effort to make it easy for him. As he left the room he said to the other Chinese man, "Keep him here until I return."

"Hey," Breckon said slowly, "is this a shake down? Are you guys part of a gang or something? I didn't see you show me any identification. I was warned not to put any valuables in my checked luggage since they would surely be stolen. Now that the traveling public has gotten wise to your thievery and started carrying their valuables with them you simply take what you want in broad daylight. I didn't willingly come over here and you can be sure I will nev . . . . "

"Stop!" the man yelled getting up and putting his hands on the desk as he leaned over toward Breckon. "We are from state police, and we don't owe you the show of credentials. This is not your precious America where the police are fools, hamstrung by lawyers and judges. Those in authority in your country hate your whole way of life that you can't seem to throw it away fast enough. It will be a joy to see the United States destroy itself. Our leadership believes in China, and we will do what we must to protect it."

Breckon agreed with what he said about the liberal politicians, judges, media people, educators, and similar people wanting to bring down the country, not that he would admit it here. As the man paused a split second Breckon started again. "Nice speech for a robot. Do you want to hear what I think about your country? Your leadership believes in slavery and you are mindlessly doing their bidding . . . . "

"No!" The man was off his chair and around the desk. "Now, I ask questions, you give answers. Any more outbursts and I'll have a guard in here to settle you down, is that clear?"

Breckon stared at the man.

"Is that clear!" he said leaning menacingly toward Breckon.

"Yes."

"Good, because if you get beaten up here there will be no lawyers and TV cameras ready to make you a hero. You'll just hurt a lot. Now you will tell me about the incident on Lasa Road on Tuesday evening of this week."

This took Breckon by surprise. Was he going to ignore the incident at the Nanjing airport?

"You were at that street intersection when there was a terrible traffic accident. Why were you there? Who were you waiting for?"

The man calmed down and seated himself behind the desk once again looking smug. Breckon sat with as neutral an expression on his face as he could muster. They stared at one another for over a minute until the man said, "Well, nothing to say now? What's the matter, you must be hiding somethin . . . . "

Breckon started talking before he finished. "I was not waiting for anyone. I was watching."

"Watching what?"

"You. Your people, your society. Everything I had heard about China in my life made me wonder what the people in China could be like. How did life go on in a totalitarian society? Your people have lived in a despotic reign of fear for twenty-five-hundred years. I wanted to see at least a small glimpse of how you lived, and I did.

"As I stood at that intersection trying to really see what was going on, a commotion started off to my left. There were men, two or three, running down the sidewalk in my direction, shouting. Apparently, this distracted some of the drivers. People drive like madmen over here. When the company driver took me from the hotel to the job site I couldn't look out the windshield of the van, it was too scary. It's amazing anybody lives a week on your roads.

"Anyway, at least one driver must have looked in the direction of the shouts which caused him to crash into another vehicle. This led to a chain reaction in which at least a dozen vehicles were crunched before everything finally stopped. Many people were screaming in pain, but few of the bystanders made any attempt to come to their aid. One man was even thrown out of a car and went rolling down the road in the intersection. It was terrible. We have bad accidents in the U.S. as well, but I've never been standing practically in the middle of one."

The man leaned his elbows on the desk. "What do you mean, a man was thrown from a car? He ran from your side out into traffic."

"I beg your pardon, I was there. The men running and shouting on the sidewalk caused the accident. If there was someone standing beside me, I was unaware of it. People were coming and going. Someone may have stopped beside me to wait for the light to change. One or two people did go out into the intersection after all the cars stopped to offer assistance. You must be talking about one of them."

"No, no," the man said softly as he leaned back in his chair. Breckon could see he was puzzled. Clearly, he had been briefed on the accident and probably had seen the street camera tape. But, the camera was located up high and didn't show the details, whereas Breckon had been at street level and saw it at close hand. The interrogation was not supposed to go this way. They sat in silence. Before either had a chance to speak again the man returned with Breckon's computer. Glancing at the second man Breckon saw a slight shake of his head. He knew they were looking for the disk, or what was on it. It was also likely they knew they would find the answers they wanted if they could use the methods they used on their own citizens.

The man across the desk had a frozen frown on his face. Without looking at Breckon he said, "Pack your things, you leave now."

Breckon started putting stuff back into his bag as he said, "You made me miss my plane. Thanks a lot. I will be writing letters to the State

Department, my senators, and everyone else I can think of. You might be surprised what can happen in a free society. Yes, I did learn a lot about China, and most of it in the last half hour."

With that, Breckon walked out. Neither man made any attempt to show him the way out, but he found it.

He walked back in the direction of the gate for his flight. To his surprise all of the people were still there, as was the plane—flight delayed four hours due to a mechanical problem with an engine cowling. What a great trip.

The plane left Beijing nearly five hours late, which meant Breckon would miss his connecting flight from Chicago to Minneapolis. This was inconvenient, but vastly offset by how grateful he felt that he was on the flight at all. The flight path took them further south than the flight to China so they flew over the Aleutian Islands rather then the north shore of Alaska. Tracking this far north where the nights were short anyway this time of year, and traveling against the rotation of the earth, made for a night that was only three hours long.

Flying over southern Wisconsin, they were put into a holding pattern which made them later yet. There had been summer thunderstorms over Chicago all afternoon. Finally, in the terminal Breckon was surprised that the whole process of Immigration and Naturalization as well as Customs was at least as hard as in China. Due to the storms, all flights into and out of Chicago had been delayed, and Breckon was rewarded by still having time to make his connection to Minneapolis.

Having had a lot of time to think on the way back he decided to get rid of his laptop computer. He couldn't be sure that replacing the hard drive would be good enough. He was dealing with the Chinese State Police, and that must be taken seriously. They could have put an innocuous looking device, a backdoor chip, in his laptop so any time he was connected to the Internet they could enter his computer, see what he was doing, and know where he was.

Arriving in Minneapolis at midnight, he was in no mood to see the CIA thugs. Happily, he did not. He was soon out on I-494 driving west where he'd take 35W north. He was tired, but traffic was light. It was good to be back in familiar surroundings and to drink in the freedom so many took for granted. Few people give the slightest thought to protecting this precious commodity as they let more of it slip away every day.

Before he left the terminal parking ramp he had opened the cover of his computer, made sure it was booted up with the hard drive operating.

Now he tossed it out the window. In the rear view mirror he saw it roll and bounce. A second later it was hit by a truck and it bounced around more. He knew he'd have to spend nearly three-thousand dollars of his own money to replace it, but there was no alternative.

Sunday afternoon

The phone rang several times and the answering machine came on. After the message and the beep, Breckon started to leave his message on Cindy Thomas's recorder. Near the end the phone was picked up. "Hi stranger. You've been up to mischief again, haven't you? That's the only time you call. How much trouble are you in this time?"

Ed drew in a long breath. He was pleased to hear her voice, but didn't know how to start. "Yeah, I suppose you could say that. I hadn't sorted out all the past demons, but I was getting close. Now there are new ones. You suppose I could see you today?" Almost too fast he added, "If you have plans that's okay, whenever it's convenient for you."

"Oh, don't try to be so accommodating. I'll manage to fit you in." There was a hint of a giggle as she finished.

It was after six when Ed pressed the door bell at Cindy's apartment door. When it finally opened Ed was stunned at how attractive she was. The real woman was always more beautiful than the one he remembered. "Well, come on in. I fixed something to eat. You look hungry like you always do."

"Thanks. My body hadn't gotten used to China time, and now it has to readjust again. I never know when it's time to eat, and there's a lot on my mind."

She looked at him and frowned. "I'm guessing this has something to do with the FedEx envelope I received at work. That right?"

Ed sat down on one of the dinette chairs and put his forearms on the table as he nodded. They were silent as Cindy set the table for two. Finally, as she was getting a beef roast out of the oven she asked, "You want to talk about it?"

"Did you open it?" She nodded.

He held up his hands and using his thumbs and forefingers made a circle the size of a CD. Then using the thumb and forefinger of his right hand held them a tenth of an inch apart indicating something thin.

She nodded, set the roasting dish on a hot pad in the center of the table, turned and pulled the envelope from under a newspaper on the end of the kitchen counter, and laid it by his elbow.

"Let's eat," Ed said. "We'll talk later. This smells so good, I think I'll die if I wait another second. I had no idea I was so hungry."

Cindy paused a minute and silently said grace. This had always rankled Ed a little. Now, it was reassuring. Maybe it was the sense of continuity with something beyond himself it gave. Since his experience in China he had felt particularly alone.

As they ate, Ed gave a continuing commentary on how good the food was. She nodded and in between asked about China and about him, opining that he didn't look so good. Finally she said, "I think it's safe to talk here. What's bothering you . . . and don't tell me things are fine."

"Yeah, why not. The CIA, you know, the same two guys from my last trip, met me in the airport parking ramp as I was about to leave town. Well, accosted me is closer to the truth. They forced me to take a special laptop computer in my checked luggage. It was to be 'stolen' from me while I was over there, professionally stolen without my knowing it. It was a disaster as you might expect. In the Nanjing airport two guys attacked me trying to steal both my checked luggage and my carry-on—tried to grab them right out of my hands. At that time I was so sleep deprived I wasn't sure what was happening. I managed to beat them off and took a taxi to my hotel. The CIA computer was never stolen. It was obviously a ruse. But, a note had been slipped under my hotel room door, telling me to be at a meeting at a certain street intersection. I don't know why I went other than maybe I'd be told what to do with the computer. Before I left Minneapolis the CIA guys threatened to mess up my visa so I'd spend time in a Chinese jail if I didn't cooperate. The meeting was walking distance from the hotel.

"One of the things I wanted to get out of the trip was to see how the people went about their business, a little snippet of how they lived. So, I went. As I stood at the meeting place the locals walking by would give me a sharp look, but never came close to me. Suddenly there was a man, Chinese of course, beside me. He said in hushed but understandable English that I wasn't professional, or something like that. He placed a small envelope in my hand. Immediately a disturbance up the sidewalk to my left caught my attention. The street sloped down toward me from that direction. The next thing I knew the man who had given me the package dashed into the street against the red light and was hit repeatedly by vehicles. There were multiple accidents. I don't see how the guy could have lived. I was almost hit by a car trying to avoid the mess. I didn't wait around, and went back to my room as fast as I could."

Cindy listened with a mixture of pain and disbelief on her face. As Ed paused she said, "Not again. Do you think there's any connection to your last ordeal?"

Ed gave the slightest smile. "What you mean is our last ordeal. You were in that up to your neck too. And, you know, before I went on this darned trip I was starting to feel better. I liked what you told me the Sunday before I left on the trip. It was starting to sort itself out. I was getting more sleep, and life was looking a little more normal. I don't know what to think now. As for your question, I have no idea."

"Why not give it to the CIA and be done with it?"

"That's the problem. I keep remembering that rogue CIA agent in Saudi Arabia. I'll hang on to it for awhile to see what develops. They didn't give me a hint that I'd get something to bring back. The Chinese state police interrogated me at the Beijing airport, so they knew something was going on."

Ed slipped the CD out of the FedEx envelope and put it under his shirt above his belt. He got up and Cindy walked him to the door. They each had an arm around the other as they walked. "I promise, it'll get better," he said. "But, for a little while we shouldn't contact one another. People keep dying wherever those dim witted CIA clowns show up." He gave her a squeeze, opened the door, and was gone.

Monday, July 24, CIA office, Minneapolis

Mel Winger chuckled as he read the message that had landed in his in-box over night. "Hey Burl, this is good, really good. The laptop computer we sent over to China with Breckon didn't get stolen from his luggage as planned, or at least the intended recipient never got his hands on it. I knew it wouldn't work out. Now they want us to talk to him and see if he knows anything about what happened?"

Carson had a sour expression. "I'm not so sure I find that bad news. Last time we were in the dark. Nobody would say that he actually was in Iraq, even if they knew. We were the flunkies on the sidelines told to do a job without the whole story. This time we know he had our computer when he left. The guy in Chicago even verified with the x-ray machine that it was in the suitcase and personally saw to it the suitcase got on the plane headed for China. He and the computer made it to China. Now we'll find out what happened to it. Let's go."

A half hour later Burl Carson and Mel Winger arrived at Control Engineering, Ltd. They posed as engineers from the company that made the defective air conditioning panel. When Breckon arrived at the lobby he stopped short. Breckon figured he'd see them eventually so he thought he might as well get it over with.

"So, you showed up for a debriefing. Let's go outside and sit at that picnic table. It's a nice day and we could all use a couple of breaths of fresh pollution, right?" He had no intention of getting in a closed room with these guys.

When they were seated at the table Breckon on one side, them on the other, he said, "Well, you said you pay people who served their country. I did the job. What do I get?" Breckon was angry about the whole business, and especially for having to replace his computer.

Carson knew that flippant attitude all too well by now, and would have happily smashed a fist into Breckon's face. Winger could see Carson was up for a scrap so started talking.

"We came to ask you if anything unusual happened on your trip. Did anything happen that seemed odd or unexpected?

Breckon knew they were fishing. "Anything odd? As a matter of fact, all of China is odd. Unexpected? Well, a despotic communistic country is different than here. I guess that is to be expected. If you have something to ask me, why not come out with it?"

Winger cleared his throat and said, "We know the computer got on the plane to China with you, but that is the last anyone saw of it. Is there anything you can tell us about that?"

Breckon smiled. "Are you sure it didn't get where it was going? I was in my seat at the rear of the plane on the right side and saw my bag arrive in an airport pickup. The pickup driver said something to a baggage handler as he dropped my suitcase at his feet. When the man left in the pickup the handler, who was as big as a moose, tossed my bag like a shot-put to the luggage conveyor. That probably smashed the computer. You guys never get a job done, do you? All the guy had to do was show his badge and put the bag on the conveyor himself. That would have left no uncertainty. The computer probably got to its intended recipient, but in an unusable state. The translations along the way fouled things up and now you think it didn't get there at all."

It's hard to argue with an eyewitness account. It's the details that cinch it. But, even if the laptop had been damaged, there should have been acknowledgement of that. Carson looked intently at Breckon. "You know stuff you're not telling. We have people in China, and before you know it we'll have more of the story. It will not go easy on you if you're holding out on us."

Breckon was getting angry. "You said the computer would be stolen, and it was. What else can I say other than I lost my computer, too? You could at least compensate me for that. I didn't ask for the job—you forced me to do it. I can't help it if each one of you is more incompetent than the next. Now, leave me alone!" With that, Breckon got up and stalked back to the building.

Winger looked at Carson. "Well, we got a little information. He lost his computer and it seems ours was stolen. I'd be mad too if I had to pay for a new computer. Maybe our guy on the other end got confused and didn't know which computer to take so took them both."

As they walked back to their car Carson said, "What do you think about cutting him a check for a few thousand dollars? Maybe he'd feel a little differently if he wasn't losing money every time he saw us. I agree he knows a lot more than he's telling."

Carson added, "The problem is we can't tell Langley what we suspect. They want facts."

"Yeah, but I got an idea."

Back at the office, Winger got Sam Li on the line. "Sam, we debriefed Ed Breckon as you requested and got nothing other than he says the CIA computer was stolen as planned and that his personal computer was stolen, too. We propose to reimburse him for his computer and a little extra for doing the job for us."

Li was hesitant. "If he can't keep track of his personal equipment why should that be the agency's problem?"

"We were against using him on this job, because we've run into him before. We told you that at the start. I suggest you dig into the 1998 archives for an operation called *sand fire* in Iraq. The agency never solved the mystery of who the deep cover agent called Jasper Stone was. All the evidence pointed to it being our Mr. Ed Breckon who was not an agent at all, but simply an able man who was in the wrong palace at the wrong time."

As Winger paused Li interjected, "So, what does that have to do with his computer?"

"We spent years trying to dig out who he worked for and how he was trained, and came up empty handed. But, if it were he, and as I said, we are as sure as we can be without him actually admitting it, it cost him a bundle of his own money. My point is this. Every time he runs into us it ends up costing him money. Why should he cooperate?" After a short pause, "We did say we'd compensate him in some way for taking the laptop in his luggage."

"Okay. Don't do anything until I have a chance to look at that file. Thanks for the help."

When he was off the phone Winger said, "At least that gives Li something to do so he stays off our case."

— 10 —

Sunday, July 30, Chinese Embassy, Washington

Allen Wu was at work at seven-thirty this morning as usual. The Chinese did not recognize weekends, especially Sunday. China was a thoroughly godless society so any reference or connection to any of the world religions was systematically removed. This was most easily done by the structures of society, like the work week.

He had one priority message when he sat down at his desk. He saw he had to alert Roger Ling to another deployment of Dragon Fang, called operation *long dagger*. The instructions were curious. The targeting device would have to be remodeled, but Fred Wengie was a good all around engineer in addition to his communications specialty. He could handle it. Ling made arrangements for the message to be left at a dead drop in Central Park in New York City.

Roger Ling was awakened by his phone. "Yes," he said sleepily.

"Don't forget our breakfast date by the pond. See you at nine." The line went dead.

Ling slapped the receiver back on the phone and pounded his fist on the mattress. "Curses!" He had been out partying until three hours ago. He had fifty-one minutes to get to the park. The message meant he was to receive a message at a garbage receptacle near a pond in Central Park. There was little chance of it falling into the wrong hands since it would only be there two minutes. The message would be tucked under the lid of the bin. He and the person leaving the message had watches that were automatically kept in perfect time by receiving the time frequency transmitted by the National Bureau of Standards. The message would be deposited at eight-fifty-eight. This gave the depositor two minutes to get out of sight before Ling came into view of the receptacle. This way neither person saw the other.

At the park Ling was behind schedule so he did not retrieve the message until three minutes after nine. Close enough. He doubted they'd turn out anyone to check his punctuality on such short notice. Back in his apartment, he decoded the message and read it. His first thought was that it was the dumbest idea he had ever heard. What did those asses have stuck up their noses this time? He was sure Fred would be as happy about it as he was. This deployment was going to last several weeks. For Wengie it would not be a problem because he was basically self-employed. The part time man he used as a helper could work on the few contracts he had pending. After all, it didn't make any difference if Ready Communications made any money. It was a front company, so any profit or loss was realized by the Chinese funding it. But, for Ling it would be harder. He had a real, fairly responsible job. No matter. He'd have to think of an excuse.

Later the same day, Minneapolis

Breckon had thought he was getting over the trauma of his ordeal in Iraq and then this whole China thing had to happen. The dead man on the street opened all the old wounds. Sometimes he thought he couldn't stand it another day. He prayed fervently for the dead man. That didn't seem to help Breckon, whether or not it helped the man.

When he thought about the larger picture, he had a gnawing feeling that there was something wrong with his life. The events in China made this particularly acute. The ordeal in Iraq was hard to accept. But he supposed that once in a lifetime one person in a million could have something like that happen to them. Having it happen to him a second time was unreasonable.

The China trip was over but the misery wasn't. There was still the disk. He knew he should give the disk to the CIA and be done with it because he sensed it would lead to something he did not want. Still, he was so angry about the way he had been treated he couldn't bring himself to do it. If somebody would have come clean and told him what was going on rather than using him like a sack of dirt it would have helped. Part of the problem he had with turning it over to them was that it would be rewarding them for the way they had abused him. Beyond that, what would make them think he had turned over everything? They could continue to hound him worse than they were now. And worst of all, they might think he was good at this stuff and be back to force him to do something like that again. No! They didn't know he had it. That's the way it would stay.

On Sunday evening he browsed thought all the sub directories on the disk while he was eating supper. It was a readable disk and the only executable program he could find, one called Dragon, started to run and then hit a fatal error with a message he could not understand. There were strange looking files buried away with extensions he had never seen. He tried to open them with every program he had. Nothing worked, except he managed to get the raw code to print on the computer screen with the note pad program. Scrolling through the pages of strange characters he saw comments made by the programmer in English. One message referred to a routine called BLANKER which, according to accompanying text was a field debugging tool. At the end of the file was a comment giving the name and address of a software company in San Diego. This was not what interested Breckon, though. Several comments referred to .dll files, dynamic linking libraries. On a hunch, Breckon did a search of the whole disk for .dll files. He found three in a deeply nested directory. Yet, there was another directory with many .dll files in it.

On a hunch he loaded the contents of the CD on to his hard drive, and started making a few changes. He tried changing the extensions of the odd files to .dll. That didn't help. Next he moved the three deeply nested .dll files to the directory with the other .dlls and tried again. To his satisfaction the program did not hit the fatal error this time and proceeded to execute.

The first screen showed a coiled up dragon with satellites orbiting it like a pictorial of an atom with the dragon as the nucleus and the satellites as electrons. Above the pictorial were the words "Dragon Fang." The dragon moved from one coiled position to another. Breckon marveled at the sophistication of the graphics. After a minute or so Breckon clicked on the button to "Continue" rather than the button to "End."

This brought up a new screen of the earth with several nearly polar orbits around it and two satellites in each orbit. It looked something like a constellation of low earth orbit communications satellites. A bar across the bottom of the screen appeared. In the bar it said "Enter Coordinates of Target."

Breckon thought a minute as he was considering if this might be a computer game with secret information hidden in it. Maybe with the knowledge of how the game worked a person could retrieve messages or other data. As a trial, Breckon put in the approximate coordinates of Minneapolis, N45°, E93°. Instantly a second bar appeared above the first. In it appeared the message "Target Area is City of Minneapolis. State of Minnesota. Country of USA. Is target moving or stationary?" Breckon thought a few seconds and selected "Stationary." It responded with, "Is target a landmark?" Breckon thought again and selected "Yes." The next bar to appear asked, "Name of landmark." Breckon typed in, "IDS Tower." The response was immediate, "Target is recognized: IDS Tower, coordinates N 44° 58.55', W93° 15.77'. Projectile will enter striking window in 6.9 minutes, optimum strike position in 16.9 minutes, leave striking window in 26.9 minutes." The message in the lower bar changed to "Do you wish to initiate strike sequence? Yes, No." As Breckon watched the other bar with the time on it counted down in hundredths of minutes. In the display above, the earth rotated so the side facing Breckon showed the orbit of the satellite going a little to the west of Minneapolis. The satellite coming over northern Canada was blinking to point out which one in the constellation would be used.

Breckon still couldn't help thinking this was a computer game. What else could it be? So in the "Do you wish to initiate strike sequence? Yes, No" bar he clicked on "Yes." Immediately a window appeared with the message, "Telephone connection software and hardware available. Initiating telephone chain call for authentication." Immediately Breckon heard the tones on his phone being dialed.

A new screen appeared. At the top was "Authentication connection being established with Dragon Fang," and yet another graphic appeared. It was the earth again with communications satellites around it. It showed a connection to the local phone system, then to a satellite, then to another satellite, followed by a down link to Madrid, Spain. These connections occurred in a couple of seconds. He heard the oscillator making the ringing sound on the line. Immediately the phone on the other end was "picked up" followed by a five-second series of tones like a short fax being sent. This was followed by the tones of another phone dialing out. In the graphics a dot changed from gray to white on the other side of Madrid as there was a pickup sound again. This was followed by yet another call. This one ended across the Mediterranean in Tripoli, Libya. Breckon began questioning his assessment of this program as a game. If it was a game, it seemed to be playing without him.

In between bites of his spaghetti and meatball dinner, Breckon watched the computer screen with a growing sense of foreboding. The program progressively completed links from the other side of Tripoli to Mumbai, then Beijing, then to Nanjing. He swallowed as he realized that was where he was when he had gotten the CD. Since all of the connecting phone calls were left active, each computer along the way could report back to Breckon's computer how far the message had gotten. Breckon didn't understand that this made it possible for the final destination to report back to Breckon's computer that the warhead had been activated and targeted. It also made it possible for the authenticating computer to determine the phone number of Breckon's computer. The next screen said connection made, authentication processing. The signal had reached Nanjing and the map zoomed in and showed the destination of Dragon Fang as the last link. It was the athletic arena two blocks from where Breckon stayed in Nanjing, and one block from where the man gave him the CD seconds before he died! Suddenly Breckon realized it was not a game and was really happening. He dove to the floor behind his computer and snapped the phone connection out of the jack in the wall.

When Breckon got back to his chair, he saw a message in a box on the screen, "Connection From Target Designator Lost! Reestablish Link Immediately!" The last three words blinked red on white background, and then white on red background, and back. Breckon sat with his heart pounding. "This is for real! That CD lets me target things with some type of satellite weapon!" he said aloud.

What had been left of Breckon's dinner was on the floor. As he busied himself cleaning up there was something nagging at him, but he couldn't put his finger on it. Finally, it came to him. All of the messages and instructions were in English! Though there were small Chinese characters by each message, it appeared the program was meant to be used by someone whose primary language was English. A chill came over him. What if he was meant to get the CD from the start? That would mean someone all along had been intending to use him. What if it was the CIA? No. It was an accident that he had the disk. It had to be.

Monday, July 31, Long Island, New York

Cid O'Donnel sat back in his chair at the New York Highway Patrol station on Long Island. "I knew it," he said under his breath. Things had been busy following the explosion of Flight 974. The FBI had tons of leads to follow up. Much of the routine legwork was put off on the local police which left traffic control on the state highways, mostly the constant battle with speeders, up to the state troopers. In addition, there were investigations of accidents and other crimes that took up a trooper's day. As a result, the incident where O'Donnel had located a light blue van driving away from the explosion of the KLM plane had not gotten attention. He had punched up the license plate of the vehicle again this morning, and found, as he had on the terminal in his cruiser, that Ready Communications Co. was the owner of the van. This time he went further and ran a check on the company. This revealed that it had only two employees, neither of whom lived at the address where he had seen the van parked.

If they were visiting at that address, it was a strange visit because there were no lights on in the house. As he left the station, he knew he was behind on other investigations, but decided to pay a visit to Ready Communications. Queens was beyond his normal patrol area, but he was free, within reason, to go where his investigations took him.

O'Donnel found the address in a part of town where new construction stood side by side with buildings that were past their retirement age. Ready Communications was in one of the latter structures. He drove past and then swung on to the side street and parked. He walked into a dead end alley that opened into an area with loading docks on three sides that served several businesses. A white panel van with a rack and ladders on top was parked facing east twenty feet from a loading dock. The license plate was different from that of the light blue vehicle. He figured it must belong to another business that used the loading docks.

He walked to it and looked in the rear window. The interior was well lit by sunlight coming through the windshield. There were racks filled with parts toward the front. Most of the rear was empty with what looked like pads on the floor for bolting down heavy equipment. He checked his notes and compared the license plate again. They didn't match. He turned and walked toward some cracked steps formed into the concrete loading dock.

Roger Ling had stopped by Fred Wengie's place of business to discuss the message he had received the day before. It was a little past seven-thirty in the morning of what promised to be a hot day in the New

York area. Ling normally got to his office about eight-thirty to prepare for the start of commodities trading. They were seated at a table in a dusty back room office discussing the work needed to meet the new requirements. As Wengie got up to get a bottle of soda out of the refrigerator he glanced out the dirty window to the loading area behind the shop. He suddenly stood erect and interrupted what Ling was saying.

"Somebody's looking into the back of the van. Hey look at this," he said and he walked closer to the window. "I think it's a highway cop."

Ling was instantly beside Wengie. They were both moving their heads around slowly trying to find a patch of glass with the least grime on it. "Yeah," Ling said in a whisper. "That's a smokey all right. Taking a real interest in what's inside. You don't have any of the targeting stuff in there did you?"

Wengie answered in a whispered hiss. "Of course not. I'm not stupid. There are the mounting pads on the floor, that's all. We agreed there was nothing we could do about them."

"Okay. Go to the door and watch. If he walks away, don't show yourself. If he starts to move as if he might be coming in here casually walk out and pretend to see him for the first time. Ask if there is anything you can do for him. I don't want him in here snooping around. I'll go to the room with the targeting stuff in it."

Wengie walked to the back door that was propped open to let fresh air in before it got so hot they were forced to close the doors and turn on the air conditioner. As he walked he heard the latches snap open on Ling's brief case, and then the sound of the slide on a .45 being pulled back to chamber a round.

O'Donnel had taken a half dozen steps when he heard a heavily accented voice off to his left, "Can I help you officer?"

Startled, O'Donnel looked up. He hoped his reaction had not betrayed this as he looked in the direction of the voice. A man came out of a darkened door on to the loading dock. In the shade of a rickety overhang he was not clearly distinguishable. "Yes, I suppose you can," O'Donnel responded. "Are you with Ready Communications?" O'Donnel moved as he spoke so he too was now in the shade. As he walked up the steps to the loading dock he saw a medium sized Asian man.

"Ye-yes, I am."

"I'm following up on a routine inquiry. Is that white van owned by Ready Communications?"

"Yes."

"You also have a light blue panel van, is that correct?" O'Donnel was taking in as much detail of the area as he could as he kept Wengie in the center of his field of view.

Ling had rehearsed with Wengie what he was to say about the blue van if he were asked. The van had been shredded so it would never be traced to the scene where they had targeted Flight 974.

"We did, but no more."

"Mind if I come inside a minute? We like to check new businesses, your security arrangements, things like that. You haven't been here long, have you." O'Donnel knew from the company profile he had pulled up earlier that Ready Communications had moved in about six months before.

"That's not necessary. We have an alarm system that is very good," Wengie lied. "We put in security systems for other businesses. But, if you want . . . . " O'Donnel was already walking toward the door from which Wengie had come moments before.

The wooden floor creaked as O'Donnel walked in. "The Bureau Of Motor Vehicles says you still own a blue van. You must transfer the title to the new owner."

Wengie hurried past O'Donnel as they walked down a short hallway to the front room in the building. "Sorry, but the new owner is a junk pile. I had an accident. As I came to a curve in the road a car coming toward me came across the center line and I hit the ditch. The van was totaled."

"Why wasn't an accident report filed?" A box fan sat on the floor of what had once been a sales room. As one would expect there were spools of wire, brown cardboard boxes, a workbench, everything one would expect in a shop for a communications company.

Wengie walked toward the front of the room where one large storefront window faced the street. He turned and looked at O'Donnel with the window behind him, "I did not think one was needed. Our two vehicles did not touch and the other driver kept going."

Normally O'Donnel might have accepted the simple explanation, but under the circumstances it seemed too pat. "When did the accident happen?"

Shrugging Wengie looked at the floor as if thinking, "Oh, about six weeks ago, I guess."

Now O'Donnel was suspicious. He had seen the blue van a little more than three weeks ago. Continuing to ask non-threatening questions, O'Donnel noticed the man in front of him was perspiring profusely. He kept wiping the sweat from his face with the sleeve of his shirt as he appeared to be looking at something behind O'Donnel.

"Mind if I take a look in these other rooms?" O'Donnel was about to turn when he heard the creak of a floorboard behind him. Slowly turning he saw a wooden door that stood about a foot open and the room beyond dimly lit from a back window. He realized the Asian man had been looking at a companion who was in that room. From his training O'Donnel knew he was in a dangerous situation. If he even moved his hand in the direction of his gun it might be enough to get him killed. Should have called in a backup, he thought.

Looking at Wengie he said in a pleasant voice, "Guess I've taken enough of your time. I should be getting back on the road. Now be sure to file an accident report, and get that title processed so we know the blue van was junked, okay?"

"Sh-sure, I do that today." Wengie followed as O'Donnel walked out the back door and on to the loading dock.

O'Donnel turned, as he walked down the steps, "Now, don't forget."

Wengie nodded.

As he walked back into the shop the first thing Wengie did was go into the office, open the refrigerator, and grab the cold soda he had intended to get earlier. He dropped into a chair. Ling stood by the dirty window watching as the trooper left the premises. As Wengie guzzled his soda Ling got one for himself. He was perspiring, too. His shirt was sticking to his back, as drips of sweat ran down his neck.

"Th-that was close," Wengie gasped. "What if he had looked into that room?"

"He would have heard a loud noise," Ling said as he pulled the .45 out from behind his belt. He proceeded to remove the clip, jack the round out of the chamber, and replace it in the top of the clip. Replacing the clip in the pistol he opened his brief case and put the weapon in it.

"He knows there's something wrong here," Ling continued. "He or some other law enforcement will be back. We have to move fast. Back up the van to the low place in the dock, and we'll load all the stuff into it any way it'll fit."

"In the daylight?" Wengie asked incredulously.

"We have a choice? Yes, in the daylight. Cover it well. When we're loaded take the van to the rented garage on Forty-Second Street. That can't be traced to either of us. Later today do those reports the cop mentioned. We have to keep up pretenses of being good citizens. Then get started on the changes to the system needed for the deployment. You'll have to do the work in the rented garage."

Wengie looked at Ling with a blank expression. "How much can a pack horse carry? I don't know anything about horses."

In an irritated voice Ling answered, "Neither do I! We'll have to see what we can find. I'll go on the web and see what comes up. Maybe I can call somebody."

As he drove away, O'Donnel knew in his guts those were the guys that were coming from the location of the 974 shoot down. The rumors were that the airplane had been hit by something, though if the Transportation Safety Board investigators knew what it was, they were keeping it to themselves. He also knew there was something in that shop he was not supposed to see. But, would anyone believe him? He only had his gut feel, and no evidence.

Same time, NSA Headquarters, Washington, D.C.

Signals analyst Greg Daley had the message format of the calls from Long Island to China put into the real time dictionary of the Echelon System. When he arrived at work, he discovered he had a hit from the evening before. It was a simple matter to trace the call back to the originating number. The NSA has all the phone listings in the world on line so Daley could instantly get the name and address of the phone where the call originated. It was from an apartment in New Brighton, Minnesota occupied by Ed Breckon. Wow, that was a surprise! He's in a different apartment from where he was during the Iraq thing, Daley thought.

Daley ran across various pieces of information after the Iraqi incident to make him believe Breckon was the man at the site. The facts also showed Breckon was a normal guy going about his business. For a year after that Breckon's phone number had been in the watch list. Nothing incriminating came up so it was removed.

After all of the names that had appeared on Daley's computer monitor since that time when he was still an intern, it wasn't odd that he'd remember this one. That was his first real case, and his success on it had propelled him onward in his career. After Daley's training was complete his reviewer had mentioned his work on operation *sand fire*, as the clash in the Iraqi desert was called. He was told a person needed a nose for what was important in this business, and that the review committee thought Daley had that talent.

On one hand Daley wanted to say, "got you" when the chain call intercept from Breckon's apartment came up. On the other, there was something inside him that said this didn't fit the picture. Daley couldn't believe that Breckon did that thing on the A340 that killed their agent along with everyone else on the plane. Yet, he had doubts. If he were innocent of Flight 974, how did Breckon know to make that peculiar chain of calls from his apartment?

At this point, all Daley had to do to keep his career on track was to turn over this intercept to his superior. Breckon's life would forever be changed, though. What if Breckon were innocent? Someone could have gained access to his apartment and used his phone to incriminate him. And, now with identity theft, it was possible to do the same thing from a remote location given the right training and equipment. This was too common to dismiss. A person connected with drug trafficking gained entrance, either directly or remotely, to the home of someone on a hate list. He made incriminating calls and good-bye life.

Daley's quandary was made all the more acute by worry about a mole in his own organization. Prior to Flight 974 it was mainly discussed in the abstract, but there was a general feeling that they had a problem. The mole issue now had a personal angle for Daley. After the shooting down of Flight 974 there were a lot of rumors, and Daley was the subject of many of them. Since Daley was close to the operation he had been formally questioned about any unusual questions friends might have asked him, or any slip he might have made. It might have been possible for someone to have learned the flight number *mirage* was coming in on from another source. But, this was where the majority of the information was available—here and the CIA.

As a result, Daley's concern for Breckon was nothing compared to what he felt for himself and his family. This one intercept could be enough to break the case. But, what if Breckon were being used, he reported the intercept, and the mole found out? The real perpetrators would be warned. Worse than that, he and Breckon could both end up dead. He kept remembering how nobody took his idea seriously that Breckon was Jasper Stone in the *sand fire* operation. He had been told to continue on other investigations with far less evidence. In fact, he had been ordered to drop all work on that operation. It didn't feel right. Had he been getting too close to finding out something about *sand fire* that powerful people wanted to keep buried?

An annoying idea was taking root in Daley's mind. He didn't like it at all. It was too ridiculous and too dangerous to consider seriously. Yet, he found he was considering it seriously. Daley and his wife were planning a vacation to her parents' farm in rural Minnesota. The farm was near Little Falls, an hour and a half north of the Twin Cities of St. Paul and Minneapolis. What if he took a day and looked up Breckon while they were there? He wanted to find out what kind of man he was. He knew he'd get bored walking around the farm, anyway.

— 11 —

Wednesday, August 2, Chinese Embassy, Washington

The messages waiting for him upon arrival at work were puzzling to Allen Wu. It was early in the morning, and this was his fifteenth day of embassy work without a day off. There was no other way about it, he was tired. Whereas he had been trained to despise the ways of the West, he could see that there was merit in having time for rest and relaxation.

He opened the file folder containing the message he had sent to Roger Ling on Sunday morning. He read it to verify that he had not said something that could be misinterpreted. It seemed that there could be no mistaking its meaning. Yet, this message that had come from China implied Roger Ling and Fred Wengie had already deployed as far west as Minneapolis, Minnesota. In fact, they had taken up residence in an apartment under the name of Edmund Breckon. What was worse, Wu received a reprimand for not emphasizing to his operatives not to use the actual targeting sequence for a communications check. It was expected the check would be made before each deployment but there was, as he should know, a separate procedure for that. This false targeting attempt had made waves all the way to Beijing. A second communiqué had arrived from someone in a different capacity on the project giving him credit for the fast response in getting the deployment underway. They had assumed this was nearly an impossible task in the time allotted, and were pleased it was being taken in stride with such proficiency.

Immediately, Wu set about getting another message to Roger Ling though he didn't quite know how to go about it. He decided to first try to contact him in New York in case there was a mistake. Since Wu could not call Ling's apartment directly from the Washington embassy, he had to send the message to the New York embassy. From there someone from outside had to make the call to Ling's apartment to tell him to go to a dead drop to pick up another message.

Wu's message simply said to get information back to him about the progress of the preparations, and when they'd be ready to deploy. After the message was on its way he got out a map to find out where in the world Minneapolis was located.

————————

Shortly after Cid O'Donnel pulled his cruiser to a stop a Queens PD squad car pulled up behind him. They were both parked on the side street near the dead end alley that led to the rear of Ready Communications. As soon as the squad stopped both drivers opened their doors and got out. O'Donnel walked back and smiled at his friend Tom McDuggan.

"How's the best darned cop on the Queens' force?" O'Donnel said as he stretched out his hand to the stout red-haired Scott who looked O'Donnel evenly in the eye. Both men were a little over six feet tall and about the same age, having shared a royal blow-out a year ago as they turned thirty-five within a couple of months of each other. "Have you got it?" was the second thing O'Donnel asked.

Pulling an envelope out of his back pocket McDuggan waved it in triumph. "It was a hard sell, but I got it. We finally had to go to the FBI for help. They were nonchalant about the whole thing. Sounded like they were humoring us so we'd keep doing the leg work they wanted. After all, what could a couple of beat cops find that they couldn't? I trust your instincts, Cid, and it would help if we could turn something up."

O'Donnel was looking a little stressed. "My gut tells me I'm on to something, but it's been too much time. We should have had that thing," he said pointing to the search warrant in McDuggan's hand, "within two hours after I was here on Monday. I know you did the best you could, but my guess is the place will be clean."

By this time, the two men were at the rear of the building separated by twenty feet. There was no Ready Communications van this time. O'Donnel tried the rear door as McDuggan stood off to his right. It was unlocked. O'Donnel motioned for McDuggan to go around front. Neither man was too afraid of being met by hostile action, but rather were con-cerned about someone slipping out the front to avoid talking to them. After a full minute, O'Donnel swung the door open. To his annoyance the hinges squeaked announcing his entrance to anyone inside. O'Donnel stepped inside, stood to the side, and listened. There was no sound except for a box fan running on low in the front room. O'Donnel continued down the short hall on the creaky floor boards. When he reached the front room he saw McDuggan on the street. The front door was locked so O'Donnel crossed quickly to let McDuggan in.

With both men inside O'Donnel said in a raised voice, "Police. Come out?" With one man covering the other they quickly checked all the rooms and found the place deserted. Walking back to the front room where the workbench was located McDuggan said, "Looks to me like a standard communications company. Look at all of those shelves full of parts, and the boxes of various kinds of wire."

"Wonder why they left the back door unlocked?" O'Donnel mused. "I know you guys have the lid on crime in this berg, but that seems a little naïve to me. Look at all this stuff, they could stand to lose a bundle if someone walked in here and cleaned them out." As he said that he pulled on an end of shielded cable hanging out of the center on a box. It was the type of box with the wire coiled up inside and fed out through a hole in the center of the box. To his surprise, he had a three foot length of wire in his hand. He grabbed the box and looked in it. It was empty. He pulled on the wire conveniently hanging out of several more boxes with the same result. "Grab some of those boxes," O'Donnel said pointing to the steel shelving against the wall.

McDuggan grabbed a box about two feet on a side. It was light. Setting it on the floor, he slit open the brown sealing tape with a penknife. It was empty. O'Donnel and McDuggan moved dozens of boxes. All were empty. Each man looked at the other and nearly said it at the same time. "This is a front!"

McDuggan continued, "But a front for what, and where'd they go?"

"They had something in that room," O'Donnel said pointing to the room where he had heard the floor creak behind him, "that they didn't want me to see. Now it's empty. I'd bet it's not drugs, though."

McDuggan agreed. They had both seen places where drugs were cut and packaged for the street. This place had none of the marks of that. "This room looks like an office," said McDuggan as he walked to the room with the refrigerator in it. Both men set about looking through drawers and wastebaskets. Finally, O'Donnel was on his knees looking under the wooden desk. He reached his arm far back and retrieved a crumpled up paper. Standing up he brushed off his uniform and spread out the paper. There was a note scrawled on it in Chinese characters with the words "Kaplin Machine" in English. There was another character scratched out and the word "inverter" written above it.

McDuggan was looking over O'Donnel's shoulder as he said. "I've seen that before. There are words that are too technical for the traditional Oriental characters so they are forced to use the English word. Lucky for us. It could be a lead to where they went, or at least the place where they got an inverter. And, it's all we found, not much to show for a search warrant. My boss is going to be mighty upset about this."

O'Donnel gave McDuggan the most detailed description he could of the Asian man he had met on his first visit, right down to the slight stutter, and accent. McDuggan said he'd make a report on the results of the search warrant, and see if he could find anything on Kaplin Machine. They parted each agreeing to inform the other if anything developed.

———————

When the call that Allen Wu had arranged came to Ling's apartment, Ling was already gone. He had been at the rented garage on Forty-Second Street with Wengie for the past two hours. His cell phone was turned off because he did not want to take any calls there. It could trace him to what was now their only secure location. Ling had called an outfitter in Wyoming and learned what a packhorse could handle. There was no problem breaking down the telescope and laser assembly to smaller pieces. Wengie was fretting about having to reassemble them out in the wild and getting the alignment correct.

"You'll have to assemble it and then make adjustments," Ling said.

"I suppose so," Wengie agreed. "According to this whole crazy plan, we won't have to worry about other people seeing us. Imagine, outfit with packhorses for seven days in the wilderness. What kind of wilderness is this? Are there crocodiles and tigers walking around?"

Ling was sitting on a crate listening to Wengie. Now he laughed. "No, no. This deployment is out in the western United States, in the state of Wyoming. There are mountains and arid plains out there, no swamps so no crocodiles. But the outfitter warned me about bears in the mountains, especially grizzly bears. He said they are really mean."

Wengie had stopped working and sat down as he drained the last of his soda. The garage was closed and it was already getting warm. For this reason, Wengie started working at two in the morning. He was perspiring enough to make his shirt wet. He held up his empty bottle, "Did you bring bottled water and soda like I asked?"

"Yeah, it's out in the car. There's food for you too." Both men went to the car and Ling opened the trunk lid. The garage was a free standing building at the rear of an old business. Back inside Wengie picked up their conversation. "Yeah, I saw bears in the zoo in China. They were about a half meter tall. Even if one was mean, I think I could handle it with a big stick."

Ling put down the bags he was carrying as he chuckled, "No, Fred. These are grizzly bears. They are over two meters tall and weigh over five-hundred kilos. And everything that is said about them indicates they are ferocious."

Wengie's eyes were as big as saucers. "Ho-hold on a minute. I'm not going out there, not with them."

"Don't worry, we'll have guns. We'll hold our own."

"Wh-where do you get a gun? Here the police are not on our side."

"Fred, this is America. You go to a store and buy one. If you have the money and a driver's license you can buy any gun you want."

Wengie looked at Ling with a blank expression. "I always wondered where you got that big pistol."

"Yeah, I went into a store and bought it."

"In China I was told I'd find some of the customs in America strange. Man, this is a crazy country. But, I like it. Yo-you'll get one for me too, yes? I want my own."

"Sure thing. What kind do you want?"

"A big pistol like yours . . . and a lot of bullets," he said putting both hands together to form a cup.

"Yeah. No problem. Hey, Fred," Ling said changing the subject. "How good are you at reading English?"

Wengie had a stricken look. "I'm good! I was at the top of my class on English."

"Great. I bought you a couple of story books about the Old West. Read them in between times. They'll give you a feel for what it's like out where we're going."

Wednesday afternoon, Chinese Embassy, Washington

Wu insisted that the Chinese embassy in New York call Roger Ling's apartment ten times. Finally someone had been sent over to pick the lock and check. Ling was not there and it appeared from the contents of his refrigerator he had intended to be gone for a long time. Actually, Ling ate few meals in his apartment and that was the way his refrigerator normally looked. Having someone break into Ling's apartment had cost Wu a few favors, but it gave him assurance that those guys were on their way west. Darn it all. They didn't even let me know, he thought. Now he prepared a message to be sent to them at their new location. It contained a scathing rebuke for not properly informing him of their movements, and the unauthorized use of the targeting system. And it demanded that they check in with *him*. Wu also included a business matter which was revised information for their new assignment. He had to contact the Chinese consulate in Chicago to send someone to Minneapolis to set up a dead drop near the Breckon address.

At the same time Greg Daley at the NSA had gotten caught up on the most pressing of his assignments, so he started a project he had been thinking about for several days. Since finding the chain call to China associated with the destruction of Flight 974 he had been given leeway in digging into areas that his intuition indicated might prove fruitful. In intelligence work, good hunches were as valuable as a pile of data.

He reasoned that only he knew of the connection between the death of his colleague and that man's knowledge of the mole in the CIA. By extension Daley knew there had to be one in the NSA, too. The CIA knew they had a problem and would be working hard to find him, not so in the NSA. Even though his dead friend worked in the Far East Division, the enemy agent could have learned about his suspicions any number of ways.

Daley knew that a leak about the *mirage* document being on Flight 974 could have come either from the NSA or the CIA, but he would concentrate on the NSA for now. His latest idea hinged on the fact that the information about Flight 974 was probably transmitted by phone since the time was so short. In the normal course of things, using dead drops took at least a whole day. From the time the flight arrangements had been made to the plane being destroyed was less than thirty hours. The time would have been short for the enemy to take action on his friend, too. Since looking for an enemy agent in his own agency was dangerous business, he would start with his friend rather than *mirage* or Flight 974. He assumed the person who passed on information about his friend's suspicions would have done the same for Flight 974. To test the idea, he would search all calls in the greater Washington area for mention of his friend's name during the twelve hours before he was killed.

He knew from experience he had to be careful about setting up his search or he would have hundreds of hits to hunt through. He also wanted to be circumspect about the search rules he entered so if someone were watching his activities it would not be obvious what he was looking for. After careful thought he decided to search only text messages since they were limited to one-hundred-sixty characters including spaces. The computers had all the abbreviations texters used so that wasn't a problem. The results would then be matched to only NSA employees at this facility. If things went his way, he would have results in the morning.

Thursday, August 3, NSA, Fort Mead

After a mid-morning coffee break, Daley had a few minutes to look at the results of the text message search he had set up. He had no hits. It happened sometimes. His rules were too tight. Simple solution. Go back to the step before the results were matched to NSA employees. That got over a hundred hits. But, it wasn't so bad because there was a local organization that used the same name as his friend. Eliminating those he had eight. Among these he found only one that fit. It had his friend's name, and an urgent statement that the man had to be contacted that evening. If contact was code for kill it would be certain. Searching for the message sender's name led to a labyrinth of companies meant to hide the identity of the user. The identity of the receiver of the message was likewise hidden. That was the message he was sure. What he need was to catch the caller in the act. Impossible? Daley smiled and muttered under his breath, "Not where I work."

He had the exact time of the call and the cell phone towers located the call within a specific cell. But, you could do better than that if you had the resources available to Daley. The caller was located to within a one-hundred foot circle. Fortunately the man had stopped at a gas station to send the message. Daley set about checking the Homeland Security files for possible surveillance camera footage that might show the car from which the call was made, assuming he was in a car.

The public at large did not realize that the formation of the Department of Homeland Security the year after the September 11, 2001, terrorist attack on the World Trade Center towers in New York had caused a huge erosion of privacy. Ostensibly, Homeland Security was formed to unite many federal agencies under one cabinet level secretary to provide a co-ordinated response to terrorist attacks and emergencies of all kinds. The first line of defense was to stop terrorists at the border. To this end, security cameras were installed at all entry points to the U.S. Using software pried out of the cold hands of the NSA, the cameras scanned the face of each person entering, and kept it in a permanent file. Whenever that person came in or went out of the U.S. it was noted in the record. If an undesirable was in the "watch-list" and his face appeared coming across a border the individual could be detained. The camera system worked so well that it was systematically being connected to the security cameras in stores, hotels and similar places to watch for faces.

The Homeland Security's computerized camera file search took only a few minutes. At the exact time of the message there was only one car at the station. Daley zoomed in on the rear, got the Maryland plate number and did a Department of Motor Vehicles search.

Bam! Daley froze in place. He knew the guy! He was in the Directorate of Computer Services, the one who called when Daley used too much computer capacity. Clutching his hands tightly together in his lap, Daley bent forward tensing every muscle in his body as he squeezed his eyes shut. Oh, how he wished he had never done that search. It was the ultimate example of *don't ask the question if you don't want to hear the answer*. Why hadn't he thought it through first? In hindsight it seemed obvious after Flight 974 that the mole was likely to be someone who could monitor his as well as his friend's activities. The sinister part was if the mole ever suspected that Daley was looking for the leak, he would discover the search he had made. What happened to his friend would happen to him!

Daley's hands were shaking as he immediately set about erasing everything about the investigation he could think of. He knew there would be tell-tail tracks left for anyone seriously looking. As he feverishly worked he slid into denial trying to think of places in his logic where there could be perfectly innocent explanations for what he had found. At times he had wondered why his friend waited so long before deciding to report his suspicions. Now he knew. The ramifications if he reported it and was wrong were something he didn't want to consider. It would look like he was the mole and was trying to protect himself by casting suspicions on others.

What was that noise? He became aware of the phone ranging. He snatched the receiver and said, "Yeah." It was a call reminding him he was late for a meeting. He stopped what he was doing, and closed all sensitive files. Heading down the hall he tried to appear normal and hoped he had not forgotten to erase something.

Evening, the same day, Minneapolis

"Hey, Darin, this is Ed. Come on over and bring along your best spook hat. I want to know what you think about a letter I got today."

Harris laughed, "You headed back to the sand kingdom?"

"I'm not kidding. This is really off the map. Come on over."

When Harris arrived a half hour later the first thing the said was, "Okay, what's the emergency now?"

"I locked my car in the grocery store parking lot and went in to buy groceries. I know I locked it, I always do," Breckon said excitedly. "When I got back to my car the door was still locked, but this envelope was on the floor by the gas pedal," he said handing it to Darin.

Harris took the envelope, removed the single sheet of paper, unfolded it, and read aloud, "I propose a walk in the park at twilight. How about Rush Lake Park in New Brighton. Meet me at the bench by the lake near the old railroad station."

Harris sat down in Breckon's only easy chair, a La-Z-Boy, and pushed himself back so the footrest extended. Lying there Harris had his right hand above him making circles in the air with his index finger. "Mr. Breckon, it is becoming clear out of the mist. Yes. There is adventure in you future, even danger. You are part of a sinister international plot. This is the order to pick up a secret message at a dead drop. You will never see who delivered it, but you will be observed as you retrieve the message to be sure you got it. The fate of millions rest on your every action." He was snickering as he ended his fantasy.

"Yeah, funny boy. I told you about the disk I got from the forbidden planet, and how the call my computer made went to the place where I got the disk. Now this letter. They think I'm the one who is *supposed* to have the disk. Maybe it was the intent that I get it all along. You ever think of that? All of the instructions in the program are in English. How do you explain that?"

Harris sat upright. "That's good. That puts it together with one exception. I don't think you were meant to get it. They *think* you are the one who is supposed to have it. You were told to go to the meeting in Nanjing with a message something like this, isn't that right?"

"Yeah. Why me?"

"Don't you see? Somebody was supposed to get the disk. For some reason, you got the message, and hence the disk, by mistake. Then you used the disk. You didn't have to, you know. Now they know your phone number because the call went all the way to the 'home office,' if you will, in Nanjing. Now it's necessary for them to give you information on what to do with the satellite weapon. So, someone was told to get information to the person with the disk, who happens to live in your apartment. They found the address, your name, car license plate number, whatever they needed. This low level operative followed you until an opportune time to slip you this message. The person who delivered this message to you doesn't know what the correct recipient of the message looks like or what's in the message. He simply found the person living in the apartment with the phone that used the disk."

"Yeah," Breckon said slowly, "I used the first thing that came to mind for a target. They want to assign me a target they want. They mean to destroy something!"

Harris was looking at the message again. "Do you know where this meeting place is?"

"Oh yeah. I walk around Rush Lake now and then. It takes about forty-five minutes at a brisk walk. I know the bench he describes."

"I'll walk the trail tomorrow. I want to see how easy it would be for someone to observe the bench without being seen. When you go to get the message I'll try to see if you're being watched."

"There are a hundred places someone in a concealed position could watch it. They picked a good spot. If you want to check it out I'll tell you where to go. There's a trail from a nearby parking lot to the bench." Breckon added, "What makes you think I'll go to get the message?"

Harris laughed, "You'll go. Wild horses couldn't stop you. Besides, they'll be expecting someone to get it. Remember, you are one of them. Keep an open mind. It might be more than a message, maybe a piece of equipment, a camera for example, or a large envelope. I'll bet there's a garbage receptacle or something like that by the bench. Or, it might be taped under the bench."

"No garbage bin, just the bench."

— 12 —

Another hot day coming. Tom McDuggan sat in his squad car with the engine off and the windows down. He had parked in the shade of a building in the industrial section of town where he could see the front of Kaplin Machine Works a block away. The company sign above a set of double doors was fading with parts of a bird nest hanging over it. To McDuggan it almost screamed, "I have all the business I want. Don't bother me." So what did Kaplin Machine do? All the searches McDuggan had done came up empty other than for general machining.

McDuggan thought about walking in and asking, but he remembered the experience O'Donnel related about walking into the communications shop. A search warrant was a non-starter. When he submitted his report about Ready Communications he had been told in no uncertain terms that he'd need better evidence than that before asking for another warrant. So he made a habit of cruising past the place from time to time making notes of what he saw. The only thing odd was there were always cars angle parked in a small parking area on the side of the building, days, nights, and all weekend. Nothing illegal about that. He even ran the plates of the few that he could read from the street without being obvious. Nothing. They were all clean. Very clean, Almost too clean.

He was supposed to be on patrol so he knew he couldn't stay here for long. But, look. Eight-oh-five, the ten year old gray Taurus was pulling out. He'd run that plate before. Registered to Trent Clausen. Clean. Well, he'd follow until they were a couple of miles away and pull him over. McDuggan had to know. He radioed the dispatch that he was on the street again.

Five minutes later he closed the distance to the Taurus and hit his lights. The driver saw them immediately and pulled over. Traffic was light, the sun was up, and the air clear. As McDuggan approached from the rear, the driver turned and handed his driver's license and registration out the window. "What could I possibly have done wrong?" he said in a plaintive voice.

McDuggan hooked his dark glasses in his shirt pocket and said, "Nothing. Mr. Trent Clausen?"

"Yes, sir."

"Will you please join me in my squad car for a few minutes?"

Clausen said a weary voice, "Sure. Whatever."

When they were both in the squad McDuggan offered his right hand and said, "Tom McDuggan, QPD."

Clausen nodded. "I hope this won't take long 'cause I'm awful tired. Been working long hours."

"I'll try to be brief," McDuggan said. "I'd like to know what you do at Kaplin Machine. Not what you personally do, but what is their business?"

Clausen looked straight ahead, rubbed his hand over his face, and replied. "Knew it wouldn't last, just knew it. Too good a thing. Look, I've got a wife and two kids, and my wife isn't well so I need the money. I'm a truck mechanic, see, and this was too good to pass up. So, now what?"

McDuggan was a little surprised. "You are not in any trouble, as far as I know. Why don't you tell me about it?"

"You know what an armored truck is, well Kaplin makes something like that. I don't design them or sell them, I only help make them, suspensions, power trains, that stuff. Is that so bad?"

"You mean like Brink's trucks to haul cash from stores to the bank?"

"No."

"Armored limos for company executives?"

"No."

"Military vehicles?"

"No."

"What else is there? Help me out here."

Clausen frowned. "Why is this so important to you? The government is involved in this. They said they had to get me a security clearance before they would hire me. It took two weeks for them to do it."

"That sounds a little odd. But tell me, what kind of vehicles do they make?"

Clausen looked at McDuggan with a sour expression on his face. "What you're saying is you won't let me out of this car unless I talk, is that it?"

McDuggan could see his man was getting angry so he offered something. "I'll tell you a little of what I know and than maybe you can tell me a little. This is part of the on-going investigation that is distantly connected to the destruction of KLM Flight 974 awhile back. Do you remember that?"

"Yeah, of course. What does that have to do with these guys."

"Maybe nothing at all. There are leads that point to other leads. And this is where we are now." McDuggan used "we" a little dishonestly so it would sound like the whole police force was on the case.

Clausen looked out the passenger window and said, "Shoot, why not. They make special rigs with all sorts of special equipment on them like tires that don't go flat if you shoot a bullet into them. That kind o' stuff. They have guns mounted on them to shoot back if they're attacked. There's lots of special communication gear. You name it."

This is good, McDuggan thought, if he could keep the guy talking. "What do the vehicles look like?"

"Rigs, they call them rigs, or *rickshaws*," Clausen said correcting McDuggan. "They make two basic types, see. One that looks like a big delivery truck, you know a big box on the back of a truck frame. And, the other that looks like these big mobile homes that rich people vacation in. I'm tired, I'm going."

Clausen opened the door of the squad car, got out, closed it, and didn't look back as he walked to his car. As the Taurus drove away, McDuggan was making notes as fast as he could, trying to remember every word Clausen had said. This was starting to get interesting. He'd have to talk to O'Donnel.

Nanjing, China

For days Richard Yang thought about the conversation he overheard behind the curtain at the hospital in Nanjing. Though he was not scheduled to go home for two weeks he purchased a plane ticket and headed for San Francisco. He felt he had to pass along the information that Muan Yingqu was a double agent working for the MSS. He also wanted to patch up his relationship with the CIA to keep his job as watcher, but to get a firm understanding that he was never to be an agent doing things. As soon as he was through customs and away from the airport, he intended to call his CIA contact and make his report.

New Brighton, Minnesota

Breckon had gone to the dead drop the evening before and retrieved an envelope stuck in among the grass under the bench. Harris had not seen anyone watching Breckon get the letter, but Breckon had been right. There was a good quarter mile of heavily wooded shoreline across the lake where someone could have watched. This is to say nothing about many locations on the same side of the lake. Breckon and Harris had decided not to get together after the pick up. Instead, they made coded phone calls to one another, letting the phone ring twice, and then three times on the second call. This signaled that all went as planned and not to worry.

It was five-thirty p.m. on Saturday when Harris came to Breckon's apartment for supper. They were trying to figure out what the contents of the envelope Breckon had gotten at the dead drop meant. There was a letter in it with a sharp reprimand for using the operational program for a communications check and that he was never to do that again. Use the Comm Check program like you were taught! The letter went on to compliment him on setting up a new identity in a new city in an apartment, with phone service, and all the rest. Nice work, and fast too. But, always keep me informed about your movements! They, whoever they were, also liked the location, a single day's drive to the site needed for operation *long dagger*. Oh, by the way, the time has slipped by a day, and the location shifted by ten miles, see enclosed information.

The second sheet in the envelope was a transparency. On it was a squiggly line, with a small circle above it. There were numbers and letters below the line. There was a straight line across the page with a single word over it, "track." Hand written in the upper left was 2030 hours, 17 August.

Breckon and Harris were in agreement that because of Breckon's use of the disk, the person, or people, in charge of operation *long dagger* now thought Breckon was the leader of the bad guys, whoever they were.

"I hate to say it," Harris said, "but it looks like they think you are somebody else. It's only a matter of time until the real bad guys do a Comm Check and they all realize there is another disk. That means they'll be after you."

Breckon was not feeling so good. "That's about what I've been thinking. They obviously know where I live. What can I do, though?"

"You could go to the CIA. In fact I'd recommend it about now."

"I'm going to sit on it for a few days. Maybe something will happen to help me make up my mind."

Monday, August 7, CIA Langley, Virginia

It was well into the morning before ShuHo Zeng got far enough down in his electronic inbox to find the report from the San Francisco office about the debriefing of Richard Yang. The report said they had immediately notified the Shanghai embassy that Muan Yingqu might be a double agent, and as a routine matter the INS had been given Yingqu's photo and finger prints. Since he was a CIA employee, there was ample information on him.

Zeng immediately forwarded the report to Sam Li flagging it with the highest priority and added a note to come to his office as soon as he had read it.

Minutes later Zeng heard a knock on the door jam of his open door and looked up.

"Well, chief, the guys in Minneapolis apparently knew what they were talking about. They were adamant about not wanting to use Breckon to carry that laptop computer into China. Guess they were right."

Zeng told Li to close the door as he laid the file he was holding on his desk. "You think Breckon is the interesting part of this report? I sent it to you because of Muan Yingqu. Did the Minneapolis guys say why they were against using Breckon?"

Li stopped a few feet from the desk. "They mentioned that I should check the file on an operation from a few years ago called *sand fire*. I got busy and never followed up on it."

Zeng motioned Li to a chair beside his desk. "Okay, lets see what it's about." He proceeded to enter codes in his computer terminal. After several minutes of frustrating dead ends, he came up with it. "Wow, this *is* highly classified. I doubt you would have been able to get into it had you tried. It looks like one of the crazy things that knot-headed president tried." They both knew who they were talking about. That man had ruined much of the agency with his use of it to help himself politically.

Li stood up and read over Zeng's shoulder as he went from screen to screen. "The guys in Minneapolis said they thought Breckon was Jasper Stone, but I don't see that code name."

With a few keystrokes, Zeng searched for Jasper Stone. "Here it is, toward the end of the report. Looks like Jasper Stone was the guy in the secret site all along." A few screens later there was a special box of bold text with the title of Jasper Stone. It gave a profile of everything that was known about the agent, most importantly that it was not known whose agent he was, though the U.S. had been given credit for him.

"Look at that," Li said, "by the time the UN got somebody to the site the Iraqis had moved out all the men left alive who had been stationed there. That meant there was nobody that could give a description of the man."

The last paragraph of the special section suggested that Edmund Breckon, the designer of the machines, was the mystery man. It dismissed him because the feats attributed to the agent were beyond someone without a high level of specialized training. And, Breckon did not possess that training.

Li sat down as both men thought about the situation. Li began, "That report explains why the guys in Minneapolis didn't want to use Breckon. If he is Jasper Stone he's a formidable man. In addition, we do know for sure Breckon was the man at the Nanjing Airport. Not only did he put two men out of commission in as many seconds, but he escaped the dragnet of China's finest. More importantly, he was standing beside Topaz Wind seconds before he died."

Zeng was struggling with it too. "Don't forget Richard Yang sent him to the meeting with Topaz Wind. That's where our information ends. What if Breckon was given something and isn't telling us?"

Li smiled. "Our guys in Minneapolis got nothing out of him at the debriefing. But, they are so sure Breckon is Jasper Stone that they suggested paying him for losing his own computer in China, because they feel he lost a lot of his own money, to say nothing of nearly loosing his life, on that trip to Iraq. Their logic is this: how well would you cooperate if every time you come up against the CIA you lost money?" After a pause he added, "I get the feeling the Minneapolis guys are a little afraid of him."

Sitting with his elbows on his desk, and his chin resting on his laced fingers Zeng thought for awhile. Finally he said, "It's strange, one second I'm thinking Breckon can't be a super agent, and the next second I'm thinking he can't not be one." Zeng shuddered, "I have a feeling in my stomach there is something wrong with Breckon, like he causes a rend in the fabric of the universe at times."

Li sat back in his chair, "Hey boss, I've never heard you say something like that. You sure you're okay?"

"I don't know what it was but, I had the oddest feeling about that guy, just for a second. I can't explain it. One day I'd like to meet him. Anyway, for now make sure that he doesn't get on any more airplanes without our knowing about it. Make sure those guys in Minneapolis keep an eye on him. I don't want anything happening to him."

— 13 —

Monday, August 7, Camp Ripley, north of Little Falls, Minnesota

"Lieutenant Roston! It's oh-nine-hundred and I don't have the revised training schedule yet!"

"Yes, sir. I'll have it in a few minutes."

"A few minutes is not a legitimate response! Deadlines are meant to be kept! Get it to me A-SAP!"

"Yes, sir," Tony Roston replied to Captain Case his company commander as he frantically typed on his laptop computer. The two men sat on identical metal folding chairs next to identical olive drab wooden tables in a general purpose field tent. Their backs were to each other across the tent. In similar situations it might be expected that after an exchange like that they'd both break out in laughter. Not here. This was deadly serious. It was going to be a long two weeks of summer training.

Roston was from an out-state army reserve unit. Having taken ROTC in college he put in his mandatory tour of active duty after graduation. He had been lucky and spent only one fourteen-month tour in Iraq. Back from the Middle East he got out of the army and landed a job in a smallish town away from the traffic, noise, and pollution of the city. The job was to his liking but the pay wasn't. Being a little desperate to earn extra money to handle outstanding loans, he signed up with the local reserves. An armor unit had openings. The combat branches, infantry, armor, and artillery, always had the most openings so that's what he got.

During his active duty he had been in the Transportation Corps. Getting the hang of the Armor Corps had been hard during his training at Fort Hood, Texas. Now, he was up to speed, or at least he thought he was doing as well as any of the other tank platoon leaders. Roston liked the discipline of running his tank crew and the platoon. He had good men. All of them were there for the money, but along the way they got into the groove and held their heads up. They were a good team in spite of what Case always said. Capt. Hardrich Case, what a "case" of the miseries. There never was a more extreme example of a bottom feeding rung climber than that man.

What had gotten him behind with his administrative duties were fault codes on one of the four tanks that he had signed for. And, it was his tank. One light said the onboard computer thought there was something wrong with the automatic fire extinguisher in the engine compartment. The other indicated an error with the turret rotation servo system, though it appeared to function normally. By the time they got a technician from the motor pool to look at the problems the servo fault had disappeared. They were told to ignore both faults. A more complete diagnostic would be done after their deployment.

As soon as the printer finished spitting out the pages Roston handed them to Captain Case and in return received the retort, "You'll never make a tanker if you can't stay on schedule."

Rural Little Falls, Minnesota

It was Monday afternoon and Greg Daley was already bored with life on the farm. For his wife it was a homecoming. Ann's parents were overjoyed in seeing her and their six grandchildren. Greg realized it had been too long since they last visited and decided to try to make it at least every other summer in the future. Ann's mother called people so friends and neighbors dropped by in an almost steady stream. They were all strangers to Greg and he felt out of place.

The children were having the time of their lives. One by one, grandpa took each of the older ones for a tractor ride. Walking round the yard by the house and being told that all of the land beyond the yard was completely theirs, and not public property, was an entirely new concept. They were told emphatically to stay off the road past the house. There was also a warning about not getting lost in the cornfields, but how to get out in case they did. The space did not make sense until Ann and Greg took the children for a walk down the lanes and field roads to the woods with the little creek running through it. There the kids could walk in the ankle deep water and let the mud squish between their toes. All of this with no paved trails, no signs about leashing pets, no park benches, or candy wrappers that missed the refuse container. And most of all, no other people.

Greg mentioned to Ann on the flight to Minneapolis that he had found the phone number of a college buddy living in Minneapolis and suggested that one of the days he might look him up. Now he had time to make a phone call when the others were outside or busy about other things. Daley had taken the time to get Breckon's business phone number before he went on vacation. He asked the receptionist who answered for Ed hoping there was only one. Immediately he could hear the phone ringing. The phone was answered with a simple, "Ed."

Daley began, "I am looking for Ed and I don't want to say your last name. Tell me if any of this makes sense to you. I need to talk to you about a strange chain of phone calls made from your apartment to a foreign country recently."

There was a pause and then in a firm but not belligerent voice, "Who are you?"

"My name is Greg and that will have be enough for now. I come to you strictly on my own, and I need your help. I am in danger and so are you. Don't say much on the phone. We must meet."

Daley could hear the hesitation in the man's breathing as he decided what to do.

"Okay, can you make it at six-thirty tomorrow evening?"

Daley took a second and said yes.

"Figure out your directions from this. Get on I-694 in New Brighton. Take the Silver Lake Road exit. Go north. On the left will be a car dealership, and at the corner a McDonalds. There's a traffic light at that corner. Take a left and a half block later another left into the McDonalds parking lot. Go in, order a meal, and eat it there." After a pause, "Got that?"

After another pause, "Yes."

"I'll meet you. Come alone. How will I know you?"

"I am average height, black hair, Caucasian. I'll wear a light green T-shirt with blue sleeves. I'll be driving a dark red minivan. How will I know you?"

"Not to worry. I'll find you. Good bye."

As Daley hung up, he hoped he was doing the right thing.

6:25 p.m., August 8, New Brighton, Minnesota

Breckon parked in the McDonalds lot at ten after six. After a fifteen minute wait he saw the minivan park and the man who had described himself on the phone. The worried, unsure expression on the strong featured face matched what he had heard in the voice. The man had a thicker than normal neck and could have gotten flabby, but hadn't.

Breckon waited a few minutes and went in. He spotted Daley out of the corner of his eye. Breckon ordered two cheeseburgers and a drink and looked for an empty table. Most of the tables were occupied, but Breckon found one across the room from Daley as he had planned. The timing was right. The majority of the evening rush was past, but there were enough people so he was not conspicuous. As Breckon ate he was careful not to look over at Daley. He wrote directions on the inside fold of a napkin. When he finished eating, he walked past Daley's table. As he did so, he stooped down as if to pick up something and laid his napkin on Daley's table as another man came toward him carrying a tray.

Breckon said without looking at Daley, "You must have dropped this."

Daley was intent on the man approaching his table expecting he was the man he was to meet. He hardly noticed Breckon or the napkin. When the man he was watching passed his table giving no sign, Daley was let down and turned back to his remaining French fries. Then he saw it. He stared at the napkin a few seconds. His first thought was, what a dip. I'm not going to use a napkin that's been on the floor. Slowly it began to register on his consciousness. Picking up the folded napkin he looked at the under side. It was the same blank white as the top. In a strange way he expected this. As he opened it he knew even before he saw the writing that this was the message. And it was.

Daley instantly looked the way the man had gone. There was a longer line of people than earlier waiting to give their orders and he saw no one at all unusual. He sat back in his booth and thought about how cleverly it had been done. The message said, "Meet me at this park." There were lines for I-694, and Silver Lake Road. Past the freeway interchange to the south was a cross street marked 7th Street, light. Then another marked 5th Street, light. An arrow showed to turn left on 5th, and "down hill" and "Hanson Park." There was a crude rectangle with "Parking" printed in it and an arrow pointing to 'J Jim," and an "X."

Breckon saw Daley get out of his car and looked away as he assumed Daley would head for the Jungle Jim where he sat on a park bench. Three kids were scrambling about on the park toys. Two were obviously siblings, while the third was a lonely single. For some reason the thought of an only child left Breckon depressed. A few seconds later Breckon lifted his arm straight up without glancing Greg's way. As Ed heard Greg's footsteps approach, again without looking at him said, "Let's take a walk."

As they walked across the grass toward a paved trail in a conversational voice Breckon said, "You said you needed my help and that you were in danger. Talk to me."

Daley's stomach was in knots. He had never felt so exposed. For years he had been in his safe cubical watching other people who were in trouble. Now it was he. "You are certainly mysterious. May I assume you are Ed Breckon?"

Breckon nodded.

"My name is Greg Daley, and I work for the Department of Defense, though I'm here strictly on my own."

"Work for the NSA, huh?"

"How'd you come up with that?"

"First you know about a certain phone call. And, second, normal people who work for DOD say what part, NSA guys only say DOD. Let's see the ID."

Daley pulled out his wallet and handed it to Breckon. "You're suspicious, too. That was pretty cute the way you left me the message at McDonalds."

Breckon looked at the photo ID then at Daley. Satisfied, he handed the wallet back. "I feel like a horse that's been 'rode hard and put away wet.' I'm angry much of the time and when not, I'm remorseful. In short, I'm miserable. So, what's on your mind?"

"You know, I really think you are the guy from the site in Iraq," Daley said a little hesitantly.

Without any emotion Breckon replied, "If that's what you want to think, have it that way. I don't know if you're the religious sort, but I can't even pray decently any more. Life is hard for me."

"You are the guy!" Daley wasn't sure he was glad about that or not. "I was the one who saw your first Iridium call from the desert in Libya. That was a fine job you did. We never did beak your code, and that's rare. Though things unfolded so fast there soon was no reason to break it. But, to the present. If you are the same guy and you were an unwitting player then . . . . "

"Unwitting in the extreme! I was taken there in shackles, literally."

"Wow! If you fell into that by accident, and you fell into this present mess by accident you are the unluckiest guy in the world. And," Daley said taking a deep breath, "I am literally betting my life on that being the case."

"And what mess is that?"

They walked over an arched foot bridge with scummy stagnant water under it. "If you see anyone coming near us talk about baseball or something," Daley said. He continued, "You remember Flight 974 that exploded over the Atlantic off Long Island?"

Breckon nodded.

"Well, that chain call you made to China on July thirtieth was identical to one that was associated with the explosion of that airliner. We know the association, but not how the plane was destroyed. Do you? You have something that permitted you to make that call, don't you?"

They walked in silence. Daley stopped and looked at Breckon. "Well?"

Breckon nodded.

"How was it done?"

"They use a kind of satellite weapon. My guess is it's a kinetic warhead. That is, it doesn't explode, just hits at such high speed that it does its damage with kinetic energy. I targeted the IDS Tower, a tall office building in downtown Minneapolis. The program shows a constellation of satellites and shows which one will be used. It knew about the IDS Tower because it had its exact coordinates in the program. It's a landmark in Minneapolis, so I assumed that's why it was in the program. I canceled the program before the weapon was deorbited. How they hit an airplane I have no idea."

Breckon looked squarely at Daley. "So, if you knew I had the same program as the guys shooting down Flight 974, why didn't you send the CIA or FBI to pick me up and throw me in jail? Who else knows about my possession of the program?"

"No one but me as far as I know. I haven't passed along the information about your call because I'm afraid. That's why I came to you for help."

"You, afraid? You're one of 'em."

"I'm afraid because we have a mole in the agency, and there's one in the CIA. A colleague of mine thought he knew who the CIA guy was, and the night before he was going to tell Security about it he was killed by a hit and run driver. I believe I am the only one he told of his suspicions. He didn't give a name. To make matters worse, a few days ago I may have figured out who the NSA mole is, and now I'm scared to death."

They found a park bench and sat down. They spoke in increasingly hushed tones as each from his own perspective began to put pieces together. They were now talking in little more than whispers.

Daley continued, "Think about it. The two of us now know more about what's going on than anyone else in the free world."

Breckon was working on it in his mind. "Why did they shoot down 974?"

Daley unconsciously rubbed his hand across his mouth. "This is way beyond the bounds of what I can say, but we have to figure this out before our enemies do. There was a CIA agent with a super secret document on that plane. It was passed to him in Tripoli. I don't know what was in it other than the scuttlebutt said it had to do with the big nanotechnology treaty with China that the news media are so nuts about these days. The leak at the NSA, if my hunch is right, or one in the CIA, let them know which plane to shoot down. Now one for you. Where did you get the program?"

Breckon proceeded to give a short story of his trip to China. When he finished he added, "Since when does the CIA use Joe-average-citizen to do their dirty work?"

For the first time Daley managed a thin smile. "I was wondering about that. It is possible you *are* the unluckiest man in the world. Through the mole in the CIA the Chinese learned about every good agent the CIA had in China, and the Chinese threw them all out or executed them."

Breckon looked a little relieved. "At least that explains one thing that's been bothering me."

"Why didn't you go to the CIA with the program?" Daley questioned.

"I'm not sure, other than I don't trust 'em. There are a couple of local CIA guys that think I have something, though. They've been around pumping me. In fact they might even be keeping tabs on me now."

They were both swatting mosquitoes now as it approached sunset so they started back toward the cars by another route.

Daley looked a little sheepish as he said, "I put your phone number in the NSA watch list since that call to China. The CIA, Far East Desk, also called a few days before I left on vacation and asked for the intercepts, too. So, there are a lot of people watching your phone. Notice, I called you at work."

They walked in silence. Finally, Daley said, "Maybe shooting down 974 was the only thing they'll use that weapon for and having the program will be a moot point."

"Guess again my fine friend, guess again. Life is never that easy," Breckon said in an almost despondent voice.

Daley took a short breath as he stopped and grabbed Breckon's arm as he turned to face him. "What!"

Breckon shook his head slightly and said, "Keep walking. For the time being they, whoever they are, think I'm the guy that's going to do the next job for them. They may think I'm the same guy that did 974. It's all very indirect. They even set up a dead drop to contact me. It's possible they got their wires crossed because of that time I tried the program."

For Daley this was beyond belief. "What are you supposed to hit?"

"That's the hard part. They assumed I knew where and what. They only sent me a change in location by about ten miles, and a change in time."

"Can I see what you got?"

"Why not? We're both in this up to our ears now with trusting each other. Follow me back to my apartment and see if you can make anything out of it."

When they were in Breckon's apartment he got out the envelope delivered to him at the dead drop.

Daley admitted he had never seen anything like it. He held up the transparency and said, "What do you make of this? It looks like we don't have a piece of the puzzle. This is supposed to be laid on something and it completes the picture. Maybe the line with 'track' by it is a railroad, and the curvy line is a trail. In any case, operation *long dagger* is set to happen a day's drive from here on August sixteenth at eight-thirty p.m. That's eight days from now."

Breckon sat with his elbows on the table and his chin resting in the palms of his hands. "We know something bad is going to happen. Shouldn't we tell someone?"

Breckon could tell Daley was torn, too, as he said slowly, "I don't know. I know my friend was killed for what he knew. You saw the guy killed in China. Those people are really dead!" He paused for a minute as if the awful truth of that statement had hit him for the first time. He continued. "The guy in China told you to protect the disk with your life. Did you ever ask yourself who you were supposed to protect it from? You see, if we give all this information to the CIA here in Minneapolis they will send it to Langley. If the mole gets wind of it, it's a simple matter to change the date or the place of operation *long dagger*. It still happens and nothing has changed with the exception that they know where the information came from. They'll be after us. And fatal accidents happen to people they're after."

Breckon started gathering up the stuff. "Okay, enough of this for today. How far do you have to drive to get to where you came from? I assume you didn't drive out here from Maryland to see me."

Daley smiled. "No. My family and I are on vacation at my wife's parent's farm near Little Falls. It's late and I told the wife I might stay in the city tonight. Could I crash on your living room carpet?"

"Yeah, I guess that'd be okay. I'll pull out an air mattress and a light sleeping bag. You want to give her a call?"

"That's not necessary. As soon as we got to the farm Ann turned off her cell phone so she could really be on vacation. And, there's no point in disturbing the rest of the family."

"Okay. This way we can have a beer and I'll tell you about the trip to the Montana mountains that my friend and I are planning. There are still a few details I have to work out."

Daley brightened up. "Yeah. That would be nice. A guy at work talks about that sort of thing. I get swept away thinking how grand it would be to do that. It's one of my favorite daydreams."

— 14 —

Wednesday, August 10, Beijing, China

Sang Dingfei, China's Director of Security, entered the office of Kang Jyan the Chairman of the People's Republic. "Sir, we have a problem."

"Yes. I have heard. Tell me the details."

"Sir, you remember my report about the American who was at the same intersection where Zhu Maohui was killed in a traffic accident while crossing the street against heavy traffic?"

"Yes. I do."

"Zhu Maohui was one of the lead engineers on the Dragon Fang project. We have learned that Maohui was an undercover agent for the CIA known by the code name of Topaz Wind. The name of the American who was at the corner is Edmond Breckon. We think Maohui passed information to the American who we suspect is working for the CIA. As a result, our people interrogated him at the airport in Beijing as he was about to depart China. He admitted he was at the location when Maohui was killed, and even saw it, but revealed nothing more about the incident. We searched his luggage, his computer, and a large crate of electrical equipment he had sent back to the U.S. We found nothing. The Dragon Fang team investigated Maohui's death, but they were never informed about Breckon. The MSS, for their own reasons, kept that from them. Finally, earlier today the connection was made.

"Now we have learned from the Dragon Fang headquarters in Nanjing that Dragon Fang was invoked to strike a target in the city of Minneapolis in the U.S. The authentication call came from Breckon's apartment there. They suspect that Breckon has the same program as the one possessed by the Dragon Fang targeting team."

The chairman's fears were fully aroused. "What you mean is he had a disk. Surely, he would have passed it along to his handlers by now, and someone, someplace, knows all about Dragon Fang! Curse the gods if there are any, I am finished. I was intent on having Dragon Fang available for the final sanction. Billions of yuan have been invested in it."

"Sir," Dingfei said in a helpful voice, "all may not be as bleak as that. Thankfully, Breckon terminated the strike sequence before a weapon was deorbited. It is our belief that he still has the disk, and at the time he used it he didn't know what it was for, and was, to put it plainly, fooling around with it."

"But, after that he must know what he has!" the chairman spat out.

Dingfei shook his head. "Don't forget our sources in the intelligence organizations of all the major countries, as well as our signals intercept ministry. We have made it a major priority to look for mention of Dragon Fang and operation *long dagger* since the destruction of Flight 974. Any message that references that flight is examined for mention of how it was brought down. There are a few who have guessed correctly, but there is no proof they can offer. It's been eleven days since Breckon used the disk. If he were planning to sell it or pass it along it would have been a major breakthrough for the organization that got it, and we would have detected it by now."

Jyan nodded thoughtfully. "Yes, lack of any mention of it is unusual. I have been reviewing Breckon's dossier," he said tapping his finger on a file lying on his desk, "which indicates he may be working not for the CIA, but for the Israelis, that infernal Massoud. He came to our attention several years ago during an operation in Iraq. He was a problem then."

Dingfei interjected, "When his name came up on the visa applications recently, he was watched as a routine procedure. Everything seemed to be in order so surveillance of him was light. Obviously things were missed." Shrugging, he added, "What is done, is done. If we move quickly, we may be able to intercept the disk before it is passed on to anyone."

Jyan maintained a noncommittal expression as Dingfei continued.

"Sir, there is a man named Muan Yingqu, an employee in good standing with the MSS. He had an encounter with Breckon at the Nanjing Airport, and had to have his knee replaced as a result. He knows the man and is extremely motivated to even the score. Using him would limit the number of people involved."

Jyan sat deep in thought absentmindedly rubbing one thumbnail on the other. Dingfei waited in silence knowing it was unwise to interrupt at times like this. Finally he looked up and asked, "Do Yingqu's abilities match the mission profile?

"Well enough if we assign one of our men in the U.S. to work with him."

"Do that. Also, assign an assassin to stay close to our two men and Breckon, unknown to any of them, of course. I'm concerned Yingqu might get too aggressive as you say 'to even the score.' If for any reason Yingqu is not up to the task, I want to be able to silence him and as many others as necessary before they can reveal anything. Get everyone in place, but they are to take no action until we have planned our strategy. There may be a better use for Breckon than you know. Dismissed."

As Dang Dingfei left, Kang Jyan was rapidly putting together a plan in his mind. Within two months China planned to bloody the U.S. forces in Afghanistan badly enough to make the Americans pull their forces out. It had been shown by the Tet Offensive in Vietnam on January 31, 1968, that even a failed attack that was played right in the U.S. press could be made to appear as a disaster to the Americans. With its military bases in the countries to the west of China, the U.S. was trying to gain control of the flow of oil and natural gas to the rest of the world. China was chaffing at this, but was finding it increasingly difficult to resist.

If Breckon were used properly he could be made to look like a CIA agent caught in a despicable act, and throw the Unite States into turmoil. China would use that time of disarray to its advantage.

6:15 a.m., August 9, Washington, D. C.

Allen Wu drove to his job at the Chinese embassy in Washington along his usual route. It was uncommon for an embassy employee of his rank to have a car provided by his employer, but it was necessary because of his particular duties. He would have happily relinquished the vehicle and provided his transportation out of his salary if he could be free of this responsibility, that of retrieving messages from dead drops.

Each morning he traveled this route and looked for markers in six specified places. Today he saw a piece of green ribbon tied up out of easy reach on the high wrought iron fence around an old mansion. Placed between the third and fourth post from the corner it was within the acceptable zone. He especially hated the green drop, but what was he to do?

He traveled a mile, turning twice, until he was in a rundown section of town with shops and walk-up apartments. He parked on the street and walked a half block to an alley discreetly looking for anyone who might be taking an interest in him. Casually he glanced into the garbage-strewn gap between the building. It was deserted of people, but unfortunately not barren of odors. How did people live in this stench, he thought. In even the poorest parts of China there was better removal of the garbage. Though, with less food, there was less garbage to dispose of. Still, it seemed to Wu that the Chinese had a more highly developed sense of civic pride then these people.

It had been hot, even for August, and the rotting refuse brought tears to his eyes as he turned off the sidewalk into the passageway formed by cracked concrete under his feet, dark brick walls on either side and a slit of sky at the top. He stepped behind a dumpster that shielded him from the street, and proceeded several more paces. He stopped by a boarded up window that reached from a foot above the pavement to above his head. On the right side of the window he reached for the fourth brick down from the arched top. The brick was real but the mortar was not. He pressed on two places in the soft elastomer between the bricks. Care had been taken so the color and texture of the fake mortar matched the real thing. His action released latches allowing the three inch thick by eight inch long brick to be pulled out. From a cavity cut into the brick he retrieved an envelope, and quickly replaced the brick feeling the latches secure it in place. He slowly approached the end of the alley, and seeing nothing amiss, walked to his car.

Once at his desk in the embassy Wu opened the envelope and read the message. He didn't like what he read, but things like this did happen. An enterprising young signals analyst had learned the identity of his agent in the NSA. He recognized the name of the analyst as that of the one who discovered the chain call used for authentication when Dragon Fang was used to destroy Flight 974. This man, Greg Daley, had erased all links to his discovery that were available to him. Fortunately, Wu's agent had access to activity records enabling him to recreate what Daley had done. It was the text messages that had tripped them up. While Wu had to admit the messages were operationally more effective because they permitted two way communication in a timely manner, he had been concerned about them from the start.

The note said emphatically that Daley had not done anything with the information, and that if Daley were eliminated nothing would change.

Wu expected that response from his agent since damage control would consist of eliminating Daley, the agent, or both.

The end of the message was disturbing, though. It said, "Daley out of town for two weeks. Left Washington 8 August. Sign-out says only he went to 'The Farm.'" That's all, not why or where. Wu knew this agent tended to be ambiguous when he got rattled. He considered getting word back to the agent to clarify. That would take more time than he could afford, so he went to work with other resources at his disposal. The Chinese embassy had dossiers on everyone who was important to them. Since Daley had found the authentication call from Long Island, a file had been started on him. It was not large yet, but that would change dramatically before the day was out.

No sooner had the U.S. formed the Department of Homeland Security in 2002 then the Chinese set about infiltrating it as they had every other governmental agency. Using carefully crafted procedures established by Chinese espionage agencies the embassy computer monkeys were able to access Homeland Security files. These records provided information on Daley's travels. Other databases yielded the maiden name of Daley's wife and the address of her parents and siblings. By eleven a.m. Wu had what he needed. Daley along with his entire family had flown to Minneapolis and there rented a minivan. Since neither Daley nor his wife, Ann, had any family other than the wife's parents in the area it was logical to assume they had gone on vacation to visit the wife's parents who operated a farm near Little Falls, Minnesota. The embassy had a call made to the farm from a front company. Asking for Greg Daley, the caller was told he was not there at the moment, but could the caller leave his name and number. The call was politely terminated leaving the embassy staff with the knowledge their hunch had been correct.

By late afternoon the head of clandestine operations in the U.S., Koa Yaobang, had arrived from New York and a meeting at the Washington embassy was in progress. Rarely had the Chinese had such a valuable source in any U.S. agency, and never before in the NSA. He was worth saving.

Yaobang was a decision maker. He led the meeting with an autocratic style that rankled even those accustomed to the top-heavy leadership style of China. "It is simple. We dispatch an assassin and eliminate him! Why was I called here for so simple a decision? Are you all fools? Did we not rub out that NSA man a short time ago for the same reason?"

Though Yaobang was standing at the head of the table, his short stature made him look like he was sitting.

Just like the little runt to really screw things up, Wu thought. "Sir," Wu began as meekly as he could. "This situation differs from the last one. To begin with, this man has proven himself to be uncommonly resourceful. More importantly, since we all agree we do not want him to return to Washington, we have to kill him where he is now. That presents a problem."

"Poof," Yaobang retorted. "The place you showed me on the map is a backward, rural area. Why are some peasants such a worry to you?"

Yaobang was now sitting and it made Wu want to laugh, though he knew he'd lose his head if he did. The man's chin was only inches above the table. With his scrunched up expression he looked like a gnome from a child's book.

Mayling Guo, a youngish researcher with a pretty face, held up her hand and fluttered her slender white fingers asynchronously to get Yaobang's attention.

Yaobang nodded at her, "You have something to offer?"

"If it please you, sir, I have found information about that area of the country where this man is. It is a strange place by our thinking. First of all, nearly fifty percent of all Americans own guns. In that state of Minnesota where the farm is located the per-capita ownership of guns is even higher. To put it in perspective, sir, in the fall of the year when they hunt the deer that run wild, there are so many men walking around with loaded rifles in Minnesota that only six countries in the world have more men under arms in their armies.

"To add more difficulty, there is little crime, as the number of guns would suggest. 'Bother me, and bam, bam, you're dead.' Ha, ha."

Yaobang didn't laugh and the scrunched up expression didn't change. "So?"

"Well," Guo continued clearing her throat trying not to show the embarrassment she felt, "the police don't have much to do. When a call comes in that someone, especially a federal employee was shot down in cold blood, all the police from a hundred kilometers around will converge on the place. And, cutting the phone lines at the farm won't help. The NSA man and his wife in that house have cell phones. If the assassin doesn't kill all of them quickly, he will not get away. If he is apprehended, we must assume he will lead the police to us."

Yaobang sat back in the padded armchair leaving his head at eye level with the tabletop. "You all have done a fine job of convincing me we must kill this man, and at the same time you have convinced me we cannot accomplish it."

After a silence Wu said, "Sir, is it possible I could meet with you privately? There is a possible solution."

Yaobang agreed telling the others to leave the room momentarily. When they were alone Wu began, "You and I have discussed the *rickshaw* program since this area around the U.S. capital is the most likely place the vehicles would be used. We are in agreement it may not be a worthwhile project as now envisioned. Is it possible that a *rickshaw* could be sent on this mission. It would have firepower to kill everyone quickly especially if this farm is a safe house and is defended. And, with the built in self-destruct system we would be certain that if things went wrong nobody would be left alive to talk. I am aware of a unit that could be ready to leave the New York area on 15 August, and the job could be done on Thursday, 17 August. We would strike at first light so everybody would be at the farm. It would give us the highest possible assurance of a successful operation."

Rickshaw was the code name for vehicles of various types being readied for a plan by the Chinese to keep the United States bogged down in the Middle East. The time would come when China intended to make military moves in the Far East. Prior to any such action, the Chinese would use these vehicles to shoot down airliners, possibly with senators and other VIPs on board, and make sure the Arabs were blamed. This would, as the thinking went, cause the U.S. to rashly over commit resources to the Mid East leaving them unable to counter any of China's moves.

The special vehicles had high speed rockets launched vertically out of them, and guided to their target by a coded laser beam. The plan was to recruit and train Moslems. This was done all over the world with little difficulty. After the plane went down, the two man crew would move the vehicle about as much as possible, and shoot down police and news helicopters arriving on the scene using more rockets. A rapid fire gun on a turret raised out of the roof would cause more havoc. The crew was promised a clever rescue when the mission was accomplished, though it would never happen. The *rickshaw* would self-destruct killing the men inside, leaving evidence to show it was a terrorist act done by Islamic fanatics.

The decision Yaobang now faced was something he had not counted on. He was certain his superiors would know the value of saving the mole in the NSA. The *rickshaw* program was one he had inherited from his predecessor, and one with which he felt uneasy. In all likelihood the *rickshaw* available for use on this mission would be lost, but the self-destruct would conceal its real purpose. The factory in Queens, New York could be burned so the trail would end there if the FBI got that close.

Yaobang nodded and called the others back into the room. "What are the roads like? Not like rural China, I hope."

Guo fluttered her fingers again, and was acknowledged. "The rural roads in this country are excellent. We see it as a main reason why food is so plentiful here. No crops are spoiled due to lack of transport to processing facilities and then to consumers. Russia suffered the loss of a large portion of the food it grew due to lack of roads. China is not a lot better."

"Yes, yes. I don't need an economics lesson. Leave me. I must make a call to China."

A half hour later Allan Wu following Yaobang's instructions gave orders to send a *rickshaw* and a backup. It was unlikely the backup would be needed so it would not be exposed. But, Yaobang was a cautious man.

— 15 —

Breckon was making pancakes when Daley asked to see the envelope of materials from the dead drop again. After examining them he said, "My guess is the number in the corner of the clear overlay is a map number. They are of the same format as those on the maps we were looking at last night. It's my job to connect unrelated information, and if I do say so, I'm pretty good at it."

With the pancake turner in his hand, Breckon walked to the bookshelf with the mountain trip materials on it and pulled out the map folder, laid it by Daley, and went back to his job. "If you're right, I'd have to chalk one up for the NSA," Breckon said flatly.

"You don't have a very high opinion of anything the government does, do you?"

"Nothing personal, but no, I don't."

Daley nodded and started unfolding maps. "The numbers aren't exactly the same, but it wouldn't surprise me if they were U.S. Geological Survey maps similar to the ones you and Darin will be using. It looks like the numbers aren't complete. If we knew the general area we wouldn't need the whole number either."

Breckon put a plate of cakes in front of Daley, "Eat 'em while they're hot. Since your guys are watching my phone line, what would they think if I went on the Internet and looked for a map of that number?"

Having gotten serious about eating Daley wasn't doing much talking but he managed to say between bites, "These are really good. My compliments. Have you looked for maps like that on the net before?"

"Yeah. Sure. That's how I got the maps for our trip. I might be able to put in general areas, and hope to get lucky. The USGS site lets you select the area of the country you want, and then it gives a patchwork of rectangles showing the individual maps. That way we might be able to pick out the map without having to enter the actual map number, assuming that really is a map number."

Daley thought as he ate. "So, if we found the map, what would we know. What does the information on the overlay mean?"

Breckon flipped pancakes, "That's easy. If the numbers really mean a map, then the curved line would be part of a contour line that when matched to the right contour line on the map would orient the overlay to the features of the map. I remember a World War II movie where the Americans captured a Japanese solider who was carrying a map overlay. There was a contour line on the overlay and symbols indicating gun positions. If the contour line could be properly fitted to the map, it would show where the guns were located. It wasn't even meant to be a code. But, it took hours for them to find where it fit. They solved the puzzle in the nick of time to destroy the guns as an assault on Japanese position began."

Daley sipped his cup of coffee as he finished his pancakes. "It seems like a lot of work to blow up a train, though. Maybe it's a satellite, or of course, another airplane they're after. I wonder if the president is scheduled to travel that day."

Breckon began eating and Daley started another batch of pancakes. "We're still getting ahead of ourselves," Breckon said. "What do the bad guys do when they get to the spot marked on the overlay?" Suddenly it hit Breckon. "We might find out if I ran that Dragon Fang program again. There were many places where I had to make selections before it started dialing the phone to get confirmation. It might give us some clues." Breckon looked at his watch. "We have a few minutes before I have to leave for work."

Breckon let his computer boot up as he finished eating. When he got to the part where the program asked if the target was moving, Breckon clicked on the "Yes" button. It asked if on land, sea, or air. Breckon picked "Air." The program responded, "Enter coordinates." Breckon entered the coordinates of Minneapolis the same as last time. The program responded, "Area is Minneapolis, State of Minnesota, USA. Fang will enter striking window in 6.4 minutes, optimum strike position in 16.7 minutes, leave strike window in 24.1 minutes. Do you wish to initiate strike sequence? Yes, No." Daley stopped what he was doing and watched over Breckon's shoulder.

Breckon said, "If I click on "Yes" at this point it starts dialing the phone to contact the headquarters in Nanjing. I guess we didn't learn anything." Breckon stopped the program.

Daley began cutting thin slices of summer sausage as he spoke. "There must be something the guy does to guide the projectile. Otherwise, he has no purpose. Someone could designate a building like the IDS building you used from anyplace in the world. That overlay means the shoot down guy has to be at a certain place at a specific time."

"Wait a minute," Breckon said, "if they have all of those satellites up there, wouldn't the U.S. telescopes that track space junk see them?"

Daley shook his head. "No. Not likely. The Chinese would have thought of that. They would have made sure all of the surfaces were rough and black so they'd reflect no light. They would also make them highly radar absorbing so there would be no radar return from them. There is probably a shell that the actual weapon slips out of after the de-orbit rocket has fired. The shell burns up in the upper atmosphere like a small meteorite as the warhead proceeds to the target. I was thinking about that last night. There's nothing that I can think of that prevents these things from working as we've assumed."

As they chatted, Breckon worked on the Internet looking at the U.S. Geological Survey site. After the first try, Breckon saw the USGS program gave the names of the maps, not the map numbers. He would have to download each one and look at the map number.

"This won't work," Breckon said in frustration.

"Why not simply put the number from the overlay in the search box on your search engine and see what comes up."

Breckon shrugged and entered 45109a5. It came up with several hits. On one it had "Silver Run Peak---45109a5." "Maybe Silver Run Peak is the map name," Breckon said almost absent mindedly as he typed that name in to the search field. It hit again and after a few more tries he had the low resolution version of the map downloaded on his computer. Zooming in on the map number he said, "Look at this, the 45 is the latitude and the 109 is the longitude. As I recall, that longitude is right for the mountains in Montana." Rifling through his map folder, he came up with a large U.S. Forest Service map. It covered the whole mountain area where Darin and he were going on their vacation. He got the coordinates of 45° 00' and 109° 30' which were at the lower right corner of the Silver Run Peak map and found them on the Forest Service map.

"It looks like that map is right in the Absoroka Beartooth Wilderness. Let's see." Breckon went back to the computer screen and zoomed in. "Thunder Mountain is on the Silver Run map. Can you find it?"

Daley scanned the large map laid out on the table, and Breckon came to help. Finally Breckon said, "Here you go, right here." Breckon put his index finger on the spot. "Look at that. There're glaciers all over that area. That's really out of it. It's in the middle of a high rugged plateau. No trees in this whole area," he said sweeping his finger around over a large part of the map. It makes sense that they would pick a place like that. If they were on top of a single mountain and someone figured out they were up there, they'd be trapped. Here they could come down any number of ways. It would be tough, but they'd have a better chance of escaping.

"We were planning on going into that wilderness from the north. It's a brutal climb, but there are almost no people. That's why we do it."

"Could you get to the area of the overlay by going that way?"

"Oh sure," Breckon said slowly, "but it would be a real back breaker. We had talked about taking the road southwest out of Red Lodge that goes to the northeast entrance of Yellowstone Park. That gets you up high so there isn't so much climbing to do. But, there are a lot of camp-grounds and people along that road so we dismissed it. That would be the easiest way to get there, though."

Daley sat back in his chair thinking. Breckon had to leave for work soon so he had to make a decision. And, he did. "Ed, somebody should go up there and see what these guys are up to. It's a week from tomor-row. I know you were planning to go on vacation a couple of weeks later. Could you move it up to leaving this coming weekend? And most of all, would you take me along?" There he said it. His wife would probably have a fit. But this was a chance to do a little field work, and he really wanted to see those mountains!

"If it turns out we get useful information, the government might be willing to underwrite the cost of the trip." On second though Daley real-ized that was unlikely, but didn't say anything.

Breckon was silent for a minute. "I was thinking about moving up the trip myself. As for you, how much of a pilgrim are you?"

Daley was puzzled. "What?"

Breckon laughed. "Like John Wayne, Darin and I call city slickers in the wild without a clue, pilgrims. Have you ever slept in a tent, been in a wilderness? Have you ever packed up mountains all day and then made camp in the rain?"

Daley smiled. "You guys are serious about your pain, aren't you. I've slept in a tent and climbed a few steep trails in the Virginia mountains as a day trip. I've never backpacked." He finished half laughing, "I walked all the way up the Washington Monument once. Does that count?"

Breckon drew a long breath. "Not for much. I can understand how you want to come, but I'll have to talk to Darin. Tell you what. I'll make a guarded assumption that you can come. We will leave Sunday at about six a.m. Do you have good boots?" Breckon went to the closet and got out his pair of boots.

"Not like that," was all Daley could say.

"Okay, I'll tell you where to start. Keep going from store to store until you find what you want. Get them large enough for two pair of wool socks. You must buy them today so you have time to break them in. Walk miles every day in them, but don't allow blisters to form on your feet. Plan to spend at least a couple hundred dollars. You must have good boots! Be sure they have an aggressive tread on the bottom," Breckon pointed to the soles. "Slipping and falling isn't even to be considered. You can't call 911.

"I'll make you a list of what clothes to bring. I'll get together a frame pack, sleeping bag, sleeping mat, and stuff like that for you. Bring whatever personal items you want, and we'll go through it and take out ninety percent of the stuff before we hit the trail. We'll be gone ten to twelve days."

Breckon paused and said, "We do have a problem with transportation, though. I have a pickup that doesn't seat three comfortably. Darin has a small four door sedan, but with three of us and all the gear it would be too tight."

"Not a problem there," Daley said. "I have the rented minivan I'm driving. We got it to haul the kids around, but I'll make other arrangements so we can use it."

"Okay. You really want to do this, don't you? You up to the boots and everything?"

Daley nodded. "Yeah, I really want to go. I'll be ready."

"I'll get together with Darin this evening and we'll start working on the food, and other stuff. Give me your phone number, and I'll call if something comes up. You have mine."

7:00 a.m., Thursday, August 10, Chinese Embassy, Washington

It had been a short night for Allen Wu. He had gotten out of the embassy after ten the previous evening and now was tired and irritable.
When it was discovered a second targeting disk existed, he was impli-
cated because he had sent the updated targeting details to the wrong person. Over the last few days he had avoided the backlash by carefully
putting together all of the instructions he had received while quoting
standard procedures. Through this period he was racked with fear that he
would take the fall. Now he was thoroughly exhausted. The passion to
nail someone to the wall for the screw-up had gone all the way to the top
in Beijing again, and wrath had fallen on hapless individuals like Wu all
around the world.

By the time the dust had settled the Dragon Fang organization learned
that in all probably an American named Edmund Breckon was in possession of a duplicate targeting disk. Breckon's use of it would have verified
to him that he had a valuable commodity, and the Dragon Fang team
surmised that he was acting alone. The assumption was that he would try
to sell it to the highest bidder. This in turn meant that it might still be
possible to recover the disk and not compromise the Dragon Fang operation. As a result, Wu was dispatched to Minneapolis to find Breckon. He
was to take such steps as were necessary to recover the disk and silence
Breckon, in that order.

Wu's flight left early the next morning. He planned to respond to
messages that came in during the night, get caught up on other work, and
leave the embassy early in the afternoon. The first message he handled
contained the information he needed to dispatch the targeting team to the
Mountains in Wyoming. He was ordered to use the same targeting information as that which had been sent in error to Breckon. Wu worried
about this, but knew in complex operations like this there were likely to
be other considerations that made another change impossible. It put
greater urgency on his mission to stop Breckon.

It was the second message that made him wake up. Wu was ordered to
meet someone from the MSS who would arrive in Minneapolis a couple
of hours after he did. He instructions were to assist the operative in finding Breckon and recover the disk that the Dragon Fang operation wanted.
He chaffed at the thought of being an assistant to a MSS operative. Obviously, this was a case where two organizations had not taken the time

to coordinate activities. The MSS message stated emphatically that Breckon was the cause of the mistaken instructions Wu had received, while Dragon Fang had only assumed that. It was already late evening in Beijing so he was unlikely to get this sorted out in the time available. But, even if he did question it, his orders from Dragon Fang would surely be over ridden. After all, Dragon Fang was only a technical operation versus the prima donna MSS organization.

8:00 p.m., Queens, New York

Roger Ling drove as he and Fred Wengie left the garage on Forty-second Street. Traffic was becoming tolerably light as he made his way to the George Washington Bridge. From there he'd take I-95 to I-80 which would take them all the way to Cheyenne, Wyoming. "Get your backside set for a long stretch of driving," he said as he entered the on-ramp. We have eighteen hours before we stop. Are you sure you didn't forget anything?"

Wengie shrugged, "Ask me that when I have a chance to think. We packed so fast I can only hope we got it all. We got the important stuff, that's for sure. Those crates were packed two days ago. What's the hurry?" Wengie asked as he settled in. "We don't do our job until a week from today."

"Yeah I know. But, we have a long way to go in that week. When we stop tomorrow afternoon we'll be about half way to Cody, Wyoming. Then we'll have two easy days to get to Cody. Out of Cody by seven the morning of August fourteenth, and at the ranch by eight. That's when I said we'd be there.

"The guy at the outfitting ranch said there was no way he'd agree to rent us the pack horses unless we had at least two days of training from him. Finally, I agreed to put up enough deposit to buy the stupid horses if we don't bring them back. Anyway, go over in your mind the stuff we packed before we get too far in case something was missed."

Friday, August 11, Lindbergh Terminal, Minneapolis

Allen Wu's plane arrived at Minneapolis shortly after nine a.m. He waited in the terminal for two hours for the plane from Japan to arrive. One of the passengers on that flight would be Jin Rongji, the alias Muan

Yingqu was using. Wu knew this would be a difficult job since they each had orders from different organizations. Rongji was expecting Wu to assist him, and would not be interested in the orders Wu had received.

Wu had been in the U.S. for over three years and was familiar with the way things worked, and the ways things did not work in American society. He had been told in the message from the MSS that this knowledge was the reason for his being selected to help Rongji. Wu would do all he could to see that the mission succeeded. His posting to the U.S. was to his liking and successfully completed assignments were the surest way to continue on here. He hoped their two missions were not at cross purposes making success impossible.

Sarah Little had worked this station in the Immigration and Naturalization Services hall at the Lindbergh Terminal for six years. She had seen her share of people coming from the ends of the earth. Everybody wanted to come to America. Many came to start a new life in the land where hard work and good citizenship paid big dividends. There were also those who came with no good intentions at all. Many were visitors, too. She tried not to be judgmental, but from the attitude of some of the foreigners, it was hard not to be suspicious. Most of the people in the crowd now filling the Immigration hall had finished a long trip and many were understandably out of sorts. She tried to be forgiving of that. The woman she had just processed was Japanese and seemed to have a chip on her shoulder. She had been most difficult, but finally the impasse had been solved and Little was glad to see her on her way.

The young Asian man approaching her station smiled and said good morning in heavily accented English. He appeared rested and at ease. Jin Rongji was on the passport, from the Peoples Republic of China. His visitors visa was in order for his vacation to visit relatives in the St. Paul area.

Little liked her job when the person in front of her was pleasant and not pushy. He seemed like a nice young man. So nice in fact that she almost handed his passport back in spite of the small amber light that was flashing. The light was set back under the counter where the passengers placed their passports so only she could see it. Amber was bad enough, but flashing too! For a moment her smile disappeared, and then self consciously she pasted a smile on here mouth as she said, "I'm sorry, Mr.

Rongji, the computer didn't read the barcode on your passport properly. That thing has been finicky today. Wait a second while I scan it in."

In actuality, the barcode reader had read the passport flawlessly. There was nothing amiss with the passport or the equipment. The alarm was from the innocuous little camera at each of the stations that nobody noticed unless they knew where to look. It was the result of the Department of Homeland Security at work. Flashing amber was the highest warning, which meant fingerprints were needed. Little scanned the passport for fingerprints as well as all other pertinent data. The date, time, and location of a "hit" were immediately transmitted to the agency that had placed the face on the hot list.

After a minute Sara Little held out the passport to the smiling man and said, "Have a nice day Mr. Rongji."

3:00 p.m., CIA Headquarters, Langley

Sam Li was surprised to see Muan Yingqu's face appear on the INS intercept list at the Minneapolis Airport. That he was using an assumed name, that of Jin Rongji, would be expected. The Homeland Security software had already associated the alias of Jin Rongji with Yingqu. As a check, Li compared the photo of Yingqu from the CIA's files with that in Minneapolis. There was no doubt it was the same man. The data base on him would grow exponentially in the next hours as records of his movements were collected and stored in the Homeland Security computers.

Considering the report Richard Yang had made, it appeared all too likely that the arrival of Yingqu in Minneapolis meant he was after Ed Breckon. This in turn meant the Chinese also thought Breckon had received something from Topaz Wind. He dismissed revenge as a motive. No world class agency would dispatch an agent for that purpose. ShuHo Zeng was out of the office for the rest of the day so Li called Minneapolis and explained the situation to Carson. Not surprisingly, Carson asked for Richard Yang's report to be forwarded to him. Li scrubbed it of nonessential material and sent it along.

Wu, being a Chinese embassy employee, was already in the system. The CIA information on Yingqu, now Rongji, was connected to the Homeland Security data base after Richard Yang's report of his connection to the MSS. When Allen Wu met Jin Rongji at the Minneapolis Airport, the cameras and system software connected the two men. As they rented a car the license plate number as well as the make and color were associated with them. Any appearance of either men or the car would be flagged and a report sent to the Minneapolis Joint Terrorism Task Force office to the attention of Messrs. Mel Winger and Burl Carson.

CIA offices, Minneapolis

Carson leaned back in his swivel chair as he read Richard Yang's report of Breckon's trip to China. It started with a chuckle and soon he was laughing so hard he had to wipe tears from his eyes. "We told 'em. Yes we did," he managed to say before he went into another peal of laughter.

Winger feeling left out said, "Okay, what's it this time?"

Still chuckling Carson managed to say, "When the CIA guy came to recover the computer we made Breckon take over to China, Breckon thought he was stealing his suitcase. He smashed our agent's knee and broke his collar bone right in the airport terminal in front of a crowd of people."

"No way," Winger almost shouted, "lemme see that."

Carson flipped the report on Winger's desk. After scanning the document, Winger began reading the last part with interest. "It's not so funny if you carefully read all of it. It says after the altercation in the terminal he managed to escape the Chinese police. And, get this, the CIA guy he took down was really working for Chinese Intelligence. The CIA didn't know he was a double agent. The question I have to ask is how did Breckon know? I tell you there's something funny about that guy. And, did you see the cover letter?"

"Yeah, I saw it. We're supposed to protect Breckon. What a joke. How are we going to do that? At the same time we have to keep tabs on those two Chinese guys, who are stalking Breckon." All humor was gone from Carson's voice.

Winger went to the coffee maker and filled up his cup. "Having to cover twenty-four-seven with only two of us leaves no choice but to let the software do most of it."

Carson nodded in agreement, "You have that right. Let's get started and figure out the rules we want."

The software Winger referred to was the offspring of what was called "Enhanced Promise." That software was originally developed in the nineteen eighties for the U.S. Criminal Justice System to track criminals. After the 911 attacks, Homeland Security applied it to the entire population of the United States with the cover story of looking for terrorists. Software obtained from the NSA that recognized faces was combined with the latest version. The problem was, the program naturally had to assume everyone was a potential terrorist or a criminal.

Enhanced Promise was nothing more than an extremely efficient data base management program. The example frequently used to justify the program was the case of locating terrorists. Assume there was a known terrorist leader, but there was not enough evidence to arrest and deport him. Enhanced Promise had access to all the data bases in the entire society such as bank records, money transfers, utility records, medical records, telephone calls, major purchases, and credit cards. The example went on to demonstrate that using utility records one could predict upcoming terrorist activity.

If the water, power, and other utilities of the terrorist leader suddenly went up, and looking at the utility records of the leader's known associates one or more were seen to have their utility usage fall to nearly zero, as if the person were not home, the assumption could be made the associate was now living with the leader. If this information were corroborated by freeway camera data detecting the associate's car in the part of the city where the leader lived, a compelling case could be made for the collection of terrorists who were presumably working on a plot.

Freeway cameras were a ready made aid to Homeland Security. In the nineteen nineties a large investment was made in putting metering lights at all the entrances to freeways in large metropolitan areas. The idea was to keep the rush hour traffic flowing better by keeping "plugs" of cars from entering freeways from ramps when traffic became heavy. To manage the traffic it was necessary to place cameras at each interchange. Using the cameras to watch the traffic flow, human controllers could adjust the timing of the metering lights. It turned out the metering system was largely ineffectual in helping the flow of traffic. This was demonstrated by those experiments when the metering lights were turned off for a few weeks. But, the cameras were in place and that was what mattered. As technology improved the original cameras were quietly replaced with ones having improved resolution that could read license plate numbers of vehicles as they moved along the freeway. These cameras could have been used to issue speeding tickets, too, since they were good enough to recognize a driver's face. But, they were not used for that so as not to alarm the public about how much of their freedom had been lost.

Carson and Winger entered a set of rules for the tracking of the two Chinese men and their car. They wanted to know if they were seen in hardware, electronics, or sporting goods stores so as to warn them that the targets might be buying items from which to make weapons. Also included were all means of transportation to be sure the targets did not leave town. Any association with foreign nationals, criminal elements, or suspected terrorists would be flagged. An alert would also be sent if the men were seen near Breckon's apartment or place of employment. However, that was unlikely because if they meant harm to Breckon, they surely would not do it in either of those locations. The Chinese men would assume those locations would be monitored. If the rules were violated both Carson and Winger would be alerted wherever they were, day or night.

— 16 —

Tom McDuggan and Cid O'Donnel sat on a park bench at the Queens Valley Playground watching a couple of kids trying to fly a kite. It wasn't a good day for that sort of thing because the winds were variable. They'd get the kite up for a few minutes and then it would flutter to the grass. As it descended the child with the string would run but the wind wouldn't cooperate.

Both cops were off duty wearing civilian clothes. McDuggan turned his head in all directions. "He said he'd meet us here on the 76th Avenue side of the park. Wonder if he'll show."

"Wouldn't surprise me if he didn't," O'Donnel replied. He had been in a bit of a depression ever since the search at Ready Communications with the warrant had been a disaster. "My guts tell me we're on to something. Why can't we make it click? Admittedly, we only have fragments of the story. But, you'd think if they were intent on solving the plane explosion, your report would have been taken more seriously."

"Yeah. You'd think my report was covered with anthrax. They refused to put it into the system so nobody has been able to connect it with other information."

"If we can get more out of this Clausen we can amend your report. By the way, I drove around and got the address of the house where I saw the light blue van the day of Flight 974. I called the people that live there thinking if someone from Ready lived there or if they had been installing a security system at that house the Chinese guy would be in the clear. They never heard of a company called Ready Communications. I know I got the plates right. In tests I can get the plates right at four times the distance with only a half second to see it. It was close, and I was stopped. And, Ready Communications did have a light blue van. Fred what's-his-name filled out an accident report and a title transfer showing they junked the blue van a couple of days after I saw it parked at the house. Yet, he told me he had the accident weeks before that."

Tom knew Cid was second-guessing himself because the search warrant was his idea. True, McDuggan had gotten a black eye for coming up empty handed, but he didn't like to see his friend so distressed. "Let's walk a little."

"You said this Trent Clausen had a security clearance," O'Donnel said as they started to the east. "I made the one check I know about and nothing came up. I got his Social and that would have found it. It didn't. Sounds odd. Ah . . . there's a guy with two kids headed for the swings. Let's see if it's him."

As they approached the man alternately pushing two swings McDuggan said, "Trent, glad to see you. This is Cid O'Donnel. We're old friends. He's with the State Highway Patrol."

Clausen glanced at them. Managing a little grin he said, "Things are ratcheting up, are they? What's next, the CIA, FBI, ABC, XYZ?"

"Daddy, don't talk, push me higher," the boy said, as he made noises like an airplane.

"We appreciate your agreeing to see us on your day off. It's our day off too. Mainly," O'Donnel continued, "I'd like you to look at a photo and see if you recognize it."

It was an enlargement of Fred Wengie's driver's license picture from the DMV. Slipping it out of the brown envelope he held it so Clausen could see it between pushes. The children were severe task masters. With the long hours, Clausen had little time to spend with them, and they didn't intend to be short changed.

Clausen took it, studied it intently for only seconds, and returned to his duties. After a few more pushes, O'Donnel asked, "Well?"

"Oh, yeah. I've seen him. He was at the shop once, maybe six or eight weeks ago. A little guy." Pausing a moment, "Well, about average though, I suspect for them Asians. I loaded a box of something electronic sounding in his van."

"An inverter?"

"Yeah, sounds about right."

"In a light blue panel van?"

"Yeah. But, I only saw him that once. I don't think he's got anything to do with the chink-mobiles."

"Chink-mobiles?" Tom and Cid said in unison.

"Daddy, don't talk so much. Push me!"

Clausen jumped to his job again as McDuggan and O'Donnel looked at one another.

Clausen laughed as he gave more pushes. "Suppose you guys are tied hand and foot by 'politically correct.' You'd be off to remedial sensitivity training if you used a word like that. It may surprise you that politically correct or not, things don't change. Anyway, that's what we call 'em. A Chinese dude comes in every couple of days and cracks the whip. Wants the one we're working on now on the road by August fifteenth or else.

"Wait a minute. Chinese?" Cid interrupted. "Kaplin sounds like a Jewish name. You sure that's right?"

Clausen laughed again. "That's the strange part about the company. The name is Jewish, but it's owned by someone with an Arab name. Check it out. The main customer seems to be a Chinese man. He comes in an SUV with dark widows. He drives into a vehicle bay that's always left clear for him so he's never seen outside. None of us are supposed to see him either. But, I did once."

"Dad, push me again!"

"Other guys say they saw him, too. Now, I'm sorta caught up on my stuff. That's why I'm off today so I'm not in the way of the electronics guys. Tomorrow morning, I'm back to finish the mount for the big gun."

They almost spoke together again, but McDuggan started first, "Big gun?"

"Ever see one of those with six barrels that rotate and shoot like crazy? There's a wash tub of ammo with it. They can pop that thing out of the top on a turret and shoot in any direction. This *rickshaw*, they're called *rickshaws*. They even have missiles like I've never seen before."

"They shoot shoulder fired missiles out of ports on the sides?"

"Nah. That's old fashioned. They have tubes, six, seven feet long standing vertically in the thing. The missiles pop out vertically and then are steered to targets some way. It's a cool machine that has 'don't mess around with me' written all over it."

"Hey kids, you're wearing me out. How about I spin you on the merry-go-round."

"Yeah, yeah. Spin us fast. Come on."

As Clausen followed the children to the next ride he said in a low voice, "Feel like a galley slave. Love 'em to death, though."

"Anything else you can think of?" McDuggan asked.

"That's the main stuff."

After the little would-be pilots were "pulling some g's" Clausen looked at the two men. "Now that I'm telling you about this, it does sound a bit over the edge doesn't it? Suppose you'll shut 'em down, won't you? Good-bye paycheck."

"I don't think you have to worry over the short term," McDuggan said. "We wouldn't be here on our own time if anybody was taking this seriously. Your information will help a lot, though. In any case, I'd guess they'd want the operation to continue so the FBI could see where these, ah, *rickshaws*, go. The customers would be more important than who's making them. If Kaplin was shut down, somebody else would start up. Anybody ever say what these things are for?"

"Nope."

"Any ideas? You must have seen or heard something."

"Oh, I heard a comment now and then, and I can guess a little. Having little kids you find there isn't much on TV fit for youngsters so we watch a lot of nature shows. The downside of them is their fetish with photographing animals screwing. When else in all of history could you watch a couple 'a beluga whales copulating in your living room? Anyway, awhile back we saw a show where a coyote killed a rabbit. Before he could eat it a wolf came along and took it away from him.

"Seems to me that if somebody like the Chinese want to steal something valuable, you know, parts of a spy satellite or somethin' like that, they want to hang on to it. Because if they want it, others do too. If they go to all the expense and risk of doing the stealing, and before they can do anything with it someone else steals it from them, who'll go to the cops? That's my idea—no wolf's gonna eat my rabbit."

"Yeah. That makes sense," O'Donnel said. "We'll be off now. Thanks for the info. Enjoy your kids."

5:00 a.m., Sunday, August 13, New Brighton, Minnesota

It was almost fully daylight with an overcast sky. Allen Wu had been sitting among the boughs of a twenty foot blue spruce whose branches came to the ground since ten o'clock the previous evening. He watched the parking lot and garages of Ed Breckon's apartment building while Jin Rongji got caught up on his sleep. Rongji had information that Breckon might leave town in the next few days. Both Chinese men considered it best to be well beyond surveillance cameras of the city before they accosted

Breckon. Wu would have called Rongji on his cell phone if he saw Breckon leave, though they considered that unlikely during the night time hours.

Maybe Rongji was short of sleep, or maybe there was something else that made the man so difficult, Wu thought. He hoped things would go better today. Without a word Rongji had called a taxi the previous morning and was gone most of the day. He returned in the evening carrying a metal attaché case giving no hint as to where he had gotten it or what was in it.

Allen Wu saw his partner pull to a stop in the parking lot not far from where he waited. Wu worked his way out of the spruce boughs and went to the car on the driver's side. Rongji slid over to the other seat. He closed the door with as little noise as possible. Wu liked the car. He had always wanted to drive a Buick. It had a nice luxury feel to it. They'd figure out a way to explain the greater expense for it when they were doing the expense report. If they were successful in recovering the disk, there wouldn't be any questions. "Successful" was the operative word. They had considered barging into Breckon's apartment and getting the job done. The fact that Breckon could act in such unpredictable ways gave them pause. The problem with the front door security was another thing. If they called his room on the lobby intercom, their thick accents would make Breckon suspicious, and he'd never push the button to unlock the door. And, they couldn't risk standing around trying to get in when someone else came or went.

Wu pointed to the spruce and said, "That's a good place to sit. The branches conceal you and there is a good view of the apartment building. I sure could use a cup of hot coffee. Take up your position and I'll make a trip to a fast food place. See you in twenty minutes. Call me on the cell phone if anything happens."

As Wu drove off Rongji took up his observation post. With a stiff breeze and the overcast sky, it was chilly even though it was August. The I-694 freeway was to his immediate left. The spruce tree was at the edge of the parking lot for a four-story office building to the west of the apartment buildings. He worked his way in among the branches gritting his teeth as the sharp needles pricked his skin. He crouched down into a stooping position as he was fond of doing. Immediately his new right knee began to hurt forcing him to sit on the damp ground. Curse that man Breckon. The replacement joint was far better than hobbling around on crutches, but it was nothing like the one he was born with.

The replacement knee joint was the latest model made of carbon composits and ceramics with no metal. His bosses allowed the expense so he would not draw attention to himself going through metal detectors at airports. Rongji knew there was more to it than that. This mission was his test case. Not only was it his first foreign assignment, which was tough enough, but they wanted to know if the knee would keep him from being effective. If he failed it would end his career.

The plan the top bosses in Beijing had devised for Breckon was crazy by his thinking. It was too involved. If he could pull it off he would be a hero. Against this he balanced his burning grudge against Breckon. During his training, Rongji had talked with other field agents. When they were candid they said operations seldom went as planned. The main thing was to come home with an identifiable victory. A dead Breckon would be less than perfect, but it would be sure.

Pondering his situation he frequently glanced at the traffic on the street to his right while keeping a vigilant eye on the parking lot. He blinked and it registered. There was Breckon. He'd know that face any where. The palms of his hands tingled with the anticipation of evening the score with him. He knew then he'd settle for less than a perfect score, and it would be so gratifying. Breckon and his companion were loading a minivan with packs and boxes. When they went back in for another load, Rongji punched up Wu on his cell phone.

Wu had gotten the food and coffee so he had to set his bags down on a table near the entrance of the restaurant to answer his phone.

Rongji spoke in Chinese. "Allen, is that you?"

"Yeah."

"Get back fast, they're loading a minivan with what looks like back packs and stuff. There's two of them."

"I'm on my way."

When Wu got to his car he was dismayed. A big pickup truck with a trailer behind it was stopped in the traffic lane blocking several cars. The diesel engine was running but there was no one in it. He put the food in his car, approached the pickup, and tried the doors. All were locked. Looking around in puzzlement, he couldn't understand why someone would do that. Then he saw a small sign saying employee parking. In his effort not to let his car stand out in the sparsely filled parking lot, he parked among a group of cars. Too late he realized he should have used the drive-up.

He returned to the restaurant to see if he could find the driver of the truck. As he looked through the glass door he saw there weren't many people in the restaurant. There appeared to be an argument between a large man and the person behind the counter. Wu walked to his car. As he unlocked the door his phone buzzed. It was Rongji again.

"Where are you? They are driving away!"

"Darn the luck! My car is blocked by a truck in the parking lot. They will probably get on the freeway. The nearest entrance is a couple of blocks behind you. Run behind the brick building until you can see the street that crosses the freeway. Watch which way they go." There was no answer and Wu heard a dial tone.

Rongji was in good shape and he ran as fast as he could with his right knee hurting more with each step. I'll get that dirt bag if it's the last thing I do, he thought. The grass was uneven and it slowed him down in spite of his need for haste. A thick wall of brush blocked his view of the freeway. As he passed the west end of the office building he saw the minivan on the street seventy-five yards to his left. There was an opening in the brush where he could see the overpass and the entrance ramps. He stopped. Sure enough the red van came into view as it crossed the freeway and made a left turn. Under the bridge he saw it merge with traffic headed west on I-694. It was five-twenty-five.

At the fast food place, Wu was going crazy. A police car had pulled up and stopped next to the door. The officer was not going in for breakfast. Now it could really be a delay. Once again, Wu looked at the possibility of driving over the curb to get out of his situation. It wouldn't work. He thought about smashing a window on the truck. What if it had an alarm system? It was an expensive truck so it likely would. And, with a cop on the premises, that would not be a good idea. All he could do was wait.

At seven minutes after six the police officer came out, got in his car, and sped off. A few minutes later the big man came out carrying a piece of paper in his hand looking glum. As much as Wu wanted to curse him out, it looked like that would not be a good idea. The man got in his truck and didn't move. Wu approached the truck and asked the driver as nicely as possible if he would pull ahead as his vehicle was blocking Wu's car. The man nodded slightly and drove away.

Wu drove off as fast as he could. He found Rongji pacing back and forth on the sidewalk in front of the office building. As soon as Rongji had his foot off the pavement Wu had the car moving. "Which way?"

"Keep going until you cross the freeway, then left on the far ramp going that way," he said as he pointed to the west." As they sped down the on-ramp Rongji demanded, "How could you let yourself get held up that way! We probably lost them!"

Wu knew this was bad. All he could offer was, "I was never trained as a field agent, I thought I was doing the best thing."

Soon they were approaching the Mississippi River bridge with signs for East River Road, West River Road, and Highway 100, as well as the continuation of I-694. Rongji fumbled with the map from the rental agency. "Which way would they go?"

"Two men in a minivan with backpacks . . . how many backpacks?" Wu asked.

Rongji tried to remember. He had spent so much time dwelling on Breckon that he had not watched closely.

"Come on, you're the one who's trained in field work, how many?"

"Ah . . . two."

"Two men and two packs, they aren't likely going to pick up anyone else. They both spent the night in Breckon's place, so they are headed out on their mission. We want I-94 going west out of the city."

Puzzled, Rongji asked, "You said mission. What mission? What haven't you told me?"

"I haven't kept anything from you. I simply put the facts together. Breckon has the Dragon Fang disk, and he figured out how to use it. From what I have gathered, that was no easy thing to do. So, he isn't stupid. Then he got the change of time and location information by accident. The project people may have thought they had a good code with that map contour. For Chinese it might have been good enough. But, not in America, not for Breckon. He has probably been to the mountains before and is familiar with contour maps. It was not difficult for him to figure it out. Now he and that other guy are on their way to the mountains to stop operation *long dagger*."

"If it is as you say, why don't the police or the FBI stop operation *long dagger*?"

"I have no idea. We may find out soon enough. In any case, they have a good lead on us and I have to watch the speed. I'll push it as hard as I can, but we don't want to be stopped by the police. Sunday morning is a bad time for that. We'll have to make few and short stops to close the distance on them."

The phone was ringing and Burl Carson slowly regained consciousness. Finally, he realized it would not stop ringing since he had disconnected the recorder before he went to bed. He fumbled with it, nearly dropped it, pressed the receiver to his ear, and said, "Yep."

It was the duty officer for the Homeland Security office. "The rules you put into the system for the people you are charged with put up an alarm. You want the message?"

"Yeah, put it on."

The synthesized female voice came on the line after a few clicks. "Subject rental car, Minnesota plate number GNR-683 has left the metro area. At 0629 hours local, subject vehicle went through the last metro surveillance camera at Rogers heading northwest on I-94. That was," there was a slight pause as the computer calculated, "six minutes ago. Press one to repeat this message."

Carson pressed the reset button and called Mel Winger. He found they had both gotten the same message as expected. According to prior arrangement Winger would drive to the Homeland Security motor pool and pick up the vehicle they had reserved. He would then pick up Carson and they would give chase. They would have to move fast to catch Wu and Rongji.

The formation of the Department of Homeland Security had combined many agencies such as the U.S. Customs Service, INS, The Transportation Security Administration, Secret Service, parts of the FBI, and the Coast Guard into one secretary level department. It also included another twenty agencies that the public never heard about. Having a common motor pool in each large city for all these agencies was one example where economies were to be derived from the new arrangement. In reality, each agency had a unique mission so the vehicles were seldom interchangeable.

It was nearly a half hour before Winger pulled up with the black Suburban and they were off. Carson had used the time waiting for Winger to put together sandwiches and make coffee. They, at least, didn't have to worry about a speeding ticket as Winger pushed it up to ninety in the sixty zone on I-494.

It made sense the Chinese were after someone so Carson called Langley on the secure sat-phone in the vehicle. He had them do a data search with the Enhanced Promise software. Ten minutes later he was rewarded with a call. The program had searched thousands of databases and had formed a likely association. The display on the Suburban's built in computer terminal came up with the following.

Targets:

> Allen Wu, Chinese national attached Chinese Embassy, Washington, D.C. Language expert, suspected intelligence operative.

> Jin Rongji, a.k.a. Muan Yingqu, Chinese national, arrived 11 August to visit relatives. Chinese intelligence operative.

> Vehicle: MN plates GNR-683, gray Buick, Hertz rental, to Allen Wu, 11 August.

Rules :

> Depart metro area, Minneapolis, MN
> Association with Edmond Breckon (SSN: 354-33-6754)
> Association with criminal elements
> Association with suspected terrorists
> Spending habits

Most Likely Association:

> Ed Breckon, electrical engineer, in vehicle with Greg Daley, NSA employee, headed NW on I-94.

> Breckon vehicle: MN plates MER-923, Chevrolet minivan, color: maroon, Avis rental

> Breckon vehicle 44 minutes ahead of target vehicle as of 0729 hours local

Rendezvous suspected

> Rendezvous positive?
> Rendezvous negative?

Database records accessed to form Most Likely Association

> Database: MN camera checkpoints

> MN plates MER-923 at camera check point 412,
> Rogers, MN 0545 hours, 13 August headed NW
> Database: Avis Car Rental
> MER-923 Rented to Greg Daley, 5 August
> Database: U.S. Government Employment
> Greg Daley employed NSA
> Database: MN camera checkpoints
> MN plates MER-923 at MN camera check point 382,
> exit I-694 at Long Lake Road, 1548 hours, 12 August
> Database: Minneapolis street addresses
> MN camera check point 382 freeway exit closest to
> domicile of Breckon
> Database: U.S. INS
> Breckon travel to China 13 July to 22 July
> Database: U.S. INS
> NSA interest Breckon's China travel
> CIA interest Breckon's China travel

There were two more screens of database references that Carson ignored.

After scanning the Most Likely Association, which in this case meant the likely reason the target vehicle was leaving the metro area, Carson whistled softly. "That's one I never thought of."

Winger switched lanes to pass "slow" moving traffic in the left lane. "What've you got?"

"In the Most Likely Association it makes the assumption Breckon is in a rental car with an employee of the NSA that is forty-four minutes ahead of the Chinese guys. The fact that they are chasing Breckon doesn't surprise me too much. The NSA guy is a wild card, though. The program also assumes there will be a rendezvous between the two groups. That's not a surprise either. But, it asks if the rendezvous will be positive or negative." They both knew that a positive rendezvous was for mutual assistance, or where one operative passed something to another. A negative meeting meant one party intended harm to the other.

"What if the Chinese got to Breckon when he was in China, and he's working for them?"

Winger was driving faster than was safe and paid attention to Carson only part of the time. "Breckon in bed with the Chinese? Not a chance. I stand by what we originally came up with. He's not working with any-body. And . . ." Here Carson hit the brakes, the horn, and the flashing lights in the grill to get the car in front of him to pull over from the left to the right lane so he could get by. "And, the more he runs into the likes of us, the more likely he never will work for anybody in this business. Count on it, if our targets catch up with Breckon it won't be a friendly visit."

Carson clicked on the plate number for Daley's rental car and all of the data on it was available. This included the people that had previously rented it, and its maintenance record. He further clicked the vehicle data. It showed a picture of the van in true color, the VIN number, and the accessories it had. Carson pivoted the display toward Winger and said, "That's the minivan Breckon's in."

— 17 —

By early afternoon Carson and Winger were driving across North Dakota on I-94 exceeding the speed limit when a car passed them.

"Did you catch the plates on the gray Buick that just went by us?" Carson asked.

Winger was leaning back in his seat with his eyes closed. "No. What about it?"

"That's our guys, the Chinese, Wu and Rongji. Really moving too. Must have stopped for lunch for us to have gotten ahead of them. Oh, no," Carson moaned, "what if we got ahead of Breckon too. We've really been pushing it."

The gray car was a quarter mile in front of Carson and Winger when they saw its brake lights come on and it shifted into the right lane. Carson pushed the gas pedal to the floor insisting, "The only reason those guys would slow down is they found Breckon."

"Or a state trooper," Winger continued. "But, if it is Breckon, we have to close in and see that our charges don't get wasted." As Winger spoke he pulled his standard government issue SIG-226, 9 mm, pistol out of his shoulder holster and put a round in the chamber. He ran his window all the way down.

Breckon was in the driver's seat of the minivan with Greg Daley in the passenger seat. Darin had a last minute family emergency and was forced to stay home. Daley graciously agreed to supply the transportation in any case. Breckon had seen the car coming up fast in his rearview mirror. "Hey Greg, that gray car was really burning up the road and a hundred yards back he hit the brakes and pulled in behind us. I don't see a smokey, do you?"

Daley craned his neck around to look. "Well, he seems to be closing the distance to us now. Maybe he dropped a cigarette on his lap or something." The car pulled out to pass and Breckon glanced over at it. He recognized the face as the gun came up, and an instant later his foot was on the brake pedal to drop behind the gray car. As soon as he had the front of the van even with the rear of the gray car, he jerked the wheel and pulled in behind it, hitting the gas as he did. He guided as far to the left shoulder as he could to use the rear of the gray car as a mask from the man with the gun. Two loud snaps left neat round holes in the upper right windshield. Another shot produced a jagged cut along the top of the right fender as a bullet ripped into the composite body of the Chevrolet. A fourth bullet did in the rearview mirror on the passenger side. Breckon stayed as close to the rear of the Buick as he could.

Other cars were forced to brake hard and pulled into the right lane honking their horns. Unaware of the deadly interchange, they assumed it was a case of two drivers using vehicles at seventy miles an hour to let out their frustrations on one another. A big black vehicle rushed up beside Breckon in a blur. As the Suburban got alongside the minivan a man leaned far out of the passenger's side window with his arm in front of the windshield. He had a gun in his right hand. Both Breckon and Daley saw the gun jerk each time a shot was fired. Breckon hit his brakes and fell back. The Suburban slid into Breckon's slot behind the Buick as the shooter in that vehicle fired one more shot and then pulled back into the car.

The Suburban fell back fifty feet and the shooter in it put out both rear tires of the gray car sending it into a skid toward the median. The Suburban driver hit the gas and sped past the Buick. They nearly collided as the Buick began recovering from the skid and came across both lanes. The Buick driver now had the car reasonably under control. By then the shooter in the Buick was leaning out of the window, again pumping off shots at the fleeing Suburban opening the distance with all the black vehicle's engine would give. Breckon was down to less than sixty miles an hour and was swerving to avoid chunks of rubber flying off the rear tires of the Buick.

Allen Wu and Jin Rongji had lost valuable time when they fueled up at a large Petro station on the west side of Fargo. All of the pumps were being used. They had no choice but to pick a pump and wait in line. It would not do to draw attention to themselves, even when another car cut in front of them. Worst of all Rongji thought he saw the minivan leaving the same station after they were in line. When finally back on the road they felt there was no choice but to travel as fast as possible to overtake their target. Wu was driving as they topped out on a rise. In the long sweeping valley ahead Rongji spotted the dark red spec on the ribbon of concrete a mile ahead of them.

"That's them, I'd guess," Rongji said, "behind those two trucks near the top of the next rise. At the rate we're going we'll catch them in less than a half hour."

Time seemed to stand still as they bore through the moderately heavy traffic. Finally, they were a couple of hundred yards behind the red van. Rongji had a gun in his hand. "Stay in the left lane and as you pull up beside them I'll take out Breckon," Rongji said almost trembling with anticipation.

"No!" Wu snapped back. "I'll pull up beside them and you shoot at the engine. We want them to stop. If you kill Breckon we will never get the disk because we won't be able to go back and look for it. People in other cars will summon police with their cell phones. We want the car to stop. Also, be sure you verify this is the right van. You must positively identify him!"

Wu's plan was to disable the van and then stop to help. They would bind the men, and hustle them into the back seat of the Buick and head for the next deserted exit. This would be easy since most of the exits along this stretch of road had a sign stating "No Services." Once off the interstate they'd get on a back road, force Breckon to tell what they wanted, and leave them dead in a field.

Along side the van Rongji saw Breckon and yelled, "That's him!" He had his gun up in anticipation of a shot at Breckon when the van driver planted his brakes. The van quickly fell behind, and slipped in close behind the Buick. Wu was watching the road and didn't know what had happened until the van appeared in his rearview mirror practically on his bumper. Rongji leaned out of the window and shot several times. But shooting accurately was impossible. He was forced to use his left hand with a seventy-five mile per hour wind impinging on his head and arm. And, this section of road, while free of potholes, was extremely wavy causing the vehicle to bounce up and down. He was lucky not to hit the Buick with the van so far to the left shoulder of the road.

Rongji's attention shifted to a large black vehicle coming up in the right lane. An arm swung out of the right front window around in front of the windshield. He saw in horror that it held a gun pointed right at him. Rongji shifted his aim and let off one shot. After the shot the slide of his automatic stayed open indicating the clip was empty. Immediately he pulled in his arm and slid down in the front seat as he scrambled for another clip.

Wu felt the car pulling to one side as a rumbling noise increased in intensity. The car was headed into a skid toward the median. Frantically, he hit the brakes, saw that braking only exacerbated the skid, so he stomped on the gas as he swung the wheel to the right. He saw the black vehicle shoot past them. "That guy in the black truck shot out our rear tires," Wu screamed as he saw the man with the gun in the Suburban. He was having a hard time getting the car under control with both rear tires completely flat. As he recovered from the skid Rongji was reloaded and shot repeatedly at the retreating black vehicle emptying the clip again. The Suburban kept going. Allen recovered his skid to the left, but he over compensated as he came across both lanes to the right. He kept the vehicle under control staying on the right lane and the shoulder until he had the speed down to thirty.

He eased into the sloping ditch where he pressed the gas pedal again. Since the Buick was front wheel drive it would still move, dragging the shredded rear tires. On the far side of the flat ditch was a slight rise. Wu smashed though the freeway fence and over the crest of the bank. A hundred yards past the rise was a gravel topped rural road. Wu bounced across the grassland and came to a stop beside the road.

When they were stopped Rongji said, "Nice going. How are we going to get any help here?"

"Listen stupid," Wu snarled. "We have bullet holes in the car. What would we say when some nice dip stopped to help? And, what would we tell the police? I had to get us out of sight of the freeway. When someone comes by on this country road we'll wave them down and take their vehicle. We'll be gone before anyone knows what happened."

———————————

Breckon was back in the right lane and up to sixty-five as they passed the skid marks left by the Buick. No one spoke for a few minutes as they recovered from the shock of what had happened. Daley brushed bits of glass off himself as he gently put his finger into the slot in the roof where one of the bullets had exited. Finally, Breckon said glancing over at Daley, "You don't look so good. Ever been shot at before?"

Daley, physically shaken, continued brushing pieces of glass off his clothing. He stared straight ahead as he replied in a deadpan voice, "No. And, I don't like it much." It was occurring to him for the first time that he had gotten himself into something he desperately did not want, yet knew he was unable to stop it. Looking at Breckon he asked, "You're better at this than I am. What happened?"

"Seems pretty simple to me. The guy in the gray car with the gun was an Asian, I'm guessing Chinese. He even looked familiar. They pulled up beside us to positively identify me. If you had been driving it might have been different. I looked at him and he was sure. So, he was going to put a bullet in me. If they wanted us alive they would have hit the engine so we would have been forced to stop. Then they would have stopped, too, taken us away at gun point, forced me to tell them where the Dragon Fang CD was, and then killed us both.

"The guys in the big black Suburban were the CIA guys that have been after me. They suspect I have some thing or other information that I'm not telling them about. Their orders are to keep me, or us, alive until they find out what it is. Once they have it they won't care what happens to me. As an aside, now I'm sure it was a good idea not to give them the CD."

Daley was incredulous, "You put all of that together from what happened in ten seconds? I think you have too much imagination."

"If you have a better explanation, I'm listening."

Daley fell silent for awhile. Finally he said, "I have to admit, if you hadn't hit the brakes and gotten behind the gray car the way you did, we'd both probably be dead, though you nearly killed us doing it. With that violent maneuver, I thought for sure we'd roll over in the median. At seventy-five miles an hour it would have been bye-bye. It seemed to me the right wheels lifted way off the road. You cut it awfully close. My God, you really live on the edge, don't you. You can't expect luck to save you every time. And, what would have happened if that black van hadn't been there at that exact second?"

They drove on in silence again before Breckon answered, "We are alive, admit it, we are. I don't know what happens to me. It isn't luck. I have time to plan. We had to get over to the left as far as we could, and as close up behind them as possible so we'd be out of the line of sight of the shooter. After I swerved to the left, I had to cut back to the right to avoid going into the median, and I had to speed up to get close behind him. The right front tire came off the road only a couple of inches. I knew that would happen. There was no real danger of us rolling over. As for the timing of the arrival of the CIA guys, all I can say is they were there. And, I don't think that was luck either."

Daley had a strange expression on his face as he looked at Breckon. Finally Breckon asked, "What are you staring at? I'm nothing but an ordinary guy who keeps getting into the darnedest scrapes. I don't have an answer for you!"

Daley finally turned to the front and slumped back in his seat. "So, what do we do now? I suppose calling the police is out of the question."

Breckon snickered. "If the police should be called they have been. The CIA would have taken care of that. I hope they manage to pinch the guys that went off the road. In any case I suggest we continue on to Glendive and camp at the park as we planned. One more thing. I'm feeling better and better that Darin let us take his lever action thirty-thirty with us. Somewhere along the line I intend to buy more bullets."

In the Suburban the two men were also putting together the events that had so rapidly unfolded. Carson shook his head a little. "You have to hand it to Breckon. His maneuver of getting behind the gray car was the only thing he could have done to save his bacon, and it worked. He could have caused a massive accident in the process, but I doubt that was on his mind. I suppose we should call the North Dakota Highway Patrol and tell them to stay off Breckon's ass. This is getting to be a thing with me. I want to talk to that young man again. We'll also tell the highway patrol to look in on our two Asians that went through the fence."

"Pull off at the next exit so we can wait for our charges to catch up with us. While we're stopped I'm going to get out and look under the car. I smell gasoline."

Carson pulled on to the next off-ramp with a sign of "No Services." As he pressed the brake pedal to stop at the road crossing the interstate he said, "Wow, we took a hit some place. It feels like the brakes on the right side are out." He pulled across the road and stopped on the on-ramp. Winger got out and inspected under the vehicle. When he got back in he said, "Let's go. We're leaking gasoline pretty bad. Punch it down so we can get to a decent sized city before we're out of gas. That guy put some lead into this crate."

Jin Rongji stayed in the car while Allen Wu sat on the front fender looking first to the west than to the east and back again. Off to the northeast he saw the dust of a vehicle heading south toward the interstate.

"There's a chance a vehicle is coming our way from the dust going up over there," Wu pointed. "Have you been thinking about the black vehicle that came to the rescue of Breckon?"

"I've been thinking of little else. No sense in that. If they were there to protect them why weren't they right behind Breckon all the time?"

"That's what bothers me too. They were nowhere in sight until a second before we made our move. They could not have known where we would make our attack, we decided that."

"Maybe our car is bugged. You ever think of that?"

A small flatbed truck came over a rise less than a half mile away.

"No." Wu said almost desperately. "In any case, if we can get this truck to stop, and we can get back on the interstate before police come, we'll have a vehicle that isn't bugged, that's for sure."

Checking his appearance, Wu waved his hand above his head. The driver pulled to a stop beside the Buick.

A big man of about fifty sat behind the wheel of the truck, and leaned over with his forearm on the window jam. His smile revealed yellowish teeth. "Ya took the road too fast, eh? Driving on gravel tain't the same as pavement. Buggered 'er up pretty good, didn't ya. Come on, hop in. Tain't goin' far, but far enough ta where ya can call for help."

Wu approached the truck while reaching behind his back to pull the pistol from his belt. He swung it up, and aimed it at the man's face. "Get out of the truck." The man didn't respond at once as Wu could see he was working through his options. After a few seconds Wu flicked the gun barrel slightly to the side indicating the man should get out.

Rongji had gotten out of the car as the truck approached, but stayed crouched on the side away from the driver's view. With the truck stopped, he walked up on the road behind the truck. Finally the man responded, "Wall if this tain't somethin'? Stop ta lend a hand and all ya get is a ration 'a guff. If 'en ya want the truck, guess ya gonna take it."

Wu heard the door unlatch, and slowly open. As the rear vertical bar of the window swung between Wu and the man the door sprung open as the man lunged out at Wu. For the man's size, his agility took Wu off guard. A huge hand swung up and knocked the gun from Wu's hands. Wu took a fist in the face as the man took a rock to the head as Rongji came from behind. Both men were down as the rock thunked against the graying and partially bald head two more times.

Wu scrambled away from the fallen man shaking his head. "That was really stupid. Why did I stand so close?" Rongji picked up Wu's gun and handed it back without a word. Rongji knew Wu was thinking this was a lesson hard learned, and the mistake would not be repeated.

Rongji got up on the bed of the truck that had twelve inch sides, but no rear board. He moved several sacks of grain. "Here. We'll dump him between the sacks. When we come to a culvert, or something, we'll stick him in it."

In minutes Wu was driving as they headed west. They found an entrance to the interstate in less than a mile. "This is a lucky break," Wu said, as he went up the on ramp. "If we get back on the interstate before any police arrive, they won't have any idea that we took this truck so won't know what to look for. This thing is kind of junky but the perfect disguise. We couldn't take a chance on renting a car since before long all of the rental places in this part of the country will be alerted to be looking for us. We'll have to figure out where to dump the body along the way."

In Dickinson they stopped for gas. While Jin Rongji was filling up Allen Wu bought a dozen candy bars and tourist maps of Montana. Leaving the gas station, Rongji drove while Wu studied the maps. "We've been on the road for over ten hours. My guess is Breckon will stop and camp. This Theodore Roosevelt National Park in western North Dakota is a possibility, but my guess is they'll go further. In any case we'll want to go further to be sure we're ahead of them. Thirty miles into Montana is a town called Glendive with campgrounds. About dark we'll drive around and look for Breckon. If we don't find the red van we'll look for a place along the Interstate to watch for them to come by in the morning. This big road is the only way to get to the mountains. They'll have to use it."

———————————

As soon as they were on the road again Winger made a call on the secure sat-phone to Langley, Virginia, to report the events of the day, and find out where they could get another vehicle. It was necessary to get this one off the road and under cover. They were not pleased to learn there were two choices, Bismarck, North Dakota, an hour and a half behind them, or Billings, Montana, six hours ahead. Carson said, "We can't go back. We'd be out of the game. If we drop this at the Dickinson police department and try to rent something we'd lose our sat-phone, and who knows what we'd get."

Carson pulled off the road at the first exit in Dickinson with a filling station. "Get the coordinates for the Dickinson police department . . . no get the airport. Plug the coordinates into the GPS (Global Positioning System receiver). We've enough gas to get there. We'll see what we can get and tell the police to pick up this thing. Even if we fixed the fuel leak, it's too dangerous to drive with the brakes messed up."

"The airport's five miles south on Highway 22."

"Let's go for it. The gas gauge still registers a little, I think we'll make it."

Budget was the only rental agency at the airport, and as luck would have it, the only vehicle at the airport that Carson would fit in was a huge blue Dodge pickup with a crew cab. It had just been returned, and contrary to their ardent pleadings, the agency would not let it go until it was washed, cleaned, and fueled up. It seemed they could have licked it clean with their tongues faster than the place operated. Of course, the frustration of being off the road made time seem to crawl.

While Winger and Carson waited, they checked on the situation with the two Chinese men. The Highway Patrol had stopped and found the Buick, but not the men. It meant those two were still at large and still a danger. They would be in a different vehicle now.

As soon as the rental was ready they transferred as much of the special equipment from the Suburban as possible. This left them with only a hand held secure sat-phone for communication.

It was after six-thirty Mountain Daylight Time when Winger and Carson were on the road again. At seven-thirty they pulled off the road at Glendive. The sign for a campground a block to the right caught their eye and that's where they headed. There was a campsite available along the south fence that bordered the on-ramp to I-94 west bound which suited their purposes.

As Winger and Carson waited for their rental truck in Dickinson, Breckon and Daley pulled off the interstate at Glendive with Daley driving. "Take a left," Breckon directed. "We'll go to the state park. It has a camping area much like the commercial one to the right. The campsites are small, and there's water handy, except there are no showers. There're also the outback campsites with fifty yards between them, but no water. That's where I want to go. We'll fill up water bags as we drive into the park. There's another facility the state campground has that I'm interested in."

As Daley drove though town minding the thirty mile per hour speed limit he said, "Okay, I'll bite, what's this other facility?"

"A rifle range," Breckon responded. "We need some practice with that 'dog leg' I packed."

— 18 —

As Breckon and Daley had driven though the area of Theodore Roosevelt National Park in western North Dakota a short time before, Daley remarked about how he wished they could stop to do some sightseeing. The land there consisted of a prehistoric seabed from the late Cretaceous Period about seventy-million years ago. As the seabed rose due to the shifting of the continental plates and the water evaporated, sediments formed many layers of clay and limestone. Over the eons erosion of the landscape yielded an almost endless tapestry of beautifully sculpted hills and ravines. Breckon mentioned at the time not to worry, Daley would get his chance to see it.

Now they were driving into Makoshika State Park southeast of Glendive. Daley was amazed to see that this was a continuation of the same country. Only now they were right in it. The road into the park made its way along a portion of land with dry gullies ten feet deep around it. Beyond the arroyos rose the hills with the striped relief of the layers of sediment visible. The earth here was mainly gray clay and limestone with colorations added by impurities. The park was frequented by paleontologists in search of fossils, and it yielded several spectacular finds.

At the entry point Breckon told Daley to stop and grab a registration envelope and a park map from the holder. They'd have to drive to the back of the park, pick a campsite, and return the envelope with the payment giving the campsite number. Past the main campground that contained about fifteen small sites the road wound through the strange terrain and then abruptly started up a steep switchback to the top of a mesa. Once on top the paved road gave way to gravel. Breckon had camped here once before so he knew where he wanted to go. Using the map he guided them to the place with the outback campsites.

"That's the one," Breckon said as they neared a place to park the car to the right of the single lane road. Daley parked and they both got out and stretched. The air conditioning in the van had been doing its job, and now they realized that the time and temperature sign along Merrill Avenue in Glendive had not been in error. It was hot. The sign had read ninety-eight degrees and it felt all of that now.

Two-hundred feet east of the road the land fell steeply for a couple of hundred feet. Along the slope scrub pine trees clung where they could. Between the car and the trees was a flat open place to pitch a tent. The picnic table and fire pit were up against the trees with a ten foot high upthrust of rock next to it to add a touch for character.

After so much time in the car, and the deadly assault made on them, the two men simply walked around, each with his own thoughts. Breckon ambled down the road fifty yards to the truly rustic outhouse. The road continued for another two-hundred yards and ended in a turn around with two campsites perched on a fifty yard wide finger of the mesa. Sheer cliffs fell away to the west, north, and east of these sites. Not a good place for sleep walkers. Daley walked along the edge where the land fell off to the east of their campsite. Around them lay a valley a mile wide sculpted like the land they had driven though in western North Dakota. It was so quiet and peaceful. Warm wind blew from the southeast. Daley noticed large black birds soaring in the lift provided by the rising air current along the ridge line. When Breckon returned Daley mentioned the birds.

"Vultures," Breckon replied. "Probably scouting us as prospective carrion. Don't look too down-in-the-dumps. We don't want to give them false hopes."

Daley couldn't help laughing. "You are one complicated guy. I halfway think you enjoy all of this, the driving, the danger, the whole package."

"You have to admit there's a certain elation in realizing you narrowly escaped death. I've felt it several times. Now, after that episode, I'm sure you have, too. Winston Churchill remarked about one of his experiences in the First World War, 'Nothing is so exhilarating in life as to be shot at with no result.' The feeling wears off fast, though. Then you start to worry."

They sat on the benches of the picnic table, one on each side as Daily spoke. "What do we do now?"

"First we should see about patching up the car." On the way through town Daley let Breckon off at a hardware store and drove around the block, not wanting to park and draw attention to their vehicle. Breckon bought a roll of masking tape and a red felt tip marker that sort of matched the color of the car. He also purchased fifty rounds of ammo for the gun.

After messing around with tape and red marker for twenty minutes, it wasn't too obvious what had happened. The holes in the windshield looked like they had been hit by stones off the rear tires of a truck. These were covered with masking tape.

Breckon and Daley set up a tent to show the campsite was taken, filled out the envelope, added the money, and put the stub under the clip on the post. They drove back to the cluster of little campsites, dropped the registration into the locked steel pipe provided for that purpose, and continued on to the rifle range. The range was within view of the road entering the park.

Breckon got out the lever action thirty-thirty carbine he had borrowed from Darin. They had thirty rounds of ammunition that Breckon had brought from home and decided they could shoot most of it. "We'll pack twenty or thirty rounds with us into the mountains," Breckon said. "If we need more than that I'm afraid it'll mean we're outgunned. Ever done any shooting?"

"Never," replied Daley.

"I've never fired one of these, but I've used a twenty-two a lot. We'll see how it goes. It's nice there's nobody else here so we don't have to coordinate our trips to the targets with them. If the bad guys come in they'll see us, but at least we'll be ready."

Breckon gave Daley the basic lesson of shooting a rifle which is remembered by the acrostic BRASS, Breath, Relax, Aim, Slack, Squeeze. To get an accurate shot off you have to take a breath, let most of it out, and then hold it. It's impossible to shoot accurately while inhaling or exhaling. With the breath held, relax. While doing this fix the sights on the target. Breckon had scratched out a large diagram in the sand showing the sight picture, how the bead on the end of the barrel must rest in the cradle of the rear sight while resting on the target.

As the sights are brought on to the target the slack in the trigger is taken up. After that, a steady squeeze of the trigger should result in the rifle firing in a "surprise" shot. If the shot is anticipated there's a natural tendency to jerk the trigger and pull the sights off the target.

Experienced riflemen cheat on that last step a little. After a lot of shooting with a given rifle he learns how much squeeze it takes after taking up the slack before it fires. He slowly squeezes about seventy-five percent of that amount. With a target the same size or smaller than the bead on the end of the rifle he waits until his natural motions bring the sight on to the target and then gives the slightest additional tug to send off the shot. Needless to say, Breckon didn't go into fine points with Daley.

Breckon put up a target on the nearest target board, and had Daley practice squeezing off shots with an empty gun. For a target Breckon used the back of the park map, a standard stationery sheet. He pinned up a dark piece of a cartridge box about two inches in diameter in the middle of the white sheet of paper, and returned to the shooting stand.

There was a roof above the shooting stands that reflected the sound of the shots to a painful level. Since neither one had earplugs each held his fingers in his ears as the other shot. The shooter had no choice but to take it.

It took a half hour to go through thirty rounds with frequent walks to the target to see how they were doing. Breckon used a pen to mark off the holes each time so they could tell the new ones from each round of shooting. The learning curve is steep when you start from nothing. As a result, Daley got the feel of the gun in his hands, and how it felt when it went off. After twenty shots he felt he could hit the side of a barn if pressed to do so.

Back at the campsite, Breckon got out his Coleman camp stove and started frying hamburgers. "Have you ever thought of putting these things that happen to you into a spiritual context?" Daley asked. "I mean, maybe God is trying to tell you something. It sounds crazy, I know, but you have to admit, the probability of your getting into two completely unrelated situations like this is way off the probability map."

Breckon was thoughtful as the burgers sizzled in the pan. "Maybe they aren't unrelated, ever thought of that?"

"Yeah, a time or two, but that's hardly possible. You have an idea of how they'd be connected?"

"Nope." He watched the frying meat intently, then continued. "Other than it seems to have started when I was almost crushed to death in a freak accident a few years ago. I was on a job troubleshooting the controls of a crane. Something went horribly wrong. At first I was convinced I was going to die. Then my thinking abruptly changed. I could figure out how to save myself. It was a strange feeling to realize I was considering dozens of possibilities in seconds. At the precise moment I was able to do what was needed.

"This saved me from immediate death. But, I was stuck between the crane beam and the building wall with a crushed leg. It was incredibly hot in there. I could hardly move my chest enough to breathe, and expected to die. Twice I passed out and was walking toward a light when it started to rain. The rain was water my rescuers poured into my confined space, or coffin as it seemed, to revive me. They finally got me out.

"As for God or His plans, I doubt it. Since that accident, and through all the rest He has seemed so far away. When I was a kid I could pray— my parent's influence, mostly my mother's. Now I feel like a small toy that a child playing in a sandbox tired of and carelessly threw into the tall weeds, never to be found again. I try to think of it as a mortification to atone for rotten things I've done."

Breckon scooped a burger out of the pan and placed it on the waiting bun in Daley's hand. He did the same for himself. As he ate he said, "It's amazing how the bun makes the hamburger, isn't it? I fry hamburgers in my apartment, but use a slice of bread since I never have buns. It's just not the same."

"Come on," Daley prompted, "you're changing the subject. So this is something that goes back before the *sand fire* operation. I have to say, how ever you got it, whatever it is, it's a gift. What you did today was magnificent. In a second you decided what to do, which in hindsight appears to be the only thing that would have worked, and then you executed it flawlessly."

"Well, not so flawlessly, I actually hit the gravel on the side of the left shoulder a little. Any more and I might have lost control."

"I won't let you get away with that," Daley retorted. "It was perfect. In case you didn't notice, a couple of those bullets didn't miss me by an inch. If you hadn't hit the gravel, I'd be dead."

Daley noticed Breckon was getting withdrawn so didn't push the subject further. "Tell you what. I'll give you directions to my in-law's farm. After we get back, you're invited out to see the family. We'd all like that." Daley proceeded to draw out a rough map on the back of the campsite receipt.

Daley's mind returned to the events of the day and their present situation. "What do you think happened to the two guys that shot at us?"

Breckon fried the second round of ground beef as they ate their first hamburgers. "That's the flip side of these things. They're still on the loose, I'm sure of it. This will grind along to an unknown but fateful climax. And, as it's going on we'll only have a partial idea of what's at play. If you want out, now's the time to speak up. It'll get worse before it's over."

Daley didn't reply so Breckon continued. "The role of the Cs is uncertain. We'll have to corner them sooner or later and find out what's on their minds." Breckon and Daley had taken to calling the two CIA agents, Winger and Carson, the Cs.

After they had finished supper, and cleaned up, Breckon walked part way down the bank to the east of the picnic table. The ground fell off steeply but was negotiable with care. He located the rotting trunk of a tree fifteen inches in diameter, and six feet long with part of the stump still attached. He proceeded to wrestle it up the bank and left it behind the picnic table. Daley didn't ask.

"Here's the plan," Breckon said as he caught his breath. "We bed down like normal as soon as the sun falls behind that butte." He pointed to the fifty foot rise of land on the west side of the road. After it's dark, we take our sleeping bags and sleeping mats out of the tent. We leave this log on the air mattress I'll have in the tent. After that we go up on the butte for the night."

"Seems a little paranoid to me," Daley said scratching his head. "But, I'm in no position to argue."

———————————

It was nearly eleven when two tired men turned off I-94 at exit 215 in Glendive. Allen Wu was driving and not talking. That MSS piece of dirt, Jin Rongji, was really getting on his nerves. Shortly after crossing into Montana, Rongji thought they were being followed and ordered Wu to exit at Wibaux. There was an interstate rest stop which they by-passed. They drove south and got lost, eventually ending up back in North Dakota. Finally, Wu stopped listening to Rongji's directions as he headed north by any road in that direction. Eventually he found an interstate entrance ramp and headed west once more.

The only positive thing about their unintended wanderings was they found a deserted stretch of road, which wasn't so hard to find in those parts. They shoved what they thought was the body of the truck's owner in a culvert. The tough Swede would live to thank God for his thick skull.

They both saw the campground and motel across Merrill Avenue to the northwest. "We'd better check that out," Wu said pointing to the campground, "and see if there is anybody we recognize spending the night."

"And if they see us as we are looking for them, we are caught!" hissed Rongji through his teeth. "There are too many lights. We must go to the state park with the funny name that is southwest of this town and see if we can find them. There will be few lights in that place. If we don't find them there we must find a place to watch for them on the highway to-morrow morning."

Wu shrugged his shoulders and turned left on to Merrill Avenue. Entering the state park Wu stopped, took an envelope, and proceeded to read the rate schedule on the poster.

"Why are waiting so long here," snarled Rongji. "We must be off before someone sees us!"

Wu looked over at Rongji and said, "Okay. This isn't working. I was assigned to go with you because I have been in America for a few years, and you have never been here. I have an understanding of how this society works. This isn't China! It is not clear from that placard if I should put money in the envelope for one night to camp, or if I have to pay for a day permit as well as a camp. From the way it is written most people would have the same question. So, what I am doing is normal, and will not draw attention to us. I must have the envelope, and know what to do with it, so if we are stopped it will look like we are normal travelers looking for a place to camp. Am I making myself clear?"

Rongji's expression was sour, but he nodded.

"There was no risk checking into the campground by the highway either. Yes, there are lights there, but they were not bright. Plus, we are in a different vehicle. You could have slid down in the seat as we drove around. Most people are in their tents or camp trailers sleeping now. It would not make any difference if we had given the campground attendant the license number of this truck to rent a camp space. Eventually, we'll drive past a scanner on the interstate highway and anyone who wants to know where this vehicle is will know. We can't do anything about that. And, one more thing. Any time we are not on the road with the windows closed, speak English. Speaking a foreign language nobody understands will instantly draw attention to us. I have seen that many times. Heavily accented English is less of a problem."

With that, Wu drove into the park being careful not to go faster than the posted twenty miles per hour. At the cluster of small campsites he slowly made a loop through the area being careful to follow the one way signs. Not finding their quarry he stopped under a light and looked at the map of the park.

"There is another camping place further into the park. We will drive in and see who is there."

Rongji was about to say something, but didn't. The road wound through the strange landscape until it suddenly started up a steep hill. The truck windows were open. The perspiration running down the men's faces was as much from the fear of the unknown as the sultry air. The full moon cast shadows making the strange terrain appear even more sinister. The road seemed to go nowhere forever. Finally, at the top of the climb the road surface became gravel. At each fork in the road Wu stopped, turned on the lights inside the cab, and consulted the map. Rongji was ready to explode.

"Calm down," Wu said in as even a voice as he could. "We are doing what anyone else would do." After what seemed a long time, they followed a downgrade on a single lane road when the headlights caught a dark red minivan.

"That's it!" Rongji whispered. "That's Breckon's vehicle." As they crept past he said, "Yes, that is the license number. Go past twenty meters and stop."

Rongji picked up the large metal attaché case from between his feet that he had been so carefully guarding. Wu stopped. Rongji got out of the truck with the case and closed the door as quietly as he could. He laid the case on the two foot high vertical cut where the side of the road abruptly ended. Wu could hear him open it and the sounds of metal on metal. Rongji returned the case through the open window and laid it on the front seat.

"Proceed on down the road and turn the vehicle around," Rongji instructed. "Turn off the head lights when you return. There is a moon so you can see. Stop twenty meters past the red van and wait for me."

As Wu drove away, Rongji quietly walked up the slope on the dry grass clutching his weapon. There was enough breeze to mask the sound of his movements. Moonlight flooded the scene of the tent setting peacefully on the flat. His knee hurt, and would probably end his career in any case, so now was the time to settle the score. Rongji positioned himself up the slope from the van. His breathing became faster in anticipation. He wiped his palms one after the other on his shirt. He had broken his orders to make the attempt on Breckon on the interstate so why stop now. Revenge was eating him alive. What was taking Wu so long?

After letting off Rongji, Wu proceeded another two-hundred yards down the grade and discovered there was a culdesac with two camping places on it. One was occupied. As he made his turn around a man was getting out of a tent to use the outhouse located in the center of the loop. Wu was sure that turning off his headlights as he proceeded up the road would draw attention to him, and it did.

The man stopped where he was and watched the truck move slowly away. What a strange thing to do, drive down the road with lights on and then turn them off when returning. The road was narrow and even with moonlight the driver could easily ram into the bank.

Wu knew when he stopped after passing the campsite his brake lights would come on, something Rongji had not considered. He shifted into park and waited as he saw the shadowy figure of Rongji on the up hill side of the parked van. Suddenly a stream of sparks spat out in front of Rongji accompanied by the staccato sound of a silenced automatic weapon. It fired in one long burst. The bullets ricocheted from the hard clay earth as well as the rocky up thrust by the picnic table. As the whine of the bullets died in the night, air could be heard escaping from an air mattress. Suddenly there was a call from down the road. "Stop! What you are doing up there? You can't shoot out here!"

Startled, Rongji gave one more long burst into the tent, ran to the truck, and got in. "There. That's done. Let's go."

Wu turned on the headlights and was off as fast as he could handle the vehicle without going off the road. Over the crest of the hill from the campsite he slowed. "You killed them, you fool! Our instructions were to get the disk, and then kill them!"

Rongji proceeded to disassemble the gun as he replied, "Those may have been your instructions. Mine were to eliminate Breckon at all costs. That I have done. Recovery of the disk can be handled by others."

Wu, driving more cautiously said, "But, did you do that? You did not check your work!"

Rongji slapped the parts of the weapon into the foam cutouts in the case. "We had to leave or the man down the road might have come up to investigate. If he had, I would have had to kill him too. And, I know I did the job. Night firing with automatic weapons was part of my training. They are dead!"

Wu retorted, "Did you think that maybe the man who yelled was one of them from the black van on the interstate this afternoon? Why didn't you do it with a knife then you would have been sure? Or aren't you good enough?"

Rongji chaffed at the personal remark. "You drove down there. Was there a black van?" When there was no reply Rongji continued, "That's what I thought. Stop making up stories. Now, we must find a place to park for the night so we can get a few hours sleep. We are still charged with providing backup support for operation *long dagger*. Though, with Breckon out of it, we may not be needed."

As soon as it had gotten dark, Breckon and Daley put the log in the tent and took their bedrolls to the top of the butte west of the campsite. They bedded down fifty feet back from the brink of the butte that looked down on their camp. Daley was pleased as he looked up at the stars with the full moon lifting into the sky to the east. "Just what I always wanted to do, sleep out under the stars with the soft warm wind blowing across me." He laid back on his sleeping pad. There was the far away cry of a coyote calling to the moon. "Wow. Is that really what it sounds like?"

"Yep. That's a genuine coyote, all right. It's the reason the camping fee is as high as it is. Coyotes are getting scarce so the park rangers have to chase around finding them to give that authentic 'out west' feeling to the campsite." Daley chuckled lightly. Within minutes Breckon could hear heavy breathing of a man in a deep sleep. Breckon smiled as he thought about how Daley's enjoyment of his life long wish certainly hadn't lasted long.

Breckon decided against mentioning that people seldom slept outside of a tent for fear of attack by rabid skunks or bats. It was possible there was a rattle snake nearby, too. What was the point, though? They had to take the chance, or was all of this foolish? Thinking back to the problems of the day, Breckon found sleep elusive. He laid one way and then another. He looked at the sky and listened to the soothing rustle of the breeze in the knee-high grass around them. In the distance the coyote continued to call from time to time. He had to admit, it was perfect.

Out of the stillness he heard it. The sound of tires on the gravel road. He shook his head slowly. It always amazed him how people could drive until late into the night and then pull into a campground. They'd proceed to set up camp in the dark, and cook a meal, all the while slamming car doors, yelling at the kids, and kicking the dog.

Breckon sat up and listened as the vehicle proceeded slowly past the small butte. Getting up, he walked the few steps toward the edge. He saw a small truck almost stop by their campsite. It proceeded a short distance and stopped. The dome light came on, maybe someone was checking registrations. No. That wasn't right. The camp attendant had come by shortly before sundown to check the fee envelopes against the occupied campsites. The vehicle started moving again.

Breckon returned and laid back on his pad and sleeping bag. He heard the vehicle returning up the grade. This was not uncommon, either. Someone checked out the campsites, and decided this was too rustic. But then it stopped again. The next sounds sent a chill through him, the sickening sound of bullets tumbling as they spent their energy on the air. He knew instantly who it was and what was happening. And, he had left the rifle locked in the van. How stupid! Yet, it was best to stay hidden. He crouched as he made his way to the edge of the butte. There was a call from down the road, more bullets whining in the night, running feet, a car door slam, and gravel spitting from under tires.

The vehicle sped up the grade and over the brink. From his vantage point Breckon watched as it slowed. Would they search the area? Motionless, he watched the vehicle that looked like a good ol' boy truck the best he could make out in the moonlight. It proceeded slowly. He followed it with his eyes until it was lost from view. It appeared they were confident enough of their success to leave, and would not check the inside of the tent. The man who called from down the road had saved their lives by scaring the attackers away.

Breckon returned to his bed. Daley was still breathing deeply. Well, let him sleep, he thought. There was nothing to be gained by waking him. He noticed his hands were trembling as he realized how earlier he had thought his insistence that they sleep on the butte was a little melodramatic. All he could think of was that it had happened again. He was alive when he should be dead.

— 19 —

Monday, August 14

At first light Breckon nudged Daley until he woke up. "Time to greet the new day and see what it holds for us," Breckon said. As they stuffed their sleeping bags into the stuff-bags Breckon continued, "We had visitors last night."

Daley stopped what he was doing and looked at Breckon. "I didn't hear a thing. Can't remember when I slept so well." Watching Breckon carefully he said slowly, "Why do I think I'm not going to like what you have to tell me?"

"Well, the good news is they now think we're dead. Come on, let's go down and look at the tent."

While Breckon fried pancakes Daley sat silently on the picnic table seat thinking. Into his second plate-sized pancake Daley finally said, "You eat a lot of pancakes, don't you."

"I'm a bachelor, and cooking isn't a big thing with me. If you want to cook, I won't hold you back."

Daley managed a smile. "No, thanks. This is fine. Let's talk about what's been happening. This is out of control, and there's nobody we can go to. We're trapped. If I call anybody back at the NSA it could get to the mole, and then they'd know they failed last night, and be back to try again." Daley was still into denial that the mole could be the man in Computer Services, so he said nothing about it.

"If we tell any level of police it will immediately get back to the FBI, CIA, and whatnot. Sooner rather than later it would get back to the leak at either agency. You know, at work we frequently talked about spies in the system, but it was mostly in the abstract. This has really changed a lot for me. What do we do when we run into the Cs? And, what's going to happen up on the mountain that's so important?" He continued eating in silence as he stared at his plate.

Breckon sat down with his plate and started into his pancake. "As for the Cs, we'll simply have to ask them."

Daley was about to say something, then didn't.

Breckon continued, "We have a pretty good idea about what will happen up on the mountain. They plan to shoot down an airplane. Which one and why is the part we don't know. Maybe the Chinese will have a small army up there, who knows. For us, we have to decide to go or not. What do you want to do?"

Daley took a deep breath, "I have a feeling this will haunt me if I don't see it through. I have a family, and I want it finished. That means I say we hit the road, find the trailhead, and start hiking into those mountains."

Breckon replied, "Let's do it." He sounded resolute, but was far from it. Daley's life had been on the line during both attempts on their lives. Still, he knew he was the intended victim. The shooter, though a little inept, was coming after him with deadly force and had shown himself to be persistent. He would try again. Was there no way he could neutralize his assailant first? He stopped short of focusing his thoughts on the subconscious urge to kill.

Leaving the park, they drove at the posted speed of twenty miles per hour. Breckon would have been driving faster except for the car in front of them that seemed insistent on driving strictly the speed limit. It was annoying, but what could he do. At the first city cross street after leaving the park was a stop sign. Across the street looking back the way they had come was a police car with its radar on.

"That's a cute trick," Breckon said. "Where else in this little berg could the cops be sure of giving speeding tickets to only out of town people. They're using this state park for local revenue enhancement."

Turning on to Merrill Avenue Breckon intently watched the rearview mirror. "There's another police car behind us. We'd better forget about the replacement tent you suggested. We need gas. As soon as I stop you start pumping and I'll go in the store and stand ready to pay. I don't even want to think about the local constabulary seeing those bullet holes in the van. Besides, I packed patching supplies that'll handle most of the damage to the tent."

An hour later, Jeb Stearman stood by the corral with his forearms resting on the top rail watching a half dozen city dudes get the quick course in how to saddle a horse and mount it. He looked to his left as Stubs, his nearly all black border collie, began to bark. A white panel van was coming up the gravel driveway toward the corral. He spat a stream of tobacco juice as he turned his broad shoulders, covered by a sun-faded plaid shirt, and watched as the van pulled up and parked on the hard packed earth next to the other four vehicles. Stearman's stout frame was only marred by a bit of a bulge above his belt. Dropping his foot off the bottom rail, he walked to the van.

An Asian man of slight build got out of the driver's side as the last of the dust raised by the vehicle's approach wafted over them. Peering from under a large gray cowboy hat Stearman said, "Hush, Stubs," which caused the barking to stop but not the dog from sniffing the man and the van. "Stubs tells us when we have guests," the man said in a pleasant voice with a hint of a drawl.

A second Asian man appeared from the far side of the van and stopped cold in his tracks as the dog sniffed around him. "I hope he will not bite me," Wengie said, afraid to move.

"Nah. Never bit anybody in his life. He's a people dog. You must be the fellers who want to rent a couple of pack horses. I'm Jeb Stearman," the man continued as he extended his right hand first to Roger Ling and then Fred Wengie. "Welcome to the L-Bar-A Ranch. Come on over to the corral. These folks are learning how to saddle a horse. They'll be off for a ride in a few minutes. Then we can get down to handling your needs. If you need one, there's a toilet in the bunkhouse over there," he said pointing to a low building behind them.

The new arrivals stood at the corral watching for a few minutes and then Wengie nudged Ling and motioned to the bunkhouse. When they were out of earshot of Stearman, Wengie said, "Those horses are bigger than I thought. How can we make them do what we want?"

"Don't worry so much," Ling replied, "people have been handling horses for thousands of years. These people will tell us how it's done. It will work."

Wengie's expression showed he wasn't convinced. "I read those books about the West you gave me. If a man has the same horse for a long time it goes good. Otherwise they can be difficult. We will be new to these horses."

As the two men walked away Stearman turned slightly and looked after them. There were city dudes, and then there were real down and dirty city dudes. What on earth would prompt a couple of guys from Queens, New York, to call and ask to rent horses. He took a deep breath. Now that he had seen them, he wondered how they'd make out with the horses he intended to sell them. When the guy asked about renting horses his initial reaction was no, especially for this particular week. It was one of the few weeks all summer that he was fully booked. It had been a lousy summer and his business was down. It had started out a little less than normal and then it got dry. The national news kept reporting on the large forest fires resulting in several cancellations. Even with a fifty percent payment when booking a reservation, people would let it go. City people didn't understand how big the western states were. Even with large fires it was less than a miniscule fraction of the forests that burned. All the time his operating costs were nearly the same with or without guests at the ranch. With the drought he was buying hay for his stock.

Since the inquirer had been so persistent he thought about a pair of nags he had picked up a year ago. He knew they weren't perfect at that time he bought them. But, his son-in-law was one of the best horse trainers around so he thought he could get them to settle down. In this business the horses had to be gentle above all. Few people knew how much work went into breeding horses, even common everyday riding horses, so they would be manageable. Somewhere splashing around in the horse gene pool were seldom seen recessive genes that made a horse mean and ornery. By some genetic trick these genes turned dominant and these two showed up. After a year's work, both he and his son-in-law agreed he'd have to get rid of them.

As the man from New York kept trying to convince him to rent two horses for a week or two it occurred to Stearman that he could sell them the horses. The sale would eliminate any liability problems. Still, he tried to switch them to the week before or after this week, but to no avail. It had to be this week. These guys wanted to take large cameras and other stuff up to the high country and get background footage for a movie. Seemed like a crazy idea to begin with, so why was the timing so darned important?

The horses he had in mind were strong, well set up horse flesh, but their free spirited willfulness made them worth less than a few hundred dollars each. He'd sell them to these guys for upwards to two-thousand dollars a head. So, if they brought them back they'd only pay a rental of six-hundred each. But, would they get them back? There'd be a good chance they wouldn't.

When the other party was off for their first ride, Stearman led the two horses out of the barn. He had given each a small handful of Valium pills with their morning feed. "This here one's a gelding, his name is Clyde," he said patting the dun on the shoulder. "This other one here is a mare named Bonnie." The roan with a white splotch on its face rolled its eyes and shook its head like it was trying to shake off a hangover. "They're good solid horses that'll go the distance."

Ling approached the one called Clyde. The horse shied and appeared about to rear up on its hind legs as Stearman kept an iron grip on the reins. "They seem, how would you say, restless, I think. Those other horses were not like these."

"You gotta remember you gents asked for pack horses, those were riding horses. There's a whale of a difference," Stearman said defensively. He was surprised at how quickly they'd noticed the horse's wild streak. "You lead a pack horse so they're much easier to handle. The big thing is they're strong, and from what you said your camera equipment is heavy. They've been in the barn for a few days and are eager to be on the trail. They're mountain horses, you know, and like to be out."

Earlier Stearman had been unsure of how much Valium to give them, but the dose was clearly not enough. He had to come up with something. "You gents wouldn't be interested in a cup of coffee, would you? About this time of morning I wilt without one. How about joining me. We'll see if we can scare up a little something to go with it, too."

Roger Ling and Fred Wengie saw they really had no choice since Stearman had tied the horses to the corral rail and was walking away. Wengie shrugged looking at Ling. As they walked behind the horses a hoof shot out at them. Luckily, they were out of reach of the horse's leg. Following some distance behind Stearman, Wengie whispered to Ling, "I don't like those horses. They are wild."

Ling whispered back, "I don't see that we have any choice in the matter. We have to get the equipment up the mountain. We'll *have* to handle them."

As Stearman walked past the barn he said something to one of the hands. Engaged in their whispered conservation, Ling and Wengie made nothing of it. Stearman had told Daryl to give each of the horses another handful of pills. Daryl was the only one on the ranch who was in on what

Stearman was planning to do. Everyone else that worked here was relation in one way or another. They would have a fit if they knew. This wasn't the first time Stearman had done something a little shady. The others didn't understand what it took to keep the place going. A couple of the bills were overdue and to cover them without getting another mortgage on the place he needed money, now.

In the house Stearman had the two men sit at the kitchen table and placed a large mug in front of each. Next, he set a plate of freshly baked cookies in the center of the table and poured coffee into the mugs. "While we're taking a break, we might as well get the financial stuff out of the way. Here's the list of what you ordered and the expenses," he said placing a sheet of paper in front of Ling. Both men looked at it. All of the items were listed, the purchase of the horses, the charge of hauling them to and from the trail head, ten days of food, feed for the horses, rental of equipment, and a couple of hours of training. The total came to just shy of five-thousand dollars.

Ling took a deep breath. Letting it out slowly he said, "It seems like a lot of money. But, we find ourselves pressured by our schedule, and must be off on our business. We will agree to it. Do you have a bill of sale for the horses prepared?"

"Yes I do," Stearman replied producing another paper and placing it in front of Ling. It was already signed, which made Ling a little worried. "The number describing each horse is its registration number. We use the microchip system that nearly everyone uses now. The chip is inserted with a hypodermic needle under the mane. This little gadget," he motioned to a small plastic device on the table looking something like a TV remote, "reads out the number. We'll verify that before you leave."

Ling knew about the microchip ID system. It was amazing what information a guy could get off the Internet if he worked at it. In the days before they left New York he had spent hours at his computer.

Ling proceeded to take an envelope out of his pocket and slowly counted out fifty one-hundred dollar bills in piles of ten. Stearman could hardly believe his good fortune. He'd have Daryl take the horses to the trailhead, while he paid visits to those of his creditors who were the most demanding.

Stearman took the bills, rolled them in a tight wad, and put them in his shirt pocket that buttoned shut. "Well, thank you gentlemen. Now I'll take a few minutes to show you how to set up your tent, and use the cook stove. Anybody can eventually figure out how these things go, but after a hard day it goes a lot better if you've seen how it's done."

Stearman wasn't sure how long it would take the extra pills to take effect. Since this demonstration was part of the package, he thought it was best to do it now as later. On the brown patch of grass in front of the house Stearman unrolled a tent, and with the assistance of Wengie, put it up and took it down. Likewise, he showed them how to fuel and use the cook stove. After that, he led them to the barn, going in the east end and walking though. Near the west door he picked up a packsaddle and went out into the corral. This little maneuver was to show his guests that the barn was empty. They would have seen by now that there weren't any other horses anywhere in sight outside. If they wanted horses, Bonnie and Clyde were the only two left.

As they approached the horses they were standing with their heads hanging down. "Look at that," Stearman said is a light mood. "Horses have personalities much like people. When we went for coffee they thought they were being left behind again. Now they're all hang-dog. They'll perk up, though, once you hit the trail. Here, let me show you how to put on a packsaddle. Then I'll let both of you do it. After that we'll take them over to your van and figure out the best way to get your equipment placed on the saddles."

After an hour of putting the saddles on and taking them off interspersed with leading the horses around the corral, instruction on using a feed bag, and numerous other tips on the care and use of the horses they were ready for loading the equipment on the horses. This took the better part of another hour. Thanks to the ingenuity of Wengie in reducing the size of the laser equipment before they left New York, this equipment along with the camping gear, food for the men, and feed for the animals was managed with the two horses.

With the horses still under the influence of Valium, Stearman wanted them delivered to the trailhead as soon as possible. "I suppose you gents are eager to be on your way. I know how it is once you get close. You can't wait ta hit the trail and be away from civilization. Those mountains seem to pull on a man. We'll unload the packs and saddles and put the gear in the bed of the pickup. Daryl will drive the horses up to where you gents want to be dropped off. You follow in your van. He'll help you get packed up and on the trail." A boy had come out a few minutes earlier with a brown paper bag. "We've even packed you sandwiches and sodas so you can have lunch on the way. How's that for service?"

Fifteen minutes later they were driving away from the ranch eating the sandwiches. Wengie said, "Didn't it seem like he was eager to have us out of there? I don't know what to make of it."

"You worry too much, Fred. Maybe there was a group of his other customers coming in from the trail. He might like to have the parties separated. It was good there weren't a lot of people standing around laughing at us as we were learning how to do things. Anyway, I'm glad we're getting an early start. This is four hours sooner than I had expected to get on the trail." After a pause Ling continued, "The only thing that bothers me a little is the price of the horses. They were less than two-thousand dollars apiece. I checked prices of horses on the net before we left. Those are young strong animals and should be worth more."

"I don't like any of it," Wengie persisted. "Why didn't you go to a place that rents horses for a business?"

"One good reason. We likely won't be coming back the way we go in, and probably will not bring the horses back. Think of it, after a big airplane crashes in these mountains there will be helicopters and people all over the place. That means we had to buy the horses so we could do anything we wanted with them. That guy needed the money, he told me as much on the phone. He was only too glad to take cash. Did you note that we gave absolutely no identification? Renting horses would have required leaving a damage deposit, credit card numbers, and all kinds of stuff. Buying horses from a normal outfit would have required identification for official records. This was nice and clean. No paper trail."

When Breckon and Daley turned on to the westbound ramp to I-94 at Glendive, they failed to notice the man watching beside a large blue pickup truck in the campground. Daley turned on the radio. "I'd like to get a weather report. We ought to be close enough now so Montana reports will let us know what to expect." When the top of the hour news came on there was national news that led with the nanotechnology treaty. China's diplomats, many of the high officials of other member nations to the treaty, and the three scientists would fly on a special Air China 747 from Washington, D.C., to San Francisco and then be driven to San Jose, California, on the sixteenth. The application of the last signature to the treaty, that of China, would be three days hence on the seventeenth.

The weather report gave them a nice day, but by evening it would turn rainy. "That's the way it goes," Breckon said after the report. "You take your chances. Keep in mind the weather in the mountains is always unpredictable, except that nearly every afternoon there's a chance of showers. On a different subject, what do you know about that treaty with China? The news media are really hyping it. They are counting down the days. Is it all that big a deal?"

Daley had a sheet of cardboard on his lap with the Silver Run Peak map laid out on it. He used the transparent overlay trying to match the keying contour to it. Since Breckon and Daley started on the trip they had taken turns trying to solve the puzzle. They had discussed how the terrorists would know where the contour would match, and decided those guys must have prior knowledge of the situation.

Daley thought awhile before answering the question not wanting to reveal any classified information. "Yes, apparently it is a big deal. The foundry is to be built in Taiwan which means China will forever have to forget its plans of uniting the island with the People's Republic. Personally, I'm a little surprised they agreed to go along with it for that reason alone. There are less obvious reasons that seem to make it a bad idea for China, but giving up Taiwan is the biggest."

"What about that business about changing the Taiwan dollar to the Taiwan yuan? Doesn't that mean Taiwan will be united to China? They seemed to think so when I was in China."

"It's hard to figure that one out. Without the treaty it might be important. But, after it's signed that'll be meaningless."

"What if China is acting in bad faith and they don't intend to live up to the treaty?"

"Wouldn't work. The rest of the developed world wants this nano thing too much. Once it's signed, and the plant is built, they'll hold China's feet to the fire. China's only hope is not to sign it. In spite of that, it sure looks like they will, so go figure."

They drove in silence for awhile. "I think I found it!" Daley whooped, "in a place I never suspected."

"You going to hold me in suspense all day," Breckon coaxed.

"Yeah. Give me a minute. I was making sure it was a good fit. I really do think this is it. The contour match is on a 10,800 foot contour, about a half mile north of Donelson Lake. This puts the path of the airplane on a more or less east-west line over Sky Pilot Mountain. The "X", which we could assume is the location of the guys with the Dragon Fang disk, is by some small unnamed lakes south of Donelson Lake."

Daley took out another map and by folding back the border matched it to the one he had been using. "Looks like your idea of starting out at Island Lake will work." Consulting another map Daley verified that Island Lake was the most logical approach.

"What about other ways to get there?" Breckon asked. "If the guys with the targeting disk are the same guys that shot down the plane off Long Island they might be coming from the East Coast. I think the shortest route for them would be to come through Cody, Wyoming."

For the next fifteen minutes Daley folded maps and placed them next to one another. Finally he said, "There are trails leaving from a campground on Beartooth Lake a couple miles down the road from Island Lake. There you start about six-hundred feet lower than Island Lake so anyone who reads the maps wouldn't use that trailhead. Another mile further west from Beartooth Lake there are trails starting west of Clay Butte that are at about the same altitude as Island Lake. You'd go to the west of Lonesome Mountain from there. We'll go to the east of it."

After a silence Daley said, "I see what you're getting at. We could arrive at the trailhead at the same time as the shooters and not even know it. With that in mind, where do you suppose the guys are that shot up our tent last night? You suppose they're the guys that shoot down airplanes?"

"That's possible, but I doubt it," Breckon said. "What they did on the interstate was risky. If somebody is intent on shooting down an airplane they'll want a sure thing, like getting the agent on the plane out east. I think it's somebody else. Don't forget about the possibility that there could be nobody out there. We'll hike all the way back into the wilderness and all we'll see are mountains. That's what I'd like best."

CIA, Langley, Virginia

Wow! Maybe, just maybe, we got a break, ShuHo Zeng thought as he scrolled through the report on his computer monitor reading it for the second time. He was reading Tom McDuggan's report about the *rickshaws*. There was mounting pressure from the White House to find answers to Flight 974. Other than the initial trace of the chain calls to China by that NSA analyst there had been no progress. The China connection put Zeng at the center of attention. His people had scrubbed the intercepted calls associated with the shooting down of 974 and there seemed no doubt that was the connection. The order had come from China.

Press reports about the destruction of the plane were all bogus—gas fumes in empty fuel tanks again, give me a break. The wreckage showed the plane had been hit from above. There were a hundred theories about how that could have been done. This was fine, it showed people were thinking. Except that none of them led to where the projectile had actually been launched. The projectile itself seemed to have been completely consumed in the explosion.

By feel he punched numbers in to his phone. "Yeah, Sam, I'm reading the account of those two cops you forwarded to me. Come in."

Sam Li arrived a minute later carrying a hard copy he'd pulled off his printer. "I had Department of Homeland Security check freeway camera files from Long Island for the afternoon of July sixth. That light blue van got on I-495 at Manorville at the right time. It couldn't be better. Sometimes I think we should let the local cops have access to the DHS camera data. But, who knows, the abuse could be as bad as we think it'd be."

"This is starting to flow. I think it'll get legs," Zeng said smiling. "Imagine, a mobile home with a Gatling gun and missiles in it. It's unlikely missiles like that got the plane, but this is all connected, I'm sure. Now we have to keep tabs on that thing. Let's find that Chinese man from Ready Communications and follow his movements, too. Contact the cops and have them find out from their man when the *rickshaw* will leave Kaplin Machine. Let's be careful not to get too close to this outfit, though. We don't want to spook 'em."

―――――――――――――

An hour later Li walked into Zeng's office shaking his head, "You think this is starting to make sense? Well, here's a kink that'll twist your brain. I had a search put in DHS for the current location of Ready Communications' white van. Guess where it showed up."

Zeng looked over his glasses with the corners of his mouth turning up in the start of a smile. "So, tell me."

"It was seen leaving Cody, Wyoming, this morning headed northwest. Fit that one into your flow. What can possibly be out there?"

"That's the wrong way for Cheyenne Mountain," Zeng replied. "I suppose that's the good news."

Li glanced at Zeng's face. He saw the mouth drop open, and the eyes stare straight ahead. Slamming his fist on the desk Zeng said, "No, that can't be, but what if . . . . Remember, Winger and Carson from Minneapolis reported they were off on a wild chase out I-94, and the shoot-up on the interstate yesterday? Breckon, the NSA guy, and the two Chinese guys that Winger and Carson are following are all headed out West. Now this guy that we are almost certain is connected with Flight 974 is headed into the mountains. What if that's where Breckon's going? Winger and Carson were sure he knew something he wasn't telling. When those two call in again, tell 'em to stick with Breckon, no matter what."

— 20 —

Daryl got his charges to the trailhead, packed up, and on their way without incident. He didn't like the idea of sending two greenhorns out with those horses. He'd hate to be the wrangler on that trip even with his experience. Yet, they forced it upon themselves by being so persistent about buying horses from the L-Bar-A Ranch. There were places that specialized in renting horses. He had given them all the advice he could think of including that it worked best with the mare in back.

On the trail running along the northwest side of Clay Butte, Roger Ling and Fred Wengie had the reins of Bonnie tied to the saddle of Clyde as both men walked in front. Wengie led Clyde with the rein wrapped firmly around his gloved right hand. Stearman had advised them to have leather gloves for handling the horses and packs. Of course, he had a supply of gloves at forty dollars a pair. At a place in the trail where they could walk side by side Wengie said, "These horses don't seem glad to be on the trail. They look like they want to sleep. I think that man drugged them to make them placid. When the drug wears off we will have trouble."

Ling shook his head wanting to say something to the effect that Wengie worried too much, but he had said that enough times already. "I'll walk in back and keep a watch behind us," Ling said at last.

"No. Not in back, drag," corrected Wengie. "You will walk drag. That is what it is called out here."

The trail led along the slopes of Clay Butte staying close to the same elevation. At times they walked through trees, but generally it was open. It would be wrong to call it grassland because the grass was thin, and interspersed with bare patches of clay mixed with crumbled limestone. To the right the butte rose several hundred feet above them. In places near the top of the steeply pitched land there were sheer cliffs a hundred feet high. They stood like battlements of a long gone city guarding the approaches to the high country. To the left the downward sloped undulating terrain met a tree line a quarter mile away. From there began a heavily forested valley that fell and finally rose again to meet the mountain peaks in the hazy distance. The trail was, not unexpectedly, hard packed clay. The air was calm and the cloudless sky let the warm sun keep pace with them as they walked. Once they stopped to drink from the one-gallon canteens, one of which hung from each packsaddle. After an hour they neared the northern tip of Clay Butte. Wengie begrudgingly admitted to himself that things were going quite well.

They stopped where a small stream crossed the trail leaving a pool of water. Here they let the horses drink. "The horses are very thirsty," Wengie remarked. "Why were they not allowed to drink before we left the ranch?"

Ling shrugged. "Maybe horses always drink a lot. How would you know?"

From here the trail headed north into mountain country. There were trees now, though not dense forests. All were either pines or spruce, and the trail was rocky. And, they started to climb. The first lake they saw was Native Lake off to the right. Suddenly Wengie felt a sharp jerk on the reins. He had grown complacent and nearly lost his grip. Of the two men, Wengie was by far the strongest having been raised in rural China where physical labor was hard and never ending. Ling with his desk job exercised regularly, but was not hard like Wengie.

Twisting around, Wengie pulled hard on the reins. Almost on cue, Bonnie began to pull on her reins and stomped off the trail to come up alongside Clyde. Ling ran up beside the mare and grabbed her reins up close to her mouth like he had seen Stearman do. Wengie shot a sharp glance at Ling. The horses settled down and they started off again. In fifty steps Clyde was giving trouble again. To avoid complications Ling untied Bonnie's reins and led her some distance behind Clyde.

A hundred yards further on Clyde jerked his head and tried to rear up. Wengie held the reins with both hands snapping Chinese words at the horse. The third time it happened Wengie got the horse under control and swung off the trail to where there was a small tree where he tied the reins securely. Searching around he found what he was looking for, a sturdy tree branch three feet long. The next time Clyde got unruly the horse felt the club on the side of his head. He calmed down, but not for long. After several repetitions of this sequence Wengie was beginning to think the horse was impervious to pain.

Not far ahead where a small stream trickled out of the west end of the next lake along the trail, a young woman sat in the shade of a pine tree. Her Forest Service uniform has lost much of its crispness of the day before. Char Muggens had been aptly indoctrinated into the liberal doctrine that the earth was her mother, and that people were its enemy. From her earliest memories in daycare, this line had been drummed into her. Now at twenty-six she was alone on a God-forsaken mountain, without anything to look forward to but more of the same for the next forty years. Standing at five foot seven, she was in good physical condition, tending toward a stout frame. Her light brown hair was pulled back in a ponytail. With makeup and her hair done right, she imagined she was not bad looking. Her clear complexion and well balanced features set off with large hazel eyes had made more than a few heads turn while she was in high school and college.

Her disposition was another thing. Her mother, being a career woman, had stressed the need to keep the upper hand around men. Never give them an inch, was the admonishment she got at every turn. Predictably, this turned away any potential suitor. Her father traveled a lot, which made him a non-factor in her upbringing other than to make sure there was always more money than was good for anybody. There were times like this, alone in the wilderness, when she knew there was something missing in her life, though she couldn't articulate what it was. It felt like she had been cheated.

A helicopter had deposited her in the clearing west of the outlet of the unnamed lake between Native Lake and Surprise Lake early the previous morning. It wasn't until the next morning that she would be pulled out. The mountain air was only steady enough for helicopter operations early in the day. The afternoon clouds that frequently led to erratic winds, and rain made it too hazardous to attempt a landing after midday.

Her purpose in life at the moment, if one could call it that, was to stop parties coming along the trail, and make sure they were properly instructed in hanging their food in a tree at night for fear of bears. She also warned them of the dire consequences of making a fire due to the "dry conditions" even though it rained almost every afternoon. She would also tally the numbers going in and out, and generally glean as much information as she could about the "pests" abusing the beautiful mountain. She had a sat-phone to report any suspicious behavior, especially if she saw smoke from a campfire. A few hundred yards to the west of the trail the mountain fell away sharply into the valley. From there she could see ten miles to the west and southwest. Her other duty was to carefully scan that forested valley with binoculars every hour for signs of smoke.

Most of the hikers coming along the trail were cooperative in answering her questions, but not all. A half hour before three young men had brushed her off and given her no information. One asked if she were going to give them a ticket for failing to signal a turn, or that maybe they were exceeding the speed limit. They laughed and continued on. She stood her ground and made threats to no avail.

Now she heard a voice to the south. It was of a man barking commands, but she could not make out the words. She positioned herself behind a large rock along the trail concealing all but her head and shoulders. Looking to the trail coming down the fifty-foot hump of rock on the south side of the lake she saw two men emerge from the trees into the clearing. The lead man was having trouble with a heavily laden packhorse. She stood perfectly still and remained unnoticed until the party had crossed the small stream. Stepping from behind the rock on to the trail in front of them, she said in a stern voice. "Hold it there a minute. I want to talk to you."

Wengie was carrying the heavy club in his left hand as he maintained a firm grip on the reins with the right. He glanced at the figure standing in the trail. As he did Clyde took the opportunity to try to rear up. Wengie turned, and whacked the horse beside the head with the stick, yelling a command in Chinese. The horse shied, and was still for the moment. A trickle of blood ran down the right side of the horse's head.

"What are you doing to that poor horse!" Muggens shrieked. "Stop it at once!"

"We rented horses, and they are wild!" Wengie snapped back at her in heavily accented English. "And, what business is it of yours?"

Muggens bristled at the rudeness of this little foreigner who stood several inches shorter than she. "You will not speak to me that way!" she retorted. "I work for the U.S. Forest Service and everything that happens in these mountains is my business. Now, put down that stick this instant. I intend to see what's in those boxes on your horses. If you don't comply immediately, I'll make a call on my satellite phone and have a helicopter come to take you out of here under arrest. They will be here in minutes!" she bluffed.

Coming along behind Wengie, Ling was having his own problems with his charge. He could hear the exchange of harsh words, but was unable to

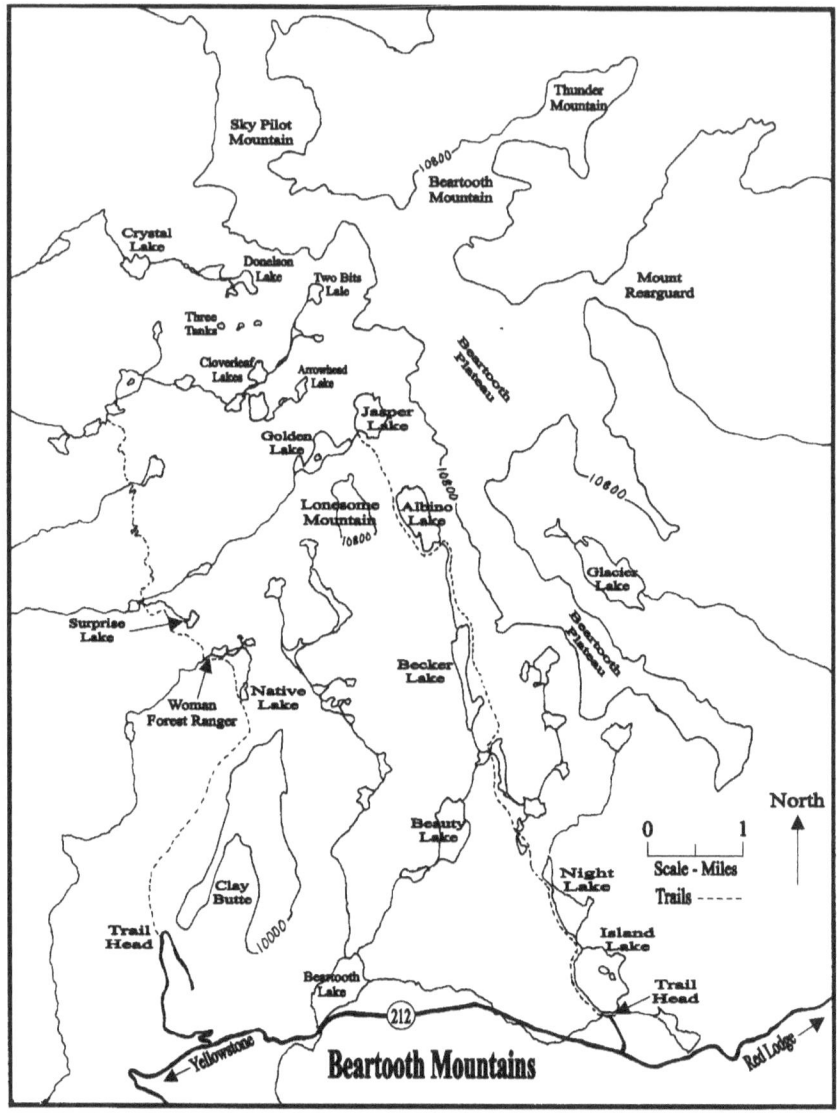

intervene. He turned long enough to see the woman lift an oversized cell phone to her mouth. An instant later Wengie's stick made a rapid arc through the air that ended with it landing squarely on the woman's head. Muggens crumpled to the ground unconscious.

Wengie immediately looked both ways on the trail. Nobody was in sight. He savagely pulled on the reins and barked at the horse to move. Maybe it was the urgency in the voice or maybe the snap on the reins, but Clyde did not object. Wengie told Ling to follow as he led the horse fifty yards up the grade into the trees out of sight of the trail. "Sta-stay with the horses," Wengie stuttered, a hint of panic in his voice. "I will get the body out of sight."

He ran back to where Muggens lay as he continually glanced in both directions at the trail. He grabbed the radio and flipped the power switch off. Taking a limp arm he heaved the woman on to his shoulders. Staggering, he followed the nearly dry stream that ran out of the lake until he was behind a stand of small spruce trees. Dropping his gruesome load, he knelt down opposite the head. With a sharp twist he broke her neck with a sickening snap. He stood and caught his breath. Good, still nobody on the trail. Checking around the area to the west and south he found where the woman had made her camp. It was near a steep drop-off with the treetops at eye level. He decided to throw the body and the radio off the cliff in the hope that it would look like an accident.

With the deed done he returned to the trail by the route he had taken. To rub out any tracks or other signs, he picked up a fallen spruce branch. When he arrived at the place of the altercation, he used the branch to wipe out marks in the dust on the trail. He carefully checked that no personal article from any of them was left in the area.

When he returned to the horses Ling asked, "What were you doing back there?"

"I threw the body over a cliff so it would look like an accident. Then I wiped out signs of what happened on the trail with the branch. That is what they always do in the western books you gave me to read. With the hard dry ground there will be no tracks in the grassy areas. I had no choice but to do what I did. She was going to call in helicopters. Now we must move fast and get out of sight."

A half mile further on Clyde suddenly jerked his head and reared up. Turning to face the horse Wengie tripped. Falling among rocks he lost his grip on the reins. The horse bounded off to the right, through a marshy area near a small pond, around an outcropping of rock, and out of sight. Ling had been following a hundred yards back and still had Bonnie under control. Nearing Wengie he could see he was bruised and scraped.

"This is war!" Wengie hissed between curses. "I will break that horse!"

"First, we must catch it," Ling said in a concerned voice. "It caries most of our targeting equipment."

Breckon pulled into the rest stop near Hathaway, Montana. He watched as a large blue pickup sped past. Pointing to it Breckon said, "That pickup has been behind us for the last fifty miles. It pulled up pretty close to us and then dropped back. I think it's the Cs. I'll bet when we get back on the road it'll pull on behind us from an exit somewhere along the road."

Fifteen minutes later they were back on the road with Daley driving. He wasn't sure he should say anything but thought he'd try again. "Ed, it seems possible there's something going on with your adventures that you either don't know or are blocking from your mind. I hate to pry, but what do you have for a religion? You mentioned a couple of times that you pray."

Breckon again was reticent to discuss it. Finally he said, "I believe in God, if that's what you mean. My parents are good Bible reading people. They never seemed to find a congregation that suited them, so they drifted from one small church to another. I did my share of Bible reading when I was young, still do a bit here and there. I pray for those guys I killed in the underground bunker. Don't know if it does any good."

Daley couldn't help interjecting, "There, you did it again."

"Did what?"

"You mentioned back at Glendive that you thought of your spiritual darkness, when God seemed far away, was a mortification. Now, you mentioned praying for the dead. Protestants and other Christian sects generally don't believe in either of those."

"Must be a carry over from my mother's youth. She was a Catholic when she was growing up. I was sort of raised a Catholic for the first few years of my life." Breckon stared out the right window into the distance for awhile. "At times it seems to me there must be a purpose for these messes I've been getting into, though I usually come to the conclusion that's what I want to believe."

"I'd guess that when it comes, you'll know it, but probably not before."

"My sometimes girlfriend told me about divine providence a few weeks ago. She said that when a person does something immoral, evil, God would not permit that evil if He didn't cause a good to come from that very evil, and that we usually won't have any idea of what the good is until we're in eternity. Maybe it's that simple."

"Not quite that simple," Daley broke in. "The evildoer is still accountable to God for the wrong he has done. Did she mention that?"

"Yeah, she did. But maybe that explains it. Everything, including my China trip and this trip. We'll never know what's going on."

Breckon rubbed his forehead and was becoming agitated so Daley asked, "What do you know about nanotechnology, not the treaty, but what they'll do with the stuff when they get it?"

Breckon perked up a little. "Nanotechnology in its purist form deals with making things at the molecular level, one atom at a time. To start with they'll make extremely powerful computers. But, that's just the beginning. The average person might see something like the replicators used in the science fiction series *Star Trek, The Next Generation*. I remember a scene where Captain Picard goes to the replicator that looks something like a microwave oven built into the wall and says, 'A cup of hot tea.' There were sparkly lights in the machine and then a porcelain cup filled with hot tea appeared. It made the whole thing, the cup filled with water that was flavored with tea. You see, with the super, super nano-computers they can catalog every atom in a tea cup, and with the right force fields, energy beams, or what have you, they could place each atom in its correct spot one at a time as they build the cup."

"That seems like a good deal. You could ask for a roast beef dinner and in a few seconds have it. That right?"

"That's about it. But there's a down side. What will the government do with it *to us*, the average folk? Right now a new bar code system is starting to be used to label products. This code is ninety-six bits long. That makes it possible to tag eight-thousand-trillion-trillion items each with a unique number. That's an eight with twenty-eight zeros behind it. These labels have the ability to transmit their number by means of radio waves when interrogated by a reader. With this system, each individual tube of toothpaste or each apple you buy will have its own unique serial number. Ostensibly, this is to insure you are never sold a product that has an expired date code, things like that. That's not so bad. Next, they'll demand you have an interrogator in your home. This way the toothpaste manufacturer can determine how long you keep the toothpaste in your linen closet before you use it. Still not so bad, but it gets worse."

"Wait a minute. Who do you mean by they?"

"That's a little hard to define exactly. Start with the fact that *they* don't count me among their number. They are basically the government and all its employees. Certainly, not all of those people are out to enslave the rest of society, though when each one gets done doing his or her little

job that's what happens. Many are drawn to those jobs precisely because
of the power that goes with them. Keep in mind, there's a measure of ego
in all human actions. The temptation to push people around is always
there, and government employees have the full authority of that juggernaut to back them up. Try going into any government institution, be it a
city office, public school, or any such place, and tell them you want
something special, or that you don't like the way they do things. You'll
find a brick wall. If you make a fuss, all other government agencies will
close ranks to stop you. Since it's the government, in most cases they
have a monopoly. That's who *they* are.

"Let's get back to the subject. With everything coded and readers everywhere, the garbage man can tell if you put something in your garbage
that should have been recycled and cause you to pay a fine.

"Another hot item for the liberals that control our society is guns. To
avoid the uproar of taking guns away from people they will put a code on
each one. They would also bury a unique code in every bullet. With code
readers in homes, cars, office buildings, along every street, they can track
where every gun and every bullet in the country is. If a bullet kills someone, its whereabouts from the time it left the factory until it entered the
victim can be recreated. This should give an idea of what's ahead.

"Moving on, if they can keep track of trillions upon trillions of products, it'll be a simple matter to keep track of a few billion people. The
government would one way or another implant a tag in each person and
would know where you are at every moment, and who you are with.
They will know what you buy, and where the things are you bought.
They will know everything about everyone on the planet.

"But, it gets still worse. Notice how the cell phones have caught on?
What if the government decided that everyone should have a cell phone
implanted in them? Of course it wouldn't be a cell phone but smart dust.
This is where micro-miniature electromagnetic sensors are made as small
as a piece of dust. Each one is actually a computer, not too capable, but
there are thousands of them. They communicate with one another and
self-organize into wireless networks that can broadcast at least a thousand
feet. They could be injected into you or you could inhale them while being unaware of it.

"Pretty soon, everyone is communicating with everyone else, and of
course, the government is eavesdropping. Back to *Star Trek, The Next
Generation*. In that series there was a race of beings called the Borg who
were part machine and their minds formed a collective intelligence. They

communicated with one another and operated much like bees in a hive. With us in the United States, I think it would be more like a collective *unintelligence*, but that's another story. With everyone connected to everyone else, all decisions become group decisions, with those in power subtly causing the results they want. This would be nothing more than an extension of politically correct thought. We could assume there would be a pain mechanism in each person by which the group could punish the nonconformist. People would hardly be human any more."

Daley was scarcely thinking about driving as he took in what Breckon was saying. "By not being human, what you mean is they won't have free will. That's a big part of the Christian message. A chill went through me as you were describing what could happen . . . . "

"Will happen," Breckon stated.

"Okay, will happen, if you insist. Ed, you may think what I'm about to say is unrelated, but hear me out. I'm a Catholic. I don't know what your thoughts are on Catholics, but let me say this. Someone once said, there are about a hundred people in the United States who hate Catholics, and about a hundred-million people who hate what they *think* Catholics are. The misunderstanding in this regard is monumental. At its most fundamental level the Catholic religion holds a few basic doctrines about what we are, and why we are here. These are as follows. We have one life to live, and this is it. We have free will and can choose to lead good lives or bad ones. Due to original sin, choosing the good is sometimes hard. When we die we are judged as we are at that moment. Based on how God finds us at that fateful meeting we go ultimately to heaven, unimagined bliss, or to hell, horror and pain beyond our present ability to understand. These states will last forever with no provision to get another chance. Finally, and this is the big one, nobody knows for sure if they will go to heaven or to hell until after they are dead, at which point there is no chance to change things. That's it. All the rest of being a Catholic is there to help us achieve the good outcome from our lives rather than the bad one. You know people do go to hell. The Bible's clear on that.

"In every other religion there's an attempt to fudge on that last item, to either get another chance, as in reincarnation among the Buddhists and Hindus. Or, know before death that you will go to heaven, as in the Moslem who dies fighting the infidel, or being one of the predestined to go to heaven as Calvin preached, or being born again. The list goes on. Finally, there's the materialism of developed nations where the plan to beat the game is a creed that says there is no life after death. We must make ourselves happy here in an earthly paradise which for each individual lasts only a short time. In that way they neatly escape the problem of eternity altogether.

"I say all of this because of the Borg connection you made. You're right. There would be an erosion of free will until there was none. Without free will, there would be no point in being virtuous and helping others. I'm afraid God would intervene before that happened. And, God tends to be awfully severe in things like that."

"That's interesting," Breckon interrupted as he intently looked in the rearview mirror on the passenger side, "even a bit profound. And, I hate to interrupt you while you're on a roll. Notice the blue pickup that came down that on-ramp. It's them again. It must be the Cs, so there's nothing to worry about. If it were the Chinese, they would have made a move on us by now. The traffic is light and they could have easily done us in."

"I see 'em. I'll keep an eye on them. You don't agree with a thing I've said, do you?"

"Quite the contrary. I've long felt that technology has moved too fast for society to assimilate it. This has resulted in our losing our heritage of freedom and independence. You've mentioned a few things that I hadn't considered before that I'll have to think about."

Breckon reached behind the seat and grabbed a light jacket that he bunched up and laid between the seat back and the doorjamb for a pillow. "I didn't sleep much last night so guess I'll take a little snooze."

He was fatigued like he thought he'd die, but he couldn't relax. Something was bothering him. That Daley was a nice guy. Why did he have to be so pushy about being a Catholic? He talked like he was the only person who had ever thought about those things. Yet, most of what he said was close to what Breckon had always believed. And in fact, many non-Catholic Christians believed that even if the official doctrine of their denominations didn't. Where was the catch? He turned and looked at Daley.

Daley looked over at him and said, "I know you have something churning around in that noggin of yours. Why not let it go for awhile? Try to get some sleep—you look something the cat dragged in."

"Thanks buddy. I really needed that."

"Okay. You look like you could use a little nap. How's that?"

"Better."

— 21 —

About noon Daley pulled off I-90 at Laurel, made a right and pulled into the Conoco station on the east side of the road. He nudged Breckon to wake him up. The blue pickup took the same exit and pulled into the station across the street. Breckon watched them from behind the van as he filled the gas tank. "That big guy is Burl, I'd bet anything," he said to Daley who was rubbing the bugs off the windshield. "Take your time. We want to be sure they have time to get their tank full. That rig has to be really sucking up the gas. We'll have a meeting with them in a few minutes."

Again, Daley didn't ask.

When everybody seemed ready to go again, Breckon drove out of the gas station and headed south toward Red Lodge. The blue pickup followed. Traffic was moderately heavy on the paved two lane highway. Two cars managed to get between them and the following pickup. After about twenty miles they approached Joliet. At the crossroads in the little town Breckon turned off to the right on to Highway 421, and immediately speeded up. A mile later after going over a rise he made a hard stop, and turned around bringing the van diagonally across the centerline. Seconds later the blue truck topped out on the rise and hit the brakes. Breckon had allowed room for them to stop safely if the driver were alert. He was.

With the pickup stopped fifty yards away Breckon got out and waved to them to come. The pickup started to move. Breckon motioned no. He yelled, "Walk." They drove to the shoulder, parked, and both got out. Daley slid into the driver's seat, moved the van to the shoulder of the road, and got out to follow Breckon. Each party walked toward the other. As they approached Breckon said to the two men he now recognized, "CIA, meet NSA," he said motioning to Daley. "We might as well get to know one another since we're working together."

Introductions were made, a little stiffly, Breckon thought, after which Winger replied a little indignantly, "We are *not* working together."

"Well, that was a nice piece of coordinated action we did on the interstate yesterday for people who aren't working together," Breckon said. "Further, may I ask what your interest is in us?"

Winger had a squished up expression on his face as he answered. "Not both of you. It's you, Breckon. We've been told to see that nothing happens to you, and that you don't leave the country, or otherwise drop out of sight. Can't say it would matter one way or the other to me."

Breckon had the thought to say something to the effect that life could be so unfair at times, but decided against it. Instead he said, "There are probably a few things that you have not been told that would make sense out of this. Tell you what. About twenty-five miles to the south there's a picnic ground on the right side of the road where we intend to have lunch, let's stop there and have a chat. That okay with you?"

They both nodded and walked back to the truck.

Now there was no reason to keep a discrete distance behind the red van so Winger stayed a safe distance back, but close. At the rest area Breckon got out the box of groceries as Daley grabbed a brown paper bag and the water. Once they were settled at the picnic table Breckon said, "Since we intend to be hiking in the mountains for a week, most of this food will spoil, so help yourself." Breckon sliced what was left of the summer sausage for sandwiches as Daley started making some with peanut butter and jelly. The apples, grapes, and bananas along with the cookies and doughnuts also had to be eaten.

Winger and Carson burrowed into the food like starving cats. "You guys haven't put on a feed bag for a while, have you?" Breckon quipped.

With a mouth full of food Winger replied, "Keeping track of you guys hasn't been easy. You can stop and go as you please, we have no idea what you'll do, or when, which means we always have to be ready to go."

"Well, in spite of what you think of me," Breckon replied, "thanks for the help on the freeway yesterday. You saved our butts. However," Breckon paused for effect, "there might still be a tiny problem. The authorities didn't get the guys that shot holes in our van, and who, I suspect, put a few bullets in your big Suburban too. That's why you're driving the Dodge, right?"

"Yeah. Right. We thought the state police would get the perpetrators. How come you think they didn't?" Carson asked somewhat surprised.

"Because they shot a hundred holes in our tent last night, that's how we know!" Daley snapped back. "A fine job of law enforcement you guys managed to do." Both special agents looked at Daley. Carson even stopped chewing for a moment. "Of course we weren't in the tent at the time. Breckon knew they'd come. How he knew I don't know. But, he knew."

Winger looked at Breckon and said, "Okay Breckon, time to come clean. What did you get, or what did you learn in China that makes those Chinese guys so all fired eager to get you? I know you've been holding out on us from the beginning. The next time they may succeed in killing you and then nobody will know. So, what is it?"

Breckon was rustling through the box looking for nuts he knew were there. Pulling out a plastic bag of almonds he said, "I'm not going to spill my guts to you guys because the whole intelligence and law enforcement juggernaut in this country is made up of people that have one thing in mind, namely their careers. I don't know if that includes you, but I suspect it does. If I tell you something that I suspect, only suspect mind you, in ten minutes you will be on a secure phone to Washington and everybody will know. Some career monger will take actions to solve what he *thinks* is the problem. He'll probably be wrong, but that won't matter as long as he's seen as taking decisive action. This will result in dozens of robots on steroids dropping out of helicopters. In a crap shoot like that I'll end up dead, and no one will care in the slightest.

"Not apprehending the guys that shot at us, and you, by the way, on the interstate yesterday, really drives the point home. You want to know what's going on? Catch 'em and make them talk, even if you have to beat it out of them. But no, you'd rather beat it out of me. How could you stupid asses let them get away?" Breckon started crunching nuts as he tried to settle down. The whole thing had him steamed. "At least now they think we're dead," he said in a more even tone. "Where do *you* think they are now, and what are *you* going to do about it?"

Winger hated being in this position, and knew Breckon had a point. "Did they check your tent to see if they got you?"

"No. A camper from down the road yelled at them and they drove off after spraying our tent with a silenced automatic weapon. I didn't sleep well so I think I'd have heard if they came back."

"I'd think they'd head back to Minneapolis," said Carson. "With you dead, they'll gain entrance to your apartment in hopes of finding whatever it is you won't tell us about. Now, what's the reason the two of you are on this camping trip? It seems unlikely you've been fast friends for years. Something brought you together."

"Daley and I plan to go hiking in the mountains starting this afternoon. We are interested in gathering information. It's not likely anything will happen, and that's all right with us. Mostly we're on vacation, and intend to see some mountains and relax. If you guys intend to tag along, I suppose there isn't much we can do about it. It's a free country, or mountain, as the case may be. After we eat I'll show you what you'll need. You'll have to buy it in Red Lodge and pay blood for it. That won't bother you, of course, because you'll be using the tax money that's taken out of my paycheck.

"If you want to be let in on what might be going on I'll give you a place to meet us in the mountains tonight. It isn't all that much, I assure you." With what was left of the food packed away, Breckon used his gear to show the agents what they'd need, and told them what not to get.

As they were leaving Breckon said, "One other thing. Bring along any guns and ammo you have. You don't want to take a chance and get eaten by a bear or mountain lion."

Winger and Carson stayed at the picnic ground awhile after the other two left. One put together a shopping list while the other made a call to Washington, and then to the North Dakota Highway Patrol. When they were back on the road, Carson said, "There's something up. Did you hear him say he didn't think anything would happen? That means he thinks something could happen. And, the part about bringing along guns and ammo. It's not bears he's talking about—he knows something!"

"Yeah. I know," Winger replied. After a pause he added, "Breckon was right about one thing, though."

"Yeah? What's that?"

"We *will* be using his tax money to buy our grub and outfit. And, we *won't* scrimp."

As Breckon drove through Red Lodge Daley said, "There's a hardware store, drop me off and go around the block a time or two. I want to get something." Breckon shrugged and stopped. There was no point in thinking about parking since the streets were crowded, as they always were in this tourist town. On the second time around the block he saw a man wearing a big black western hat raise his hand and wave. Taken off guard Breckon took a second look and realized it was Daley. He jumped in the van knocking off his hat as he did. He grabbed it and got in again with a big plastic bag in his hand.

"So what did you buy besides the hat?" Breckon asked. "Looks too heavy for a box of Kleenex."

"I got to thinking about what you told the Cs. So, I took the opportunity to accelerate the arms race," he said smiling as he pulled a box out of the bag. He opened the box and took out a Colt .44 magnum revolver.

Breckon laughed, "That's enough to scare me to death. And look at that, a hip holster complete with belt. There are even cartridge loops on it. With the hat and the gun, you'll be the meanest looking hombre on the mountain. How did you beat the waiting period for a hand gun?"

"The NSA picture ID along with 'national emergency' did the trick. Of course, it took the store manager to finally make the decision."

"Hmm. Should I call you Dirty Harry?"

"Guess Dirty Greg doesn't have the same ring to it, does it?" Daley replied sounding a little dejected.

"Ya gotta go with what ya got's all I can say."

Daley had out a box of cartridges and was filling the loops on the belt. "They fit awfully tight. I can barely push them in. Wonder if they sold me the wrong belt."

"I wouldn't know. But, it makes sense they should be snug. We don't want to leave a trail of cartridges up the mountain like a modern day Hansel and Gretle."

Breckon couldn't let the moment pass without a comment. "I think it's a good thing that you managed to get the gun. You just may need it. But, if my need had been a hundred times greater than yours, I would not have gotten it. That makes you one of *them* that we discussed earlier."

"Yeah. But, you have a gun."

"That's because the laws apply to me. I have to plan ahead."

Twenty minutes later the same store manager was staring at a CIA ID as the stern man in front of the counter purchased several boxes of nine millimeter ammunition along with camping gear. The manager mentioned the NSA guy that minutes before had purchased a handgun. He thought to ask what was happening to his quiet little town but decided against it. This man did not appear to be in a chatty mood.

———————————

Wengie and Ling rounded the boulder that had blotted out the escaped gelding from view. They saw a mountain ravine a hundred yards wide that headed up hill. There were trees, brush, and plenty of knee high green grass, but no horse. Now it was Ling who had the negative attitude. "We will never find that horse in here, and we cannot complete our mission without the equipment he is carrying."

"It's not so bad," Wengie replied. "See the steep walls on the sides. Clyde would not go up them. He went up this ravine. You go on that side," he motioned to the left, "and I will go up this side. Be quiet. If you see him tie up your horse and we will try to corner him. He ran hard with a heavy load. He will be tired."

The two men worked their way up the grade scouring the small stands of thick spruce, and bunches of brush. For flat landers, it seems like everything in the mountains is up hill, and the "up" goes on forever. Finally, Wengie came along the side of a hump of gray granite with spruce and pines surrounding it. In front of him spread a lake. As he walked into the fifty yard low area between the rock and the lake he saw Clyde, his reins tangled in brush. He spoke softly as he approached. The horse jerked his head up and backed off. Wengie snatched the reins just as they pulled free of the branches.

"Over here, I caught him," Wengie said as Ling appeared around the other side of the rocks. Ling approached, a look of relief on his face. Wengie motioned in the direction they had come, "There are tight bunches of trees on the other side of these rocks to hide the horses and equipment in. We will camp there tonight. And, the lake will supply water. After we unload the horses I must work with this one."

Ling searched Wengie's determined face. "What can you do with that wild horse?"

"We will see, we will see. We are lucky he did not break our equipment. Next time he will, assuming we even find him next time. He must be made more manageable. After we unload the horses, I must walk along the lake." He repeated his earlier statement. "I will break that ornery horse. I'm pissed."

An hour later Wengie led the roan out to the west side of the lake with Ling at his side carrying the items Wengie had taken out of the packs. Wengie found a heavy stick with a short sharp branch protruding from it near the large end. Stopping at the place he had selected he tied the reins securely to a small tree. The water immediately dropped to three feet deep just off the bog where they stood. The lake gradually got deeper until fifty feet from the shore there was a shear drop-off. The clear water made this easy to see. Wengie proceeded to take off his boots, hat, and shirt. "Okay," Wengie began, "I will point Clyde toward the lake. Then I will grab his mane and pull myself up on his back. As soon as I'm up you hit him in the rump as hard as you can with the sharp prong on this stick. I want him to leap into the lake. Do you understand?"

With a look of disbelief, Ling nodded.

Getting Clyde to stand still was hard. On the first try the horse stepped to the side away from Wengie who fell on the ground. After several attempts Wengie got the horse to stand beside a rock that nature had gratuitously placed beside the lake. For his part Clyde appeared to know what was about to happen, and had lots of practice preventing it. He threw his head, snorted, and stomped his feet. Finally, Wengie had him settled down for a moment with a firm grip on the reigns. He stepped up on the rock grabbing a handful of mane as he did. He leapt on to the horse. "Now!" he yelled at Ling.

The horse was poised to buck Wengie off as he had done with every other would-be rider. The sting Clyde felt on his hindquarter as Wengie landed on the horse's back was totally unexpected and he half bucked, and half fell into the lake. As he leapt the horse had started to turn toward the land, and fell forward on his side in the water. Wengie was thrown off, but maintained his hold on the reins. As the horse righted himself Wengie was once again on his back, jerking the horse's head toward deeper water. The water made bucking impossible and soon the horse was beyond the drop-off swimming with only his head above water. Wengie hung to the mane as he let the horse turn toward shore. As soon as its hooves gripped the edge of the submerged rock ledge the horse pulled himself up and attempted a mighty buck. But the water dampened the action so Wengie managed to stay aboard.

Thus, they fought. Wengie was thrown once but managed to hold on to the mane and swing himself up again. Clyde was frantic, twisting, and thrashing. Wengie kept him in four feet of water as much as possible. Finally Clyde stopped and stood still in the lake. Wengie let him turn slowly to the shore. As he was about to pull himself up on the shore, he went into action again. For the horse's part, he tried a little too soon. Wengie pulled savagely on the reins, and the bit dug into Clyde's mouth and turned him back into the water pitching about wildly. At last, giving up his struggle, the horse stood motionless in three feet of water. The cold water and feverish effort were having their effect on both horse and man. After a full minute, Wengie pulled on the rein and turned the horse to the shore. He encouraged him on. Slowly the horse walked through the water to the boggy shore. He put his front hooves on the soft earth and tried to pull himself up, but could not. He was played out. Sliding off the horse's back, Wengie took the reins over the horse's head and proceeded to crawl up on to the bank. He pulled as he encouraged him in a soft voice. This time the horse managed to get himself up. His head hung to the ground as he still puffed for breath.

With teeth chattering Wengie grabbed for his shirt and threw it over his back. "Roger, quickly, get me my dry pants you carried out here. That water is really cold. Also, get the horse brush and that box of sugar cubes." When Wengie had his dry clothes and boots on he instructed Ling to use the brush to wipe the water off the horse. Wengie put several sugar cubes in his pocket and returned to where the horse was tied. He lifted the horse's head. It was bleeding where the bit had dug into the skin at the rear of his mouth. Wengie offered a couple of sugar cubes to the horse. Unsure at first, Clyde took them from the offering hand. Due to his abrasive personality, the horse probably had never received a treat before. Wengie took the brush from Ling and brushed Clyde's neck and mane all the time talking in a soothing voice. Handing the brush back to Ling, Wengie pulled gently on the reins and the big gelding followed with no objections.

By four-thirty, the sun had gone behind the hundred and fifty foot high buttress of granite that guarded them on their immediate west. An hour later the deepening shadows offered a feeling of seclusion. Wengie worked at starting the camp stove and cooking one of the prepared meals Stearman had packed for them. Ling read the instructions that came with the Global Positioning System receiver he had purchased in New York. At the time he bought the instrument he was not sure it was something he'd need. This was the most expensive model they had. It displayed a map of the area from its memory. It seemed this was the most useful feature, and he now was thankful he had it, if he could get it to work. He had no idea how far they had come on the trail, and with chasing the run-away horse he was feeling hopelessly lost. After a half hour of fooling with the instrument, he identified the lake where they were camped as Surprise Lake.

Checking the paper map, he could see that the trail ran to the west of the rocks blocking the sun from their present position. With all of their seemingly endless wandering they were less than a quarter mile from the trail. On the trail they had passed close to Surprise Lake unaware of its existence. When the horse bounded free it had doubled back. In all they had not traveled as far as he had planned this day. Though, they still had enough time to get into position if the horses behaved.

As they ate the heavily seasoned meal Ling asked, "Where did you get the idea of riding the horse in the lake?"

"In the books," Wengie answered flatly. "The Louis L'Amour stories you gave me to read. I even bought more of them. They are fun to read stories. The good guy always beats the bad guys, and at the end gets the pretty girl. One story was set in mountains that could be these very ones. Along the way he describes many things, about how people lived in the Old West and how they did things. The cowboys always broke horses by getting bucked off until the horse was too tired to buck anymore. But, some of the Indians learned a better way. They took the horse into water. This meant the horse could not buck as hard, and if the rider were thrown off the water kept him from getting hurt. I think I broke Clyde today. One place in a story a man made the observation that any horse is stronger than any man, and it's the man's job to keep the horse from knowing that. I hope Clyde now thinks I am stronger than he is.

"The books also tell about how the men took care of their horses. They were kind to them, and at least in the stories, the horses responded by working hard for their masters."

3:10 p.m., Mountain Daylight Time

Daley was driving and Breckon checked off the landmarks. "That's Little Bear Lake ahead. Once past it, watch carefully for a turn off to the right. Boy, it's been a long time getting here, but we're almost ready to hit the trail. I can hardly wait. There, that must be it. And a little ways up this gravel road . . . yes, there's the sign for the turn to the trailhead parking off to the east."

Seconds later they stopped in the crushed rock parking area with small poles spiked to the ground as lane markers. There were spaces on the west side for single vehicles and in the middle for trucks with horse trailers. In all there were fifteen cars and four trucks with trailers. Breckon was immediately out of the van. He quickly jogged around to all the vehicles and felt the hoods.

"Checking to see if anybody else arrived recently. They're all cool except for the one that young couple just left," Breckon said nodding to the two hikers starting on the trail.

Twenty minutes later they set off. The trail headed west along the south side of Island Lake past a National Forest Service campground. They crossed the lake's outlet river by stepping from rock to rock. That was a nice thing about August trips to the mountains, the streams and rivers were low. Earlier in the summer hikers had to take off their boots and wade across in the freezing water.

From there they took the trail along the west side of that lake and then past Night Lake. The going was easy with a well established trail and level ground. There were a few marshy places, but they made good time.

An hour later as Breckon and Daley were hiking north of Night Lake Allen Wu and Jin Rongji arrived at the trailhead with Rongji driving. There were now a half dozen people in the parking lot either coming in from the wilderness or preparing to go out. Rongji hit the brakes so hard gravel spit from under the tires. Heads turned. Rongji moved on after the pause, and parked near the end of the row.

"Surprised to see Breckon's van here, are you?" Wu said unable to keep a note of smugness out of his voice.

Rongji said nothing. The weight of the retribution he would face for having killed Breckon against orders had been gnawing at him. Breckon's presence meant he still had a chance to exact his revenge in the mountains where cover stories would be easier to fabricate. It did bother him that he had missed twice, though. Another thing he knew— Allen Wu could not be allowed to return from here alive lest he report the first two attempts.

He got out of the truck and said little as they finished packing their gear, food, and the rifle with scope into the frame packs. They had done their shopping in Billings thinking it was a larger town and they would be less likely to be remembered. Most of the gear like tents, clothing and ponchos came in either bright colors or camouflage, so they chose camouflage.

When they were ready to leave, Rongji looked at his Beartooth Butte map purchased at the same place they got their gear. "Breckon being here changes things a little. They would most likely take the trail on the west side of the lakes," he said in a hushed voice. "We have to assume their helpers are here, too. That means we should use the east side of the lakes to avoid an ambush so close to the cars and that camp ground over by the lake." Wu could see nothing wrong with the logic of this so they headed out without further comment.

Rongji thought he might still have a chance at Breckon later along the trail, but he was becoming cautious. The man had a magic life. The pack he was carrying would have given him no difficulty if it weren't for the knee. Better to get Breckon sooner than later, he thought. But, if all else failed he would attempt to trap him as his bosses wanted.

The going was slower on the east side. Even where there was a trail, they frequently left it since they tried to stay under the cover of trees. In mountains, if there are trails, take them if they go anywhere close to your line of travel. They were probably first laid out by animals. Where there is a dead end, there is no trail. At the very least, trails show the easiest route to get from here to there, count on it. Wu and Rongji were learning this. After forty-five minutes they dropped their packs and rested.

Keeping his voice low, Rongji said, "I've been thinking that you were partially right about the man that yelled at us when I shot into Breckon's tent. It wasn't someone from the black van, but the man with Breckon. The tent was a ruse. Breckon was nearby since his vehicle was there at the campsite. They wanted us to report that we had killed Breckon. Those in charge of operation *long dagger* would then think the target designation team was safe, and order us to break off the chase. That would leave Breckon free to stop the operation without hindrance."

"Why wasn't the location of the intercept changed a second time when it was learned Breckon had the disk and the new intercept location?"

"Changing the intercept location meant other plans had to be changed. There was not enough time to do that before the team was dispatched. We know the NSA monitors all communications, so we had no choice but to give the team their orders and let them plan and execute their mission. This meant we would not contact them once they set out except to cancel the operation."

"Do you know the intercept coordinates?"

"Yes. Breckon has the coordinates too, and that gives him an advantage. But, I think he does not suspect we are here and that may cause him to get careless. Enough talk. We must get moving so we can close the distance to them by dark."

— 22 —

5:50 p.m., Monday, August 14, Absoroka Mountains

Roger Ling and Fred Wengie had picketed the horses on a patch of good grass and were making fair progress with setting up the tent. It was easy when Stearman did most of it. Everything seemed different now that they were doing it alone for the first time. Finally it was taking shape. They had chosen a place down the ravine from the lake because the tent was well hidden, even though the site was not as level as it should have been. They'd learn the problem that caused when they bedded down for the night. The sky began to darken as heavy clouds moved over. Suddenly a huge shaft of lighting struck the rocks near the lake. It was followed immediately by a deafening clap of thunder.

"Finish the tent," Wengie said, "I'll bring in the horses." He ran first to Clyde, untied the lead rope from the fifty pound rock used to tether him in case the animal got funny ideas. He led the horse into an open space shielded on three sides by a tight wall of spruce. He followed with Bonnie. Huge drops of rain exploded on rocks as Wengie dashed for the tent.

Ling seemed to have the tent done, and both men dove in as the rain came in earnest. Cracks of thunder split the air as pea sized hail pummeled the mountain. There were small air vents on each side of the tent up under the rain fly that could be zipped open leaving only the mosquito netting. Each man was up on his knees looking out the vent nearest him. The sound of drumming on the tent left their heads numb as in amazement they watched the ground became white with hail. They could hear the wind whip the trees on the top of the rocks on either side of the ravine. The tent shook and flapped, but their snug position in the sharp gorge provided shelter. Ling could make out the horses in the adjoining clump of trees. They were pressed up against the trunks of trees so the branches broke the fall of the hail.

Wengie rifled through a duffel bag, and at last pulled out a medium weight parka. "I thought Stearman was crazy when he insisted we take these things along," he said as he put the coat on and zipped it up. "The rain has made it cold. We must also locate our ponchos so if we have to go out in the rain we don't get wet. My other clothes are still soaked from the lake. If you get wet you will die quickly from the cold. I wonder how the horses can stand it."

At four-thirty Breckon and Daley arrived at the place where they said they would meet the Cs. They found a good campsite well hidden from the near-by trails. To the south of Becker Lake were several small lakes. Their camp was on a rise to the west of the most southerly of them. The upland area they occupied was wooded with small marshes in the flat areas among the trees. Around the lakes below them to the east was open land. After camp was made Daley watched the trail for their buddies while Breckon did his best to patch the tent. He always brought along a tube of flexible glue and swatches of rip-stop nylon to patch tents, packs, water bags, boots, and anything else. He patched the holes highest up first. When he had used up all of the materials the tent looked like a teen-ager with acne after shaving with a blade. By folding over the edges of the ground cloth inside the tent the equipment around the edges under the un-repaired holes would be kept dry.

His task done, Breckon joined Daley and they observed the trails in the valley below them. They were surprised to see the number of parties coming and going. In the space of an hour they saw three parties going in and two out. One group of four coming out had two lamas as pack animals. Daley mentioned how he thought that group had the right idea. He had aching muscles after only a few miles of packing. They were eating a cold meal when the rain came, so they finished in the tent.

A little before dark the sky cleared. Watching the gathering darkness Breckon commented on the mountain to the east as it caught the last rays of the sun.

BANG! A gun shot in the trees a short distance to the south shattered the stillness of the evening. Both Breckon and Daley fell flat on the ground. They were well hidden so didn't think the shot was directed at them. Daley had his revolver and was about to start making his way in the direction of the shot when Breckon whispered in his ear, "If you see movement be careful what you're shooting at. You could hit a stupid camper who shot at the sound of a mouse in the dark."

Breckon was familiar with how noisy the small creatures of the wild can be in the still of night. He eased off toward the west in the direction of their tent. A few minutes later Breckon heard the crunching of brush followed by a muffled "Ouch," and recognized the voice.

Breckon was lying behind a tree as he said, "If you promise not to shoot us, you can come into camp."

"That you, Breckon?"

"Yeah, and you can only be the cavalry. Keep your voices down, not that it matters much, now."

Twilight was nearly ended and the moon, one day past full, was about to rise. Breckon saw the shadowy figures and went around some bushes to guide them to camp. It was terribly hard walking in the woods in the dark, and here, with half the land setting on end, it was nearly impossible.

When everyone was accounted for Breckon asked, "What did you shoot at? You could have hurt somebody in the dark. And, you told everyone on the mountain where we are."

Winger was feeling a little foolish. "I thought there was a bear coming toward us, but I guess it was only shadows."

"I was kidding about being eaten by bears. There aren't any in these parts. I'll show you a place to lay out your pads and sleeping bags. It won't pay to try to get your tent up. It won't rain any more tonight. We'll talk in the morning."

———————————

Allen Wu and Muan Rongji coming around the east side of Night Lake discovered that it was mostly open grassland north of the lake. Staying under cover of trees where they could, they made it to a point a half-mile north of the lake and a quarter-mile east of the trail. Here, they had no choice but to cross two-hundred yards of open area. They were nearly across when the rain hit. They raced for the trees and were soaked by the time they found their ponchos and got them on. They shivered under a large tree until the rain slacked off.

"We had better move back into the trees and find a place to spend the night," Wu suggested. Rongji nodded. It was occurring to both men that simply surviving out here was going to be difficult. They had done no climbing yet, to say nothing about accomplishing their mission.

As the sky cleared they decided not to try to figure out how to set up the tent, and were chewing beef jerky in the gathering night when they hear a shot off to the northwest. The two men looked at one another. "That must be Breckon," Rongji whispered. Having kept under cover as they traveled on the east side of the lakes they had seen no other hikers. This led to the feeling they were alone on the mountain with their enemies. "Now we know where they are. Sleeping here is good. We will get up before dawn, and move up on their camp. This time I will not fail."

4:45 a.m., August 15, Absoroka Mountains

Daley had been awake for nearly an hour. The reconstituted dried food they had eaten for supper was salty for his taste causing him to drink a great deal of water. Now he decided he simply had to leave his warm sleeping bag and go out to relieve himself. Moving as quietly as possible in the dark he slowly zipped open the tent, set his boots and revolver out, and slid out himself. Immediately his socks were wet on the soles of his feet. When he sat down to slip on his boots his pants got wet. He wrapped the laces around the upper parts of his boots and made a simple tie. Standing up he brushed himself off feeling his wet behind. The rain and the heavy dew had left the ground soaked.

Shoving the gun behind his belt he wasn't sure he believed Breckon about there being no bears in these parts. Since he had bought the thing, and was paying the price of its weight, he might as well feel the comfort of having it at hand.

The moon had set behind the mountain to the immediate west which left the area in little more than starlight. His eyes were fully dark adapted so he thought he could see quite well. The exposed rocks were light gray with everything between them pitch black. He soon learned his depth perception was not good. A gray spot could be a rock flush with the ground or one knee high. In between the rocks the land was unbelievably uneven. In an unsteady gait like a man half drunk he made his way to where Breckon had dug a cat hole behind a tree for a latrine.

Having his job done he walked out from under the tree and stood in the stillness looking up at the stars. Suddenly from the marshy area to the southwest of him he heard a sucking sound of a foot being pulled out of mud. As silently as possible he maneuvered behind a large tree peering intently in the direction of the sound. Moving his gaze to the left and right he saw a movement out of the corner of his eye. He hadn't been trained in night work. If he had he would have known it is fundamental that the rods at the edges of the retina are more sensitive to dim light than the cones in the central area.

Looking directly at the spot of the movement he saw nothing. Looking away he saw it again. A twig snapped, and he glimpsed another movement further back. He estimated they were fifty to a hundred yards away. He didn't want to wake his companions if the sounds were caused by deer or elk. The thought of the shooting on the freeway, and the tent full of holes came to mind. He had to take the chance.

In a level voice he said, "Who is out there?"

He no longer heard anything, and try as he might he could see no further movement. Maybe they were animals. He slowly crouched down. With his right hand he pulled the revolver from his waist band, and with his left felt around the ground for something to throw. His hand came to the edge of a rock. As he pulled it out of the ground it scraped on another rock. He gritted his teeth. Too much noise. He stood and looked around the left side of the tree again. Nothing. In an underhanded motion he threw the rock in the direction of the movement he had seen. It hit one of the tree's branches six feet from him. Immediately the crack of a rifle not a hundred feet away sent a slug cutting through the branches.

He jerked behind the tree, raised the gun, and fired on the right side of the tree at the place of the muzzle flash. The unexpected recoil of the gun almost caused him to lose his grip. Stooping down he grabbed the barrel with his left hand, pulled the hammer back, and slowly stood again holding the gun with both hands.

In the camp he heard quick movements and the sound of slides chambering rounds. The tent zipper sounded like tearing fabric as Breckon was obviously getting out fast. Daley also heard the sound of the lever action on the carbine. Where there had been no sound to his front he now heard stumbling steps retreating from him. Moving his eyes around the area he caught a movement near where he had first seen them.

"Who's there?" It was Carson's voice.

"It's me, Greg." Daley said in a low voice.

"You hit?"

"No. I think our visitors left. I heard steps moving away. Don't shoot me, I'm coming into camp."

As Daley neared the tent he said, "Where's everybody? We have to keep track."

"I'm over here by the rocks to the east," Breckon replied. "Mel headed to the north. We have to stay quiet and listen until it gets light. No talking."

Daley went back to his tree near the latrine. The sky to the northeast was showing the first tinges of dawn so it wouldn't be long.

Forty-five minutes later it was nearly full daylight. They took turns scouring the areas in front of their positions to insure there was no threat of another attack. Breckon built a fire and began cooking oatmeal to go with dried fruit and turkey jerky.

Carson sat on a rock looking out over the valley to the east. "They sure turned tail easy. No fight in them a'tall."

Daley smiled, "It sounded like an infantry company back here with all the guns getting ready for action. They're not stupid. They may have gotten one or two of us, but we'd have gotten them."

"Do you think they're the same guys from the freeway?"

"Does the big bear crap in the woods?" Breckon asked rhetorically. "Did you make a list of the vehicles at the trail head like I asked?"

Carson pulled out a small notebook and started reading them off. When he came to a red flatbed truck Breckon stopped him. "That's them. If there were any question before, there isn't any now."

It took a two day ration of oatmeal and brown sugar topping to feed the crew, but the way they licked it up, Breckon thought it was worth it. He'd get something from the Cs in return.

As they finished breakfast Winger said, "Okay Breckon, you going to tell us what's going on? We know one of those guys has a reason for killing you, but this goes beyond that."

"Why would a Chinese man want to kill me?"

"Because you smashed his knee when you where in China, that's why. He has a mechanical knee and isn't too happy about it. Now, what else is going on?"

"Small world, isn't it. He tried to steal my suitcase at the airport, did he tell you that? Anyway, have you got a satellite phone that you could use to call back to civilization?"

"Yeah. So what?"

"Let's see it."

Winger opened one of the side pockets of his frame pack and pulled it out.

"Okay," Breckon continued, "here's the deal. If you give me that, I'll tell you what we know. I simply won't have you in on anything where you'll be reporting half-baked assumptions back to Washington every few hours. What do you say?"

Winger and Carson looked at each other in long silence. Finally, Winger handed it to Breckon. "Let's hear it."

"Do you remember KLM Flight 974 that exploded off Long Island in early July?" They nodded. "From information Daley and I have put together, we suspect that someone on the ground targeted the airplane probably with a laser so a small deorbited satellite could home in on it to destroy it. The information put out by the Transportation Safety Board about why it exploded in flight is misinformation so the public won't panic. There was a special CIA agent on the flight that the Chinese wanted to destroy, and they did.

"Now we have information that points to the fact that they plan to do that trick again tomorrow back in these mountains. We don't know if it will be an airplane, but from the location it could hardly be anything else. Maybe it will be a B2 bomber and will set off a hydrogen bomb, or a commercial airliner with VIPs on it, or a special private plane. We don't know."

"Who knows about this?" Carson asked.

"You guys are the third and fourth people on our side. I suspect there aren't many more on the other side. The location may have been changed, and we may be going up the wrong mountain. Who knows? The fact that those two guys are so keen to stop us tells me we're on the right track."

"Hey. You mister NSA. Why haven't you told your superiors about this," Winger said sharply to Daley. "Seems like a clear case of dereliction of duty to me."

"Not as clear cut as you might think," Daley replied. "There's a mole in the CIA, you know that. That's why you had to use Breckon to carry the computer to China. There's also one in the NSA. If we told someone, at least one of the moles would find out and know we knew, and they'd change the targeting location. Nothing's gained. With this wilderness, a change of a few miles is as good as a hundred. Now the only people that know besides us are you. If things go bad, we'll know who to hunt.

"A friend of mine thought he knew who the mole in the CIA was. The night before he planned to report it he was killed. We aren't going into this for fun—we're trying to save our lives. They will assume because you are with us that you know what we know, and so you do. Now, you'll be trying to save your sorry asses too. Join the club. And if I might offer a suggestion, follow Breckon's lead."

The Cs didn't like what they were hearing. They never guessed things were this deadly. Nobody said anything for several minutes. Winger went to the tree to relieve himself. When he came back he asked, "How do you see it Breckon?"

"They know who I am, and by now possibly Daley. They would not likely recognize the two of you, is that right?"

"I suppose so."

"You take the trail up to Albino Lake. Scout around for a defensible secluded campsite, in the event we need one. Daley and I will have to take the hard way over the rocks to the west of us. We'll come on to Albino from the southwest. Be watching for us and try to spot the Chinese guys. The maps don't show a trail, but it looks like there will be one on the west side of Albino. When we join up, Daley and I will stay several hundred yards ahead or behind you guys. We'll continue on to Jasper Lake yet today if we can. Don't give any sign you know us. I'm guessing that will be open country, but there's no way to avoid it. Any comments?" There were none so they packed up and set off.

After their aborted attack on the camp, Wu and Rongji made a wide sweep to the south and east before they started up the east side of the valley toward Becker Lake. They assumed that Daley had been a sentry. They were also shaken by the number of weapons they heard being readied for action. They now recognized the two of them could not expect to make an effective attack on the combined enemy force. Even if they put two or even three out of action before being taken down themselves, it would leave the targeting team at risk. The only alternative was to join up with the targeting team so they also had the numbers for sentry duty and combined firepower.

— 23 —

Camp Ripley, Minnesota

Lieutenant Roston had his platoon of four tanks out on a maneuvering exercise. It trained the crews to work together as a team. In normal deployed formation each tank in a squad of two covered one another, and each squad covered the other. In open country this wasn't too hard. But, where the terrain was hilly with stands of trees about, it got harder. It was still more difficult with choke points. These were places where all the tanks had to traverse a particular place, like a river that had only one place to ford. It was all too easy to end up with a traffic jam at places like this which would be a tempting target for the enemy.

"Blue 1. Your lead squad is too far ahead. You'll lose sight of them in the trees ahead!" the radio snapped. It was Captain Case, of course. He was along in his command tank micromanaging the operation. He was on his radio so often that Roston scarcely had time to direct his tanks.

Roston had no choice. "Blue squad 1, close the distance to squad 2." The long two weeks were winding along at a snail's pace. It was finally Tuesday of the second week. Would Case please get promoted and move on to another job? Please, God!

Roy Hatley arrived at the Beartooth Ranger District office in Red Lodge, Montana at quarter to seven, more than an hour earlier than normal. In his mid-fifties, he had gotten his district posting less than a year ago. He had spent the greater part of his life working for the U.S. Forest Service busting his back in the wild improving trails, working forest fires, and all the rest. He loved the mountains as if he were born to them. He was a stout, strong man. Though he was hard and brown his hips were giving him increasing problems. It was obvious to him he couldn't keep up his past pace until he retired, and was pleased when he got promoted to the district office.

He had called Char Muggens repeatedly the evening before, and again before he left home. He was genuinely worried. It had been his idea to put personnel into the mountains to warn hikers of the fire danger, and have spotters in case anything started. He desperately did not want a major fire in his district. With so few people and so many trails, there had been no choice but to have each one operate alone. The men he didn't worry about so much, but putting a woman out there alone bothered him. Yet, it didn't seem right to force the guys to take all of the nasty duty, while the gals rode around in trucks all day.

After another call to Muggens with no answer he called Dirk Swensen, a young man here for his second year. It was Swensen's day off and Hatley promised him compensatory time. He told Swensen to come by the office and use the Forest Service truck. Hatley would have him take the spare sat-phone along on the assumption there was a technical problem with Muggens'. It was a forty minute drive up to the trailhead, and an hour's walk to the lake where she was stationed. Swensen would be back before noon.

Two hours later the phone rang and Hatley answered it. It was Swensen. "Hey chief, this is Dirk." There was a pause as Hatley heard heavy breathing. "I found her. You'd better be sitting down for this. You sitting down?"

"Yeah, what is it?"

"She's dead. Broken neck. Looks like she fell off the rocks to the south of her camp. It looks like an accident, but I don't think so."

"You sure she's dead?"

"Yeah, she's stone cold. Must have happened yesterday before the rain. She's all wet and the ground under her is pretty dry."

Hatley was stricken with self-recrimination. His guts had told him not to put her up there. Why had he done it?

"Wait a minute. What did you say? You don't think it was an accident? Why not?"

"There was no reason for her to be near the edge where she went over. If she were looking for smoke in the valley there's a better place. The rain washed out a lot of signs, but it appears there's a place she went regularly to look for smoke. And, her binoculars are still in her tent. What do you want me to do?"

"Stay there for now and keep the phone on. Don't disturb anything more than you already have. You've done a good job. I'll get the state police out there as soon as I can. By the way, stay by the trail and note everyone you see going in or out. Especially question anyone you see coming out about who they might have met on the trail. Understood?"

"Consider it done."

A mile to the northwest Roger Ling and Fred Wengie were making their way along the trail through heavy forest. Much to Wengie's surprise the horses were behaving. They had taken to talking to them almost constantly in a low soothing voice. At this point Bonnie was giving the most trouble. But, with Clyde under control, she was manageable.

They started early knowing the woman's body would be found by midmorning at the latest. They passed a small creek that ran from Throop Lake to Thief Lake. Ling was getting experienced in reading the contours on the maps and his GPS receiver. He knew that not far ahead was a steep five-hundred foot climb. He hoped to get to the top before they met anyone on the trail, because once on top they would leave the trail and head out to the northeast for the Cloverleaf Lakes.

As they were about to start up the daunting switchback, they met three women going in the opposite direction. Ling cursed under his breath as he realized their chance of going undetected was gone. And they would have to be women. Guys would look at the horses and at the equipment a little, but not normally much more. The women would take in all the details of the horses, the gear, and especially the two men.

Almost as if reading Ling's thoughts, Wengie watched the women. As soon as they were past him he pulled the silenced automatic out of a saddlebag on Clyde, slipped a round into the chamber, and killed the women.

Ling's stomach turned, but his mind didn't. He realized as did Wengie that since they intended to destroy an airplane and kill as many as two-hundred people a few more didn't matter. He just didn't like being so close to it.

"I'll tie Bonnie's reins to Clyde," Wengie said. "Let's hope they behave. Get them to the top of the climb and leave the trail to the right until you are out of sight. I'll clean up down here and then find you."

Ling nodded and started up. When he got to the top the horses were panting, but Ling urged them on until he found where he could get off the trail and out of view of hikers that might come along. Here he waited for Wengie while letting the horses rest. The rain had not been nearly as heavy this far into the mountains so the horse's tracks were not readily visible in the hard earth once off the trail. Some time later Wengie joined Ling and they started off again. By late morning they were east of Liver Lake and swallowed up by the mountains. Here they stopped by a small stream, and unloaded the horses for a one-hour rest.

Shortly before noon the sheriff from Cody, Wyoming, arrived on his horse accompanied by a deputy. The lake where the apparent altercation occurred was a half mile south of the Montana border, so was still inside their state. Dirk Swensen had yet to see anyone coming down the trail out of the mountains, and said it seemed unusual. With the concurrence of Hatley and the sheriff, Swensen started up the trail into the mountains to see if there were any signs of anyone having come this way. He decided he'd walk for an hour and a half and then start back. It would probably rain again in the afternoon.

He saw where Ling and Wengie came on to the trail with the horses. He hoped he could overtake them to inquire about what they might have seen or heard. When he got to the base of the steep switchback, he thought he should turn back since he had quite a distance to go. From what he could see looking up through the trees, the cumulus clouds were building already. As he sat and caught his breath for a few minutes, he noticed the horses' hoof prints were missing from the trail. Scouting off the trail he saw blood signs and eventually found the body of one of the women.

"Hey Roy, you ready for this?" Swensen said as soon as Hatley came on the phone.

"Now what? Where are you?"

"Southwest of Throop Lake. I don't know how to break this to you, but I found another body."

Swensen could hear a long breath being let out. "What's happening up in that wilderness? What else can you tell me?"

"Well, it's another woman, still a little warm, so it happened today. Shot several times. And, get this. There were a couple of horses on the trail this morning going in. They came on to the trail a little north of Surprise Lake. The tracks continue up the steep switchback from where I am. The horse tracks are wiped out in the area of the body. It's hard to tell if they were pack horses, ridden, or one of each. There are boot tracks on the trail, but they might have been made by another party. That's about it."

"Time you started back. Can you mark the spot?"

"I can blaze a tree with my knife at the place to go off the trail. She's not hard to find."

"Okay. Do that. Then head back, and be careful. We don't know what's going on up there. I'll notify the Montana authorities. See you when you get back."

———————————

Wengie and Ling were learning the hard way the value of following trails. A few hardy hikers liked to go across country because of the challenge and the solitude, but it's risky leaving the trails. In the high Absorokas it was not like climbing a single mountain such as Mt. Rainier. It was more like a couple hundred square miles of high plateau that was very bumpy with two-thousand feet from the bottom to the top of the bumps. In this rugged country a hiker can easily make a hundred foot climb with full pack only to end up at a shear rock face rising in front of him, or find himself on the edge of a cliff requiring an equally hard return. With horses the animals carried the weight, but getting them turned around and down steep slopes was difficult. From the point of view of keeping one's footing, it was much easier to go up than down.

By four-thirty they found a place to camp north of the most westerly of the Cloverleaf Lakes. They crossed a well used trail coming up from Rachel Lake and managed to avoid a party of four hikers. Keeping out of sight had been hard work. The horses were tired and so were the men. With the last of their strength they unloaded the pack saddles and stripped the gear off the animals. Wengie did the best job he could of rubbing down the horses. Ling worked at the tent. A rumble from the sky in the west reminded them there would be no time to relax.

Wengie put a feed bag on each of the horses as Ling finished with the tent. And then the storm came in its furry. Having left the trees behind they found there was no shelter here. The elements were free to do as they pleased with anyone or any thing. Both men were on their knees in the tent holding on to the fiberglass tent spars to keep them from breaking. They pushed until their muscles ached, and yet it continued. It ended as suddenly as it started. The landscape was wet, though less than a quarter inch of rain had fallen. In this alpine tundra that was common. It was part of the reason why there was so little vegetation. The other reason was that six to eight months of each year the ground was covered with snow.

The day had gone hard for Breckon and Daley. Going across the mountains to the west of Becker Lake had given them the same hardships as Wengie and Ling had encountered, only there were no horses to help Breckon and Daley. Not knowing where the next attack would come from kept them continually looking at the landscape near and far. It also kept Breckon from concentrating on their travel resulting in their climbing more than necessary.

It was two o'clock when they topped the rise to the southwest of Albino Lake. They hurried over the crest to avoid being skylined. Pausing a moment they saw a party of three coming south on a trail along the west side of the lake so they headed toward it. As they approached the trail two guys who had not been visible entered the trail a hundred yards ahead of them, Carson and Winger.

Breckon said, "Wait" in a voice just loud enough for them to hear. Carson and Winger stopped. As Breckon came past them he said, "We're all played out. Go over the saddle ahead and find a campsite on the east side of Jasper Lake. We'll be there in a couple of hours. We have to take a breather." Breckon and Daley hardly stopped as they passed. A short distance further on Breckon turned off the trail and started up the grade toward Lonesome Mountain. When he found a sheltered spot among large rocks he stopped and dropped his pack.

Breckon and Daley sat down leaning back against their packs. It was still sunny, warm, and comfortable where they were. Breckon could see the other two slowly making they way up the climb to the saddle between Albino and Jasper lakes. Breckon tilted his hat forward to shade his eyes and let his eyelids fall.

After awhile without opening his eyes he asked, "What if you're wrong?"

"Wrong about what?" Daley asked.

"What you were talking about in the car yesterday, about our purpose and destiny?"

"That's simple. On one end assume you plan for one life and then judgment when you die, and the Hindus are right. So, you get another try. What have you lost? Or look at the other extreme and the atheists are right. If you plan for a life hereafter and there is none, again what have you lost? But, if you believe as they do and I'm right, you could be in a world of hurt not for a long time, but for time without end. I'm not wrong though, and you know it. Everyone knows it. People spend a lot of time, energy, pain, money . . . their entire lives, trying *not* to know it.

"Look at the way people buy insurance on their homes, health, cars, life, and whatever else. What are they doing? They're erring on the side of safety. In the best case, they'll never need any of it. In dozens of other ways they err on the side of safety. For example, they look twice before driving into an intersection, just in case they missed something. But, with the most important thing in their whole lives, their eternal destiny, they wouldn't think of erring on the side of safety. It's crazy."

"Yeah. But, everybody's not like that. What about someone who does good things for others because it makes him feel good. That's not a bad person."

"That's true as far as it goes, and I'm sure there are people like that. But, it's only the positive side of the hedonist philosophy of 'if it feels good do it.' What if your hypothetical person runs into someone he doesn't like and is mean to him because that feels good? The Christian idea of loving your neighbor goes beyond doing good until it feels good, but doing good until it hurts—hurts you."

"Guess I've heard that a few times," Breckon replied. "It really surprised me, though, when yesterday you said that all the stuff about being a Catholic wasn't important."

"Oh, no. I didn't say it wasn't important, but that it wasn't part of the basic reason why we're here. I said it was there to help us get the good rather than the evil result out of life. Look at it this way. There are three things everyone will come to learn sometime, sort of a foundation of life. They are: there is a God, it isn't me, and I will live forever. It so happens that the Catholic Church is the structure that fits the foundation."

"You saying you have to be Catholic to get to heaven?"

"No. I didn't exactly say that. Someone who through no fault of his own has never head the true message of Christ can still get to heaven though it will be difficult. Some say it's too hard being a Catholic. In certain ways it is, I guess. But, it's more an adventure of hope. The stakes of life—how you'll spend eternity—are so high I'm stupefied by how little people even think about it."

Breckon was looking across the lake at the mountain on the other side. There were rock slides that came down into the lake along most of that shore. "I'm going to change the subject. Notice how those slides across the lake look like rocks are rolling down them all the time. It's rarer than you'd think.

"A few years ago we were up above the tree line like this, and after supper I was looking across a meadow at a fifty foot up-thrust of rock a hundred yards from me. There was a knob about thirty feet in diameter jutting out from the rock face. The bottom half of the knob had broken off leaving the top half hanging there. The remaining part was cracked all around as evidenced by a dark ring. Where the lower part had fallen away the granite was dark in contrast to the light gray of the rest of the wall. The dark color looked like dirt that had run into the crack before the piece fell off. It appeared as though the part had fallen off in the last few years, and I wondered when the rest of it would come down. As I looked, it occurred to me that the broken part wasn't there. The meadow was too flat for it to have rolled away. Obviously, glaciers had carried the fallen part away, and it had been ten thousand years since the last glaciers came through those parts. It's not much of a story, but is reminds me that things happen slowly up here.

"By the way, I've been meaning to mention the great job you did this morning. I should have thought that we needed a sentry. And that was good thinking to guess they'd come at dawn."

With a smirk Daley replied, "Yeah. Well, I guess there's more Injun in me than you guessed, huh?" A little sheepishly he continued, "The truth on the matter is I was afraid my bladder would explode and I was out tending to that—got lucky."

Breckon laughed. "There are those rare times when it's better to be lucky than good. Enough of this sitting around. We should get going. The rain'll be here before sunset."

An hour later they found the Cs on the southeast corner of Jasper Lake. The campsite they had selected was good, but further up in the mountain than Breckon and Daley would have liked—more climbing. They had a cold supper. There were no trees. Even if there had been they would not have chanced giving away their position with a fire. Based on the experience of the night before they set up a schedule where each of them would take a fourth of the night as sentry. The wind and rain came and went giving way to a clear night.

— 24 —

ShuHo Zeng and Sam Li were having an early meeting before the demands of the day took over all of their time and most of their sanity. The long hours Trent Clausen worked at Kaplin Machine Works made it hard to contact him. They had learned that the special mobile-home was there when he left at seven the evening of the fourteenth, and it was gone when he got back at seven the morning of the fifteenth. Trent told the Queens police officer that occasionally they drive them away, but more often they load them on low flatbed trailers, tarp them completely, and truck them out.

"I did a search of all the freeway cameras in that twelve hour period," Li was saying, "there was nothing close to what Trent described, in any paint scheme. As for it being trucked out, there are a lot of wharves on the east side of the East River in that neighborhood. A lot of freight goes out tarpped on flatbed trailers. Truckers like to depart during those night time hours to avoid traffic. I hate to say it, but it looks like we lost it."

Zeng nodded solemnly. "Bad luck. Put *rickshaw* in the NSA watch list. It'll slow up. What's happening with our Minneapolis guys heading out West?"

Li laughed. "The day after the shoot-out on the interstate, Breckon actually stopped them and fed them lunch. Breckon and his pal from the NSA were headed up into the mountains on a camping trip like nothing happened. I don't believe that guy. Mel Winger, he's the suspicious one, thinks they're up to something but Breckon wouldn't say what. By the way, they lost their good com set in the shooting so they only have the hand held sat-phone now. Sometimes it works, sometimes not. They went to a trailhead by Island Lake as directed by Breckon a few miles west of the Bear Tooth Pass. Here, I got a Wyoming map."

Li and Zeng studied the location. "They left their vehicle by this lake and started hiking into the mountains to the north. After dark on the fourteenth they met up with Breckon back in the rocks. Winger said it was out in nowhere. Nothing but rocks and a few trees. We haven't heard from them since. Maybe the phone died."

Zeng shook his head at the story. Li continued. "You know, I mentioned the DHS cameras picked up the white Ready Communications van leaving Cody, Wyoming early the morning of the fourteenth. It was headed northwest. Look," he said pointing to the top part of the map, "if they took Highway 296 and then turned east on 212, they'd get to the same place as the rest of them!"

Zeng gave a snort, "You know, and I know something's going to happen on that mountain, and I don't think there's anything we can do about it. We can't call out the National Guard with the speculative information we have."

"What about this *rickshaw* vehicle?"

"They're hiking back into the wilderness. You couldn't get that in there. I'm sure it's connected, but not out there. The only good thing I can think of is Breckon's out there." He held up his hands, palms facing Li. "And please, don't ask me why I think that's a good thing."

6:10 a.m., Wednesday, August 16, Jasper Lake, Montana

Everyone was up greeting the cold morning. Being on the east side of the lake, they would not feel the warmth of the sun until they walked out of the shadow of the mountain. Between eating and breaking camp there were a lot of eyes studying maps. Breckon showed the Cs the overlay and the other information he had received by mistake.

Winger said, "I'd guess the reason we didn't have any trouble last night is because the two guys after us went on ahead to set up a defense of that hill south of Donelson Lake. Whatever it is, it happens tonight."

"What can be so all fired important?" Breckon asked to no one in particular.

"Something occurred to me," Carson said. "The guys after us are Chinese. We know that for sure. The signing for the big nano-treaty is in Washington today, with the last signature, that of China, being put on tomorrow in California. They will all fly in an Air China 747 to San Francisco later today. What if that plane is some how directed to fly over say, Sky Pilot Mountain, tonight after eight? Maybe a faction in China doesn't want that treaty and will destroy the plane. This is a good place to do it."

They all stopped what they were doing for a moment stunned as they thought about it. It made too much sense.

"And the whole world would blame the U.S. for it," Daley said.

"What a perfect dirty trick," Breckon added. "I'll bet there are others arriving at that spot today with whatever they need to target the plane for the satellite weapon. That means we must split up. One pair of us must go on up to Two Bits and Donelson Lakes. The other pair will have to go along the north side of Golden Lake to the Cloverleaf Lakes and see who's over there. They might be coming up past Crystal Lake, but we're too far out of position to cover that."

"Who goes where?" asked Winger.

Breckon stooped over and picked up a couple of pebbles putting one in each hand. He held out both closed fists. "Large pebble goes the Golden Lake route. You call it Mel."

Winger hesitated a second and pointed to the left fist. Breckon turned it over and opened his hand. He did the same with the right. The larger pebble was in the right. "Guess we get Golden," Breckon said. "Remember, any shot will give away the approximate location of the shooter, though the echoes can be deceiving and the sound travels forever. We'll converge on the spot shown on the overlay midway between Donelson Lake and the north Cloverleaf Lake. Be careful. We don't want to shoot each other."

With that, they gave one last look around, heaved their packs on to their backs, and set off.

Breckon and Daley hiked along the south side of Jasper Lake while Winger and Carson went the other way until they came to the valley that came into the lake from the north. Traveling was normally done in single file. If the guy in front made it over a rough spot, those behind followed. There was no point in testing a second path. Daley was in the lead this morning which gave Breckon time to think. He should have been more concerned about the day ahead of them. By its end any or all of them could be dead.

Breckon couldn't help marveling, as he always did, at the stark beauty of the landscape. The traveling was easy except for a stretch along the northeast side of Golden Lake. Here the trail was nothing more than a few rocks sticking out of the water with a rock wall pressing close. A few places they had to get on their knees to crawl over the next rock. Any slip would have ended in a cold swim in the lake.

But, his mind was not free. At times the foreboding mental state of what was happening to him closed in. He even thought there might be a sinister spiritual plot against him. The many close scrapes he had experienced in the last several years, in fact the last few days, weighed on him. He was even nagged by the thought that today was different. He was going into a known dangerous situation when he could simply have said no, and not gone. All the other times he had more or less fallen into them against his will. Would this be the one that undid him?

The third attempt on his life—he saw it as aimed at him even if others could have died too—had been almost miraculously thwarted. What were the odds Daley would be out of the tent at that exact time yesterday morning? His antagonist had to be stopped, killed. There was no longer any shying away from the obvious. Only one of them would survive. Why should it be that asshole with a grudge.

He was brought back to reality as they came into view of the Cloverleaf Lakes a little after nine o'clock. They had taken the valley up from the center of the north side of Golden Lake to the saddle that would lead down to the lakes to the northwest.

If they walked directly down to the lakes, whoever was of a mind to see them could do so, but only if they were watching that approach at close range. Other than that, it was uncommonly hard to spot a man in the mountains even if fairly close. Beyond a quarter mile it was almost impossible without binoculars.

There are four things that got one noticed in the mountains. By far the most important was noise. Sound traveled so well in the thin air that on a still day even normal conversation could be heard for a half mile. The second was walking across snowfields. Since most clothing was fairly dark, the snow set it off. Light clothing would be less noticed on the snow, but highly visible the rest of the time, which leads to the third which was bright colors. A blaze pink strap would be seen long before a whole person complete with pack. The fourth was being skylined. This would normally be the least important because for a given observer and observed the conditions were right for only brief periods. Beyond that it is natural for movement to attract the eye. But, the background was so rugged and multihued that movement in this setting was not as noticeable as elsewhere.

Breckon was vaguely aware of all of this but not dwelling on it. Being skylined was so obvious a problem that they crossed over the saddle as quickly as possible and stopped among boulders to rest and observe the valley below. Only by taking time to look for out of place colors or other signs could they hope to see their enemies.

————————————

There was no chance Breckon and Daley would see the men they sought because these men were already at the targeting location shown on the map overlay. Fred Wengie and Roger Ling had rightly figured that with the discovery of one or all of the bodies they had left behind there would be a determined effort to find who had done it. They assumed, also correctly, that the tracks of their horses would be something the authorities would be likely to link with the murders, if for no other reason than few of the hikers used horses. And, horseshoes left marks in the soil where boots didn't so there was a trail to follow.

For these reasons Wengie and Ling were up loading their horses at three a.m. They had only a mile of travel though the land was intensely broken. On the undulating ridge between the Clover Leafs and Donelson Lakes there were three small lakes, or large tanks, in an east to west row.

As they entered the hollow around the center of the three unnamed tanks before dawn they were surprised to be hailed in hushed Chinese. This left little doubt whose side they were on as Allen Wu and Jin Rongji made their appearance. Wengie had meticulously sealed each major item in watertight plastic before crating it. Using boards from one of the crates they tried to dig into a snowfield on the north facing slope of the basin to bury the equipment. To their consternation they found the snow was nearly solid ice with a couple of inches of crystallized snow on top. So they laid the equipment in depressions along the edge of the snowfield and scraped the layer of snow off the ice to partially cover it. After it was camouflaged as well as possible Wengie, Wu, and Rongji took up positions where they could watch the approach from the north, east, and south. It fell to Ling to get rid of the horses and then take up a position guarding the approach from the west.

Roger Ling led the horses northwest to Donelson Lake, and then to the west end of Maryott Lake. The sun was peeking over the mountain tops to the east as Ling stripped the gear from the horses. He swatted each on the rump with a board. The horses were off like a shot. Happy to be free they ran until they were lost from sight headed down the mountain to the west. Ling watched in satisfaction because he wanted a lot of distance between the targeting equipment and the animals. He stashed the gear from the horses up against a north facing rock so it would be in shadow most of the day.

From the beginning Ling had seen that it would be difficult to get out of the mountains after destroying the airplane. With their job done they would have the remainder of the night to get as far as they could from the scene. As a result, he had taken the precaution to include medium sized backpacks in the crates they brought from New York. Now he loaded a poncho, food, and a coat into his. His 9 mm pistol was in its shoulder holster. Then he started slowly making his way back to Wengie's position.

Leaving bodies lying along the trail had definitely not been part of the plan. This worried him. It meant the authorities would be scouring the area even before the plane crashed. As he mulled this over he heard the sound of a light plane in the distance. Crouching in the shadow of a rock he watched the plane pass a little to the south of him. He was about to move when a helicopter came down the valley from Donelson Lake. He wasn't sure if a helicopter could hover and land at this altitude, but he didn't want to find out. He sat motionless in the shadows and it passed over. He knew if they made a determined effort to search the area they'd spot the horses, and maybe even him. If only those cantankerous beasts could make their way down the steep slope to Crystal Lake before being spotted he'd feel safe.

At the place selected to target the plane, Wengie found a sheltered spot in the rocks not far from the snowfield where they had buried the equipment. With the dawn he saw he was on the southeast end of the middle of three tanks about seventy-five meters long and thirty wide. He saw the same light plane that flew over Ling and knew he had not been spotted. He was in the shade and his clothes matched the terrain. He had food, water, heavy clothes, and the forty-five pistol Roger Ling had purchased for him before they left New York. He had never fired it but it made him feel good having his own gun. At times he pulled it out of his shoulder holster and imagined shooting an attacker. He was ready for what was to come. All he had to do is sit tight until dusk.

Breckon and Daley were now about a mile as the crow flies from the suspected targeting location. The easiest route of travel was to go down the slope to the Cloverleaf Lakes and then up to the site. The route up was a gradual slope according to the map. In reality it had many small ridges and valleys that could conceal their approach. However, if there were men watching that approach, they would be seen and easily killed. Therefore, they veered off to the right and stayed on higher ground by heading toward Arrowhead Lake. According to the contour map, northwest of Arrowhead was a high point of rock from which they could look down on the targeting site from a quarter mile away. Between this point and the site was a deep steep walled ravine.

Breckon was surprised to learn as they made their way that there were numerous errors in the maps. Sometimes where the map showed even contours, there was a large hump of rock. Beyond the inaccuracies, the spacing of the contours gave little idea about whether the terrain was actually negotiable. Their map showed a rise of rock just south of the middle tank so the small body of water would not be visible to them when they arrived at their intended observation point. But, it was clear that anyone guarding the middle tank would position himself on that high ground less than a hundred yards south of the tank because from there one would have a commanding view of the surrounding area.

By noon, they were in position to observe the area of the site. The hump south of the middle tank was there, sort of, but the middle tank was partially visible to him. Breckon knew from experience it would be difficult to determine if anyone was on the rocks across the ravine. Even though the overlay had a dot on the map, their enemies could presumably be anywhere in the general area. At a quarter mile a person looks like a small red ant at your feet. Once located, a person can keep track of a hiker who cares nothing about being observed. But, if he isn't moving and is taking precautions not to be seen, it's nearly impossible to locate him. If their enemies were over the ridge north of the tank toward Donelson Lake, they would be out of his line of sight all together.

They took up a good position being careful not to reveal themselves. Predictably, they saw no one. If by some stroke of good luck they saw a glint of sunlight from a shiny object, they'd have them located. The sky was beginning to cloud over and their chances dimmed. When they arrived it had been their plan to stay here until late afternoon and then make their way back down to Arrowhead Lake and from there to the Clover Leaf Lakes to the west and come up on the site from the southwest in twilight.

At the sound of any aircraft engine they pressed against rocks and sat motionless. There were several helicopters working the area to the southwest. Every half hour or so an aircraft came over. They all seemed headed to the same general area.

For three hours Breckon and Daley took turns watching the place marked by the spot on the overlay. They saw no sign of anything but rocks and were beginning to think this was all a figment of Breckon's overworked imagination. A little after three o'clock they saw cumulus clouds building to the west. They decided to throw it in and began making their way down to the three lakes.

When they neared the level of the lakes a helicopter swooped down and began circling the area. The air was getting rough from the forming clouds. The helicopter briefly set down, a figure got out, and it was up again. Then they saw the reason in it. The man from the helicopter was headed to a couple of hikers who had stopped to watch the aircraft as the pilot skillfully worked the changing air currents. The man from the helicopter hurried to the hikers. He talked to them for ten minutes as the helicopter circled. It came directly over Breckon and Daley twice as they sat motionless among the rocks.

The man from the helicopter ran back to he high point of rocks on a loaf of ground between two of the Cloverleaf Lakes. Here he waited for the helicopter to retrieve him.

The helicopter made its approach only to be hit by a gust of wind from the north that sent it off over the lake as the pilot gunned the engine to gain altitude. The helicopter was near its altitude limit to hover.

On the second and third attempt it was driven off by unpredictable air currents while still fifty feet in the air. On the next try the pilot got to within a few feet of the rocks, but before the man on the ground could get to it a strong gust of wind hit the helicopter. Driven sideways toward the southeast lake it rolled into the down draft on the lee side of the rocks. The tips of the rotor blades flicked up water as the pilot rammed the cyclic control, used to control how much or how little the craft tipped, to the maximum to level the craft. Righted, it sank until the belly was in the water. Now with the engine red lined he put the maximum power into the collective control that was used to make it go up and down, to pull it out of the water. Doing this he sacrificed power to the tail rotor thus loosing tail rotor authority and the helicopter started to rotate. Newton's law stating that for every action there is an equal and opposite reaction is absolutely king in the flying contraptions called helicopters. The small vertical rotor in the tail offsets the torque of the main horizontal rotor to keep the helicopter from rotating in the direction opposite that of the main blades.

This was clearly unacceptable so to gain control of the craft, the pilot headed into the wind and tried once again to lift off. It stayed in the water. Water had seeped into the belly and it was too heavy. Partly in the water, the pilot maneuvered to the southeast end of the lake. Heading into the wind, and applying maximum power he headed toward the northwest. Slowly the machine began to lift higher in the water. The goal was to get enough air speed to gain transitional lift. That was the point, at about forty knots, where the spinning rotor began to act like a solid wing and additional lift was generated. At last it happened. The helicopter lifted free of the lake. It slowly gained altitude while water streamed from its innards. Taking a circle over the lakes to get high enough to avoid downdrafts as he cleared the immediate mountains, he headed off to the southeast not daring to attempt another recovery.

The two hikers had taken off at a good pace in the direction of Golden Lake. The man on the ground looked after them, but in the fading light they were lost from view.

Breckon and Daley watched the saga of the helicopter trying to snatch the man off the rocks. "That's the last we'll see of helicopters today," Breckon said. "Now we'll have a loose guy bumping around the mountains tonight. It looks like the weather will get nasty so we'd better try to meet up with him. It doesn't seem like he intends to go anywhere."

―――――――――――

Allen Wu had the rifle with the scope. At the time he bought it he had not anticipated the value of the scope simply as a telescope to scour the mountains for people. It was easily detached from the rifle and he used it to systematically watch the mountains around him. He had seen Carson and Winger come into the area of Triskele Lake in the morning. He could not be sure if they were random hikers or part of the force coming against them. When they continued on toward Two Bits Lake he lost sight of them. About noon he caught sight of movement in the higher rocks across the deep ravine to the southeast. Being careful to keep the lens of the scope in shade, he saw other movements in the same area.

At one thirty he told Rongji he would take his rifle and work his way down to the outlet of Triskele Lake and then up to the position of the those watching from the rocks. They had to be some of the men sent here to stop their operation. There was no other reason why someone would spend the afternoon hiding in the rocks looking at this particular area of the mountain. Rongji with his silenced Uzi had been watching the area to the northwest. Wengie was there to take up Wu's duties so Rongji was not concerned about Wu's leaving, particularly because it might make Rongji's job easier in the end.

Wu worked his way up to the top of the rocks where he had seen the movement. Being cautious and keeping under cover behind rocks as much as possible was more time consuming than he had planned. Every time he had to expose himself to the line of sight to the top he had to pause and try to determine if he were being watched.

When he finally got to a point where he should have been able to see those who had been spying on him he found nothing. Searching the area he found boot marks in the dirt where someone had knelt behind hip high rocks. Putting himself in the position he could see that by kneeling straight up he could see the entire position across the ravine. It was obvious they were watching the place where Wengie would deploy the targeting device.

He realized he was now out of position to help defend the site. But, if he could find where they had gone he might be able to come up behind them unawares and finish them off before they even got near the site. He hurried across the relatively flat plateau until he could look down on Arrowhead Lake and the Cloverleaf Lakes. After five minutes of intently watching the area below him he spotted movement. Two figures were making their way down the slope, though they were too far away for an effective shot. Immediately he started after them not noticing the third man. Soon they were masked by a hump of rock so he could move fast to close the distance to them without fear of being seen.

The first bank of clouds passed over with no rain, and the wind slacked off. After four o'clock another line of clouds formed and the wind began to stiffen. When Breckon and Daley were a quarter mile from the lone man they heard a light plane. It was high to stay out of the wind currents created by the mountains. As it came over the lakes a green flair could be seen falling from it. It soon became obvious the flair was attached to a bundle hanging from a small parachute, obviously assistance for the man left on the rocks. As the chance of the air currents would have it, it landed in the northern most of the three lakes. The plane made that one pass over the area and was gone working its way around the strongest storm cells.

The package was buoyant enough to float. The lone man walked to the point on the shore where the wind would deliver it. A hundred yards from him its progress stopped. The lines from the parachute had snagged on submerged rocks. The man spent several minutes watching and hoping. Finally, giving up, he started walking toward Golden Lake. After a short distance he hesitated and looked back. Breckon waved to him.

— 25 —

Dirk Swensen was discouraged as he saw his life support supplies land in the northwest side of the north lake. He got up on the highest rock in his immediate vicinity hoping to see it floating on the surface. There it was. With a strong wind blowing his way, it would float to shore quickly. As he watched he could see it making steady progress with the wind whipping the surface of the lake. His heart stopped as he saw the rock sticking out of the water. After watching the direction of the waves a few minutes he was relieved to see it would pass to the north of the obstruction. Hurriedly he moved to a point on shore where it would arrive. It got steadily closer, and then didn't seem to move. After five minutes he climbed the rocks behind him and carefully studied the surface of the lake. At first he wasn't sure, but finally he had to admit that there was a small peak of rock he could make out in the troughs of waves. There were more submerged rocks, and the rigging has snagged on them. Finally, he decided to follow the two hikers he had talked to in hopes he could find their camp and ask for assistance.

Starting off to the south toward Golden Lake, he looked back again at the lake where the package sat bobbing in the water. His eye chanced to catch a movement up on the rocks to the east of the lake. One of the figures raised his arm as if waving to him. What luck. More hikers, and they had large packs. Things were starting to go his way, he thought, as he started toward them.

The two men were making their way down a difficult slope opposite the intersection of the three lakes. Swensen hurried to intercept them at the bottom of their decent. As he approached, he saw two well built men. One wore a stiff brimmed black western style hat, and the other a floppy tan hat. The one in the floppy hat said, "We saw the helicopter pilot having his problems. He's lucky to be alive. I'm Ed Breckon and this is Greg Daley."

Swensen extended his hand and said, "Glad to meet you. I'm Dirk Swensen with the U.S. Forest Service." Daley put out his hand and had it grasped by one twice its size. Taking note he saw Swensen was well filled out, and not with fat. About six-two, he'd come in at two-thirty or a little more. "I'm not wanting to cause you any inconvenience," Swensen continued, "but it looks like the weather will be getting bad before long. I'm wondering if you could let me sit in your tent until the storm passes. From the looks of those clouds to the west this could be a real blow."

Breckon nodded but said nothing.

Swensen now prodded, "I'm not wanting to be forward, but you really ought to be looking for a place to set up for the night."

"In good time," Breckon said. "What was all the airplane and helicopter traffic about over to the southwest all day about? Why did you get out of the helicopter to talk to those two hikers at such great risk? Something important must he happening."

Swensen looked to the sky to the west unable to conceal his eagerness to get on with setting up a tent. Looking back at Breckon he said, "I don't know that I can tell you. It's being kept pretty secret until we have more answers."

Daley reached in his back pocket and pulled out his wallet. "We really need to know what's going on. I'm with the NSA, and there is a party of men from the CIA on the other side if that mountain," he said jerking his head in the general direction of the northeast as he presented his picture ID. "We hope you will be cooperative. We need to know."

Swensen could feel his stomach muscles tense. Not only was he uneasy about the approaching storm, but now another level of apprehension gripped him. "I might have know it had to be something big. What's going on, anyway?"

"You first," said Daley. "We'll tell you enough. You're in on it now whether you want to be or not. That 'care package' dropping in the middle of the lake saw to that."

"Hadn't we better look for a place to pitch your tent? I assume you have one," Swensen persisted looking at the increasingly ominous cloud banks moving in on them. The lightning flashes were almost constant now, and the thunder rolled across the lake.

"Talk!" Breckon almost screamed.

Swensen's anxiety was now replaced by a fear of the two that stood before him. "Okay if you insist. We found the bodies of four women along the trails. One of them was a Forest Ranger. There seems to be a madman up here some place. The hikers I talked to . . . . "

"When did they die," Breckon interrupted, "not when did you find them, when did they die?"

Swensen was wary, trying not to reveal information he had promised to keep secret, yet this situation seemed a more immediate peril. "Well," he began, "one died on the afternoon of the day before yesterday. Back near Clay Butte. The other three died yesterday morning a couple of miles southeast of here. All were on trails."

"Anything else?" Breckon persisted.

"There were a couple of horses along the trail yesterday morning. May have been packhorses, or ridden, we're not sure. Somebody must really hate women."

"No," Breckon replied. "They happened to be in the way." Turning to Daley he said, "If there were any doubts that there is another party up on the mountain, there isn't anymore." Looking at Swensen he asked, "Do you have a weapon?"

Swensen pulled out a formidable looking hunting knife.

Breckon shook his head, "As they say, never bring a knife to a gun fight. And, this is shaping up to be a bloody one."

The three Cloverleaf Lakes were arranged so the first one was to the north. The second was directly south of it, and the third was to the west of the second. The three men were now up against the steep rocks on the southeast corner of the north lake.

Breckon found a place out of sight where they stashed their packs. Breckon and Daley had their parkas on since the wind was blowing cold in front of the even colder rain that was even now starting to obscure the western side of the basin. Breckon pulled out his light jacket and the tent without the poles, and handed them to Swensen. "Put on the jacket and when the rain starts wrap the tent around you. We're not pitching a tent tonight." Looking at Daley again he said, "We'll use the storm as cover to get up the mountain. The slope is gradual in most places."

Swensen looked at the tent and then at Breckon and said, "This is no help. This tent is full of holes. And, who put you in charge, and . . . . I still don't know what's going on."

Daley turned on Swensen, "It's a good possibility the guys who killed the women were the same ones that shot that tent full of holes. By the way, they thought we were sleeping in it at the time. Breckon figured out what would happen. As you can surmise, we weren't in it. I have this to say to you. First, don't mess with this guy! He destroyed half an army single handed. Second, listen to him, he knows what he's doing. He saved my life and his twice in the last few days from these guys. What else can we tell him Ed?"

Breckon shrugged. "There are at least four men up on the mountain to the north of this lake," he said pointing to the north. "They are intent on targeting a jumbo jet with a laser so a missile from earth orbit can destroy it along with two or three-hundred people on board. These men are all heavily armed, and have tried to kill us three times. Daley in his modesty left out the attack on us he foiled yesterday morning. They are highly motivated professionals. And I might add, by this time also highly pissed because of their failure to neutralize us."

It was registering on Swensen that he wished he wasn't being told this, but Breckon continued. "I think we can use you. As soon as somebody goes down, you'll have a weapon. Want to come?"

If it hadn't been for the dimming light caused by the approaching storm, they would have noticed how pale Swensen had become. And the physical darkness was only a fraction of what Swensen felt inside. He was afraid, but his pride was also on the line. "Ah, ye-yes, sure. Of course I'll come. Yo-you mean I'll get a gun off a dead man, is that it?"

"That's precisely it!" Breckon's words hit Swensen like bullets. "Okay," Breckon continued, "Greg will start out between the lakes and go up the west side of the north lake. Dirk, you stay about a hundred yards behind him. When the shooting starts get your head and your ass down. It's going to be miserable in the rain. I'll go around the east side of this lake and work up the steeper rocks to the southeast of their position. By the way, the guys we're hunting are Chinese. And, be sure of your target when you shoot. The two CIA guys are over to the east or north some place. Let's go."

Breckon and Daley both had their ponchos on as the rain started, lightly at first. Swensen threw the tent fabric over him the best he could as he watched both men start off. The going was slow because the rocks were slippery. Suddenly the thing that had been sticking in the back of Swensen's mind came to the fore. Who did Breckon work for? He acted with such authority, it scared him. Swensen started after Breckon with the intention of clearing up the point. Breckon had not gone far, but Swensen would have to run to catch him. After twenty steps Swensen had nearly fallen twice so decided it might not be such a good idea after all. There'd be time for such things later. Turning he started back only to see another man had appeared from the rocks and was pointing a rifle at Daley. Swensen cupped his hands to his mouth and yelled, "Daley, behind you."

Swensen was closer to the shooter than the man was to Daley. The man with the rifle immediately whirled around and Swensen heard a whap an instant before the report of the weapon as the bullet went through the tent fabric an inch above his head. Having had the tent pulled up over his head in something like half a teepee it made Swensen look taller than he was. The bullet was intended to put a hole in his face. Swensen fell to the ground and scrambled behind a rock for cover.

Daley had been walking with his poncho open on the right side and his hand on his gun. He didn't know why, it just made him feel better. At the warning from Swensen, he pulled the gun from the holster, turned, and fell to one knee pulling the hammer back while holding the gun with both hands. At the sound of the shot toward Swensen, Daley fired. The man lurched. Daley pulled the hammer back and carefully squeezed off another round. Much to his astonishment, the man fell. Daley pulled the hammer back again as he slowly rose and walked toward the fallen man.

Daley arrived over the man and saw steel gray eyes alive with fire looking back at him. He kicked the rifle away and yelled, "Dirk, you okay?"

"Yeah."

"Come on over here."

Swensen approached and looked in horror at a dying man. Prior to the day before yesterday he had never seen a dead person except in a casket at a wake. Now he was seeing them everywhere.

"Pick up the rifle," Daley said in a conversational voice. Swensen did so with the words Breckon had spoken only minutes ago ringing in his head. *As soon as somebody goes down, you'll have a weapon.*

Daley knelt down beside the man and said, "Dirk, see if you can get that tent to keep the rain off us. I want to talk to him."

The eyes looking back were now amused, almost taunting. Allen Wu had fallen by a rock and Daley tipped him up so his back rested against it. "I am going to die. I took one in the chest and one in the guts," the man said with an Asian accent. "You did right good for a city kid. He," he said looking at Swensen, "called out to you. He said 'Daley.' Gregory Daley, I presume. Glad to make your acquaintance." The last was more of a sneer than a courtesy.

Swensen spread the tent enough to shelter the three of them. As the rain pattered on the fabric, Daley looked at the man in disbelief. "How do you know my name?"

The man coughed and blood came up. "I work for the Chinese embassy in Washington. You work with a man in the CIA who works for us. I also work with someone in the NSA. I know all about you."

There was an exceptionally bright flash followed immediate by thunder that almost split their eardrums. The man lurched and coughed again. More blood. Daley was about to say something but didn't as the man, living his last moments, continued. "Too bad you are here" he continued with labored breathing. "Before I left Washington two *rickshaws* were dispatched to destroy the safe house where you went. You found out about Dragon Fang, and worse, you found out about my carefully recruited source at the NSA. You had to die." He closed his eyes as he twisted his face in pain.

Daley felt a terrible dread dawn on him. "*Rickshaw*? What do you mean? And, what safe house? I didn't go to a safe house."

A thin smile came to Wu's face as he partially regained his composure. "No ruses now. Too late. The one by the military base in Minnesota, by that town, Small Falls."

Daley swallowed hard. "Little Falls," he almost whispered.

"Yes, Little Falls." Seeing the horror on Daley's face the dying man laughed a hideous laugh "Of course. They wouldn't send you alone. They'd send your family too." Another cough. More blood ran out of his mouth and down his chin staining his shirt. "I lose track of the days, today or tomorrow safe house will be destroyed. All there will die." He made a last cough that issued a torrent of blood, he tensed, and then went limp.

Daley reached over and felt the artery in Wu's neck. "Dead," was all he said.

"What was all that about?" Swensen asked.

"He was mistaken. That is not a safe house. It is my wife's parents' farm. My wife and six children are vacationing there waiting for me to return. We have to get up that mountain and find Breckon. He has the satellite phone. I have to call someone and warn my family if it isn't already too late!"

Breckon heard the shot. He stopped and turned. Two more shots. At first he saw nothing. There, he saw one figure rise, walk, then stop. Another appeared and moved rapidly toward the first. The second looked like Swensen with the tent pulled up over his head. Breckon took a few steps toward them, but he too stopped. With no time to lose he felt he could not go back.

Turning his back on his comrades, he started off with a grim determination. The line "I set my face like flint" stabbed its way into his mind. He knew where it was from, but why now? Then another random line came to him. "I fled Him down the labyrinthine ways of my own mind." He knew where that was from too. What was happening? Had he lost his sanity? He marched resolutely forward. It seized upon him that he would die in the coming hours. Strangely, that thought didn't bother him.

A half hour later Breckon was at the base of a steep front of rock. It was probably on average only a fifty-degree slope, but the difficulty came in the word "average." At times he would have to work his way around vertical faces. In places it was a certain bone-crushing tumble to the river far below if he lost his footing. But, this was the approach that would be less watched on a night like this. He knew he could top out on the flat above before his companions were within range of the defenders. This would put him in a position to provide covering fire for them. So, the climb was his to make.

He started his ascent as the rain slacked off. It had been a steady pelting rain since he had left Daley and Swensen. The poncho kept the rain off him, but its plastic construction prevented moisture from escaping leaving his shirt soaked with perspiration. He paused briefly to catch his breath. To the west was a black wall of clouds. A nearly straight shaft of lightning thrust out of the cloud to the rocks. At home in Minnesota lightning appeared as thin fingers of light. This was many times thicker, like a forearm in comparison. He could feel the force of the thunder as it broke against the side of the mountain. The higher he climbed the closer and more energetic the lightning became. He felt electricity flow through him an instant before a bolt hit a couple of hundred feet above him.

Taking the warning he found a wall of rock and pressed himself into the lea of it until the worst of the electrical energy passed. He was amazed as he saw the frequent strikes systematically walk across the mountain toward him. As the full furry of it came over him, he pressed his hands against his ears, closed his eyes as he sat on the rocks. The sound and flashing were beyond what the senses could tolerate. Electricity flowed through him a couple of times. If he took a direct hit, he would be toast.

Finally, the majority of the flashes moved past him. He started up again. It was now dark, but with the lighting flashing every few seconds, near and far, it was not hard to plan his climb. With less than twenty feet to go the wind and the rain came like the wrath of avenging beasts. At one point a gust of wind almost tossed him off the rocks like a dry leaf.

Breckon carried his rifle barrel down under his poncho. It hung from a makeshift sling over his right shoulder. Now with only a short distance to go before he topped out he unslung the weapon. He levered a round into the chamber and released the hammer to the safe position. In the carbine, a replica of the Old West saddle gun, the lever ejects the round in the chamber, chambers a new round, and leaves the hammer back in the firing position. To release the hammer to the safe position, the hammer is held back with the thumb as the trigger is pulled. Then the hammer is gently allowed to swing forward on to the firing pin. This was in effect the safety. To "remove" the safety it was necessary to pull the hammer back with the thumb until it clicked into position.

Taking several steps sidewise he looked for a way to get around an eight-foot ledge. Intent on finding an opening he missed his footing. Flailing his arms to break his fall he lost his grip on the rifle. He landed by slamming his arm and side on the rocks where he had been standing. Rolling over on to his stomach there was nothing under him. Only his right hand rested on anything solid. His fingers engaged a small cleft.

With a strength begotten of terror his fingers latched into place as his body swung down and pounded him against the rock face. Dangling on his arm his left hand searched the surface for a life saving hold. At last, it had a grip. He hung suspended on the side of the mountain. The wind tore at him and the rain was relentless. Breckon could pull himself up a few inches, but no more. He glanced over his shoulder as a flash illuminated the canyon below. If he fell he was dead. With certainty, he knew he would fall.

A moment after Allen Wu died Daley was up. "That Breckon has the sat-phone. I want it! I should have insisted on carrying it. What makes him think he's the boss?" Daley spun around to head in the direction

Breckon had gone minutes before, paused before the rough ground, and then started in the direction of the west side of the lake.

Swensen had a bad feeling about the way things were going. What was wrong with this picture? Daley was suddenly angry with Breckon, who he had highly praised a short while before. Of course, learning that your family was dead, or about to be killed would send most men off the deep end. But, of all the times for this to happen, unless . . . .

It was hard running because of the slippery rocks. Finally Swensen came to a stretch of grass, or what passed for grass, clay with lichens on it, and it was better going. Still, he almost fell a couple of times. When at last he came up beside Daley he put his hand on his arm and said, "Wait. He might have lied."

Daley jerked his arm loose and kept going. Rebuffed the second time, Swensen put Wu's rifle down, dropped the tent off his back, and running up behind Daley, tackled him. High school football did have practical applications in the real world. Swensen was heavier than Daley and he was on top of him.

"Greg! Listen! Think! What was wrong with all of that back there?"

"Get off, you jerk! My family may not matter to you, but it does to me!"

"No. Listen. Guys like that are supposed to bite on a cyanide capsule rather than reveal information like he did. There was no reason for him to do that unless he wanted to make you crazy. What if he was lying, and wanted to get you steamed so you would do something rash, and get killed. Or maybe he was playing with you because he knows you are not going to live out the night anyway. In either case, there's nothing you can do until we finish what's ahead of us. Acting like a madman isn't gonna help."

The rain was steady and lying on the ground they were getting soaked. Finally, Daley stopped struggling. "Okay, okay. Get your fat ass off me."

Swensen let him up and went back to get the rifle and tent. As they set off again Swensen said, "You're right. I don't know how you feel. But, dead you'll do your family no good, so be careful. When we get past this lake I'll stay off to the left. You angle over toward where Breckon might be. That okay?" Daley nodded as they slopped along getting wetter by the minute.

From the direction they were traveling Swensen could see he would come to the suspected targeting site from the west and Daley would come at it from the south with a mound of rock between them. He wasn't sure that was the best tactic. They should operate as a team so they could cover one another. But, they had to cover as much terrain as possible. It might work out.

Jin Rongji had given up hope of Allen Wu doing him any good as he scanned the valley to the southwest. When Wu left, Rongji took Wu's place, and Wengie went to the north side where Rongji had been. Rongji sat in an observation post with a panoramic view. Through the rifle scope that Wu had left with him he was able to see the area between the Clover Leaf Lakes. At one point he thought he had seen movement, but had no idea who it was. The thunder masked any sound of the shots that might have reached him. Between him and the clover Leaf Lakes the rock lifted up so that after a man was half way past the northern most lake he was hidden from view. If someone were coming from the south he wouldn't see him until he was much closer. As he watched, Wengie came up behind him.

"I have to start digging out the equipment and setting it up," Wengie said. "You'll have to divide your time between both posts."

Rongji agreed. It didn't matter much, though. The terrain was so sliced and crossed with ridges, piles or rock, and ravines that it was impossible to see where anyone was. He was only partially aware of how extreme this was. Looking out over this landscape even in bright daylight it might seem one could see all the land between himself and a particular rock feature. In reality, there could be several hidden dips in the terrain from two to two-hundred feet deep. If there had been a tree on the near as well as the far side of a ravine it would give scale to the width of the depression. There were no trees, not even a bush, and rocks came in all sizes. One might assume a fifty-foot wide rock on the far side of an obscured area was a five-foot rock much closer.

Wengie was setting up on the south side of the middle tank. Rongji was forced to cover attack from both the north and south. In a new position looking to the south, he could turn to see the basin containing the middle tank with Wengie to his rear forty feet below him and some distance away. By going two-hundred feet around some rocks to his rear he had a good view of the approach from the north. From here he could also see the east tank and the approach to it.

Rongji saw that Wengie had all of the equipment unpacked and was starting to assemble it. If the plane came on the track indicated by the overlay, it would be easy to target, unless this heavy weather lingered. Lacking a visual sighting of the plane he should be able to aim on the collision avoidance beacon. The laser could penetrate average cloud cover. But, there was a limit to any technology. A massive electrical storm with towering thunderheads would make any targeting impossible since it would cause the pilot to divert around the storm and out of range. As the wind and the rain became more intense Wengie was forced to cover everything with plastic sheets and wait it out.

Taking one last sweep to the south with his scope, Rongji hurried to his post on the north side. Arriving at his chosen spot a little out of breath he saw them crossing an open space, one fifty feet behind the other. It was a long shot for an Uzi so he fired a long burst. One man fell. The other man was instantly behind a rock and firing back.

Winger and Carson had arrived at Triskele Lake in mid-morning. If all of their assumptions were correct, it was fairly certain they were being watched. With this in mind they traveled in depressions where possible. They stopped at times to rest and used their map and compass to try to determine which pile of rocks was their destination. There was nothing but rocks and they all looked the same. Neither of them had any experience in a wilderness like this with uncertain reference points. There were no radio towers, church steeples, or other unmistakable features. Even the lakes didn't seem to have the same shapes as on the map. They decided to pass by Triskele and head for Two Bits Lake like normal hikers. Once there they made a determined effort to stay hidden as they made their approach to the suspected enemy position that was then to their southwest.

There was no sign of their adversaries, rarely a sign of anything human. Carson commented that it was like being a kid again, playing cowboys and Indians with imaginary Indians. At one point Winger pointed to boot prints in what weeks earlier had been mud. They looked around half expecting to see a rotting corpse. What nut would come up here voluntarily?

Finally, the going became too hard to continue with their packs. They stashed their gear, except for a small pack with ponchos, and food, and each carried his weapons. Carson had the rifle he bought in Red Lodge, and each had his service pistol.

Through the afternoon they worked their way from one ledge of rocks to another. At one place the climb was steep, but going up was not hard. Then the land gave way to a gentler slope. It swept upward with narrow patches of grass weaving among the lumps and terraces of rock. For normal hiking it was perfect landscape with enough bare rocks for pleasing scenery, yet with care in planning the route, an easy gradual climb on grass. These were not normal times for Winger and Carson. Not knowing how many they faced, or where their enemy might be waiting, made the day long and stressful. They even faced the possibility that they were on the wrong mountain.

With the worsening weather in the late afternoon it made their concealment easier, but the same was true for the enemy. Now there was no hope of seeing anyone on the rocks above until they were nearly face to face. They were near the top of a rise and had no choice but to cross one last open space. Carson went first. When he was halfway across Winger followed. A burst of automatic weapon fire caught Carson. Carson went down and Winger fired his pistol at the source of the shots as he ran for cover. Carson lay groaning on the ground as Winger worked his way toward him keeping covered by low rocks. By the time he reached him the rain had started in full force. Winger pulled Carson up behind a rock ledge and examined him. He had taken one bullet through his side below his ribs and one in the toes. Using handkerchiefs and parts of shirts, he managed to stop the bleeding in both places. Carson still had on his poncho but was shivering uncontrollably. Winger moved up beside him and pulled Carson's legs up under his poncho the best he could as they waited out the rain.

Breckon hung by his fingers. From eons of weathering, the rock face had a rough texture to it. Frantically he tried to find a place to hook the toe of a boot. The wind became increasingly strong and gusty. Drops of rain stung his face like pellets of ice. He could feel his fingers slipping inexorably out of their holds. Seconds . . . seconds measured the remainder of his life. No fancy foot work here. No last minute quick thinking to save him this time. This is how he'd end having left nothing behind.

Many times he'd thought of that. To some it was given to leave the world a better place for having walked its paths. Not to him. He resolved that if he were to live, he'd make a concerted effort to change. A quick look down revealed nothing but a black void.

His forearms were becoming numb. The oxygen and nutrients needed to fuel the muscles were depleted. Humanly, there was nothing left. A surge of despair engulfed him as a fierce gust of wind whipped against him, and the fingers of his left hand slipped from their hold. His whole weight swung to his right hand and those fingers slipped too. He fell . . . less than a foot. He stood pressed against the rock as his bleeding fingers searched for a cleft. Yes. First one hand and then the other found a grip. Panting he could feel the blood flowing to his arms once again.

Hope. Now hope replaced despair. There was hope. With no conscious thought he said aloud, "Oh! That was cute!" Seconds passed. With each one something welled up inside him until he shook. Jerking his head back he screamed at the air above him, "God. That's not fair! You knew that ledge was there all the time!" Not surprisingly, there was no reply.

Returning to his practical situation, he carefully started to feel the ledge with the toe of his boot. It was narrow, and his hands and arms were tired. It was almost completely dark and the rain drops still smashed against his face. He blinked continually to keep the water out of his eyes. The wind gusts would blow him off the ledge after all if he didn't get to a safer place. He thought the rock face became less inclined to the left so that's the direction he moved. Carefully he moved one foot and hand at a time. The rock was becoming more flawed as he progressed giving more hand holds. His optimism grew as it looked like he would make it.

Becoming more confident, he put his weight on his right foot as he released his right hand hold. The shard of rock under the foot tipped ever so slightly away from the cliff. The twist to his ankle caused a turning moment in his leg with the foot as the pivot point thus imparting an impulse to his center of gravity in a direction away from the wall. Nerves sent signals to the brain. The left foot wanted to step out and stop the motion, but conscious thought over-rode that command knowing there was nothing there for the left foot to land on. To counter the movement instinct caused the hands to flail at the air to force a reverse moment to that caused by the ankle.

An instant later the cognitive part of the mind concluded it was lost. All possible corrective actions had been brought to bear, and the tipping motion away from the safety of the rock wall had not been arrested. He would fall . . . to eternity, with a horror that he was ill prepared. Without knowing why, Breckon turned his will toward God and put himself in His care.

A violent wind hit his back and slapped him against the rock and held him there with such force he could hardly breathe. The storm had nearly passed, but as frequently happens the turbulence at the rear of the thunder cell had spawned tornadoes. These were weak and ill formed due to the jagged terrain. But, for two minutes Breckon could not move. He squeezed his eyes shut to keep dirt from being driven into them. When the violence of the storm had passed the winds fell to a breeze within seconds. As he dared to open his eyes, they were met by a yellow light illumining the rocks. To the west the black veil had lifted a crack to reveal the orange disk of the sun slipping behind a peak.

With the light to help, Breckon made his way to safety. He sat with his back to a rock feeling wrung out. He closed his eyes and drew in a breath of the clean mountain air. It felt good simply to be living. Pulling off the shreds of what was left of his poncho, he was amazed to see his clothing was nearly dry. The intense wind he was exposed to at the last must have dried him. What had happened to him was no mystery but it left him with an edge. Looking up he saw a few stars peeking through breaks in the clouds. He said aloud, "Thanks a lot, God." It was partly a thank you for having been saved, and partly a cynical complaint for the terror he'd been put through—twice!

— 26 —

The storm was at its height as Dirk Swensen approached the hump of rock that separated him from the southwest side of the basin there the targeting device was supposed to be. Feeling the hair on his head tingling, he immediately hit the ground as a lightning bolt struck higher up on his right. In his time with the Forest Service, people had told him about the hazards of being on a mountain during an electrical storm. As he lifted his head more distant lightning illuminated the area. Rock chips stung his face. He might have passed off the report of the gun as more thunder if it had been a clean miss. He dropped again and shuttled to his right to get more cover from a rock. There he stayed, thunder crashing, torrential rain beating on him, and the wind acting like it wanted to throw him off its mountain.

Roger Ling had seen Swensen making his way up the slope, a little closer with each lightning flash. When the man was a hundred and fifty feet away he got up on his knees ready to fire. The close strike momentarily blinded him. When he got his vision back the man was gone. In the flickering light he saw him again, close to the ground. As the head came up he shot. With the next light the head was gone again. Cautiously, Ling stood up to get a better angle on the man lying on the ground. He wanted to be sure of his kill. He stretched out the pistol holding it with both hands waiting for the next flash. Intent on his target he ignored the tingle on his skin, and the electricity starting to flow through him.

Swensen was starting to raise his head again when the world became a blaze of electric blue light even though he wasn't looking in the direction of the strike. He bounced as the ground retched beneath him. The last thing he remembered was rocks thumping and rolling around him.

Consciousness returned minutes later. Slowly reorienting himself, he remembered where he was and why. But, why had the rain suddenly stopped? What was the pecking all over his back? It dawned on him that it was still raining, but he couldn't hear it. The rain was letting up, as the wind became more intense, blowing from first one direction then another. He passed it off as an effect of the thunder cell passing over the mountain.

The sky was getting light in the west so he could see his surroundings clearly. With considerable relief his noticed his hearing was coming back. He crawled into a position of better cover so he could partially sit up. Examining his rifle for the first time he found it was a clip fed, bolt action, thirty caliber made for high accuracy, long range shooting. How dumb of me, he thought, He realized he had failed to check the load. Pulling back the bolt he found the spent cartridge from the shot Wu had fired at him. He ejected the empty casing and slid the next round into the firing chamber. Now, where had the shooter gone? While he was unconscious his enemy could easily have killed him.

He twisted around looking first one way than the other trying to reveal as little of himself as possible. For a brief moment direct sunlight fell on his position. For the tenth time he looked in front of him in the direction of the shot. The sight of the toe of a boot close in to a rock made him pull down. Immediately he brought his gun into position. Hardly breathing he raised his head aiming at the top of the rock. The boot had not moved. Maybe the lightning had knocked the owner of the boot unconscious, too. Up on one knee poised for a shot he swept the muzzle of the gun around the area. He stepped around the rock and advanced half the distance to the boot. Again, he looked quickly all around expecting to hear a shot and feel a bullet at any instant.

The wind had dropped to a breeze, the light was dim, but adequate. The caustic smell of ozone hung in the air. Holding his rifle at the ready, he advanced so he could see over the hip high rock by the boot. Instantly he pulled back. What he saw made him want to vomit. The yellow light revealed a scene right out of a horror movie. An exceptionally energetic lightning bolt had struck the man. The head was all charred. The eyeballs had burst, the lips and nose were gone, and the teeth were burned to black jagged stumps.

Swensen dropped to his knees, and hunched back on the heals of his boots taking deep breaths. It kept getting worse with every man he saw. He struggled to keep from screaming. It was as though he had been thrust into the abode of the doomed, a macabre world of evil and death. Daley's flaring up was becoming understandable to him. There was a limit. He didn't want to move, but the desire to get away from this spot set his resolve. He'd see the job through. Not wanting to look over the rock again he turned, got up, and cautiously made his way toward a low place in the rocks to his right.

Winger had stayed with Carson through the tempest. Though he encouraged Carson, he was expecting him to die at any moment. With the external bleeding stopped he had him stabilized as much as possible under the circumstances. On the east side of the mountain, the twilight was little better than total darkness. When he spoke to Carson softly there was no response. There was still a weak pulse so it meant he was unconscious.

Deciding it was imperative to get help, Winger stuck Carson's 9 mm SIG behind his belt and with his own pistol in his right hand he started in the direction the automatic fire had come from. At this point Breckon with the sat-phone was his goal, and whatever was in between was nothing more than an annoyance.

During the height of the storm Wengie and Rongji hunkered down trying to stay alive and dry. When the worst was past the first had been achieved, not the second. They were cold and irritable. The rain had nearly stopped, but the wind, though dying, still brought cold gusts chilling Wengie as he got back to his job of putting together the equipment. He had planned to use one of the crates as a bench to sit on to look through the telescope and sight on the target. But, in the early morning as they rushed to get the equipment out of the crates and camouflaged with snow the crate had been broken. As a result, he used a flat rock as a seat. As he did a trial sighting through the eyepiece, he found the rock had the annoying habit of tipping when he shifted his weight. After several attempts to arrest the problem, he gave up. Glancing at his watch he saw the plane was due in less than twenty-five minutes and he still had the generator to set up.

Grabbing the small motor-generator and the cable he started out at a run to the west and promptly took a fall. The generator tumbled on soft ground. Picking it up he moved more cautiously and located a level spot fifty feet away. Tearing off the sealed plastic bag, he connected the spade connectors from the end of the power cable while holding a small flashlight in his mouth. Walking back to the rest of the equipment he let the wire unreel behind him only to discover there was still half of the wire on the reel. The other ends of the wire were at the core of the spool so he pulled the rest of the wire off leaving it lying on the ground where it fell. Once again with the flashlight to guide him he made the connections.

With the can of gas he returned to the generator being careful of his footing. Wengie removed the caps from the can and fuel tank and filled the tank. It ran over spilling gasoline over everything. With no time to waste he replaced both caps and set about starting the generator. Flip the on/off switch to on, close the manual choke, and pull. On the fifth pull the motor caught and started to run. Soon it started to cough and spit. What's wrong now, thought Wengie? Oh yes. The choke. Opening the choke it fell into a smooth cadence.

Wengie ran back to the telescope and turned on the computer. He had outfitted the computer with a touch screen to eliminate the need for a keyboard and mouse. It booted up and Dragon Fang came on line. He went through the sequence of steps and the phone automatically dialed the sat-phone to start the chain call to Nanjing, China. A message came up saying, "First Leg Of Chain Call Not Complete. Check Local Phone Connection." Irritated, he realized he had forgotten to align the twelve-inch parabolic antenna to the satellite. He was unaccustomed to working in such a chaotic environment. What else had he forgotten? With the antenna aimed properly, the message updated to tell him the chain call was initiated.

With this done he flipped on the laser. Instantly he heard the governor on the generator open up as the four-cycle motor began to work. The laser was the main power-using component in the system. He sat on the rock, it tipped, but this was anticipated. He sighted through the eyepiece at the top of Sky Pilot Mountain. Seeing the laser spot through the infrared eyepiece he was satisfied everything was working, and glancing at his watch saw he had done it with fourteen minutes to spare.

Breckon was collecting his thoughts when he became aware of the sound of the generator. Strange sound for an airplane, he thought. The roughness in the throbbing as the choke nearly killed the engine drew his full attention. The one thing one does not expect to hear is an airplane engine running rough, especially over country like this. No. That wasn't a plane . . . it was a small generator! Of course. A generator to power the targeting equipment. A pack horse could easily have carried one in.

Breckon was up. The carbine. Where was his carbine? Being careful not to fall over the cliff, he tried to locate the place he had come up. With the half light he could see well enough. Moments later he had it in his hands, dirty and wet. He wiped it off as best he could on his shirt. He started off to the northwest as fast as the dim light and slippery ground and rocks allowed. The generator was beyond the thirty-foot high hump of rock in front of him.

Rongji divided his attention between watching Daley make his way toward his position from the south, and Wengie putting the equipment together off to his right rear. The man before him was being cagey as he managed to keep rocks between himself and Rongji most of the time. It was almost as if he knew where Rongji was. Allan Wu would not be acting like that, so he assumed Wu had lost it down in the valley. Glancing over at Wengie, he saw Wengie looking his way. Seeing Rongji, Wengie gave him a thumbs up. This meant the system was ready to go. The storm had swept off to the southeast leaving the sky to the north clear except for patchy clouds.

As Breckon approached the top of the rise to the southeast of the hollow Wengie's movements caught his eye. Someone was intently working on something, and the dim glow of the computer screen left no doubt about what it was. He lifted his rifle in both hands and pulled the hammer back. Being more intent on his target than what he was doing, he did not have sufficient pressure on the hammer. It slipped out from under his thumb and the rifle fired. Stunned by the unexpected report of the rifle, Breckon momentarily lost his concentration and froze. Wengie pulled his pistol from the holster under his jacket as he turned and fired at the shadow on the rocks. Breckon dropped as he felt the sting of a bullet graze his upper left arm.

Rongji heard Breckon's rifle shot to his left. From the sound, it did not seem as if it was directed at him. Could Daley have gotten this close already? Maybe so. Rongji glanced at his watch—minutes to go. It didn't matter who was shooting, he had his last job to do. Hurriedly he made his way down to where Wengie stood, gun in hand. Wengie looked to his left as he heard Rongji approach.

"Who's that?" Wengie asked.

"Jin Rongji. How's the system working?"

"I was afraid you might be one of the others. Maybe the one who shot the gun."

"I don't know," Rongji said unable to keep the irritability out of his voice. He didn't like what he had to do, but orders were orders. The unknown shooter up in the rocks didn't help his mood either. "I asked, how is it working?"

"Fine, everything is working as it should. I hit the man who shot," he continued excitedly. "Pulled out my big pistol and let him have it! It makes a loud noise."

"Concentrate on the mission! Have you made contact with Nanjing?" Rongji asked to insure he did not act too hastily.

"Yes, yes," Wengie said excitement still in his voice. "Less than a minute ago we achieved deorbit. It is on its way. And, the plane is on schedule too. It's still too far away to target, but through the infrared optics, I glimpsed . . . . "

Wengie did not finish his sentence as a single slug from the silenced Uzi went through the side of his head.

Breckon held the carbine in his left hand as he clasped his right hand on his wounded arm reproaching himself for his ineptness. In a stooped position he back tracked down the slope away from the hollow.

Winger heard the shot from Breckon's carbine, followed by the return shot. If that's where the action was, that's where Breckon would be. He set off with a grim determination. He was moving too fast for safety in the dim light and wet conditions, but screw it. Carson needed help fast and there was only one way to get it. As he came around a large rock he saw a figure moving some distance away. Running nearly as fast as he could Winger tripped and went tumbling on the rocks loosing his grip on the gun. Hardly feeling the bruises he was up. Grabbing Carson's gun from behind his belt he continued on. He could no longer see the man.

The sound of the gun clattering on the rocks had caused Breckon to duck low behind a rock. If the man Winger was moving toward wasn't Breckon he was in trouble. "Breckon," Winger said in a loud whisper. "It's me, Mel."

Breckon recognized the voice. As Winger approached Breckon asked, "What's been happening? I wondered what happened to you two."

"Burl's been hit, bad. There's a shooter up in the rocks with a silenced automatic. Give me that sat-phone! I'm calling in help, no matter what you think. If I would've had the phone we'd have help by now!"

Breckon stopped. "First grab the handkerchief out of my back pocket and bandage my arm—hurts like crazy."

"You hit too! Hope we're getting some of them. Here, let me at it." In a minute Winger had the bandage on by tearing the shirt sleeve and using it to hold the wadded up handkerchief in place over the wound.

Breckon opened the pouch on his belt and handed over the phone. "Make your call," he said. "This'll be over before they arrive."

Both men dropped as they head foot steps to the south. "That you Breckon?"

Daley had taken a big chance too, borne of necessity, to speak while he was still half running. Both Winger and Breckon recognized the voice. Immediately Winger started pressing buttons on the secure satellite phone.

Breckon walked a few steps toward Daley. "Ed, that you?" Daley said again.

"Yeah," Breckon replied.

As Daley approached he said, "I need that sat-phone! I shot one of the Chinese guys. Before he died, he said he had ordered hit squads to kill everyone on the farm where my family's staying. He thought that's where I'd be. Gimme that phone!"

"Mel has it. Burl's been shot pretty bad, and Mel's calling in help. Work it out with him. We still have a war to fight up here. With all of us clustered together out in the open, they could wipe us out with one burst from an automatic weapon."

Breckon left them to their problems and started up the rocks again.

Rongji caught Wengie so he wouldn't fall and disturb the equipment. He pulled him off to the side and laid him on the ground. He was a good man, he thought. It was a crazy world to be doing this. For one of the few times in his life he let the thought enter his mind. He questioned whether it was all worth it. And worse than that, he wondered if what he had done was wrong. Had he done something where the excuse of obeying orders would not satisfy? There was no clear idea in his mind about who might know his thought, to say nothing of deciding his guilt. The feeling was as unexpected as it was brief.

He went immediately to the computer monitor and spent a few seconds checking screens to be sure the authentication had been completed and the projectile was on its way. When he touched a small icon on the corner of the display, the picture of a computer keyboard appeared. He pressed keys to write a short message. Then, carefully pressing a five letter sequence he pressed Enter again. The screen returned to showing the time left to intercept.

Off to the west he heard a rock scrape on rock. It might be Roger Ling, but maybe not. Rongji skittered off to the northeast to the place he had stashed his pack. Quickly he pulled a smaller pack out of the main one. This was his egress survival pack. His attention was fixed on a shadowy figure making its way along the south side of the water. The light jacket told him it was not Ling. At the same time he heard movement to his left. He stopped breathing as someone came into the basin fifty feet away from him moving as silently as possible from rock to rock. As the two figures approached, one from either side of the equipment, they both stopped. A hushed voice said, "That you, Ed?"

The reply was, "Yeah."

Okay Breckon, let's see you do it, Rongji thought. Would the big risk pay off?

10:37 p.m., Alexandria, Virginia

ShuHo Zeng was brushing his teeth in the hopes of getting to bed early for a change. His wife answered the phone. From the bedroom she said, "It's for you sweetheart, it's work. It's urgent." The tone of her voice portrayed a resignation that had come with years of urgent calls late at night.

"Zeng here."

"Two messages came in on a secure sat-phone from agents in the field," the duty officer said. "They've been transcribed, and are on your secure channel sir. Could be something you've been looking for."

"Can you stay on the line?"

"Unless there's another emergency, I'll be here."

Zeng put his password into his computer that was always booted up while he was at home. In a minute he had the messages on the screen.

MESSAGE ONE

Agent Burl Carson injured in the line of duty, near death. Extract immediately. Location this phone.

    0424 Zulu (2024 hours MDT)

    Location of Call: N45° 2.62', W109° 36.74'

MESSAGE TWO

National Security Agency employee Gregory Daley learned from dying Chinese national that *rickshaws*, I spell, R-I-C-K-S-H-A-W-S, were sent to rural Little Falls, Minnesota to kill Daley's family. Stop *rickshaws* at all costs. Meaning of *rickshaw* un . . . .

    Signal lost.

    Message Two came immediately after Message One. Voice analysis shows same speaker. Time and location same as Message One.

Zeng grabbed the phone. "You still there?"

"Yes sir."

"We'll handle message one first. This is a vital national security case with an 'officer down.' The location is inaccessible, and that officer must be extracted alive. In your Standard Ops book go to Section G. It will direct you on how to initiate a *fallen star* operation. Any and all DOD assets necessary are to be used to extract this agent. They'll want approval so put them through. I'll be here. Is that clear?"

"Yes sir, I have Section G open."

"We'll deal with message two later."

With that Zeng hung up to let the poor guy on the other end wrestle with his assignment. It may have been overkill calling for a *fallen star*, but when his agents were at stake he was of a mind to ask for forgiveness rather than permission.

Immediately Zeng pressed a speed dial on his phone. After a few rings there was an answer. "Sam, get on your secure line. There are two messages from our guys on the mountain. I've handled the first one.

Hope I didn't overdo it. We have to decide what to do about the second. The duty officer is sending the message transcripts to your computer. Take a look, I'll wait. "

Ten minutes later Li was back on he phone. "Sorry I was so long. I called up a contour map of the area of the call. Your response was correct. That's a truly miserable location. I wonder what they got into."

"To handle number two, I'm afraid we'll have to go into the shop. We're both pretty sure what's going down, but it'll take some arm twisting to get the response we need in time."

"Agreed. See you there."

— 27 —

Breckon recognized the voice as that of Dirk Swensen.

Dirk arrived at the computer first. "Ed, get down here. There isn't much time."

Breckon moved in and they both surveyed the area. "You run into anybody to the west?" Breckon asked.

"Yeah, one guy. Got himself fried by lightning. It's horrible. You know what to do here? This thing seems to be counting down," Swensen said looking at the computer display.

Breckon unconsciously looked around the sky, but saw nothing. Seeing the body on the ground he nudged it with his toe. "Did you get him?"

"No. Didn't hear a shot either." Swensen reached down and touched Wengie. "His face is warm and dry. It happened after the rain."

Breckon got down on both knees by the computer, "That means the guy with the silenced weapon is still around."

"But, whose side is he on? This one looks Asian."

"Don't know, and don't have time to care," Breckon said as he started punching buttons on the touch screen until he found the view he wanted. It said, "Fang has deorbited, on track to intercept in 9 min, 58 sec." The seconds were counting down. Toward the middle of the screen was a message, "Fang has locked on target. Target moving. Target airborne." Further down was another message. "Target found on predicted track minus 2.3 miles. Nearest alternate target 26.2 miles. Probability of correct target: 98.61%. No illumination needed."

Swensen knelt beside Breckon and read over his shoulder. "Wow! You were right. A missile from space. Who's in the plane anyway?"

"Far's I know it's a Chinese plane with diplomats on it."

"There's something wrong here Breckon," Swensen said quietly. "What if the storm had come a half hour later? There would have been no chance for these guys to target the plane. Now look. It's doing it all by itself anyway. And, why was this man shot through the head? Why all the fuss and expense of getting these guys and equipment up here?"

"As a backup, I'd guess, in case there was another plane too close to the intended plane for the missile to find the right one?" Breckon's voice did not sound convincing, and he knew it. "Worry about that later. We have to get it to miss the plane, and I don't know how."

As the evening deepened the remaining clouds reflected the sun's last light on to them making it possible to see better than normal at that hour. Breckon said, "Dirk, look through that telescope and tell me what you see."

Swensen got into position by sitting on the rock behind the telescope. He aimed it at the rocks a few hundred feet away. As he did so he shifted his butt on the rock and momentarily lost his balance. His foot shot out to stop himself from falling over. "Oops. Kind of a tippy seat here," he said. "This thing is putting out a spot of light that I can see though the eye-piece, and . . . ," he looked up, "I can't see otherwise."

"Okay. Good," Breckon said. "It makes sense. It's infrared. Would have shown through clouds better than visible light. Aim it at one of the mountains to the north. What do you see?"

"Still a spot."

"Find a snow field or smooth rocks that give the brightest reflection and hold it there."

As he spoke Breckon punched buttons on the computer screen. Finally he noticed an icon down in the corner that looked something like a keyboard. He pressed it and a picture of a standard keyboard appeared. He pressed in the word "abort" followed by Enter.

What appeared next made him gasp. There was a message in large letters filling the whole screen that said,

> We've been expecting you, Mr. Ed Breckon. Welcome to the mission. You will be responsible for shooting down an Air China 747 with diplomats from around the world on it. You have done well as an agent for the People's Republic of China.

At the sound of the gasp Swensen looked over at the computer monitor. After the seconds it took him to read the message he said, "Breckon, what's this?"

No sooner were the words out of Swensen's mouth than the message disappeared from the screen. The screen returned to showing the time left to intercept, 9 min, 3 sec.

Breckon stood up and stomped about pulling his hair, groaning in obvious anguish.

"Ed. What's happening?" Swensen asked. "Stop it! We have to prevent the hit on the plane." As Swensen attempted to rise and go to Breckon the rock he was sitting on tipped again and he fell over, his foot hitting the telescope and laser. The optical equipment tumbled in disarray as Swensen fell in the loose pile of extra cable from the generator. Extricating himself from the wire, he caught up to Breckon who was still in a sort of stupor.

Rongji watched the scene below him with total satisfaction. It had worked! He had not thought there was a chance in a thousand of that. When Breckon started working with the computer, it invoked a special program. Soon signals would be sent by sat-phone to the Dragon Fang headquarters in Nanjing. Only this time, not by the chain call but directly. They would be coded, but in a way that could easily be broken. The NSA would collect the message that would implicate Breckon as a Chinese spy. The Chinese operatives would be seen as hauling the equipment up the mountain with the purpose that Breckon would use it. When the CIA recovered the equipment he was now using, it would subtly reveal Breckon's presence all over the place. After all, the information and messages from the Dragon Fang program were in perfect English and distances were in miles rather than kilometers. What other reason than for an American to use.

Enough of this being a spectator. He had to make sure the others did not spoil the plan. Moving to the east he heard voices and then saw movement. Two figures stood in the dusk a hundred yards away. They were intent on something. It occurred to him they were calling in help. He rested his Uzi on a rock and squeezed off a single round. One of the figures fell. He was met with return fire from both men, but it was directed randomly. He started off to his left toward the area where before the storm he had shot the man rushing his position. Nearing that area he was no longer in sight of the two men making the call. He unscrewed the silencer and fired a long burst at the rocks to draw the two men his way. Replacing the silencer he moved further west.

As he walked he noticed his knee wasn't bothering him so much. The doctor had mentioned that he had to use it to stress the bones the mechanical knee was mounted on. This would hurt, but the bones would rapidly strengthen in response to the new requirements. When he started into the mountains the uneven ground plus the weight of his pack had made for tooth-grinding moments. Now with only a small pack, he felt almost normal. Moving slowly so as to make no sound, he moved toward the targeting equipment to watch the operation play out.

Breckon was in too much torment to see Swensen approach him. Swensen put his hand on Breckon's upper arm and said, "Ed! What's wrong? You have to stop acting like this 'cuz we've got work to do. We have to stop that missile from space, or you have to. I wouldn't know where to start."

Breckon shook his head as he squeezed his eyes shut. When he opened them he was back. "Okay Dirk, let's beat 'em." Returning to the equipment he found it hard to dismiss the man with the silenced weapon. There were more shots to the east. Maybe Winger or Daley had gotten him. In any case, they didn't have time to hunt him and still have any chance of affecting the pending disaster.

Breckon surveyed the damage and said to Swensen, "See if you can find a flashlight and get this stuff set up again."

At the computer screen once again Breckon had the keyboard image up. Something was tugging at his mind, something he had seen when he was viewing the code files while trying to get his version of Dragon Fang to work. What was that strange word? It started with a "D." Dagger, dragger, danker . . . yes, blanker, that was it. Not a "D" but a "B." He punched it in and pressed Enter.

It responded with a message at the top of the screen "Blanker Invoked." Now what the heck was Blanker. He saw a group of Chinese characters near the bottom of the screen with no English equivalent. Not knowing what else to do Breckon pressed the Enter button. A window opened that was black with white characters. At the top of the screen in English read, "Blanker, A Routine To Adjust Program Variables On The Fly." Oh yes, Breckon thought. The field debugging routine. The writers of the program had been forced to use a standard Western language for program comments since the compiler could not handle Chinese characters. English had been used. The programmer that had done the portion for Breckon's use was fluent in English anyway.

The screen contained a series of options each preceded by a square. Breckon pressed the square in front of the "Targeting Modes" option. Breckon studied the next screen intently. It was filled with what most people would see as encrypted data, but Breckon recognize the code of an assembler program when he saw it. Years before Breckon had done programming in assembly language for an Intel 486 computer. The computer being used here was an advanced member to the Intel Pentium series, but the basic instruction set appeared similar.

Yes. Among other things, he recognized a conditional jump instruction. The Blanker function had brought him to a decision point in the program where he could change the program. Depending on the value of a variable, the jump instruction directed the flow of the program to any of a several different subroutines. Using the page down key he saw various short subroutines. Each set up a series of variables making the program behave a certain way.

At the bottom of the screen was a small window showing the time remaining, 7 min, 32 sec.

The header of each subroutine started with a line of asterisks to delimit it from the previous one. There followed a line saying what it did, and a number. He found one that said "Illuminate With Laser, Use Chain Call." That would take too long. He hoped he'd find one that did not use a call, but there were none. The best he could do was one that said "Illuminate With Laser, Use Direct Call." It had the number 0B after it. In the conditional jump instruction was the variable OPERATION_MODE. This variable had to be set to 0B, but how?

Breckon pressed and held the "page up" button. The pages flashed past until he was at the beginning of the Balnker section. There under the series of options where he had found "Targeting Modes" was another option called "Program Variable Table." Breckon pressed the square in front of it. The screen filled with a list of variables in alphabetical order. Paging down at least ten screens he went past it. Going back he found it. To the right was a column headed "Binary Value." Pressing the line-up key he got the OPERATION_MODE variable as the top line. Then by pressing squares above the bit values he could toggle them from zero to one and back. There were sixteen bits in groups of four. The group of four on the right was 0100 indicating a binary four. The other twelve bits were zeros.

So, he only had to set the lower four bits to the binary equivalent of the hexadecimal character "B." Breckon thought a second, because it had been years since he had done any work in hexadecimal. The number 8 was 1000, then 9, A, B so B was 1011. He changed the least significant bits to 1011. At the bottom he pressed the square in front of the statement, "Accept Variable Change." If he were right, the next time the program cycled to the conditional jump instruction, which should be in less than a microsecond, the program would branch to the Illuminate With Laser mode.

The little window at the bottom of the screen read 5 min, 56 sec.

Yes! The series of screens he had seen in his apartment appeared. He answered the questions as fast as he could. When it asked for the coordinates of the target he was stumped. These mountains were at about 45° north, the same as Minneapolis. From looking up maps on the Internet he remembered the maps were in the vicinity of 109° West. He entered N45°, W109°. He hoped that was close enough so he pressed Enter. The message came back "The Present Location Of Targeting Device Is N45° 2.62', W109° 36.74'. Use These Coordinates?" Breckon pressed the square in front of the "yes" assuming there must be a GPS receiver in this stuff someplace.

He continued through the questions answering that the target was not moving, on land, and not a landmark. To the question "Do you wish to initiate strike sequence?" he answered "Yes." He was about to press Enter when he realized this would never work. It had to look like he was sorting out targets so the warhead would hit the right airplane. He returned to the page and selected moving, and airborne. He finished by pressing Enter.

The window at the bottom read 4 min, 42 sec.

The computer appeared to be processing the information until a message came up, "First Leg Of Direct Call Not Complete, Check Local Phone Connection."

Swensen had the telescope and laser set up again, and was watching over Breckon's shoulder in amazement. He wanted to ask what he was doing, but from Breckon's intense concentration, and occasional curse, he thought it wasn't a good idea. As Swensen saw the message he quickly switched on the flashlight and looked around. Sure enough, about ten feet from the rest of the equipment was a small dish antenna lying on the ground. Somewhere in all the fuss the cable had been pulled tipping it over.

"There," Swensen said, "that small antenna must be what it needs." He was at it in an instant, setting it up and adjusting it so it pointed in the direction he had seen other dish antennas, about 45° above the southern horizon.

Breckon pressed Enter again. No more messages appeared. "That seems to have solved the problem. Now we wait," Breckon said. "This system has to communicate with its headquarters in China to get approval for a hit. I hope we get it in time."

"How do you know that?" Swensen asked.

"It's too long a story for now. Be sure you're ready to aim that spot of light at a nice bright part of the mountain. Oh, by the way, I just thought of something. Slowly and as evenly as you can move the spot along the mountain. The target is supposed to be moving. Keep the spot near the top so the light reflects into space in all directions. The satellite could be coming from the north or the south."

The little window said 3 min, 10 sec.

"I see the strobe light of a plane to the northeast, That must be it," Swensen said.

"Yeah, I suppose so," Breckon replied. "Come on, you guys, give us the approval." Still they waited. The faint rumble of the plane could be heard. A message appeared on the screen, "Connection Made, Authentication Processing."

Almost immediately came another message, "Fang Already Deorbited For Primary Mission, Use This Weapon?" Breckon immediately pressed "Yes" and then Enter.

The little window said 2 min, 43 sec.

Fifteen seconds later came another message, "Probability of correct target is greater than 99%, illumination is not needed. Why change?"

"Oh, boy. I'm talking to them in real time," Breckon said. "What do I say."

"How about a stealth fighter in the area," said Swensen.

"Suppose they'd believe it?" asked Breckon. "Yeah. It's off-the-wall enough that they might."

In the space provided Breckon typed, "Stealth bomber in area confusing target selection. Need immediate approval," and pressed Enter.

The little window showed 0 min, 54 sec.

The plane was obvious now. "Come on, you jerks. Give it to us!" Breckon said. It was down to 28 seconds. "Get ready Dirk. Sweep the spot from east to west, and move it about as fast as the plane is going.

Breckon looked up for a sign of the smart rock making its reentry. No matter how good the heat shield was, it would at least glow. It was dark enough to see stars. Glancing back at the computer he saw, "Approval granted. Illuminate target."

"Dirk! That's it. We got it." To the south Breckon saw an orange star moving silently across the sky. "I see it. It's coming from the south. Start moving the spot. Ten seconds to go. Be sure you don't go so fast you run out of mountain."

Breckon turned to see where the plane was. Swensen looking though the eyepiece at the mountain was oblivious of all else. From the angle of the telescope it looked like it was pointing right under the plane.

"Look at that," Breckon said under his breath. "That plane is moving right between the missile and the spot on the mountain." Glancing at the screen he saw four seconds left. Three, he glanced up, two . . . a shower of sparks fell from the horizontal tail surface of the plane, and a second later there was a blinding white light as several cubic yards of granite were vaporized.

Breckon put his hand on Swensen's shoulder and said, "It's over my friend. You did a terrific job. Thanks. She looks a little wobbly, but she'll make it." The plane was still trailing an occasional spark, but it seemed to be doing all right.

"Stand away from the equipment!" It was Winger.

"It's okay, ol' stick," said Breckon. "It's only us. We managed to keep the plane from being destroyed."

"I know it's you, Breckon, and you are under arrest. I saw you working that system to shoot down that plane. What you mean is, you screwed up and only managed to get a piece of its tail. It's lucky you're so incompetent. Who's your accomplice there Breckon!" The voice had pure hate and malice in it.

"Whoa. Wait just a minute!" Swensen retorted. He didn't know what was going on, but being accused of helping to kill hundreds of people made him flush with anger. "I'm from the U.S. Forest service, and that plane would have been destroyed if it had not been for this man. I was with him all the time. That missile was on automatic control. It didn't even need this stuff to destroy that plane!"

"Well, we'll let the judges figure that out. For now you're both under arrest. I wondered why you took our sat-phone. Now I see. You wanted to be sure your plot wasn't messed with."

The light had faded until the men were little more than shadows. Swensen slowly got up and as he did picked up the extinguished flashlight keeping it at his side away from Winger. He stepped away from Breckon. Winger approached being cautions because of the dim light. "You," he said. "Get back by Breckon." Swensen raised the flashlight holding it at arm's length out to his side, and turned it on. The light shone directly into Winger's eyes. Winger shot at the light, but before he could think to shoot again a large hand grabbed his gun wrist. A split second later the gun clattered on the rocks.

"Wait a minute. I'm a federal . . . " that's all he said as a huge fist to the face turned out Winger's lights. When Winger woke up, he was tied up like a mummy in a piece of electrical cable that had run from the generator to the laser. There was also a rag in his mouth.

"What's going on down there. I heard a shot." They recognized Daley's voice from up on the rocks.

"We're all right. Come on down," Breckon said. "Mel's gun went off by accident."

"Come on up and give me a hand. I'm shot in the leg and the pain's killing me."

Swensen immediately hustled up to help Daley. Since it was painful for him to walk, Daley opted to stay where he was until help arrived. He still had his revolver in case one of the Chinese came back. Swensen got him as comfortable as possible and returned to the equipment.

Breckon knelt by Winger and asked, "Mel. Where's Burl, anyway?"

Winger struggled for a minute, and then gave up. "He's hit bad. I came over here to be sure things were under control before I went back to him. Who's the gorilla?"

Breckon made introductions. "Mel of the CIA I'm pleased to introduce Dirk of the U.S. Forest Service. I'm surprised you don't know each other. You work for the same employer." Breckon couldn't keep the cynicism from his voice. More seriously he said, "We didn't try to shoot down the plane. As Dirk said, we did just the opposite. The 747 didn't crash, if you failed to notice. Somebody will tell you about it later. We'd better see how Burl's doing."

They untied Winger who promised to behave since he couldn't find his gun in any case. The three headed off to find Carson.

The groans made it easy for them to home in on him. Breckon and Winger knelt by Carson as Swensen stood back a short distance to listen for sounds of anyone approaching. Carson was delirious and shaking uncontrollably. Breckon felt his clothing.

"He's still wet and cold. We have to get his body heat up. Here, let's put my parka on him. There's a stocking cap in the pocket. Put it on him, and get the hood pulled over his head." Moving Carson as little as possible they got him into the parka. After five minutes he seemed to be resting easier. "When's help coming?" Breckon asked.

"The battery was nearly dead so I called until it crapped out and then let the battery rest a little and tried again. Through a series of short calls I think they got it. Sounded like they're sending out something to get him. Should be here about 2300 hours if I got it right. It was pretty scratchy at the end. That's a long time for Burl."

"There's a small generator back there," Swensen said. "I left the tent full of holes over the rise to the southwest of the laser. Maybe we can arrange it to direct the hot exhaust around his lower body."

"Good," Winger said. "Take the flashlight." With his partner's life in the balance he was willing to handle the two malfeasants later.

Swensen and Breckon headed back to the small basin in the top of the mountain. As they made their way up the rocky terrain Swensen asked, "What was that all about with that message on the computer screen? Somehow, I don't take you for a Chinese spy. And, who do you work for, anyway?"

Breckon was taking deep breaths since the climb had gotten steep and they wanted to assist Carson with as little delay as possible. "I feel like I'm a hundred years old," Breckon said between puffs. "To answer your last question, I'm an electrical engineer. I work for an engineering company doing electrical engineering stuff. That's all."

They topped out and could see the smooth water of the tank as a sheet of black. Breckon said just loud enough for Daley to hear, "Greg, it's Dirk and Ed. Don't shoot."

Starting toward the tank Breckon continued, "As to what I'm doing up on this mountain at this time? Well, I'm on vacation doing what I like to do on vacation, namely hike in the mountains. But, it's not that simple. You can see that. Tell you what. Some day I'll let you buy me a beer, and I'll tell you about it."

They stopped by Daley and he asked about Carson as they asked about him. Continuing on, Breckon stopped at the generator and Swensen went to find the tent.

— 28 —

Using extreme care, Rongji had moved to within a hundred feet of Breckon and Swensen as they worked with the computer. He knew they couldn't change the coming destruction of the 747, but his explicit orders were to stay close until the plane went down. As things progressed he had become less certain of the outcome. In the still air he heard them clearly. Breckon's propensity of talking to the guys in China like they were standing beside him kept Rongji informed of the progress. When the plane failed to explode his shock quickly faded to horror and then anger. He was about to spray the area with bullets killing the two men by the computer, but he paused. Doing a quick mental total of the number of shots he had fired, he realized there were only a few rounds left in his magazine. Putting his hand on his survival pack he closed his fingers on the various items in it. To his dismay, the characteristic shape of the spare magazine was not there. With so much going on he had forgotten to transfer a magazine from his big pack to this one. His first thought was to return to the pack and retrieve the magazine. But, with the pressure of stopping the destruction of the plane gone, the two men would be alert to the slightest noise. There was little chance of finding it without revealing himself. And, it was too dark to shoot single shots with any certainty.

Mel Winger's arrival changed things. Now, there were three of them, all armed. He decided if they discovered him he'd shoot single shots and get as many as he could. But then Rongji's hopes rose. Of all things, the CIA agent actually assumed Breckon was a Chinese spy, anyway. Breckon was even placed under arrest. The plan would still work! A few minutes later he wasn't sure again. They had formed a common cause to help the wounded man.

With the three of them gone, Rongji thought of finding and killing the man he had shot in the leg to finish that job. Yet, he'd be moving and in the dark could easily make a noise and get himself killed. In any case, it was Breckon he wanted so he waited. In a few minutes he heard voices again. They were talking normally so he knew what they intended as they talked to Daley. It had become dark except for starlight, though the moon would rise before long. He slowly made his way toward the approximate location of the generator. He crouched ten feet from it as the two men approached. Breckon took his time getting the electrical cable detached from it as Swensen continued on. At this range it would be easy to shoot Breckon, but that would be too generous. It was important Breckon knew who was killing him and why. Having the advantage of surprise on his side, Rongji had no doubt he could take him.

Rongji waited for Breckon to pick up the generator. This would encumber him with a load as well as give the other man time to get far away. His full attention was fixed on his attack. At the precise moment he lunged, but as he did his foot slipped on a thin layer of wet moss and twisted his leg sending a searing pain through his knee throwing off his timing. Breckon was startled by the nearby scrape on rock and the slight grunt from the pain. He turned to see a shadow surging in on him. Dropping the generator he stepped back, caught his foot, and fell. Rongji tumbled over the generator giving both men time to regain their footing. Rongji renewed his attack. Breckon was skilled at confronting an assault from his months in self-defense classes. He anticipated the height of the center of gravity of the approaching mass, and stooped lower, leaning his weight toward it. His shoulder caught Rongji at the hips. Breckon straighten up, and sent his opponent flying over his back. The gasp indicated the landing on the rocks was not gentle.

Immediate scurrying sounds of clothing scraping on stone told Breckon his shadowy attacker was still in the fight. Rongji chanced over a patch of clay with grass and lichens growing on it. In the starlight this was black and concealed him. A second later Breckon was hit in the side by what felt like a boulder. He was down with his enemy on him. Again training came to the fore. Breckon flipped his legs up and crossed his ankles under the man's chin. As he threw his arms against the ground to gain leverage to thrust the fiend off, his hand fell on something smooth and tubular. It was the silencer of the automatic weapon. Clutching it as he heaved Rongji off, he rolled forward and rammed the stock into the abdomen of the attacker.

With a grunt Rongji fell back. Breckon, in a half squat, swung the weapon over his head at the moving shadow. It missed and smashed against a rock in a screech of metal. A part clanked free on the rocks.

Breckon homed in on his antagonist by the sound of heavy breathing. At that moment Rongji stepped in front of a large white rock and Breckon saw his arm come up with something in the hand. He fell on the ground as the rock clipped the top of his head. Immediately he came up and held the weapon, muzzle forward. Rongji attacked, catching it in the solar plexus, and fell backward. Lunging on him, Breckon caught his opponent's right wrist and twisted it. To relieve the strain Rongji turned on to his stomach, permitting Breckon to bring the man's arm up in the mid-back as he threw his weight on him. With his left hand he grabbed the neck with his fingers pressing on Rongji's throat. In seconds the struggling mass beneath him was still.

Breckon, in a rage, pressed harder. A convulsion of the man under him made his hand slip off. Each man struggled for his life. In a labored gasp Breckon heard, "Do it . . . do it."

Once again Breckon had his stranglehold as he pressed his fingers to end life. The slimy sweat on the skin combined with the fatigue in his forearm caused his fingers to lose their force—more struggling for air. "Kill me. You . . .want to." Labored breathing. "Kill me. Make you . . . feel good . . . broke my knee . . . finish it."

A renewed flow of adrenaline and Breckon had a final grip. All resistance ceased. Panting from the exertion, Breckon knew he had won. It was over. Except . . . searing through his mind were Daley's words about hedonism and doing what feels good. If Rongji had used any other words . . . but he hadn't. Unconsciously, Breckon lessened his tension on the wrist and the neck.

Rongji's first thought was that he would die, and that Breckon would drag it out as long as possible giving him just enough air to keep him struggling, like repeatedly forcing his head into a pail of water. His words were to inflame Breckon and cause him to inadvertently strangle him quickly. He couldn't fake death because of his rasping uncontrollable fight for air. Suddenly to his surprise he felt the tension on his right arm lessen. He was catching his breath, but he still gasped like he was near death. His left hand was lying on the ground and the palm rested on a lump. Slowly between gasps he tightened his left fist. The rock moved. A weapon.

He had no idea how much strength he had, but Rongji knew it had to be now. Twisting, he heaved. To his surprise Breckon tumbled off.

Rolling over he raised the rock. It was heavier than it should have been for its size. Rongji's arm shook with weakness from his near suffocation. He let it fall in an uncoordinated blow on Breckon's head. He struggled to lift the rock for another attempt. A call by Swensen from a couple of hundred feet away galvanized him to a new threat. Dropping the rock he crawled on all fours and struggled to gain his footing. Each breath was agony as his lungs convulsively sucked air though his wounded throat. There was no time and no point searching for his gun. He had heard the sound of twisting metal and the part fall free. It was clearly damaged. Keeping low, he faltered as he made his way clumsily up the rocks to the north. Without having thought about the small pack, he almost fell as he stepped on it—small favors. Grabbing a strap he dragged it along. Over the brink, he paused as he labored to get enough air. Badly bruised, he had no broken bones that were readily apparent. It was painful to swallow, but he sensed he'd survive. He heard Swensen call to Breckon again. A chill came over him as he heard a halting groan and reply. It didn't really surprise him, though. He knew he had been too weak to deal a deadly blow. Besides, that man had nine lives.

With no weapon and little strength he had no choice but to get out of the area. After several minutes of slowly making his way to the west, he stopped and sat down. He had escaped death, but to what end? The plan had failed, Breckon was still alive, and he was in the middle of a mountain wasteland. What was the point in struggling? No point, other than to get as far away from that place as possible. Dying in the mountains was far better than being captured and put at the center of a media circus. On reflection, he realized that his people would kill him before that happened. With those happy thoughts to encourage him, he plodded on.

———————————

Swensen hurried to Breckon. "What happened? You hurt?"

"Part of the long story. In China a guy tried to steal my luggage. I smashed his knee. He was here. Nearly killed me. Got away. Another lump on my head." The short sentences came out of a woozy haze.

Crouching lower Swensen whispered. "He the guy who shot the others? Where is he now?"

Breckon's head was clearing a little. "Yeah. I think so. Don't think he's a problem. I smashed his gun on a rock in the fight. Help me over by Daley. Afraid you'll have to carry the tent and generator yourself. First go over by the computer stuff and find my rifle. I laid it there some-place."

When Swensen was off with the tent and generator, Breckon sat down beside Daley and leaned his bruised back against the rock. "You got your cannon handy?" Breckon asked.

"Yeah. Here in my lap."

"Good. Keep your hand on it." Breckon levered a round into the chamber of his carbine. He wasn't sure if he was ejecting an empty casing or a complete cartridge. He couldn't remember where he was. But, this guaranteed a live round in the chamber. He carefully lowered the hammer on the firing pin. Then he related his encounter with Rongji.

Daley was only half listened being occupied with his own problems. When Breckon finished his story Daley said remorsefully, "I should have been home with my family. Why did I have to go off to see a mountain. That was really selfish of me."

Breckon could understand how Daley would reproach himself. "Come on. You're right where you're supposed to be, doing your job. Did you manage to call them on the sat-phone?"

"Mel got a message out to somebody in the CIA to rescue Burl. He told about the attack on the farm, but the battery was nearly dead. I don't know if they understood what he was saying, or even how much of the message went out." They sat silently under the stars each with his own thoughts.

Daley shifted his position and groaned. "How's the leg?" Breckon asked.

"Hurts a lot, but that's not the worst. I keep thinking about my family. Wonder if they're still alive."

"Don't you see, it's happening to you. Why were you so taken by the guy's talk about the mountains back on your job? Where else could you have found out about the attack on your family? If you were with them and the attack came, you'd be dead, too."

"I'm not buying that crap."

"Keep the faith. They're all right. I don't know how, but they'll be safe." Getting up stiffly Breckon considered his options. He was cold and starting to shiver. But, finding his way to his pack in the moonlight was a long shot. Walking around on the rough terrain in the dim light was risky, too. In the end he decided to stay and keep Greg company.

Breckon wished he could be walking out, though. He didn't trust Winger. The man apparently still carried a grudge from the time Breckon took his gun away from him and punched him out. Talk about touchy. He was glad Swensen and Winger were with Carson as he and Daley huddled against the rock in the cold moonlight pressing their shoulders against each other for what little common warmth they could get. Ed continued to encourage his friend with his feeling that his family would be all right. As they talked Daley filled him in with what he could surmise about the *rickshaws*, and what he believed was happening to his family, or maybe had already happened.

They were silent for a time when Breckon said, "I had it in my power to kill that scum bag. Why didn't I? What good can come from letting something like that live?"

"Take it easy, buddy," Daley said seriously. "That's a human being you're talking about, not a bear or a bug. Maybe he wasn't ready to die, and you gave him a chance to change."

"Yeah, that's easy for you to say. In the last few days you were nearly killed, too. But, it was only because you were with me. He's after me! In a few hours you'll be on your way, and we'll probably never see each other again. Meanwhile, I'll be walking around with a target on my back."

"Still, you can't play God. Remember the thing about divine providence?"

Breckon managed a chuckle. "You're saying God's going to make something good come from my letting that dirt-bag live? It's a good thing He's infinitely powerful, 'cause nothing else could do it."

"Don't get cynical. Yes. I'm saying something good will come of it."

Breckon laughed out loud. "Like a guy in the Andes Mountains *not* getting gored by a yak?"

"Ed, there are no yaks in South America."

"There ya go."

Daley chortled. "You're a hard case, Breckon." After a pause he returned to his morose state and said, "I'm going crazy worrying about my family, and my leg is killing me! I keep thinking I'm bleeding to death, and the bacteria are breeding like flies to infect it."

Breckon shook his head, though it was unlikely Daley saw it in the moonlight. He said, "The mind's a terrible thing. It can cause more pain than anything nature can do. I'm an expert on that. The blood in your wound has clotted or you would've bled to death by now, and the micro-organisms aren't all that fast."

"Yeah. I suppose. Hey, Ed. Let me see if I can rake together in my mind more of what I've learned about divine providence. It might distract me from my problems a little."

Ed was about to say, sure, anything to help you out, but thought that was a little crass. The guy obviously was in anguish about his family. He said, "Sure. I can use all the help I can get." As he spoke he got up minding his bruises and scrapes. He leaned his rifle against the rock and began slapping his arms around him to stay warm.

"First, not killing that Chinese guy was not an evil thing. It was a good thing in spite of how you might see it. Beyond that, nothing in the world happens that is not willed by God, and hence, is good."

"Wait a minute. Are you saying God wills sin, and that sin is good?"

"No. I'll get to that. Let's say someone punches you in the nose because he's angry with you. Every human act has two parts, a natural part and a moral part. The arm coming out and the clenched fist striking you, like all natural things, is good in itself. God is acting through the man's fist to do something that is good. The man turning his will away from God and doing this out of malice is the moral part, is a sin, and is evil. This is the fault of the man alone who is exercising the free will that God gave him and permits him to use. He must bear the punishment for the sin.

"From your point of view, the fact that you were hit by the fist, the natural part of the act, means that God willed that you should be struck, and that in some hidden way good will come from it. More to the point, it was good *for you* but in a way you may never know this side of the grave. Look at the same act in a more transparent way. What if you were about to walk into a minefield and the only way for the man to stop you was to punch you in the nose? The natural act was the same, it was obviously good for you, but the man didn't sin."

"What if I decided to do something else, and didn't meet the angry man? In that case I wouldn't have gotten punched. It sounds like you think I don't have free will, that God forced me to be there to meet him."

"That's an old problem. Essentially what you are saying is that if God knows what I will do before I do it, how do I have free will? The philosophers use this example to try to explain it. Assume you are standing on the bank of a swiftly flowing river. There are no obstructions up stream as far as you can see until it goes around a bend. Down river there are sharp rocks poking out of the water everywhere. Suddenly you see a small boat with people in it coming around the bend up river. They have no paddles or other means to steer the boat. You see the speed of the boat, the width of the river, and other factors. You conclude that the boat must smash against the jagged rocks. Your certain knowledge of the coming disaster does not force or cause it to happen.

"If you like to look at things poetically I once saw it put this way, 'To God, time is the unfolding of truth that already is, the unveiling of beauty yet to be.'

"Aside from that, all we can say is that God's foreknowledge of our free acts involves time. We live in time and it's all we know. God is beyond time, outside of time. He created time. In God's infinite intelligence—a lot smarter than us—He decided time would be good for us. We are expected to humbly accept that we do have free will, even if it is something of a mystery. There are no proud people in heaven. Humility is part of the deal to get there."

Breckon crouched by the rock and hugged his arms about himself.

Daley continued, "Before you made reference to something good happening to a guy on another continent because you didn't kill the Chinese man. That could be the case. More likely, the good will occur a lot closer to home."

They batted this around for awhile and fell silent. Breckon moved about from time to time to work his muscles to stay warm. Daley found it hard to move, but then, he still had his coat.

— 29 —

The rescue plane was a V-22 Osprey. It had an engine nacelle and large propeller on the end of each wing. The nacelles rotated vertically to land like a helicopter, and tipped forward to fly like a normal airplane. The pilot circled the spot on the mountain the GPS system told him was his destination. Both he and the copilot wore night vision goggles which, with the aid of moonlight, made the view as bright as day. The rugged landscape was not a welcome sight. The engine nacelles were at sixty degrees giving the craft more of a hover than winged flight. Seeing first the flashlight as a signal, the pilots spotted the men by Carson. Swensen motioned with the light as he walked toward the basin of the middle tank. The area around Carson was too steep, and the flatter areas nearby were strewn with large boulders. Once over the hump between the east and middle tanks Swensen dithered the spot of the flashlight on the southwest end of the middle tank. After a complete orbit of the area the V-22 gently settled on to the soggy mountain. As soon as it was down a half dozen men were out. An instant later the engines increased power and it was gone.

It was too dark for those waiting on the ground to see the markings on the V-22 as it maneuvered and landed. If it had been light enough, they would have seen MARINES painted in subdued letters among the camouflage pattern.

The first four out of the V-22 were Air Force Commandos followed by two medics with a litter. Swensen met them. After a minute or two of confusion in the moonlight and Swensen's raised voice the commandos were off to secure the area. The two medics followed Swensen to assist Carson.

Daley's left leg was stiffening up and it hurt intensely. He tried to get up a couple of times but fell back. After the group was off to rescue Carson, he called out. They saw a shadow in the moonlight coming their way, and as it got closer it disappeared. They heard movement but saw nothing more. Suddenly Breckon saw a form appear above the lip in a depression in the rocks twenty feet away. For a moment he froze except to squeeze Daley's arm. "There," he whispered as he pointed.

Both men were in shadows and afraid it might be an enemy as they cocked their weapons.

"Air Force Commando," came a loud whisper. "Show yourselves. No fast movements or I'll shoot."

"Not so fast," Daley said in tense voice. "We've been shot-up, are cold and in a surly mood. We're both armed so take it easy."

"I can see that. I have night vision, and you don't."

"Then you can see we're not bad guys. The guys you should worry about are Chinese."

"What do you think?" Breckon whispered to Daley.

Daley responded in a hushed voice that would carry to the man, "We'll lower the hammers on our guns and raise the barrels. That's as far as we'll go." As he spoke Breckon edged away from Daley.

Nothing happened. Finally Daley said, "I'm Greg Daley of the National Security Agency. You blow me away and win or lose, your life is over."

There was uncertainty in the reply. "Okay. I'm moving up to you. No fast moves." Soon the commando crouched beside Daley with his gun pointed at Breckon.

"Put up the gun, asshole!"

"Better do it," Daley advised, "or he'll feed it to you. Don't mess with that man."

Slowly the muzzle went to vertical. In hushed tones the commando said to Daley, "Is the LZ hot?"

"Huh?"

"The landing zone. Where are the guys that shot you? Will there be enemy fire when the '22 comes back to pick us up?"

"I doubt it. We think there were four of them. Three are dead. The last one shot me, and he could have gotten more of us if he had wanted to die himself. Later he attacked that guy," he said motioning to Breckon. "It was totally dark before the moon came up. He took the silenced assault rifle away from his assailant, smashed it on a rock, and beat the stuffing out of him. In the dark that one managed to slip away unarmed and wounded. I wouldn't worry about him."

"He didn't get away," Breckon interjected. "I let him go rather than kill him. I could easily have strangled the piece of dirt."

"The CIA guy over the hill is in bad shape," Daley continued. "I think we will want to be on our way as soon as they get him here so I'd like not to hold things up. I guess I'm not severely wounded but it really hurts. Can you give me a hand getting to where the plane will land?" The commando gave a cryptic description of the situation into his radio. After an acknowledgment a strong hand grabbed Daley's upper arm and helped him to his feet.

Daley hissed through his teeth as the commando put Daley's arm over his shoulder and half lifted him with an arm around his waist. As they shuffled along the commando said, "You picked a bad place for a battle. A few thousand feet higher and we wouldn't have been able to hover. As it was, we came in light on fuel. Don't worry. A tanker's waiting for us on top. The twenty-two'll drink up as soon as we're on our way."

Breckon followed behind largely forgotten which was all right with him.

As the medics made their way down the slope into the basin of the middle tank carrying Carson, the commando with Daley and Breckon had a few cryptic exchanges with the aircraft using his hand-held radio. Daley wondered what had happened to the aircraft. It was nowhere to be seen or heard. Thirty seconds later it settled into the basin. With Daley, Breckon, Winger, Carson, and the two medics on board, the V-22 was airborne again. Swensen and the commandos remained behind to secure the site until morning.

The V-22 pilot and his copilot, both members of the U.S. Marine Corps, had stopped at Ellsworth Air Force Base in western South Dakota as they ferried the V-22 across country. They had planned to get a few beers and a good night's sleep when an urgent call came in from the office of the Secretary of Defense. The beers didn't happen.

As the V-22 Osprey headed east gaining altitude one of the medics put on a headset and spoke to the pilot. "One guy, a CIA agent, is in critical condition. He'll need the best care available. The other CIA agent back here says they're from Minneapolis, and that North Memorial Hospital there has one of the best trauma units in the country. The guy's family lives there so that's a consideration."

"I'll check it out while we're getting a sip of juice," the pilot replied. Twenty minutes later, with a full load of fuel, they were on their way to Minneapolis, ETA: 0315 hours.

2320 Hours, Mountains in Montana

Rongji was making his way west. He had stopped to rest where the high plateau fell off abruptly to Crystal Lake five-hundred feet below when he heard the beat of rotors to the east. He knew the aircraft had come to rescue the men he had shot, so would not be a threat to him. What came later would be a problem, though, if he intended to live. As he fought Breckon he hadn't cared if he died. Now, the thought of starving to death in these mountains put a different light on it, to say nothing of what awaited him if he were captured. Life had a way of asserting the will to survive, however bleak the chances looked at the moment.

As the helicopter left with its cargo he knew that if he were to have any chance of surviving even assuming he managed to get back to civilization he should report in. He had an emergency satellite phone in his pack. But, all he could report was that the mission had failed. They already knew that by now so what was the point? As he vacillated about what to do, he realized he hadn't been noticing his knee so much, not that it didn't hurt. It was just that he hurt in so many other places that it didn't stand out. Finally, he decided not to send a message. Before starting on, he found an envelope of pills in his pack. He took out three of the extra strength Tylenol and crept to the edge of the stream. It was hard to see, but the sound drew him to it. After gulping the caplets, and taking a long drink of water he crawled back to his pack. He ate an energy bar before starting the daunting climb down the steep rocks to the lake below.

It would have been a miserable climb for a man in good health in daylight. Once he tripped and rolled on the rocks arresting his downward plunge only after adding to his scrapes and bruises. At times he slid on his butt feeling his way with his feet and holding himself back with his hands. After a half hour he came upon a trail going down. It was steep and he lost it at times, but managed to pick it up again.

Chinese embassy, New York

Kao Yaobang planned to spend the night in his office in the New York embassy since the shooting down of the Air China 747 was the major clandestine operation of China anywhere in the world at the time. The plane had a transponder on it so he could follow its progress on a computer monitor with the expected point of destruction marked. For extra assurance he had someone from the embassy call the Chinese ambassador on the plane and discuss a minor point of protocol starting ten minutes prior to the intercept. This conversation was fed to a speaker on his desk. When the call ended abruptly, he'd have backup confirmation of a successful operation. It had been all too clear that the plane had not gone down. Fear of repercussions came to the fore of his thinking.

Due to the priority of this operation Yaobang could call upon any resources that China had. This meant he assigned all the signals intercept capability available to determine what had happened to operation *long dagger*. Within a couple of hours he knew a V-22 Osprey had lifted wounded men off the mountain and was headed to the suburban hospital in Robbinsdale, Minnesota. This aircraft, he knew, had the speed and range to accomplish this. The pilot had even radioed the names and types of wounds each had.

In cases like this where operations fell apart the standard procedure was to clean up the lose ends as quickly as possible. This usually meant killing those who could be made to talk. For the moment, he knew nothing about the condition of his operatives, but he knew enough about Breckon to understand that he could and should be terminated. He did not have the targeting assets in place to destroy the V-22 in flight, so he alerted his assassin to be ready at the hospital.

By one o'clock in the morning Rongji had made it down to Crystal Lake. From here on it would be easier going. This gave him a measure of hope that he would survive to get out of the wilderness. He had about a mile and a half—he had taken to figuring in miles because the map grid used miles—to Green Lake, then another two to Granite Lake. At Granite Lake he could pick up a trail for the five miles out to the road. Once there, he could hijack a vehicle and kill its occupants. His first objective was Green Lake where the trees started. However far he got tonight he'd have to lay-up under cover during the day.

While making his way, he thought about how to save himself from his people. One by one ideas began to fall into place. The nick on the tail of the 747 could be a real advantage, even better than destroying the plane.

He could see that destruction of the plane was all they could do with the projectile from orbit. But, they probably didn't realize how remote this area was. The U.S. government would refuse to let any of the news media or Chinese investigators into the area. This meant they could attribute the crash to faulty Chinese maintenance. The effect would be far less than they had planned. But, with the plane on the ground in San Francisco, China could show the whole world that someone in the United States had tried to destroy the plane. Add to this that the CIA agent on the scene had watched Breckon working with the targeting equipment. In the dark he, Rongji, had been close enough to hear the CIA agent accusing Breckon of being a spy, and had actually put him under arrest. The CIA would need a fall guy. China's plan was already taking shape without the Chinese doing a thing.

At one thirty he stopped and decided to send a message. He took the small low power satellite phone out of his pack and began setting it up. He carefully unfolded the gossamer three foot diameter parabolic antenna and set it on a rock. It had a mesh of fine wires spaced to match the wavelength of the frequency used. Using bubble levels in the base and a small red flashlight he carefully leveled it. Then he adjusted the angle to correspond to this latitude, and finally rotated it until a small red light blinked indication it was aimed at the geosynchronous satellite. The alignment has to be precise because of the low power available. All that was left was to connect the phone cable to the antenna base and he was ready to go.

He spent several minutes composing in his mind what he would say. The phone would record the message, digitize it, compress it, encode it, and sent it as a burst transmission. He started with the bare facts. The plane had not been destroyed, but had damage to the tail. One CIA agent, the NSA man, and Breckon were wounded. At 2315 hours local, a helicopter had departed the site, presumably with the wounded. He was the only Chinese survivor and could likely escape capture. He added his analysis of the situation. It wouldn't be wise to rely on someone in an office to put together the story that was born out of his own will to survive.

Inside the Chinese embassy in New York, Koa Yaobang received Rongji's transmission and leaned back in his chair. In a crazy way it made sense as far as Rongji's information went. What Rongji did not understand was that the primary reason for destroying the 747 was not to embarrass the U.S., but to kill the three nanotechnology scientists. On the other hand, it did add an unexpected twist to things. He had not known about the damage to the tail of the plane. With his own comments appended he forwarded Rongji's message to Beijing. It was afternoon there so it would receive immediate action.

3:05 a.m., North Memorial Hospital, Robbinsdale, Minnesota

With a tail wind they bettered their ETA by a few minutes. The sight of a Marine Corps V-22 landing on the roof of the clinic across the street from this suburban hospital would have caused quite a stir had it been daytime. As it was, a few hospital employees would have something to tell about their shift this day, but other than that all was serene. After Carson and Daley were on gurneys, Breckon got out followed by Winger. As they followed the other two into the enclosed elevator access on the corner of the helipad, Winger said. "Breckon, you are still under arrest until we get this sorted out. You hearing me!"

"There's no case against me and you know it. You're still pissed off, aren't you? You should do something about the attitude."

"Well, smart mouth, as soon as you're patched up, you're coming with me to a big time lockup. We'll unravel that pompous attitude of yours."

"Come on. I'm not going anywhere. And don't forget, things could turn and bite you. You forced me to take that computer to China. The radio talk show hosts would like to get their teeth into something juicy like that." Winger said no more, but Breckon knew he'd follow through with the incarceration threat if given the chance.

The elevator door opened into an underground corridor. The ragtag procession of Air Force corpsmen, hospital staff, gurneys, and assorted disheveled men traveled what seemed endless passages, finally passing under the street. This brought them to an elevator that delivered them to the emergency rooms in the hospital.

As they came off the elevator Breckon saw immediately the admitting room for emergency was overloaded. Three gurneys bearing bleeding black men were parked along the wall. A man on one of them was jabbering incoherently. "Anybody know what language this is?" a man in green scrubs asked. All he saw were shaking heads. "Any ID?"

"He was clean, like they turned out his pockets before leaving him by the curb," a man from the ambulance said.

Winger was immediately at the lead. "Make way, make way!" he shouted.

A nurse spoke up, "Over there to triage."

"No way," Winger snarled. "These are federal officers, down in the line of duty." He did a quick draw on his ID. "CIA," he said as he flashed the badge around. "These go first or I'll take control of this whole facility. Now move!" They did.

A few minutes later Breckon and Winger were in an examining room after Winger was sure Carson and Daley were in good hands. Breckon reproached himself for not ducking out while the jerk with the badge was busy. Winger flopped into the only comfortable chair in the room as Breckon peeked out into the hall.

"Watch it there. Don't even think about running away, mister."

"I was wondering what the new commotion was. Looks like they brought in a couple more. Busy night." Since Breckon was walking under his own power when he came in, nobody even looked at him. They may not even have known he was wounded. Winger grabbed this room like it was his make-shift headquarters. Nobody objected.

To pass the time Breckon said, "Ever notice how that triage notion is a communist concept?"

"How'd you know?"

"Well, look at it. First the part about 'from each according to his ability'—to pay, that is. I've been paying into Medicare, taxes, and medical insurance premiums all my life, some since my first two dollar an hour job. Now, when for the first time in my life I really need medical care I get this 'to each according to his need' stuffed up my nose. Meanwhile, this guy who can't speak a word of English, committed a felony by entering the U.S. illegally, is probably a criminal selling drugs, never paid a dime in medical insurance or any other taxes gets first class treatment while a paying customer with his insurance card in hand, namely me, gets zip. That's not capitalism, I'll tell you that."

Winger's eyelids were starting to droop, but he managed a rasping chuckle. "Suck it up, Breckon. This is nothing compared to the grief I intend to dump on you."

Breckon fell silent. He could see how sleepy Winger was. He also noticed a roll of gauze and what looked like antiseptic on a cart in the corner. "Hey Winger, if you don't mind, I need to use the john. That okay? And, I'd like to wash my hands and face."

Winger was slouching lower in his chair. Only slightly opening his eyes he gave a slight twitch of his hand and said, "Yeah. Sure."

Breckon grabbed the gauze and antiseptic on the side away from Winger. There was a restroom adjoining the room they were in. After quickly doing his job he splashed cold water on his face and washed his hands with soap. He untied his shirt sleeve and removed the shirt. Then after gingerly removing the handkerchief, proceeded to wash the wound with soap. It stung unmercifully. The bullet had traveled under the skin for an inch and exited. There would be fragments of his shirt in the hole but he couldn't help that now. He dabbed on the antiseptic to renewed pain. Finally he wound the gauze around his arm with his good hand using his chin to help until it was used up. Tucking the end under the outer wrap, he put his shirt, such as it was, back on.

There was another door on the opposite side of the room. Obviously this restroom was shared by a treatment room on either side. He didn't know how far he'd get, but knew he'd never know if he didn't try. Cracking the door to the adjoining room he saw a doctor and an attendant working on a thigh wound on a young black man. He had heard that this hospital got a lot of knife and gunshot wounds from the local area.

As he entered, the doctor turned as if to say something. Breckon held up his hand and said. "Must have gotten the wrong door. Easy to get turned around in a place like this." By the time he finished talking he was out in the hall. The gurneys were gone. The triage station was the only place with any activity.

He walked to where a woman was doing reports on a computer. "Is there a pay phone for me to make a local call?"

The middle aged woman behind the counter looked at him with eyes that seemed abnormally wide awake for this hour. "What about the arm?"

"It's nothing. I'm to call the clinic in the morning."

She didn't look convinced. Finally she said, "There. Use that phone on the counter if you're not too long," she said nodding to her left.

Breckon punched in Darin Harris's number hoping he could get him to wake up. It rang four times and the recorder came on. All the time Breckon expected Winger to come bounding out of the room, blowing a whistle, yelling for backup, and doing all manner of police-like things.

After the beep Breckon started haranguing into the phone as loud as he could. "Wake up. It's Ed. I need you to come pick me up. Come on pick up the phone." As he continued he saw the woman looking at him with deepening furrows in her brow. "He's a heavy sleeper," Breckon said looking at her. He began badgering into the phone again.

Finally he heard a sleepy voice on the other end. "This had better be good."

"Great. I got you. It is." Cupping his hand around the mouth piece and turning his back to the woman he said in hushed tones. "As fast as you can I need you to come to the emergency entrance of North Memorial Hospital. Don't bother to come in. I'll be out on the street someplace. If you don't see me drive up and down the street. I'll find you. Got it?"

"Yeah. Guess so. North Memorial emergency entrance. Up and down the street."

"Good. Hurry." In a normal tone he added, "Gotta go." Breckon hung up, and thanked the woman behind the counter. He eyed the emergency entrance. So near and yet so far. Would his luck hold?

Koa Yaobang dozed in his comfortable chair. A knock on his door and he was instantly alert. "Enter."

"Sir. A message from Beijing," a staffer said presenting a sheet of paper to him.

Quickly scanning it he dismissed the messenger as his eyes narrowed. Curses. The Director of Security had personally gotten into the operation. He seemed to think that both Rongji and Breckon, especially Breckon could still be useful. The time, he thought looking at the ornate clock hanging on the wall, the time was too short. But, he had to try. The call to the assassin had to go through two cutouts. He made his call then sat back and took a deep breath. The time was too short.

— 30 —

Breckon didn't even glance at the room where Winger slept lest mental telepathy or even the movement of his eyeballs would arouse him. He stepped out into the covered space where the emergency vehicles stopped to disgorge their cargoes of hurting humanity and was met with humid seventy-five degree August air. Two unattended emergency trucks with their engines running was all he saw. Using the trucks to mask him from the emergency entrance, he hurried to the street. Looking both ways there wasn't a car in sight. "Hope it's not a Tex Avery street," he said under his breath. It should have been funny. Why did he feel such dread?

He loped across the street to the high-rise clinic building. Down the sidewalk to his left he came to the entrance of a parking lot with a magnetic card operated gate. Stepping into the shadows on the northwest side of the building he peered back at the entrance. No movement.

The assassin was irritated which in that particular business was dangerous. And, she knew it. Closing her eyes she tried to let it go. The probability of success in this assignment approached zero. Her handler had to know that. She let her intellect direct her will and willed the control of her emotions. Placid again. Profiling targets was something the Chinese did well, but this was a bit much. Breckon was supposed to get medical care for a minor wound, then escape the CIA agent holding him, leave by the emergency entrance, and wait nearby for someone to come for him.

Having entered the parking ramp at North Memorial Hospital in her rented SUV at two-thirty, she had driven to the top to check out the possibilities. Along the way she carefully noted the security cameras. It wasn't good, but workable. The range would be less than a hundred yards which made a short barreled silenced rifle suitable.

Waiting was something that was part of her training. Having joined the army part way through college she had adapted well. Being five seven and in good shape, she handled the training easily. It was her mental attitude as much as her physical aptitude that made it work. As opportunities opened for specialized training she signed up. The dearth of women in any of the special forces cadres made her acceptance almost automatic.

She trained with men, fought with men and, of course, was used by men the way men use women. Society was blind to this reality. Out-and-out rape was a crime anyplace. Consensual sexual intercourse outside of marriage was viewed as a national pastime. It was that huge number of cases in between the two extremes that was common in the military. It caused her to develop a burning hatred of men. Her present occupation suited her well. Every assignment she had received had been to kill a man. Perfect. The best part was nobody expected an assassin to be a pretty woman.

She had been expecting the V-22 when it came. The sound of the dual rotors was familiar from the times she had been in one on operations. Five minutes later she was in position. She was wearing loose fitting light green hospital scrubs. This was a useful stratagem that went beyond hospitals so she always had the garments at hand. They were accepted in small grocery stores, gas stations, and nearly anyplace, especially at night—someone getting off a late shift. Their looseness easily concealed weapons, as well as the outfit underneath. Peeling off the scrubs would reveal a tight sweater, short skirt, and with the addition of high heals, a completely different look.

If the profile were worth anything, she allowed him thirty minutes to get patched up and give the goons the slip. If he were any good, he could do it, something she had learned from experience. Her assignment to Minneapolis several days before had come with photos and video of the man walking. Alone, he'd be easy to spot. Her elevated vantage point sixty yards back from the street left the emergency entrance just out of sight to the right. If he came out of the building and turned to his right she would not see him. If he were escaping from someone, though, he'd cross the street immediately and go to his left to get distance between himself and those he wished to elude. Her easiest shot would be as he crossed the street. But, anyone seeing the body would call police and block her escape. A shadowy place on a sidewalk would have to do.

The top level of the ramp was deserted, but she swept it with her eyes every thirty seconds for security guards. Looking back in the direction of the emergency entrance she saw movement. The face was right, the walk was right. Very good, she mused. Twenty-five minutes from wheels down to escape. Very good indeed, you unluckiest of all men. He hurried across the street. Expected. On the sidewalk. Careful he doesn't get under those branches. Slowing, he turned, stepped in the shadows beside the building, and waited. Head shot it is. Though she didn't consciously think it, she let out a breath and held it, relaxed, aimed, started taking up the trigger slack, and . . . the vibration on her hip! Only one person knew the number of the new cell phone. Irritation again. Breaking her concentration on the shot, she grabbed the phone.

"Yes," she hissed.

"Have you seen the invoice?"

Yes."

"Have you paid it?"

"In two seconds!"

"Negative. Negative. The shipment has been canceled. Do not remit. Confirm."

"Confirmed. Shipment canceled. Do not remit."

"You will be compensated as usual."

The call ended. She looked through the scope. He was still there. You *luckiest* of all rotten males. No man deserved to be that lucky—two heart beats from having his brains splattered on the building. For an instant she thought of doing it anyway. No. Then she'd end up in the sights of an assassin herself.

She was still torn as she put the parts of the gun in the case. Why hadn't she lied and done it anyway. No one would have known. Would have been risky, though. He might have moved while she was distracted. Then what? She might have lost him.

Driving down the several levels of the parking ramp she thought of how it could be done. She lowered both windows. It had become an obsession with her by the time she paid the parking fee and drove out. As always she had the silenced 9 mm under the seat. She laid it on the seat beside her. To be called off when she was so close! Starting up the incline toward the street she realized her right hand held the gun not being conscious of how it had gotten there. Slowing nearly to a stop at the street she could see he was still there. All she had to do was drive into the street, stop, and shoot through the open window—less than ten yards. For a second there was a doubt, then once again discipline directed her intellect to hold rein on her will, and hence, her emotions. Her foot rammed down on the accelerator as the vehicle skidded left into the street. A hundred feet later she pulled her foot off the pedal. What was she doing? Driving on, being careful to observe all traffic laws, she was struck with how the whole sequence from slowing at the street to tromping the gas pedal had been out of her control. She now knew she had intended to kill him. Why hadn't she? Was this job starting to affect her mind?

As Breckon stepped in the shadow the mental gloom was so thick he could hardly think. More pain . . . divine providence . . . what did a non-existent yak herder in the Andes Mountains have to do with anything? What good could come from all that had happened to him, or what he had done or not done? His nemesis had to be stuck in the mountains yet, so why the feeling of what . . . terror?

One of the emergency vehicles left as Breckon watched. A small SUV came out of the parking ramp, slowed as it neared the street. The light fell on the face of the woman driver as she looked directly at him. He felt a chill in the warm muggy air. The engine roared and the squeal of melting synthetic rubber cut the air as the vehicle made a left on to the street.

Must get spooked by Tex Avery streets, too. His mood lightened as his mind, of a sudden, slipped into a revelry. Now it was funny. It had to do with the gag in the animated cartoons shown before the main feature in movie theaters. Tex Avery drew a series of cartoons for MGM in the forties and fifties. The gag, that appeared in a number of variations, had the cartoon character come to a highway and see only an empty road disappearing into infinity as he looked both ways. The instant he started to cross the road a huge truck would come out of nowhere and roar past leaving the hapless guy spread eagled like a bug on the grill. As kids he and his brother would cross railroad tracks to go fishing. They'd look both ways to see nothing but empty tracks. One or the other would mention he hoped it wasn't a Tex Avery railroad. They'd skitter across laughing. Every time it was the same. Every time they'd laugh. What had happened to that carefree world, those laughter gilded days? They seemed to have skipped behind the summer leaves of time, peeking out now and then, but always teasingly beyond his reach. The lifting of his spirits gave way to an ache in his stomach. Would he ever feel peace again?

He glanced at his watch. What was keeping his friend? Harris drove a dark blue four door sedan, a Taurus, or something like that. There was virtually no traffic so it should be easy to spot. Finally he saw a car that looked right stop at the traffic light at the end of the block to his right. It moved slowly down the street from the northwest. It had to be Harris. Breckon stepped out of the shadows and into the street as it approached. Harris had the driver's side window down. They recognized each other. Breckon opened the rear door and dove into the back seat pulling the door closed after him.

"Keep going like you drive this street every day and don't come back past here," Breckon said. "I'll explain after we're away from here." They wandered aimlessly through the streets for a few minutes until Harris was back on Highway 81 headed northwest. Breckon reached over and leaned the front passenger seat back as far as it would go and wiggled himself into it.

"Take 81 to 100 East to 694 then north on University Avenue."

"Where the heck are you expecting me to take you? Why University Avenue? You don't live out that way. And, why are you back so soon, and why the hospital other than that patch on your arm? Why the secrecy?"

"It's quite a story. We'll talk as we go if I can stay awake. The secrecy is because that maggot of a Mel Winger arrested me, and I escaped. He doesn't have anything, just wants to make me miserable. I went out to the mountains as planned with Greg Daley, the guy I told you about, the guy from the NSA. He was shot in the leg, and the other CIA guy, Burl, got hit bad. We were picked off the mountain by a V-22 Osprey and landed on the roof helipad of North Memorial. Those guys go first class. It'll be in the papers and on TV in the morning—quite a trip. We're going up to the Little Falls area to see some people that might already be dead. With any luck we'll get there in time." Ed continued to fill in Darin for the next twenty minutes. Ed decided to use Highway 25 that intersected Highway 10 north of Becker. They'd miss St. Cloud and Little Falls that way.

0340 hours, Camp Ripley, Minnesota

Lieutenant Crawley was thrashing his way through the underbrush when suddenly his arm became tangled in vines. The vines were fixed fast and shaking him. He reached over with his other hand to pull the vines off. Now the vines were calling his name as he desperately pulled to free himself. Finally awake, he was sitting on the edge of his bunk with the duty sergeant repeating his name.

"Lieutenant Crawley, wake up. There's an urgent call from Washington. We have a *red falcon* alert."

Dick Crawley had put in a twenty-hour day before he had fallen exhausted into his bunk in the post headquarters two hours before. He was in a battalion headquarters company that had no battalion, at least not one that was ever visibly assembled except for summer training. That's the difficulty of out-state reserve organizations. He was at Camp Ripley, located a few miles north of Little Falls, Minnesota, doing advanced planning for his battalion that would begin arriving in two days. The coordination needed to insure it went smoothly was a big job, especially since he was short handed. In addition to that, he had been picked as the post duty officer for the night, fulfilling once again the adage that everybody likes to dump on lieutenants. At least, he had thought, he'd get a few hours of uninterrupted sleep. Nothing would happen in this out of the way dump.

Crawly shuffled into the next room where Staff Sergeant Kenikey was taking in rapid-fire partial sentences on the phone. " . . . have two Cobras armed and fueled, and the crews on deck by 0430 hours. Yes, this is a *red falcon* alert. When those two depart have two more ready." He paused as he listened, flipping pages in a three-ring binder. "Here I'll read it to you then, '*red falcon* is called when an imminent terrorist threat occurs that is beyond the capability of local law enforcement.'" More pause. "I don't know. We have a gob of encrypted messages here. I have . . . . " Pause. "I'm reading out of the post SOP book. I've called the number in the book and a guy's coming in to decode. What . . . no missiles? Only chain gun . . . . I don't know, depends what we're after, I guess. Here's the duty officer. Talk to him."

Kenikey had his hand over the mouthpiece as he handed the phone to Crowley. "It's somebody at the airfield. I'd tell 'em we'll call back when we find out what's going on."

Ten minutes later they saw car lights a block away rounding a curve going too fast. It fishtailed as the driver recovered from the skid. Thirty seconds later a fiftyish man ran into the office panting. He flipped open a wallet and showed a moderately impressive ID to the two citizen soldiers. "I'm the post crypto specialist. This had better be right. Where's the traffic."

Kenikey handed five messages to the man. "I logged them in as they came off the printer over there," he said pointing to an unimpressive looking device that looked like a combination printer and outdated personal computer. "It wasn't until I got the phone call from the Pentagon that I realized they were important. At least I think the call came from the Pentagon. It's kind of late and I wasn't expecting this."

"That's a decoding machine," the specialist said gesturing to the device. "It's a little outdated. This means these messages are doubly encrypted. Give me a few minutes."

Crawley and Kenikey looked at each other as the man disappeared down the dimly lit hallway with a glossy linoleum floor. As he sat down in the desk chair Kenikey said, "I knew how long you had been on your feet so I thought I'd let you sleep. But, that Pentagon call shook me. Darned if I know what's happening. Never heard of a *red falcon*."

Crawley was looking for a cup, which he eventually found. He looked into it trying to make up his mind if he wanted to use it. Finally he poured a few drops of cold coffee on the floor, wiped it out with a paper towel, and filled the cup from the pot on the Mr. Coffee. "Guess I'm glad you woke me. Wouldn't have wanted to sleep through a *red falcon*," he said with as much sarcasm as he could muster.

In a matter of minutes the crypto guy was back. "Fletcher," he said holding out his hand to Crowley.

Crowley took the hand, "For a couple of weeks, Lieutenant Crowley," he said taking the hand. "Rest of the time I'm Dick Crowley." Next Sgt. Kenikey took the hand and introduced himself.

"Now that we have that out of the way we have work to do. First, what I say now is classified. It doesn't seem possible to do the proper formal stuff on security. You'll both be debriefed after this is over so watch what you say. You leak, you pay—a lot. That understood?"

Crowley and Kenikey both said yeah.

"Okay. It seems there are people vacationing at a farm east of here that are big time government employees. At least one guy is in the intelligence business. The brass out east is worried the intelligence dude will be killed, or worse captured, by a well funded terrorist group. The bad guys are headed for that farm loaded for bear. We are to use any and all resources of this base to stop them. Have you alerted and armed the Cobras? They specifically ask for Phoenix rockets."

"Yes sir," Sergeant Kenikey said. "They've been alerted. But, we only have two Cobras here. Another two will be coming in from St. Paul later. And, we have ammo for the chain guns, but only training rockets. You know, all go and no blow."

"What?"

"The rockets have inert warheads. Wouldn't kill a gopher . . . well, maybe a gopher."

"They said they wanted the rockets! Well, I'm headed to the airfield to brief the pilots."

When Fletcher left, Lt. Crowley sat down and ran his hand over his face. After a sip on his coffee he said, "I may not the sharpest tool in the shed, but Phoenix rockets are used to kill tanks. This could be an interesting morning."

0440 hours, Camp Ripley

The post commander, Col. Russell Hamstadt, had been in the post headquarters for a half hour working in the briefing room off his office. Having government supplied housing on post, he had arrived first. Sectional maps were taped together and laid out on the table.

"Marv," he said to his adjutant, the first of his staff to get in, "any luck finding where that farm is?"

Colonel Hamstadt, known as Colonel Hammer in a past life as a hard driving brigade commander, was near retirement. His assignment as post commander of Camp Ripley would be his last. He was always at his best when the situation was the most desperate. This minor emergency, as he saw it, was the stuff of life.

"No, sir. But, we're pretty close. I have someone on the Internet looking up the name. Should have a map showing the address pretty soon." With only the Maynard Klappenbach farm to go on, they had called the post office in Little Falls and nobody answered, of course. It was outside of business hours. Klappenbach's name was in the phone book, but there was no answer, only the answering machine.

"Okay. As soon as we have a map, have the duty officer drive out there and get the people out of the house. Be sure he's got a cell phone, and a government vehicle—got to look official."

"Yes, sir."

"How're we doing with the Cobras?"

"They said shortly after five."

0455 hours, Southeastern Morrison County, Minnesota

The first tinges of dawn were visible in the east as the huge eighteen-wheeler lurched to a stop on the deserted stretch of road. Minutes before they had verified their position as they passed Gotvald's Store at the crossroads known to the locals as Gotvald's Corner. Immediately the driver killed the lights. The hiss of the air brakes was in sharp contrast to the stillness of the pre-dawn. Over the panting of the idling diesel the frogs resumed their rhythmic croaking in the slough beside the road. Silently three men alighted from the truck, and instantly set about removing the tie downs on the tarp over the load. With that done, two of them climbed up on the trailer bed behind the truck cab and pulled the tarp toward them until it lay in a heap. There it was tied down. The third man was already in the cab of the large mobile home with the engine running.

Hydraulic cylinders unfolded the ramp off the back of the drop-bottom trailer as the other two men removed tie downs from the motor home. Less than ten minutes after the truck stopped, the two vehicles parted. The mobile home headed north with two men in it, and the semi-truck continued south. The truck driver would circle around to the planned rendezvous point.

The two men in the mobile home, one Arabic, one Hispanic, had little in common, though one of them thought they did. They were known to each other only by Ahmad and Cortez, Tez for short. Tez had been converted to Islam while serving time in prison. He thought Ahmad and he were working for the greater glory of Allah, while in fact both were in the employ of the atheistic communists that ran China.

Ahmad was another case entirely. He cared nothing about Moslems or communists. Having grown up in the unrest of the Middle East he had been recruited in his early teens and trained as a terrorist. He grew to manhood killing American soldiers and groups of civilians in Iraq. As his abilities to lead operations became apparent, he was given greater and greater leeway in conducting them. He had gotten good, too good. His handlers saw a disturbing trait develop. As his proficiency at planning operations expanded his plans became ever more involved. His favorite scheme was to pick an area where there would be a lot of people. He'd set off two small explosives separated by ten to fifteen meters. A few seconds later a large explosive would detonate between the two. His stratagem was well enough known so when the small charges went off the people between them knew what was coming. As happens with people who kill other human beings as a routine matter, he developed an addiction to seeing the horror on his victims' faces when they became aware that they were about to die.

Not wanting to lose Ahmad's leadership abilities, his superiors gave him a "promotion." He was sent to the U.S. to develop and lead terrorist cells. If it ever came to actually carrying out one of the plans, he would be shunted to the side for the implementation of the operation. His old habits could not get in the way on his present assignment because he would not likely see any of his victims, to say nothing of setting them up to know they were about to die.

Both men had trained, like others, on virtual reality headsets using computers to generate a variety of conditions they might encounter. Training in driving the large vehicle was the one area where they had actual hands-on experience. Both men could handle either the job of driver or weapons control, but each was in the position of his greatest proficiency.

Ahmad was the commander of the operation and handled the weapons. Tez was driving. Each compartment of the vehicle was equipped with a speaker and a microphone so they could communicate with one another without worrying about a cord and headset. The vehicle was equipped with a Magellan GPS system that guided the driver.

— 31 —

Lieutenant Crowley had the map, actually several taped together MapQuest squares, in his hand. He was headed to the main gate of the post in a HMMWV (Humvee) borrowed from the MPs. This was nuts.

———

Ten minutes later Capt. John Miller advanced the throttle and the collective simultaneously and the rotorcraft that had been built nine years before his birth rose into the air. "Raptor Roost, Raptor 1 is airborne."

Moments later Raptor 2 was airborne as well. Miller's Cobra helicopter had last seen combat more than a quarter century before. Here's a war machine relegated to training duties for decades, he thought. Now at last it could be on its way to act in anger again. As for himself, combat was more recent. Duty in Afghanistan presented its moments of danger. But the enemy there, though motivated, was not well armed. From the briefing, he knew what lay ahead could be an unpredictable contest.

As they headed east, the sky was magnificent with the hint of red at the horizon, fading into light blue, dark blue, and then into black. As they passed over the Mississippi River Miller flipped the switch to the intercom that connected him to his weapons officer, "We'll find a hill for you to clear your gun. Try to make 'em sink in. We don't want ricochets because sure as heck they'll land in a cow." A surge went through him. You cleared your guns to be sure that when you met the enemy they'd work. But this wasn't a pile of rocks a half a world away, this was home. Those were fields of corn and hay down there. This was America. What was happening!

The pilot of Raptor 2 had positioned his craft to the left of Raptor 1. Though both pilots were from the Twin Cities, they first met in Afghanistan a couple of years ago. Since their return to the states, they had seen a lot of each other through their reserve obligations.

It was getting light enough to make out objects as they crossed the Platte River. Miller keyed his radio, "Raptor 2, we're on location. Begin your pattern." According to plan, Raptor 1 would work the roads to the south and east, while Raptor 2 worked north and west.

Miller switched to the intercom. "Lets find the farm, and be sure we're not too late."

"Roger. Ah . . . there's Big Mink Creek, bring it right. There's the road, now left. Follow the dirt road. Now coming up, there, to the south of the road. That has to be it."

The Cobra circled the farm once and all looked peaceful. A few toys were on the grass near the front door of the house. A tractor and hay bailer were parked near the barn. A pickup truck sat partially hidden by a tree.

Miller wondered if the family on the farm below had been awakened as he pounded overhead at four-hundred feet. The helicopter would wake them up if nothing else, he thought. Perhaps someone had called and alerted them and they were already up.

He followed the gravel road north to Highway 46. With roads of one quality or other on nearly all the section lines, there was a lot of checking to do. As the light became better they could go higher and make shorter work of it. The head phone crackled, "Raptor Flight, this is Raptor Roost. We received a report from the Minnesota Highway Patrol. It's kind of old, thirty-five minutes, but a flat bed truck hauling what could be one of your targets was spotted heading north on Highway 169. Raptor 1, take a sweep east and south of Pierz.

"Roger, Raptor Roost. Out."

———————————

Darin Harris reached over and shook Breckon who had been dead out of it for the last hour. "Ed, we're almost at Pierz. I need directions. Come on. Wake up."

Ed rubbed his eyes, and brought the seat back up to the normal position. He shifted around going through his pockets as he said, "I hope this isn't all for nothing . . . got a feeling about it, though. If I'm totally over reacting maybe we'll get a good ol' country breakfast out of it." Finally, he had the crumpled up camping receipt from Glendive, Montana, in his hand. Reaching up he switched on the dome light. "Okay, here it is. Go through Pierz a couple miles and turn left. The roads should be on section lines so watch the mileage."

Darin made the left turn and Ed had him slow down a mile later. When he saw the outline of farm buildings in the early dawn on the left he had Darin stop. "Go to the next road going north, should be less than a quarter mile, and take a right. Find a place to wait where you're out of sight. If this gets ugly, like it might, I don't want you, and our ride out of here, getting shot up."

"You're taking this pretty seriously, aren't you?"

"Yeah, I'm taking it seriously. It sure was serious up on the mountain. I may take off running toward you so watch for me. Now go."

Breckon jogged in the driveway and immediately saw lights in the barn. Well, it made sense. If it were a dairy farm, it would be milking time. He continued his easy trot and arrived at the barn a minute later. Walking in he heard the sound of a milking machine, though he didn't know what he was hearing. He saw a well built man stand up between two black and white cows. As Breckon approached his motion caught the man's eye. There was enough light for Breckon to make out the expression of surprise on his face. It was uncommon to have a stranger walk into his barn at this hour.

Breckon had forgotten the name of Daley's father-in-law so he had to do the best he could. "I'm sorry, but I have forgotten your name, sir. My name wouldn't mean anything to you, but I believe you son-in-law's name is Greg Daley who works for the NSA. That right?"

The man stepped over the gutter on to the concrete aisle between the back sides of two rows of cows. "Yes," he said slowly. "Who are you, and why are you here at this hour?"

"Please, I hope you will believe me when I say you and your family may be in great danger."

The man took off his cap that had a cob of corn with Dekalb on it and scratched his head. "Hold on a minute. What's this all about? Does it have anything to do with that helicopter that circled the house a few minutes ago? Was low enough that I could of hit it with a broom."

"Yeah, probably is. You mean nobody's called to warn you to get out of the house?"

"Dag nab it! We were having family time last night. With all the telemarketing calls we turned off the phones. If anybody called, it went to the recorder in my office."

"We have to get the people out of the house immediately and to a place of safety. If there's no safe place, head out into a corn field or something. You can call me a fool if it turns out to be a false alarm. But, let's not wait to find out."

Having traveled on paved roads, they were within a few miles of their target. "Approaching intersection with gravel road in one quarter mile. No stop signs," intoned the Magellan speaker.

"No, wait," Tez said aloud. "That thing isn't right. Here's the dirt road." He stopped, backed up a little, and turned left off the pavement.

Ahmad was checking all the defensive systems. On command the mini-gun rose above the roof and aimed as directed by the targeting system. The six-barrel gun was a modification of the standard GAU-2B/A 7.62 mm gun. A direct descendent of the Civil War era Gatling Gun, it fired between six-hundred and six-thousand rounds per minute. The rate of fire was simply a mechanical process that depended on how fast the six barrels rotated. He resisted the temptation to fire a test burst. The self-test circuitry for the gun and all missiles showed no faults. Using the electronic periscope he panned completely around using the infrared optics as the training had instructed him. When he was not controlling it, the periscope continued to rotate while a computer program compared images from one rotation to the next to detect anything new. That was a programming feat of some consequence for a moving vehicle.

Proceeding slowly Tez did not like what he saw. "Ahmad," he said, "the road ahead looks muddy. I'm going to back up, go a section to the north, and try there. Looks like they had heavy rains."

"Should be okay, but watch the time. We don't have any to lose."

Ahmad was alerted by a beep that something was new in the periscope images. He stopped the rotation at the image of the change. "Tez, we got company. Helicopter off to the south." Switching to visual optics, and five-power magnification, he continued. "Bad news, it's a Cobra, probably from that Camp Ripley to the west. Locking on laser illumination, might need it."

A minute later the weapons officer on Raptor 1 saw it. "There, on the road to the left, slowing down for that intersection. No, wait. That's a long driveway. I doubt that's our target."

"Yeah I see it," Miller replied. "That's one grand looking mobile home. What if it's a retired couple arriving early to visit relatives? Let's try this. Once it's off the road we'll tear up the driveway in front of it so he has to stop. If he tries to back up we'll tear it up behind him too. That way if it is the bad guys there's no harm they can do, and if it's normal folks they'll be out of our hair."

As he swung around for a pass perpendicular to the road he called in, "Raptor Roost, this is Raptor 1, found target one mile north of Pierz. Will damage road to stop. Out."

The Cobra's three barrel 20 mm chain gun spit 'em out at two-thousand rounds a minute. The road exploded a hundred yards in front of the vehicle.

"Ahmad, he's interested in us, making a run at us from the south."

"I see 'em. Don't over react. Keep going. He won't shoot without provocation."

Tez heard it first then looking ahead it was just light enough to see clods of dirt being thrown in the air. The realization came to him that they were making the road impassible. "Ahmad, he tore up the road in front of me. I'll have to back up to the intersection. Get him before he does the same thing behind us."

As the Cobra pulled up and turned to the east, both occupants saw the puff of smoke from the top of the vehicle. Miller keyed the radio, "Raptor Roost, vehicle has launched missile . . . " and the transmission ended.

"Raptor 1, this is Raptor Roost, lost your transmission. Come in."

No response.

"Raptor 2, did you hear that?"

"Roger, Roost."

"Two, this is Roost, get over there and investigate. Be careful. You heard One's last transmission."

"Roger. We're seven miles away and saw a fireball and smoke. Will proceed cautiously. Out."

"You saw it," Ahmad said, "Now we've stirred up a hornet's nest."

"Yeah, but they'll keep their distance. If you see another one get it at long range so they stay way back."

"Don't worry. I had the same training you did. Oh, and there he is, range six miles. Got a good laser lock. Here she goes." A thump shook the vehicle a second time as a missile shot up. Small thrusters rotated it to the optimal angle where a signal ignited its rocket engine twenty feet above the roof. It sped to the source of the reflected infrared laser pulses.

"Roost, this is 2. Rocket plume at six miles and closing fast. Flares and chaff away. Taking evasive maneuver . . . . Whap . . . got our tail rotor . . . into auto-rotation . . . fastest rocket I've ever seen . . . flares, chaff no effect . . . here's the ground . . . . "

As Breckon and Mr. Klappenbach left the barn they heard the beat of helicopter blades off to the northwest. They both instinctively looked that way in time to see the light of the chain gun being fired. As they were about to continue to the house the dawn sky was lit by a large ball of fire.

"That," said Breckon, "is the explosion of a U.S. Army helicopter and the certain death of two pilots. Let's move!"

They were both sprinting as they reached the house. In seconds everyone was up, babies cried, and bare feet raced across the dew soaked grass. "The storm shelter," shouted Klappenbach."

In days of yore, most farms had a below grade storage pit, called a root cellar where potatoes, pumpkins, squash, and similar vegetables were stored in the fall. It extended from a foot above ground level to below the frost line so if the produce was properly covered the heat from the earth would keep it from freezing. With the advent of modern food processing, those farms that still had a root cellar, kept it intact as a tornado shelter.

Klappenbach heaved back the oak cover that laid at a slight angle from the elevated center of the cellar to grade. With a flashlight to guide them they carefully made their way down the dirty concrete steps to the underground cavity. A look around with the light revealed a few frogs hopping around erratically, and a salamander clumsily making its way to shelter behind a small pile of cement blocks. There were squeals from the girls and "cool" from the boys. With everybody safely inside, Klappenbach said, "Gotta go to the barn for a few seconds," and started off with his head low as he ran to the open door. The sound of the milking machine motor stopped and the lights went out. He was looking after his cows and equipment.

Moments later he was back. The cover to the cellar was not hinged so it was left partially slid to the side of the entrance as Breckon and Klappenbach had only their heads sticking out.

In a hushed tone Breckon said, "If it's going to happen, it won't be long. I'd guess the helicopter was here in response to the call your son-in-law made from the top of a mountain in Montana. Seems his concern was well founded."

"Mind telling me what's going on?" Klappenbach blustered.

"It's a bit of a story. We had a shoot out on the top of a mountain. Greg was hit in the leg—he'll be fine," Breckon hastened to add. "He called in a rescue plane and we arrived at North Memorial Hospital in the cities a couple of hours ago. On the mountain he found out that a hit squad had been dispatched to kill him, thinking he was here on your farm. It looks like the helicopter was sent out to stop the bad guys. We both saw it failed. Now, they'll be coming here."

Ann Daley was now beside them having overheard most of what was said. "Where is Greg, and who are you? Why isn't he here?"

"He'll be here as soon as he can. Last I saw him he was in the emergency room at North Memorial—has a flesh wound, nothing to worry about . . . hush! I hear tires on the gravel. Get back down inside. Here, let's slide the cover fully in place."

The vehicle that came past the farm was one of the neighbors leaving the area for his job in Little Falls.

In the cellar they continued to wait. It was dank and musty. With only sleepwear and a couple of blankets, it was cool. Already there were complaints of how foolish this seemed.

The headquarters staff trickled in and now was all present. The airfield tower's radio was connected to a speakerphone in the room to keep them abreast of the situation.

In a second Colonel Hamstadt snapped a button on the phone to talk to the tower, "Keep the two Cobras coming from St. Paul out of harm's way, low and behind the horizon. Bring them in here because we don't know the range of those missiles. Got that?"

"Yes, sir," was the immediate reply.

Quickly he eyed the men around the table. "Rudy," Hamstadt said looking at his S3 operations officer wearing Lieutenant Colonel insignia, do we have any M1s awake?"

"Should have a platoon on deck to start gunnery at sunrise on the east range, sir."

"Get 'em armed and to the front gate as fast as they can go. Break all the rules, we'll pick up the pieces later. This has turned deadly."

"They've drawn ammunition by now sir, but it's training ammo. The ammo for the fifty-cal on the top of the turret and for the 7.62 coax is real."

Hamstadt thought for a second and said, "Getting them back to a bunker to exchange training ammo for real ammo, even finding someone to open the real ammo bunker . . . . No. Take too long. We'll send them with the ammo they have. Isn't it the way of things. Every modern war is a come-as-you-are war."

Mark Willis was the S2 intelligence officer. "Mark, get a set of maps the same as these four for each tank," he said pointing to the ones he meant lying on the table. "And, find a bullhorn for each tank commander in case they encounter civilians. Then get the stuff to the front gate to meet the tanks. "We'll radio the GPS coordinates to them.

"Marv," he said to his adjutant, "call the State Highway Patrol and get some cars here. Those tanks will have to go down Highway 10 for at least a ways. They'll need an escort. Oh, and call the Little Falls Police Department. If civilians call in, as they will, they must be told there is an emergency and they are to stay indoors. Call the local radio station too. We gotta keep the civilians out of the way."

"Yes, sir. What about the duty officer on the way out there?"

"Too much going on—forgot about him! If he isn't there yet, have him come back. We have to get the heavy stuff out there fast."

— 32 —

Lt. Tony Roston continued to count off the days like each was a day of torture with bamboo slivers being driven under his fingernails. It was finally Thursday of the second week. He had today and tomorrow left, and then on Saturday he'd turn in his gear and be on his way. Having a platoon of tanks could be thought of as a real buzz for a lot of people, but it wasn't for him. That's not true, he thought. He did rather like it. It was Captain Hendric Case that ruined it. What a "case" of the miseries.

Well, here he was at the front of the line of his four tanks at one of the ammunition bunkers at Camp Ripley. It was getting light enough to see indistinct shapes as his platoon was loading 120 mm training rounds for their final gunnery test. Glancing at his wristwatch he saw five-thirty-two. Look at that. Official sunrise isn't until six-twenty. They'd have over a half-hour to wait. The army'd never change, and neither would Case. In the event an ice age happened to come along, you had to be up early enough to account for it, and still get to the range on time.

The gunnery ranges were running behind schedule so the only way to get all the tank crews through the gunnery test was to use all the daylight available. They could see and shoot at night with the night vision capability they had, but to keep things fair all crews fired for the test during daylight.

His gunner was standing on the hull of the tank taking shells from a uniformed man on the ground. It wasn't light enough to make out his rank. The gunner in turn handed them to the loader who was standing inside his open hatch. The loader, whose job it was to load shells into the 120 mm smooth bore cannon during firing operations, stowed the shells in the ready rack in the back of the turret. He carefully slid each of the forty-one pound shells into a storage tube, and insured it latched into place.

In the M1 Abrams tank the ammunition was carried in a magazine outside the armored crew compartment of the turret. During operations the loader sat on the left side of the turret facing the right side. When he was called upon to load a round he pressed a large lever with his right knee. This caused the blast door separating the magazine from the crew compartment of the turret to slide to the side revealing the butt ends of the shells.

"Lieutenant Anthony Roston?" the civilian government employee said in something less than a yell as he held up the clipboard. Roston was standing on the hull of the tank in front of the turret beside the main gun.

"Here," he said as he stooped down and took the repository of bureaucratic accountability from the offering hand. He leaned over the edge of the turret and shouted, "Dillon, you got fourteen?"

Dillon Scranton, the loader, was very conscientious and Roston was very happy he was very conscientious. "Number fourteen coming in," he yelled back. Losing rounds, even training rounds like these, was almost as bad as losing one of your men. Roston scribbled his signature on the property transfer form and handed the clipboard back to the sergeant.

"Bring 'em all back," the man said. "Whole or part."

Roston nodded. This meant that after the firing they would return to the bunker and have either whole unexpended rounds or the afcaps or "ashtrays," as they were called, that added up to the total of the shells Roston had signed for. The 120 mm ammunition burned the entire shell casing except for the butt end, a metal slug four and three-quarters inches in diameter and an inch or so high that looked something like an ashtray.

Roston crawled up on the turret, knelt by the tank commander's hatch, and looked down into the turret. With his face below the rim he said in a more reasonable tone, "We all squared away?" Besides Dillon, the gunner Hank Glossen, and the driver, Jim Cushing, made up the crew. Hank nodded "Yep." So Roston hung his legs into the hatch and lowered his slight five foot ten inch frame on to his seat. This is where he stood when his turret hatch was open. He plugged his intercom lead into the jack and said, "How's she look?"

In the practiced order the crew responded. "Targeting systems up," from Glossen, "for now." "Ammo's secure," from Dillon. In his turn Cushing responded, "engine's good except for the same fault that's been there since we drew this pile of junk."

The servo problem turned out to be intermittent. When it failed, it was only for a few seconds and then came back to normal. It might seem like a minor malfunction, but they wanted the best chance of getting good scores on gunnery without having to deal with equipment malfunctions. And, the computer still thought there was something wrong with the automatic fire extinguisher system in the engine compartment.

After the report from his crew Roston switched on the platoon radio frequency and asked if they were all loaded and secured. They reported they were and he gave the order to move out. Now that they had live ammo aboard safety became an obsession. The blast door covering the magazine was closed and there was no round in the main gun. The ammo for the fifty-caliber machine gun on the top of the turret was in the ammo box attached to it, and the same was true for the 7.62 mm coax machine gun inside. The latter was set in the front part of the turret and was aimed parallel to the main gun.

Setting off on the tank trail Roston pressed the intercom button. "Jim, watch that you don't bend a blade of grass." It was a sarcastic remark but the driver knew its meaning. The post rules about protecting the environment were crazy enough. Captain Case was a fanatic. They all wondered what would happen if they actually got into a fighting situation one day. Would Case be able to make the switch and actually crush a weed in order to save his life? There were differences of opinion.

It was several miles to the gunnery range and they ambled along at thirty-five miles an hour. The drivers were still using night vision since it was nearly dark among the tall stands of trees. Roston welcomed the cool morning air on his face. This is what he liked. It had rained heavily the day before, but the morning was clear and cool. The smell of the rain washed vegetation was invigorating.

The machine moved quietly with the turbine engine, and at over twenty miles an hour there was almost no sound from the tracks. Tracked vehicles put a lot of surface area on the ground. This averaged out the bumps so the ride was surprisingly smooth. He floated through the air with a feeling of absolute authority. There were few things on a modern battlefield that an M1 feared, to say nothing of this small training base. He was king!

Of necessity Roston had the company frequency on when he wasn't talking to his platoon. Capt. Case would be on the line any minute to make certain he was ahead of schedule. As a result, it was no surprise, when his earphone snapped and a voice came on. It was a surprise that it wasn't Case's voice.

"Charlie Blue Leader, this is Wild Wind 3. Over." Roston's platoon was Blue platoon of Charlie Company, First Battalion, 94th Armor. Since there was only one battalion on the base at the present, the battalion number wasn't used. Wild Wind 3 was the base operations officer.

"This is Charlie Blue Leader. Over."

"Blue, has your platoon drawn munitions? Over."

Roston wondered why the base operations officer was getting into Capt. Case's act. "Roger, Wild Wind 3. Now nearing east gunnery range. Over."

"Blue, listen carefully to what follows. An extreme emergency has arisen. This is not a drill. You and your platoon are to drive immediately to the post main gate for instructions. You are authorized, and ordered to brake all speed regulations. Damage to terrain and property is authorized. Is that clear? Over."

Roston paused a few seconds and then pressed the radio key, "Wild Wind 3, this is Charlie Blue. No sir, not really."

"Charlie Blue, get your butts to the main gate as fast as those tanks will go! If you have to run over a car or a truck, do it. Just don't kill anybody. Is that clear? Move it!"

The tone in the voice said more than the words. There was something about it that was a little terrifying. "Yes sir. Main gate in less than ten minutes. Out." As Roston was about to switch to his platoon frequency he heard another transmission. He waited on the company net for a few seconds.

"Wild Wind 3, this is Charlie Leader. Request permission to lead Charlie Blue. Over."

"Charlie leader, request denied. Stay off this frequency. Out."

This was too good! Whatever lay ahead, didn't matter. This was a gold star day. Case got it stuck to him. With a flip, Roston was on his platoon frequency.

"Charlie Blue this is Blue Leader, listen up. There is an emergency. This is not a drill. We are ordered to go to the post main gate as fast as these things will go. Wreck or destroy anything in the way. Don't kill anyone. Don't go nuts and lose a track! We need these tanks in working order. NO RACING! Now, close all hatches and follow me. Out."

A tank can easily clip off a tree six or more inches in diameter, especially going as fast as they intended to go. The danger was when the bottom of the tree was snapped off so quickly the top didn't have time to move and fell straight down. If it fell into an open hatch, it produced unpleasant results.

Roston switched to his intercom. "Jim," he said to his driver, "let's go. See if you can teach those young jockeys a thing or two." Jim Cushing, at twenty-three, was the oldest and most experienced of the drivers. He had seen duty in the Middle East and had pushed an M1 to the limits before.

Putting the pedal to the metal was the one thing young tank drivers wanted to do more than anything, and the one thing they were most admonished not to do. Something to the effect of "God is good" came into the mind of each of the three youngest drivers. They hoped that "old man" Cushing didn't spoil it for them.

Simultaneously four tanks wheeled around. Fifteen-hundred horses in the back of each machine were pushed to the limit.

"Jim," Roston said, "you know this place as well as anyone. Use your judgment as to route." The reservation was crisscrossed with tank trails, and Cushing intended to take shortcuts between trails. After a few miles he was gratified when Roston came on the intercom. "Looks like we're opening up the space with the hotshots behind us."

It was one thing to push the tank fast across a smooth flat ground in full daylight. But, quite another to exceed forty-five miles per hour in the half light of dawn while crashing through brush on Cushing's improvised road.

Roston had Cushing slow to thirty to let the others catch up. The intercom permits the whole tank crew to hear what the tank commander says and hears on his radios. This made it possible for Roston to talk to the other tank drivers directly, though he addressed the transmission to the tank commanders. "Blue 2, 3, and 4, there are things these machines won't do, but things they will do, too. Stay with us. Jim will lead you through. Watch the brake lights." With that, Cushing pushed it again. Five minutes later, there were amazed drivers following Blue Leader as they approached the garrison area. If truth be told, some shirts were soaked with sweat.

They had to reduce speed. Crossing the airfield would give them a clear open space, but getting to it would be hard. Cushing opted for going east along the north side of the field. He was headed to the Range Control Building. As he remembered, he could cut across to the south of it and then cross the parking lot. From there, he'd have a straight shot south on the wide four-lane road to the gate. If there was too much traffic on the road he could charge down the parade ground adjoining it on the west side.

He was now on a regular road and meeting wheeled vehicles. The few HMMWVs he met hit the side at the first sight of him. The drivers of those vehicles knew a "no-contest" when they saw it. They may have been pissed but decided to live. He wheeled off the road and up a slight bank to make for the parking lot. Oh, no. The lot was half full. Most of the POVs (Personally Owned Vehicles) were bunched near the door. But, there were always those few who thought they needed extra steps of exercise or didn't want door dings. He did his best to avoid the clump. Sorry guys for the scratches, crunch, crunch. He squashed one entirely and sent two others spinning across the crushed rock. By the time the other three tanks made the transverse it was a mess.

Now headed for the home stretch he poured it to the M1. It was over a mile. Good enough space to show any onlookers how fast these babies could go. It was flat and smooth.

An MP at the first intersection inside the main gate madly waved his arms. As he did so, he moved sideways. He was not at all sure those tanks running with throttles wide open would stop where he was, and didn't want to become a wet spot on the ground. But, they did stop, one behind the other, with foliage and mud hanging from the fenders and elsewhere.

Hatches popped open as the platoon frequency came alive. "Charlie, Blue, this is Wild Wind Leader." All the crews knew this was the base commander. "I will break into your net as needed because there is no time to brief your tank commanders in a normal way. There is a terrorist threat in the form of one or more mobile homes or large cube shaped delivery trucks. Their goal is to kill a VIP who is staying at a farm about eight miles east of the post. We have identified one large mobile home as a certain threat. It destroyed two Cobra helicopters with missiles without taking a single hit to itself. It killed one Cobra at six miles so we cannot provide stand-off recon for you in the time available. We are also told these vehicles carry in addition to these laser guided missiles, a mini-gun that can pop out of the roof on a three-sixty turret.

"Your mission is to find them and kill them before they get to their target."

As Roston was listening to the transmission from Wild Wind Leader, he was getting madder by the second. At first, he didn't know why, then it hit him. As soon as the message from the base commander ended Roston was on the radio. "Wild Wind Leader, this is Charlie Blue Leader. I realize you thought it important to brief my crews personally. You have done that. From now on, you will not, ever, use my platoon net. That is for my platoon and me. There is a chain of command and such a thing as unity of command! If you do not agree to this I will get out of this tank and walk away, period! You can court martial me, shoot me, or whatever you want, but I will not lead this mission, is that clear! You will reply on this frequency so my platoon hears your answer. Over."

The pause that ensued seemed to last forever. The men in the tanks were stunned. It was like a small child chewing out his grandfather. Yet, they had all heard of unity of command as one of the principles of war at one time or another in their training. Finally, they heard the click of a transmitter being keyed.

After a pause a somewhat mechanical voice, but clearly that of the base commander said, "Charlie Blue Leader, this is Wild Wind Leader, agreed. Meet me on the company frequency. Out."

Oh boy, Roston thought. That was really dumb. That's it for me. Call me Mr. Tactful. He switched to the company frequency wondering if he should be the one to initiate the call.

The click came immediately. "Charlie Blue, this is Wild Wind Leader. The base S2 is meeting you with maps and other materials. It is not your battalion S2. Your battalion command is now being alerted. We thought the Cobras could handle the situation. Now the time line is desperately short. Until your normal chain of command is operational and briefed, you will take orders from me. Understood? Over."

"Roger, understood, Wild Wind Leader. Over."

"You will move out as soon as you have the materials. The farm, code named Home Base, is marked on the maps, and you will be radioed its GPS coordinates momentarily. You will have to stay to the roads mostly because the area you are going into is not good tank country. There are a lot of swamps and rivers. And, speed is essential. Over."

"Roger, Wild Wind Leader, understood. Out." In the radio briefing, the colonel was revved up and forceful, like this was his mission. Now the tone was reserved, even transformed, like a man who had grown old in seconds. Roston could feel an ache inside for the man, but his crews came first. The surest way to get people killed in combat was to have conflicting orders.

The S2 arrived with the maps and bullhorns. Roston found that the four Geological Survey charts had been taped together so a continuous map from Camp Ripley to Home Base could be seen.

"Okay Jim, move out," Roston said on the intercom. "Out the main gate take a left and then bear right. After a short distance south on Highway 10 take 47 east."

After this he went on the platoon frequency. "Charlie Blue, follow me. We head east on Highway 47 to the second intersection, and then south three miles to 46." Switching to the post frequency he said, "Wild Wind, this is Charlie Blue Leader. Is there any more intel on the enemy position. Over?"

"Charlie Blue, the one that shot down the Cobras was a mile or two north of Pierz. It appeared he was having trouble on a muddy road. We hope this has slowed him down. That's all we have. Out."

They had turned east on county road 46 and Roston was thinking about how to deploy his tanks when his driver called in the intercom, "Humvee headed our way." The company radio clicked. "Charlie Blue, local law enforcement in Little Falls reports a large straight job truck was seen leaving Little Falls going east on Highway 27. It's leaving town now. Over."

"Wild Wind, this is Blue Leader, will intercept. Question: what's a Humvee doing out here headed toward us? Over."

"That's from the post. He was sent to warn the people at Home Base, but was called back after the Cobras went down. Over."

"Roger, Wild Wind. Out."

———————————

"Okay. First I get dumped out of bed in the middle of the night. Then off to nowhere in cow country still in the middle of the night. Don't even know where I am. Only drove one of these outsized pieces of carp once before. Still can't find all the buttons." Lieutenant Crawly talked to himself to stay calm. "Now, don't bother. Come back to the post. I'm starting to get real irritated!" At first he didn't realize what he was seeing. Maybe a truck stopped on the road? Didn't look right. Sure seems to be getting bigger awfully fast. Oh no! He wrenched the wheel and was in the ditch which happened to be the edge of a swamp. "Tanks pounding down the road! This is crazy!"

———————————

"Blue 2, this is Blue 1. When we cross north-south Highway 45 head south to 27. Intercept a large straight truck that fits the profile. Over."

"This is Blue 2. I'm *all* over it."

"Blue 2 this is Blue 1, use correct radio procedure. Out."

"Blue 1, this is Blue 2. Wilco your last two orders. Out."

Roston switched to the intercom. "Everybody hates a wise-ass."

He knew he'd have to split up his remaining tanks if he were to cover enough territory. On to his platoon frequency again he said. "Blue 3, patrol Highway 46 between north-south Highway 45 and where 27 jogs north. See if you can find where the Cobra went down. Near there was where the target was last seen. Blue 4, patrol the same area between east-west Highways 43 and 27. I'll make best time to Home Base and patrol nearby. Out."

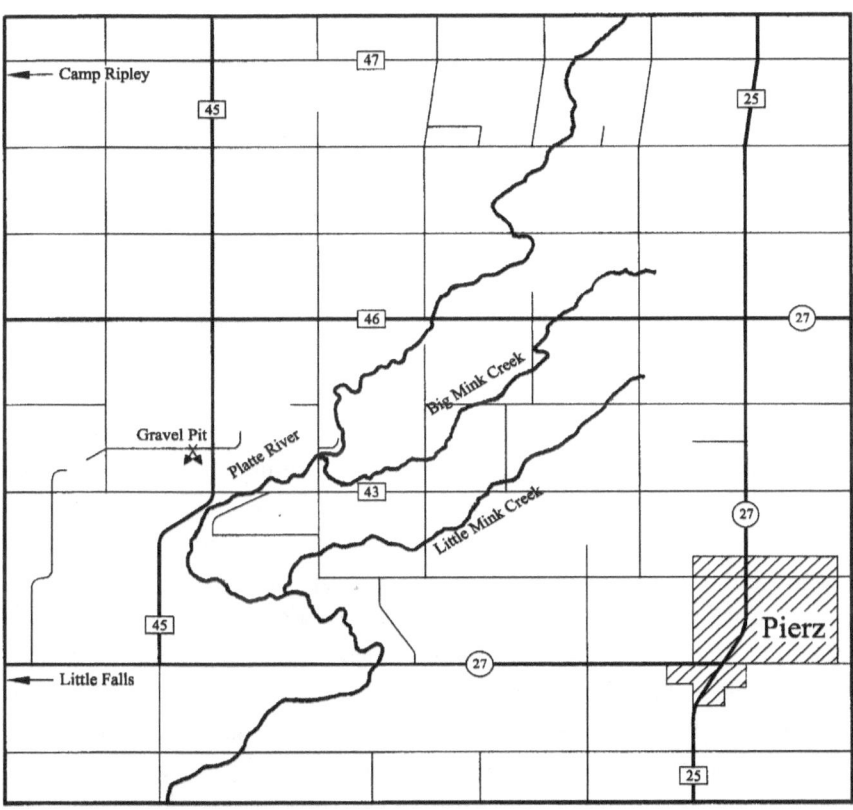

— 33 —

Jerome Haser was headed east out of Little Falls. For a summer job, this wasn't bad. He drove the All Makes Auto Parts truck out of Minneapolis to deliver parts to out-state communities. He left yesterday for the north run and got as far as Little Falls. He stayed in a motel, at company expense. Normally this wasn't permitted, but it helped that his uncle worked for the company. He used his forays out of town to scout hunting places, especially for duck hunting.

Today he wanted to check out the Platte River for hunting. Seven or eight miles east of Little Falls he'd cross it. Then he'd head north on Highway 25 until he crossed the river again. Along the way, he'd also examine smaller rivers for the same purpose. The sun was not up yet, but it was light. He had plenty of time to get to Brainerd so he was going slow not wanting to miss any prospective places.

Driving along at forty-five he was paying more attention to what was along the side of the road than the road ahead. Glancing ahead it was the smudge against the sky that caught his attention first. A quarter mile away the cause of the discoloration came out of a depression in the road and was silhouetted against the morning sky. Strange, it seemed to have the outline of a tank. A second later he realized it was not in the opposite traffic lane, but headed right at him, fast. In panic he stabbed on the brakes and the tires squealed the truck to a stop.

He wasn't headed directly at the soon to rise sun, so he could see enough of the vehicle to satisfy himself that it was indeed a tank. What a jerk driver, he though. Haser had come to a stop diagonally on the road. Before he could do anything he saw the front of the tank dip on its shock absorbers as the threatening mass of metal slowed rapidly to a crawl and moved up to align itself directly with his truck. It was intent on him! When it finally stopped the end of the main gun was ten feet from the windshield. Jerome went from bewilderment, to frustration, to anger in seconds with his final state being panic. That was an awful big gun. The whole machine was menacing. He realized that sweat was running off his face as he wiped his sleeve across his forehead.

Jerome was starting to tremble when finally two hatches on the top of the tank opened. Immediately the man that was half out of the one on the right side of the tank worked a lever on the machine gun and pointed it right at him. The other man had a portable megaphone and said. "Turn off your engine, slowly get out of the vehicle, and walk around to the front. Do it now!"

He moved so quickly he caught his heel on the step and fell to his hands and knees on the pavement. That'll leave a bloody scrape, he thought. He got up, closed the door, and cautiously limped around to the front. As he did, the tank backed up.

"Walk around the passenger side to the back. No fast moves," the megaphone said. As Haser started to walk the tank turned in place and swung into the ditch, and half into a cornfield, as it paced him. Jerome walked with a constant eye on the hard-as-rock monster vehicle shadowing him. His mind kept racing trying to think of what this could mean. One second he thought it was a sadistic game being played by lunatics. But, he could see that they were outfitted perfectly for what they were doing. If this were a training stunt, a couple of senators would hear about it.

The thing that most unnerved him was that big gun. All he ever saw was a round black hole. No matter what the tank did it always pointed right at his head. He had never heard of a stabilized turret, so he could only think the guy aiming it was a human machine that practiced with it ten hours a day.

When he was at the back of the truck the tank was up on the road again turning in place until the frontal armor was pointed to the truck.

"Now slowly open the rear door."

At this point Jerome only shrugged and opened it. He turned to the tank and yelled, "Car parts, like the side of the truck says." He held out his hands with palms up and continued, "So, what is this? You need a muffler?"

The megaphone replied, "Terrorists shot down two Army helicopters, and this truck fit the profile. Stay here or go back."

Jerome saw both men in the turret hatches lurch as the tank spun forty-five degrees, and took off. Sod and dirt flew as it rolled into the ditch and wheeled up on to the road again heading east. The speed and acceleration were shocking. It seemed to slide across the ground, like a hockey puck on ice.

———————

"Charlie Blue Leader, this is Blue 2. Straight truck on 27 was hauling car parts like the side of the truck said. Any other jobs, over?"

"Blue 2. Yes. The maps show gravel pits two miles north of 27 and east of 45. Check 'em out. We'll be at Home Base in a few minutes. I'll call if I need you. Out."

Sergeant Jay Trout, the commander of Blue 2, had his tank headed north on a gravel road when he received the order to go to the gravel pit. By the time he found the gravel pit on the map they had passed paved Highway 43, Hawthorn Road. He instructed his driver, Louis Martinez, to take the next road right and head east.

Trout, and Rod Krep the loader, both stood half out of their hatches. Trout showed Krep where they were going and Krep said, "Why don't we cut cross the open land here," pointing to an area on the map, "and meet up with the road going north of the gravel pit where it hits this north-south road?" Trout thought a minute and agreed. When they came to the place indicated he'd tell Martinez to bear left off the road and head cross country. His decision was prompted partly by the thought that there was no chance of finding anything in the pit, and partly by the fiasco with the auto parts truck. That had produced a subtle and dangerous cynical, almost carnival attitude in the crew. That last comment by the truck driver about if they needed a muffler had been cutting. Why not romp across the countryside in their ultimate "recreational vehicle?"

———————

William and Amos were both awake as it began to get light in the gravel pit. They had spent the night spelling one another so one would always be on guard duty lest anyone approach them during the night. Now they both sat in the cab of the mobile home, Amos in the driver's seat, William on the passenger side. Both had been recruited and trained the same as Tez. They were the backup unit stationed in the Milwaukee area and had driven out. They arrived at their stand-by position late the evening before.

Their scanner had picked up the transmissions from local law enforcement. The Cobras and M1s were using their standard military coded radio transmissions, which left Amos and William out. "I don't like the sound ah that," William said as they heard the Little Falls Police car report "the vehicle that fit the profile heading east on Highway 27". There followed a description. "They know something's going on. Shoot a burst to Unit 1 and see what he knows." The burst transmission was sent via a small satellite dish on their roof to a satellite in geosynchronous orbit and back.

Amos frowned, "That's only for use for priority transmissions, not some 'How you doing, I'm fine' stuff. We get our asses in trouble if we do that."

"How about I run out an' climb that bank an' look around," William said pointing in the direction of the road. "Can't see nothin' from down here."

"I don't know. We're not supposed to split up. What if I have to move an' you're out there? Nobody to shoot the weapons."

"Come on. This here's Sleepy Hollow. Nothin's happening. Sure would like to stretch my legs."

Amos thought a minute. "Yeah. Why not? Take the glasses," he said pulling a small pair of binoculars out of a case. "Take the hand radio too, an' keep it on. You come a runnin' if I squawk. Got it?"

"Sure, boss," came the reply. Amos was the man in charge so William gave him his token due.

The gravel had been dug out of the side of a hill and out of the bottom so the floor of the excavation was twenty feet below the level of the pit entry. It was roughly a circular excavation near the south side of a gravel covered east-west road that wandered past it. The road into the pit was on the northeast corner. Immediately to the right as one came down the inclined access road was a pile of tailings. Further in and to the right was a huge pile of crushed gravel. Amos had parked to the west of the tailings. This put him out of sight of the road because of the north wall of the crater. To the east, south, and west were hills and tall trees. To the north on the far side of the gravel road was a row of trees with open fields beyond.

William was jogging easily toward the wall of the pit to the north. He planned to climb out, cross the hundred yards of virgin ground and look either way on the road. Perhaps he could get high enough to see over the trees to the east.

Amos wondered at the thirty-year-old man, so strong and fit. Life had been hard on both of them growing up in the same neighborhood, but separated by five-hundred miles. As they traveled they had discussed their similar lives. All of the grief caused by welfare and the broken families it produced in the inner city black ghettos was forced on the people by a governmental system designed to produce exactly those results. Add to this a school system that cared nothing about teaching basic skills, and dwelt instead on having the students working together to solve problems in a group. William had learned to work in a group all right. He sold drugs. The group effectively solved his supplier's problem of greed, his customers' problem of addiction, and William's problem of not eating regularly.

Speaking for himself, when he got to prison he was functionally illiterate. Prisons had the only governmental educational system in America that effectively taught reading, writing, and arithmetic. Learning these basic skills opened up the world to him. It especially taught him that his drug supplier had been cheating him. He vowed to get out of prison and even the score. But, before that happened he met another inmate who had a better plan. Why waste your life settling one score with a two-bit drug distributor? He offered a religion counting a billion members that was on the march to destroy the whole stinking system. It was Islam. How could he refuse? It was the answer to a prayer he had never prayed. From the path his life had been headed there was no reason not to join.

By now William was out of the pit and ambling between a stand of small trees and another pile of tailings. And then he was out of sight. The radio clicked, "I'm goin' to jog up the hill west for a peek over the hill. Okay?"

"Yeah, guess so."

William liked to run. The morning air was clear, the sky was blue with no wind, and everything was quiet. All he could hear was his sneakers on the gravel and his breath starting to come a little faster. After the slums where he had spent most of his life with its constant ruckus this was spooky. He topped out on the hill and looked west. From here the road sloped down to the west until it made a tee with the north-south road they had come in on. The view was blocked by a solid stand of trees to the south side of the road where William stood. He could see between the few trees on the north side. Beyond the north-south road at the tee was a large hayfield. Past that in the distance were the greenest trees he'd ever seen. Farm buildings and silos poked up here and there. Songs of birds provided the only sound.

He stood a minute to catch his breath, and then took the glasses and scanned the hayfield, the cornfields, the trees, and the far horizon. The maps showed splotches of green indicating wooded areas here and there, but on the ground all he could see were trees. With the glasses lowered he caught a glint of bright red in a tree. Focusing the glasses on it he saw the prettiest red and black bird he'd ever seen, a scarlet tanager. "Never saw one o' them, before," he muttered.

He turned and looked to the east. With trees on either side of the road, he couldn't see much. Turning to the west he scanned the fields once again. There! A movement. A dark vehicle angling across the field coming his way. The shape, and the turret with the long gun on it moving from side to side. A tank. And it was hunting! His training films had shown him this.

He had the radio in his hand not knowing how it got there. "Tank comin' from the west!" His legs were moving. He ran like he had never run before. He half slid and half tumbled down the gravel slope to the floor of the pit. He was up instantly pounding dust and dirt off his clothes as he made for the vehicle.

Amos had the motor running. Swinging the door open he half yelled between panting, "Tank comin'. Headed right for us!"

"You sure it's a tank way out here?"

"Yeah. He's off the road, cuttin' through fields. Goin' right for the tee in the road. Guess it's one o' them M1s, too."

"Yeah. It's an M1 all right. That's all they got around here. Now, 'member what they taught about tanks. If we're close enough, we can get 'em if we don't fall to pieces. I'm moving over behind the other pile o' sand. I'll poke the nose out enough so's you can see the road with the gun."

The primary purpose of any tank has always been to kill other tanks. They're good against other armored vehicles, but not necessary. The modern tank, especially the M1 Abrams, was developed during the cold war to counter the superior number of Russian tanks they faced along the border between the former U.S.S.R. and Western Europe, especially in the Fulda Gap. Its strongest feature was the ability to accurately hit tank size targets at three and more miles range, while both were moving across rough terrain. But, as the Israelis learned repeatedly, they were not good for guerrilla warfare. Their big gun was all but worthless in cities and other close quarters. It was too destructive. And for close-in fighting tanks had severe weaknesses.

The armament on an M1A1 consisted of the main gun, 120 mm smooth bore, and a 7.62 mm coaxial machine gun that shot where the big gun was pointed. It also had a fifty-caliber machine gun mounted in front of the tank commander's hatch. On the early 105 mm gun M1 models, the fifty-cal could be aimed and fired from inside the tank by the tank commander. The many changes made when going to the 120 mm gun forced the operation of the fifty-cal only while the tank commander had the hatch open. The other item of "armament," if it can be called that, is the sure mass and bulk of the vehicle. Beyond this, the psychological "shock" factor on unprotected soldiers could be substantial.

The *rickshaw* that Amos and William were in sported the standard GAU-2B/A 7.62 mm mini-gun. Unless in dire peril, he had been cautioned to shoot at lower than maximum rates. The ammunition supply became depleted at an alarming rate when one hundred bullets a second went out of the spinning barrels.

Their rockets were the same advanced design as in their companion vehicle, though William doubted he'd have a chance to use them. He had the gun powered up and extended above the roof of the vehicle. The setting was for fifty percent rate of fire. He didn't want to take a chance of something failing. Amos moved the vehicle to what he thought was the best position assuming the tank appeared at the place William guessed. Both men's hands were sweating as they saw a dark shadow moving along the road. It went behind a stand of small trees and did not reappear on the other side. They saw twenty foot high trees being slapped flat to the ground as the tank drove through the trees. It wouldn't be long.

As soon as the bulk of the monster appeared, William laid on the mini-gun. "If the tank is within range of your gun, target it in this order if its main gun is pointed at you," the training system had said. "First, the optics in the 'dog house' as the little hutch on the top right-hand side of the turret was called. This housed the laser range finder, and the optics for aiming the big gun. Next, get some slugs down the barrel of the big gun. If it was fired with something the size of a 7.62 bullet wedged beside the 120 mm round the barrel might explode. Then, go for the coaxial machine gun protruding a couple of feet in front of the armor on the right side of the big gun. After that go for the fifty-caliber machine gun. Lastly, try to shoot off the radio antennas. If you are beyond the minimum range for a rocket, aim at one of the tracks. You might get lucky.

There was not much more you could do, so go as fast as you can. An M1 can exceed fifty miles an hour." Sitting in his small apartment with a virtual reality helmet in his head hadn't prepared him for this. But he was determined to do the best he could.

The gun purred as the slugs splattered against the hull of the tank. Both men saw the orange ethereal cloud of fire the size of the tank as soon as the tank emerged from the trees. Instantly there was a deafening bang as the round went diagonally through the *rickshaw* leaving a four-inch hole where it went in three feet behind the passenger seat, and a one foot hole where it went out. Since it was a training round, it did not explode. The mobile home shuttered again a second later from the shock of the muzzle flash. Too late William pulverized the doghouse and then hit the coaxial machine gun as he aimed for the muzzle of the 120. It was no easy shot at a tank that was moving.

Amos hit the gas and backed behind the pile of gravel. Slamming the brakes he stopped and swung to the right and up the ramp out of the pit. When they saw the tank again after they had passed behind the pile William was on the mini-gun again. He splattered steel-jacketed rounds on the prisms in the driver's and tank commander's hatches. They would not penetrate, but the splintered glass blinded the occupants. The turret had turned so the main gun was pointed away from him. He raked the rear of the turret shredding everything that wasn't inches thick steel.

Out of the pit and on the dirt road heading west, William said, "They ain't followin'. Think I showed 'em we ain't pushovers."

"Yeah. That's nice, but the mission's over. Never make the target now. Should o' done it last night. Now, it's me that's gotta send the message. Well, here goes." Amos proceeded to make a short spoken message as he drove, telling what had happened and that his part in the mission was aborted.

To send the message, he had only to press the send button. The onboard computer then took over. It first digitized the message, compressed it, and finally encoded it before it went out as a burst. Included in the communication was their exact position from the onboard GPS receiver. Before he could act on his intention a red light blinked beside the send button. This meant there was an incoming message for him. He hesitated, but finally pressed a blinking button to hear the message.

Down the hill headed southeast, Martinez, the driver of Blue 2, was in the shallow ditch on the right side. As a precaution Trout had ordered all hatches closed. Tank commander, gunner and driver all saw the light floor of the gravel basin through the trees at the same time.

"Swing right and go through that thin row of trees," Trout said over the intercom. Trees began slapping the ground in front of them. "Stay alert, we're about to break through," Trout barked. As soon as the words were out of his mouth, they were in the clear and they saw the vehicle. Immediately they heard the tinging of the 7.62 rounds on the armor.

Kurt, the gunner, said, "Locked on, it's yours." By established procedure, the gunner sights in the target and then releases the firing to the tank commander. It helps to avoid shooting at the wrong object.

The target was so close there was no time to think. Trout let the round go for a sure hit. The recoil sent the gun back to within inches of the rear of the turret. This was normal. As it began its recovery to firing position the breach automatically opened, ejected the afcap, and was ready to accept the next round from the loader. But, it is not in the training to expect small arms slugs flying out of the breach to ricochet around in the turret. That is what happened. All occupants of the turret were injured in seconds. The loader had foot and leg wounds. The 120 mm round he was about to load absorbed the bullet that might have killed him. He released the shell letting it fall as he lunged over to the gunner's position and hit the control to swing the turret around. It moved fast throwing him off balance and sending him falling on his two wounded comrades. But, the rear of the turret was now presented to the shooter, and with it the radio antennas.

Martinez saw the edge of the pit and broke hard. The forward pressure on the front idlers combined with the mass of the tank caused the ledge to collapse. The tank slid easily to the floor as Martinez let off the brakes. He saw nothing of the vehicle and was turning right when it reappeared from behind the pile of gravel. He had it in his mind to ram it if he could. That changed as his vision blurred. "He got my glass," he blurted.

"Louis," Krep the loader said with urgency in his voice, "when the breach opened that guy pasted us with small arms down the tube. We're all hit. Guess I'm in the best shape. We need help. I'll try the radio." With no antennas Krep couldn't make himself understood. It seemed he could hear them better than they could hear him.

After a minute Krep cautiously opened his hatch. The motor home was not to be seen. He got on the intercom, "Louis, can you drive?"

"Yeah, if I open the hatch. He sprayed my prisms pretty good."

"I could use a little help back here for a minute. Here, I'll align the slot."

When the turret was rotated to the front, there was a slot in the turret that aligned with the driver's compartment, making it possible for the driver to exit through the turret.

Martinez crawled into the turret, and together they got the bleeding stopped on the other crewmembers so they wouldn't die immediately. Their battlefield wound training made it possible for them to separate the truly dangerous wounds from those that looked bad. The turret of a tank was not a good place for wounded men. It was cramped and the only comfortable positions were the work places for each healthy crewmember. Krep was making a good show of it though his leg was badly lacerated with a slug in it.

When they had dressed the wounds the best they could Krep said, "Let's head for the hospital in Little Falls. If you see whatever that thing was button up and drive blind if you have to."

Martinez arranged the turret crew so he could not get into the driver's position through the slot. He crawled out of the loader's hatch and slid off the turret. Afraid of who might shoot at him, he scrambled as fast as he could. He started the tank moving with a grim determination that he'd get to the hospital in time, no matter what.

— 34 —

Tez and Ahmad were having their problems. Not only had Tez mistaken the driveway for a road, but the Cobra had made it impossible to go forward. In his hurry to get the big mobile home back to the main road, Tez had backed it partially into a field. He worked it forward and backward trying to get all wheels back on the hard surface. At one point Ahmad had to use a shovel to dig away the dirt in front of one of the rear wheels. After some hard work and tense moments they had it back on the driveway. Taking it much slower this time, he backed his way to the paved road and headed north. They had lost a precious half hour.

"I don't care what they said, we ain't goin' to make it on a dirt roads like that. I'm goin' north until we hit something better." The thought of getting stuck and being a sitting duck had unnerved Tez. In a quarter mile he came to the road he should have taken in the first place. Now he saw his mistake. He hated to say anything, but he had to alert Ahmad that in a few minutes they'd be at the target.

After the left turn Tez said," Okay, mile and a half to the target. Target will be on the left." Ahmad grimaced. It was fully light, but there was nothing he could do about it. Retribution would come later. Tez slowed as they neared, and started to turn into the driveway.

"What're you doing!" shouted Ahmad. "Don't go in there. I can splinter that house from the road. No need to chance getting hung up." Tez stopped and backed out. When he had the vehicle diagonally on the road, Ahmad opened up. Tez put the shift lever into drive, pressed on the accelerator, and . . . he died instantly.

Lieutenant Roston was headed east on Highway 46. He turned south on a gravel road a mile east of the intersection with Highway 45. He intended to go a mile south and then turn east to Home Base. At the planned turn point there was no road. The Platte River came through that area. There were a limited number of bridges that could be justified. This one had been omitted. Looking at the map he saw he had to go an additional mile south, east a mile and then north to get on to the road headed to Home Base. Well, an extra three miles would only delay them five minutes. When they finally reached the intended road and turned east the gunner immediately said, "Large vehicle on road, two klicks."

Roston put his eyes to his optics and at that moment the infrared image of rapid gunfire appeared. Through simulator training both the gunner and tank commander knew the signature. "That's him! Fire."

"On the way," came the instant reply as the tank shuttered.

Two seconds later debris flew from the front of the vehicle. It lurched forward into the ditch and rolled on to its side.

"HEAT," yelled the gunner. In a few seconds the loader had another round loaded.

Pressing the button to release the gun for firing he yelled, "Up," into the intercom.

"Looks like we got him, but stay alert. We especially don't want to hit any friendlies."

In the cellar nerves were getting raw. The youngest was crying nearly all the time. They had the cellar cover off to the side again, enough to see the road to the east. It was fully light and nothing had happened. Breckon was beginning to feel like a complete fool. But, they had seen the helicopter go down. Ann Daley came beside him on the steps and was about to speak

Breckon shook his head. "I know what you're going to say. Greg feels it's important to err or the side of safety, and I won't let him down now. We stay here." They heard in the distance another vehicle on the road. It came closer and slowed down.

"It's big and it's slowing down he said. Too late to close the cover. The movement could catch the driver's eye."

Klappenbach and Breckon saw it go out of sight to the west. As the tires left the gravel surface of the road for the driveway the sound changed. "It's turning into the yard," Klappenbach said.

They heard it stop. The engine increased in speed as it backed away. The ripping sound of the gun firing and the crashing sound of windows shattering reached them. "Their shooting up the house . . ." Klappenbach started to say as a thud and crash stopped the gun. Moments later a boom like rolling thunder reached them, the report of the tank gun. Then it was quiet.

Klappenbach eased his head up. "It's laying on its side in the ditch. The front part is ripped open. Wonder what happened." Minutes later the ground shook as a large machine strode into the farmyard. Twenty feet away it stopped, the turret continuously panning from side to side. It was big! Green and tan camouflage rippled across its shape. A hatch on the top opened. The upper torso of a man wearing a smooth olive drab helmet appeared. Klappenbach made a wave holding his hand at head level.

The head high above them spoke, "Is everybody accounted for? Anybody hurt?"

Klappenbach replied in a loud voice, "All safe. We're all in here." By now more heads, including some small ones appeared.

"Wow! A tank!"

"That's a good place. Stay there until we secure the area and come back. There may be more." The mouth of the head spoke into the microphone and the tank sped away through a stand of brush and up the ditch on to the road.

Roston keyed the Post frequency. "Wild Wind, this is Blue 1. We put down one of the vehicles. It's lying on its side in the ditch. The Driver's dead. Recommend we use the fifty on it to insure there are no others. Over."

"Negative, Blue 1. There are expectations in high places of getting good evidence. Guard it, but do no further damage. Confirm receipt of that order. Over."

"Wild wind, this is Blue 1. Will do no more damage to target. Out."

On his platoon net Roston said, "Blue 4, this is Blue 1, where are you?"

"This is Blue 4. I'm a half mile east of Home Base headed west."

"This is 1. Good. Come to Home Base and stay in the area. Watch the vehicle in the ditch. The brass doesn't want any more damage to it, but I'm not sure it's completely dead. I'm headed west and then south on the first road. Out." Roston was worried about Blue 2 and intended to work his way over to the area of the gravel pit. He was sure the tank commander was trying to communicate from the times he heard the radio keyed. He reported to the post on the problem, but they would not risk more aircraft until all threats were neutralized. He had been informed there could be two hostile vehicles.

Inside the disabled *rickshaw* Ahmad got up on his knees with his head between the underside of the weapons console and the floor. With no time to lose, he snatched the emergency flashlight from its holder on the wall. He released two latches and removed an access panel. The light beam fell on several bundles of electrical wiring. He felt around the side of the opening until his fingers found the switch. He flipped it off. This disabled the self-destruct system.

He knew enough about terrorism to understand that a vehicle like this would be equipped with a self-destruct that would burn the vehicle and kill the operators. On the first day of their trip from New York, he had let himself into the vehicle and spent several hours removing every access panel until he found that little switch. He wasn't sure what would initiate the self-destruct, probably any of a number of conditions. But, he knew there had to be a way to disable it during normal maintenance. Whatever time delay had been built into it had been enough.

He relaxed a little as he gingerly touched the sore spot on his head, then crawled toward the front. In the cab he saw parts of Tez splattered all over. So much for retribution.

They still had battery power so he crawled back to his station and prepared an emergency message. To transmit it, he extended the dish antenna from the roof of the vehicle now in tall grass and weeds in the ditch. He maneuvered it around until he got a satellite lock and pressed the send button.

Amos didn't know what to expect. Why would he be getting a burst message? The accented voice was as terse as it was unwelcome. "Secondary *rickshaw*, this is Primary *rickshaw*. Primary did not complete mission. You are now Primary. Proceed with all haste. End of message."

Sucking in his breath, Amos said to William, "We got ourselves a job. Guess the big shot wasn't so good after all. Probably got hisself lost." William punched the button on the Magellan for the previous destination which was the house. They were a mile north of Highway 27. He had to go south to 27, then take 27 east a couple of miles and head north at the first road.

Blue 1 had no sooner turned south on the first road west of Home Base when headquarters was back.

"Blue 1, this is Wild Wind. A woman on a cell phone heard the news on the local radio. She called in that a large mobile home was seen turning north off Highway 27 three miles west of Pierz. That was only a minute ago. Over."

"This is Blue 1. Roger. Out."

Roston fumbled with his map until he had a square foot of it showing his area. He saw the situation. The target would head north and turn east on the Home Base road a mile and a half west of it. He keyed the radio.

"Blue 3, this is Blue 1. What's you location?"

"This is Blue 3, I'm on Highway 46 headed west getting close to the Platt River."

At a glance Roston could see he had the second one covered.

"Blue 3, this is 1, you're in perfect position. We believe we've found target number two. Before you reach the Platte turn south staying east of the river. A quarter mile south of the road is a hill. Get over the brink of the hill so you can see south. A motor home will be coming north on the road you'll see there. But, make it fast! Take care. We're not sure it's hostile. Over."

"This is Blue 3, wilco. Out."

Two miles after heading east on Highway 27 Amos found his turn and went north. "Here's da ticket," he said on the intercom. Amos was doing the driving and didn't care what William thought. He was talking to keep himself calm. "Have to jog a little, but we'll get on the road that takes us a mile west of the house. We'll be there in a blink. Keep a sharp eye open."

Amos had the Magellan Navigator on and he glanced at the moving map as the audio promptings told him when to turn.

After going a half-mile south, it occurred to Roston that he knew which road the vehicle would take going north. If he could be sure of intercepting it, he'd learn its intentions. On the intercom he spoke to his driver. "Jim, the map shows good ground to the right. Head west across country as fast as you can to the next road. The crew in the turret hung on as they went though the ditch alongside the road.

Glossen, Blue Leader's gunner, panned the horizon with three-power infrared. "There, to the southwest is an infrared target. Has to be him. I can glimpse him now and again. Now I lost him." Glossen worked the turret back and forth over that general area. "Again, I got him. Let me try visual . . . darn it, that servo again—won't respond. Now she's stuck. Come on," he said coaxing the machine. But it was to no avail. "She seems to be dead for good, and at the worst time. Didn't get a visual, but it must be him."

Roston was already on the radio. "Blue 4, this is Blue Leader." Without waiting for a response he continued, "Watch to the west of Home Base, but also other directions. This could be a decoy. Over."

"This is 4, wilco. Out."

Blue 3 was off the road before the Platt. The attractive manicured lawn surrounding the newly built home nestled up against the Platt became a little less pleasant. Shrubs and small trees were crushed. A utility shed in the back of the property was flattened.

"Blue 3, this is Leader, where are you now. My turret servo is dead. It's up to you. He's coming. Over."

"Blue Leader, this is 3, have hill in sight . . . oh, oh. There's a cattle pasture in the way. Out." Switching to intercom he said to his driver, "Remi, don't break your stride, go though. It'll be messy. Then slow to a crawl as we top out on the hill." To his gunner, "Burt, tube to max elevation, then be ready to shoot." They all heard thumps as cattle went under the treads of seventy tons of charging steel. The barnyard came next. Board fences and feed bunkers splinted as chunks of wood sliced through the calm morning air.

Frank Wooder finished the morning milking and cleaned up the utensils. He was headed out of the barn to the house for breakfast. As was his custom, he watched his milk cows in a line ambling up the slight grade to the pasture north of the barn. He heard a funny crunching sound. The top of a slender tree over the rise being swept from view caught his eye. Immediately, he saw the brown-green blob heave over the hill slashing through the row of cattle. His pipe fell to the ground as his mouth dropped open. His herd of prime Holsteins was being slaughtered before his eyes. He heard himself mutter, "Hey, hey, you can't do that . . . . " In seconds it was crashing though his feed lot. It moved so fast at first he thought it must be one of those hovercraft. But no, it couldn't be. The ground was shaking. It was, yes, it was, a tank! He stood motionless like watching a wide screen movie as the war machine lunged across his yard in front of him.

Not a hundred yards away from him it lurched to a stop rocking forward on its shock absorbers. The huge gun moved and then stopped. Instantly.

———————————

"Hey Amos, there's another tank coming across a field to our right, close. Odd though, his turret isn't moving and not aimed at us. Bet it's not working. Wait. He opened his top hatch. Oh, no! He'll get us with his fifty."

"Get him with the mini-gun!"

"No time. He'll have us by the time I get it up and aimed. Launching a missile." The thump told them it was on its way.

———————————

The mobile home was due west of Blue 1's position and Lt. Tony Roston had to do something.

"I'm going to try to spook him with the fifty," Roston said.

"If he fires one of those missiles, he'll get you," Glossen yelled.

"I'll duck if he shoots," Roston yelled back as he opened the hatch. "Tell me if he launches." He pulled the cocking lever twice and opened up. The thung, thung, thung of the fifty came up as Roston directed the tracers on the road in front of the mobile home.

"Tony! Duck! He launched!"

Roston whacked his head on the rim of the hatch as he pulled his head down in time to hear a deafening explosion. His turret CV helmet absorbed most of the blow to his cranium, but he was dazed. "Where is he?" Roston yelled even though Glossen was only a foot away from him.

"Disappeared into a depression in the road."

"Jim, keep after him. Keep pressing him. We have to give him something to worry about." Slowly standing up Roston saw his fifty was sitting at a strange angle and his hatch cover was gone.

"Blue 3 this is 1. The vehicle is definitely hostile. Over."

"This is 3. Roger. Out."

———————

"Amos, he was too close, only grazed the top of 'em. Think I killed his fifty, though."

"Hope he's the last one."

———————

His legs finally came to life. Frank Wooder's ire was up, and he intended to vent a huge dose of spleen on those jerks. He had gone five steps when he saw the plume of orange fire and a deafening shock wave sent a tremor through his chest. He stopped not knowing what to do, his ears ringing.

Wooder's anger was replaced with curiosity mixed with fear. Proceeding more slowly, his gaze was fixed on the tank. It was moving as another orange flame belched from the enormous gun. A thunderous explosion reached him throwing him to the ground. As he fell he could see the tank was engulfed in smoke and flame as parts flew. A thump and clatter of metal caused him to jerk his head to the right. The remains of a machine gun rattled to a stop. His mind raced to comprehend what was happening. This was not training!

Looking up . . . what? The tank was gone. Had his eyes deceived him? Reflexively he glanced back to his right. There was the machine gun on his driveway. Cautiously now, with his head lowered, he advanced to the south. At fifty-two he was in good physical shape from farm work, but his breath came hard and his heart pounded from the shock and excitement. He thought of how moments before he was about to head for the house thinking about the work of the day ahead. In seconds his world had turned inside out. War in the heartland of America! Terrorists attacked big cities, and large concentrations of people. Here he was safe, or so he and his friends and neighbors had always thought. No enemy could possibly care about this out of the way place. How could they have been so wrong?

———————

"Okay William, I'm comin' to a rise. Look to the front."

"Looks okay." The optics on the top of the vehicle gave William a commanding view of the nearly flat farmland.

"Closin' the distance to the house fast so keep a sharp eye out for trouble. Watch the road in front, and the sky." Amos had a bad feeling in his guts, but they were committed. As he rumbled north on the gravel road he hoped they had seen the last of the tanks.

"Amos! Got IR image to the north of us. Going to visual. Got another tank sittin' on a hill. He'll pop us off!"

"No, no!" Amos yelled. "Use a missile!" As he spoke he saw the gravel rip out of the road in a straight line like a giant hand yanking up a buried cable. It was the sabot projectile from Blue 3's first shot. Gravel pelted the windshield and Amos unconsciously ducked. Seconds later Amos heard the whomp as the cylinder was ejected vertically from its launch tube. The instrument of destruction sped on its way.

They both saw the muzzle flash of the second round from the tank. A second later the windshield split at the top right and they felt the jarring of intense vibrations and sounds as the titanium rod slashed through the vehicle. Amos almost ran off the road. When he looked up the tank was engulfed in smoke. The rocket had run true. Once again, he was surprised there was no explosion from the tank round. "What happened to the tank?"

"He's still movin'."

"Did he get the missiles? They still up?"

"Yeah, yeah. Got us some fresh air back here. He hit empty tubes."

"William, shoot for a track. You gotta stop 'em. Even if he can't shoot he can ram us."

Another whomp followed. Seconds later the expected puff of smoke appeared on the tank. Amos thought how lucky it was that William had the weapons job because that man was really good at targeting those things. The tank with one track off careened to the right and slid to a stop in an alfalfa field with its rear toward them.

"Nice job, William!"

"Blue 1, this is Blue 3. He hit us two out of two shots while we were moving. He's good. He got our optics, and then a track. We're done. Out."

"Blue 4, this is Blue Leader. Over." The radio procedure was clear, disciplined, and quick.

"This is Blue 4. Over."

"Blue 4, we see the target, and you heard what he did to Blue 3. Those high-speed missiles are deadly. Get to a place where you are concealed, but can see west on the east-west road past Home Base. You don't have much time to get into position. Over."

"Wilco. Out."

———————

Blue 4 had patrolled back and forth several times on the gravel road that ran past Home Base. The call from Blue Leader came as he was to the east of Home Base. Ray Hinton the driver heard the traffic and was already off to the north side of the road in a hay field turning around when Chet Gordon, the tank commander, spoke.

"Ray, head for those farm buildings to the west on the north side of the road. Go through the corn, it'll be faster." Gordon surmised correctly that to use modern farming machinery the fields were smooth. The tank accelerated to forty-five before it entered the cornfield.

In mid-August corn stands eight feet tall which is bad news for a tank. As corn was hit at high speed corn stalks quickly covered the prisms in the driver's hatch and left him blinded. Hinton had been too eager. In seconds he realized his mistake.

"Chet, I can't see! The corn's plastered on the tank!"

"I'll guide you." Popping open his hatch Gordon was met with a sensation the caught him by surprise. As they sped through the corn his eye swept over the sea of golden brown tassels touched by the risen sun. In front of them the corn tips, a couple of feet below eye level, snapped from view as the hull swam forward. The sweet smell of crunching stalks mixed with the pungent odors or wet earth caught him unaware. The impressions common to those who worked the earth quickened his senses to where he was nearly mesmerized. After a long moment he heard a frantic cry in his headphone.

"Chet, which way!"

"Ah, swing, ah, to the right." The tank changed course. Gordon still struggled to focus. Having been born and reared in the city, this was more intense than coming to grips with battle. He had been in Iraq. The first time bullets whizzed through his tent as he was writing a letter he was left with impressions he knew at the time he'd never forget. But this was something else. The tank rocked gently as it fled across the field all the time the slapping of the stalks against the hull producing a soothing rhythm. A flock of blackbirds rose in front, veering to the right and left to avoid the charging monster.

Finally, he realized the farm buildings were bearing down on them. "You are nearing a dirt road . . . slow down, and bear left." They slowed to thirty-five. The turret crew braced themselves as they went over the road.

"In the farm yard now. Slow down. Good. To the left a little. Okay. Oops, to the right, no more. Ugh!"

Gordon instinctively raised his arm to cover his face as the left of the tank mowed down the end of a small building with white painted siding. As it flashed by he saw chickens hurled trough the air, wings flapping, feathers flying. Then it was past.

"Sorry Ray, we did in a chicken coop, I'm not used to driving. Barry, don't let the tube hit that tree." The turret swung to the right as a six-inch elm fell in front of them, trimming off limbs of other trees as it slammed to the ground. "We're in a batch of brush and small trees, nothing to worry about . . . oops." An old hay bailer crumpled under the treads.

Gordon headed for a couple of Gold'n Plump chicken barns a short distance west of the farm buildings. He guided Hinton between them.

"Okay Ray, slow to five, to the left a little. Good. Stop. Barry, use the optics to guide Ray for a good shot down the road."

"Looks about as good as I'll get," Barry said. After a pause, "How's it setting for concealment, Chet?"

"Not good. The field in front of us is soybeans or something like that. Short. Hope the building gives off enough heat to obscure our signature. Load a sabot, Dewey."

Sabot ammunition were rods of dense metal a couple of inches in diameter. To make them fire through the 120 mm gun they were surrounded by a plastic sheath that fell away in two halves after leaving the muzzle. Real war-fighting sabots were made of depleted uranium that was dense and hence carried immense kinetic energy. In addition, uranium had the characteristic of sloughing off burning slivers as it penetrated armor. Thus, if it didn't directly kill the occupants of an armored vehicle, the white hot metal fragments burned ragged holes in their flesh. These slender pointed rods traveled at slightly more than a mile a second.

Training sabots were made of titanium, a fifth the density of uranium. From the aspect of hitting a target they behaved like a uranium round.

When they hit something soft like the mobile home, they still left an ugly hole due to their high speed.

"William, be alert. I'm comin' to the last right turn."

Neither man was thinking beyond the next few seconds. The thought of completing the mission and escaping was lost in meeting each new threat as it appeared. Rounding the bend was no different. William had the infrared sensor panning back and fourth thirty degrees either side of their direction of travel.

"Got an IR of a building that's hotter to one side at a little less then a mile. Visual . . . another tank!"

"One missile left. Lay it on 'em."

"No good. Last bird's got a fault light."

"Get on the gun. Mile to go."

The buzzing sound told Amos that William was firing. The motion of the vehicle and the distance to the tank meant the rounds were scattered over a hundred-foot area. At first they all fell short until William lifted the barrels. Scattered rounds hit the tank, and many others slaughtered chickens before their time.

Blue 4 was waiting. Gordon told Barry that as soon as they identified the target that he would not hand off the target, but to shoot at will as fast as they could get rounds loaded. Gordon would man the fifty.

"That's him," Chet yelled. "Do it!" The muzzle belched flame as the beat of the fifty began. Seconds later the big gun let go with another one and, yet another.

The vehicle slid off the road after the first round, and now was on its side in the ditch. They could see dirt fly as it scraped the shoulder going in.

"Got him! Nice shooting. There's Blue Leader in hot pursuit," Gordon shouted in glee. "Oh, look at that. It's going to be tough on the guys inside that thing." They watched as Blue 1 ran over the vehicle from back to front. Pieces of aluminum skin flew off and fluttered to the ground. The tank turned around and rolled past the wreck.

"Blue 3, this is Blue Leader, report your condition. Over."

"This is Blue 3. The crew is bruised but okay. The tank is completely out of action. Out."

"Blue 4, this is Blue Leader, report your condition. Over."

"This is Blue 4, crew and tank are okay except we have the front of the tank piled full of corn stalks. Driver can't see or open his hatch. It'll take a half hour to get fully operational. Out."

"Blue 2, this is Blue Leader. Do you copy? Over."

There was no reply after repeated attempts.

Roston switched to the post headquarters frequency. "Wild Wind Leader, this is Blue Leader. Second threat is neutralized."

"Blue Leader. Are you certain?"

"This is Blue Leader. Yeah I'm sure. I ran over it. Nothing higher than three feet. He's done."

Roston heard the click as the radio at post headquarters was keyed, and a heavy breath being let out. "Blue Leader, was that necessary? Over."

"Wild Wind, when you see the condition of your tanks I'll let you decide. In the meantime, it should be safe for aircraft. I'd like to know the status of Blue 2. There's been no word from him since he called in that he was approaching the gravel pit. Over."

"Blue Leader, negative. Report condition of your platoon?"

"Roger, Wild Wind. Blue 1's turret doesn't rotate, and I have no fifty-cal, and no hatch cover. Doghouse is unusable. Blue 2 is missing. Blue 3 lost a track and all guns. Blue 4 has a half ton of corn stalks on the front of his hull. The driver can't see or open his hatch. Thirty minutes for Blue 4 to be operational. Over."

"Blue Leader, get Blue 4 operational A-SAP. Then keep Blue 4 to guard Home Base. Another platoon is leaving base now, ETA vicinity of gravel pit fifteen minutes. Out."

— 35 —

Out of the gravel pit entrance road Martinez swung left and turned the throttle to the limit as he accelerated up the hill. Coming over the top, he felt like he was flying. With his hatch open, and his goggles on, the wind in his face felt good. He determined to continue west until this gravel road made a tee with the north-south paved road. He'd turn south to Highway 27. From there he knew it was a straight shot into Little Falls. All these small towns had hospital signs on the main roads coming in to them. He hoped against hope this would not be the exception.

Martinez slowed as he swung right on to Highway 27. And then he was off. Hang on back there guys, he said softly, hoping he could will them to live. He knew it was only five or six miles to town, minutes to go.

Before he knew it he came up to the auto parts truck that he had stopped a short time before. There were a dozen vehicles backed up behind the truck, and people were out on the pavement milling around. Lewis slowed and dove into the ditch and into the field leaving them wondering what was going on.

Nearing town he had to pull off on the shoulder to avoid a tractor pulling a harvesting machine going the opposite direction. He didn't mean to hit the mailboxes, but he got a few. He entered a forty-five zone with a traffic light ahead. He was going forty-five or a little more. He kept looking for the hospital sign.

This was the junction with Highway 10. The first light was for the off and on ramps from 10 North. Under two overpasses to the second set of lights he came to the ramps for 10 South. He had a green light at the first and a red at the second. A car was coming on to 27 from the 10 south-bound off ramp and the driver was alert. He hit the brakes in time and slid sideways as the two vehicles passed a foot apart. Past the light on the left was a Burger King. A woman holding a cell phone to her ear was coming on to 27 from that establishment and was not so observant. She spun around once as the tank's left front fender hit her right front. Hope she didn't have hot coffee, Martinez thought.

He traveled down a street knowing he was going too fast when he saw what he wanted, a cop. Good. He dodged an oncoming car and broke to a stop. Here there was a lane each way and a center turn lane with no shoulder. He used his lane and the turn lane to pivot in place. He started to move only to see the police car coming toward him with lights and sirens blaring. It looked like the cop car was going to go past him so he swerved into his path. They both broke hard and stopped only feet apart. Martinez motioned for him to get out. He was met with a revolver aimed out the window at him.

Officer Clarence Tiffner had been on the force in Little Falls for twenty-three years. He mostly liked his job. There was an altruistic vein in him and he felt good about helping people. He'd been in his share of close scrapes but he accepted the danger. His present job was unpleasant, but unquestionably necessary. He was doing traffic control, or what most people would call manning a speed trap.

There was a forty-five zone on the road coming into town. Then there were the traffic lights at the junction with Highway 10. Some days he worked the forty-five zone east of Highway 10. Today he was situated in the thirty zone to the west of the interchange on a gradual down slope with his squad pointed west. He waited under a large shade tree in a quiet residential area, his favorite place. The radar was on watching traffic both ways.

He saw him coming on his readout. He caught the top of him back under Highway 10 so it must be a truck. Look at the fool. Not slacking off a bit, even speeding up a bit. Got him though, dead to rights, forty-seven in a thirty zone. He glanced in his side mirror to see what he had. It was big and ugly. Not a car, not an eighteen wheeler. What? The green-ish brown thing whooshed past him like it owned the place, and he doubted the wisdom of arguing the point. A tank, and really cooking! That thing'll kill people! In horror he thought of what he had seen on TV—the case in California where an unbalanced man had gotten loose with a tank on the freeway.

"Dispatch, this is Patrol 3. An Army tank blew through my control point going forty-seven in a thirty zone!"

"Patrol 3, this is Dispatch. Give chase, and be careful. We have been alerted that tanks are prowling around west of town due to the terrorist threat you were briefed on earlier."

Tiffner hit his lights and siren and punched his accelerator. He had gone only a half block and was up to fifty miles an hour himself when he realized the tank had stopped, and was spinning around in the street. He slowed and thought to slip past him to get out of the madman's kill zone. The tank quickly moved to block his path. He hit his brakes hard as they stopped bumper to hull. It did not look like an even standoff to Tiffner.

The driver's head was clearly visible under the huge gun barrel. Grabbing his service revolver from his holster he put it in his left hand and pointed it at the head that looked dwarfed by the monstrous hulk surrounding it.

The tank driver yelled at him, waved both hands, and pointed at the turret. He put his hands over his ears gesturing frantically. The driver appeared to have a problem and was trying to talk. Always get them talking, was the first rule when dealing with dangerous crazy people. He flipped off the siren.

"I have severely wounded men inside. Lead me to the hospital!"

"What? Wounded men?"

"Yeah. Terrible accident. Explosion. Lead me to the hospital. Please, they're dying!"

Tiffner thought at first it might be a trick, but the guy was so young, and so animated. It occurred to him that if he was a nut case like in California he could have crushed his squad by now with him in it.

"Hurry, I hear them calling for help!"

Decision time. Oh, boy. What was he doing? He re-holstered his revolver and yelled. "Get out of the way, the hospital is that way," he said pointing in the direction his squad car was headed.

Immediately the tank backed and turned. There was a bone scraping sound as it crushed the front of a car trying to sneak by behind it. The tank driver was oblivious to it as he gestured sharply with his hand for the police car to get going.

Forgetting how fast the tank had been going as it came into town, and remembering the ponderous bulk backing over the car, Tiffner started off at a brisk thirty-five miles per hour. In his rear view mirror he saw the thing about to run him down. He responded in the nick in time, and pulled ahead.

"Dispatch, Patrol 3. The tank driver says he has severely wounded men in his tank and I am leading him to the hospital. Or maybe he's chasing me to the hospital says it better. If you send backup, keep them out of the way. He's only a kid and is scared to death. Alert the hospital we're coming!"

"Roger, Patrol 3."

A half mile into town Highway 27, now Broadway, made a gentle turn to the left and then an equally gentle turn to the right with parking lanes on either side. Past the first turn a large delivery truck was entering from the left about to head west on Broadway. Well into his turn the driver saw what was coming. Hitting his brakes he left enough room for the police car to get through between him and some parked cars. But no way was there room for the "outsized" vehicle following. And of course it had to be. A woman opened the back door on the street side and was lifting a child out of a car seat.

Too late the woman glanced to her right to see the oncoming dreadnought. Instinctively she grabbed the child tightly against he body. The police car skidded behind her. Seconds later her SUV was rammed ahead in front of her pushed by a monstrous bulk twice her height. Her knees turned to rubber as the earth quaked. Her vehicle stopped moving as it smashed into the van parked in front of it. Before she could blink it was buckled and bent into nothing more than junk amid an ear-shattering squeal of tortured metal. Pieces of shattered plastic pelted her as she stood in shock not comprehending what was happening. Then it was quiet. The truck driver set his brake where he was and got out. He ran to the woman and grabbed her and the baby, gently pulling her to the side of the street. She sat on the curb looking straight ahead, but still not comprehending.

"My baby. Where's my baby?" she asked lethargically.

"You're holding it," the truck driver said.

"Oh," was all she replied as she sat gently rocking back and forth.

Martinez saw the woman in horror. He swerved as hard as he could to the right, but that much mass simply doesn't change direction easily at forty-five miles per hour. He hit the SUV and the van but thought he had missed the woman. He got a street light and a garbage receptacle. Smothering another car he swerved back on to the street. He was now down to forty. Amid the flying debris he lost sight of the police car and thought he had been left behind so he twisted the throttle. Once around the last of the devastation he had left, he saw the police car, smoke rising behind it.

Tiffner saw the truck and felt a little relief as it jerked to a stop. Then the woman. How could it be at that instant! He realized he had forgotten to turn on his siren and in panic hit his horn. He hit his brakes and the antilocks pulsed furiously as the rubber squealed. He missed the woman by a breath who fortunately had frozen in place clutching her child. His eyes were drawn to his rear view mirror wondering what had happened to his charge. There it was swinging on to the street as its right track heaved slightly over the remains of a small car, and it was bearing down on him. He stomped the gas pedal to the floor. The big police interceptor engine in his Crown Vic responded leaving smoking strips of rubber on the pavement.

For an awful moment it was still gaining on him. After what seemed forever he was finally pulling away. But, he was doing over fifty and First Street was a half block ahead, and there he had to make a left turn. His siren was blaring. Once again he left dashed strips of rubber on the pavement as his antilocks went into action. This was the last corner. Tiffner could hear his tires complaining as he rounded it, and gritted his teeth at what he saw happening behind him.

The police car skidded around the corner heading to the left at the next intersection. Finally, Martinez saw a sign for Hospital with an arrow pointing to the left so it confirmed they were going in the right direction. The problem he now had was that he wasn't sure how well the tank would slide around the corner. If he were not careful he'd lose a track so he rounded out his turn as much as possible. Angling to the left he cut across the parking lane, and the sidewalk aiming to miss the building on the corner by as little as possible. Unfortunately, there was a steel post that supported the traffic lights for that corner squarely in his line of travel. And, ah gee, there was a bicycle chained to the light post. A kid was surely going to be disappointed.

The post was solid and it caused the tank to shudder as it bent over the armor on the front of the hull. Fortunately, there were no cars in the intersection but one was approaching the light. He veered to the right in front of the car and then pressed the brake for the left tread. The tank slid to the far side of the street and shoved a car over the curb. First Street also had a traffic lane each way and a center turn lane. Correcting for his skid he straddled the traffic and turn lanes. Guess a tank will slide on pavement, he thought. The street light mast slid off the turret and got caught under the left track. The top bar of the light stand whipped over and tore off the front wheel of a delivery truck that happened to be in the wrong place at precisely the right time.

He twisted the throttle to the limit again and the police car increased speed with it. They were getting the hang of this. The going was good down this broad straight avenue. A calmness settled over Martinez as he sped along. He accepted the fact that he had done so much damage that anything more could hardly make any difference. Though he remained deeply concerned about the crew in the turret, he was getting a distinct satisfaction as he remembered seeing people along the way gaping at what was befalling their sweet little town. "We want the big weapons, and we want kids to use them. We know cities will be destroyed with them, but it must always be somebody else's city."

At last, there was the big sign for "Saint Gabriel's Hospital and Retirement Home - Emergency Entrance." A police car with lights flashing stopped oncoming traffic at the turn-off to the hospital. Martinez made a left behind the police car he was following. A block further there was another police car with lights flashing and a policeman beside it motioning to make another left. A hundred yards ahead was a small covered drive-up with Emergency painted on the overhead.

A man in a white suit motioned to Martinez to stop where he pointed at the ground. Martinez stopped exactly there. He set the brake, ran the engine to idle, and disappeared into the tank.

"Rod, how're you doing? Is anybody still alive? Sorry it took so long."

"Jay and Kurt are unconscious. They lost a lot of blood. I think they're still alive, though."

"I think you should get out with your bad leg. I'll come back and keep the civilians out of trouble."

Rod was already being lifted out. As Martinez tried to get into the turret to help he met a foot in the face, followed with, "Out of the way, asshole!"

Stunned, he crawled back to his driver's seat. Bad news travels fast, he thought. When he lifted his head out of his hatch, he was looking up the barrels of two cocked revolvers.

"Get out of the tank, now! Any false move and we'll shoot." Instinctively he hit the kill switch on the engine. The turbine wound down.

With tanks patrolling the farm and Cobra helicopters in the air, Breckon decided he should leave. With everyone's attention on a tank stopped in the farmyard, he sauntered away toward the road. Across the road he walked a hundred feet into the corn field and turned west. He intersected the north-south road and jogged north in the ditch. As he was abreast of the farmyard he saw Darin talking to the family that lived there. As he walked up he said, "Hi Darin. Think it's time for me to be getting out of here. Things seem to be under control." Darin thanked the family for letting him park in their yard and they were off.

As they drove to the north, Darin said. "Big ass tank came out of the corn field and almost squashed me in my car. Guess your hunch was right. I assume you got everybody out of harm's way."

"Yeah. For once things worked out okay. It'd be nice if I could get Winger off my back, though." At the intersection of Highway 46 they turned east.

0630 hours, North Memorial Hospital, Minneapolis, Minnesota

Carson was still in surgery. Daley's leg was patched up, though it was still numb from the local anesthetic. To everyone that came near him he asked if he could get information about his family, but everyone seemed too busy to care.

When the V-22 pilot and his copilot arrived in Minneapolis they were beyond the time without sleep to operate an aircraft under peacetime rules. They were allowed to leave the V-22 on the roof with the proviso they get it out of there if another emergency case needed to land. By seven o'clock they had both gotten a few hours of sleep in a lounge at the hospital. At the urging of the hospital staff they agreed to be on their way. After a few phone calls, it was decided they'd take Daley to his family and then hop over to Camp Ripley to stand down.

The V-22 lifted off into a clear August morning. The medic beside him had his helmet and headset on. He was intently listening. Finally, he leaned over and yelled to Daley, "There has been military activity this morning to the east of Little Falls."

Daley's complexion immediately went white. The crewman waved his hand. "No civilians were hurt. But a couple of pilots were killed and several reservists wounded. From what they're saying it was messy. They say it's resolved now, and we're permitted to proceed."

Twenty minutes after they left North Memorial they were circling the Klappenbach farm. They had been flying with the starboard door open since it was such a short hop, and the day so pleasant. The crewman next to Daley pointed first to a pair of Cobra helicopters and then to M1 tanks patrolling the road in front of the house and the surrounding fields. They could both see the overturned mobile home with the shattered cab. "Looks like your family can take care of themselves," he said with his mouth inches from Daley's ear. Daley looked at him and saw a wide toothy grin. Daley intently studied the small group of people until he was sure the entire family was accounted for. One of the children was pointing to the new addition in the sky.

For a moment Daley was stung as a strange sensation went through him. He thought back about how certain Breckon had been that his family would be all right. They were from all appearances as safe as humanly possible. Whatever had happened, the response had been massive. Even with tanks and helicopters, though, things could still go wrong. How could Breckon have been so sure? And Breckon had been right about another thing. If Daley had not been on that mountain top a thousand miles away, he and his entire family would be dead now.

As they circled the medic yelled to Daley. "You really shouldn't walk on the leg without crutches, you know. But, under the circumstances I suppose you will."

Daley grinned at him and yelled back, "Under the circumstances, I suppose I will."

The crew found the opportunity compelling. Pilots, especially military pilots, rarely got the opportunity to show regular people what they do. Families, friends, and the general public can walk through the aircraft at air shows, and see them fly off at a safe distance. But, they never, ever, got to take them home with them. Here was a case where they'd get to do exactly that. The farmyard was large enough to safely land between the house and the barn.

The pilot made his approach from the southeast toward the house where the people were standing. Their audience backed up as he came to a hover a couple of hundred of feet from them. The down wash from the rotors sent a small hurricane filled with loose grass and bits of dirt over the onlookers. Gracefully rotating ninety degrees so the door was facing the house, he settled the forty-thousand pound craft on the ground.

Daley waited for the plane to be firmly down, then swung his legs out the door, and gingerly stood beside the plane. Carefully he let go of his hold on the door rail, and started to walk. Part of his pant leg had been cut away so the bandage showed. He had his black hat on and his gun belt. Might as well make it look good, he thought. Ten days of black growth on his chin and the bandage on his forehead from when Dirk tackled him all added to make him look like an Old West desperado. He waved as he walked toward the people.

His oldest son of twelve, Jimmy, ran to him and said, "Dad?"

"Yeah, it's me Jimmy," Daley answered as he put his arm on his shoulder and they walked toward the others.

"Mom's been worried about you, but I told her you'd be okay."

Ann ran up and said looking at him. "I let you out of my sight for a minute, and look at you. What kind of trouble did you get into?"

Daley smiled and said, "I'm glad to see you too, sweetheart. Come on, give me a great big hug and a kiss."

She raised her chin and said, "You're dirty and stinky. I'm not going to touch you!" With that she flung her arms around his neck and planted the most passionate kiss on him he could remember.

"I think she's kinda glad to see you, Dad," Jimmy said.

The medic got out of the V-22 and carried a pair of crutches to Daley's father-in-law. "He'll need these when the anesthetic in his leg wears off," the man said with a wink.

The pilot broke ground contact, and rotated until the craft pointed toward the people. Power to the engines was increased and the V-22 ascended vertically for a couple hundred feet. From there it transitioned to level flight, and soon disappeared over the horizon to the west.

As they had prepared to land, an urgent message came to the Osprey to medevac two critical soldiers from the Little Falls Hospital. They would soon be bound for Minneapolis again.

Daley was overjoyed that everyone was okay. "Looks like they stopped that thing just in time," he said pointing. "They call them *rick-*

shaws." They all turned their attention to the overturned vehicle. The six-barrel gun could be seen sticking out of the roof as well as the holes from the spent rockets. "If they had shot at the house with that gun, you'd all be dead. Boy, that was close."

Klappenbach interjected. "It wasn't that close. But they did start shooting. If you look more closely, the house if full of bullet holes. We weren't in the house, though. We were safely in the storm cellar."

"Good thing somebody called to warn you."

"No, no," Ann said. "A young man arrived at dawn and made us get in the storm cellar. He was so insistent that we stay there, even after we all began to think he was crazy, said he knew you." She added a little incredulously, "Said, you liked to err on the side of safety? What's that all about?"

Slowly it began to dawn on Greg. "Describe him."

"Oh, about your height and build. Dark hair, blue eyes. He had a bandage on his arm, and a horizontal scar on his left cheek," she said making a movement with her hand.

"Breckon—that dog." Greg whispered.

"You know him?"

"Yeah. I know him. You were in good hands, very good hands. Where's he now?"

Klappenbach spoke, "Haven't seen him for awhile, now that you mention it. With all the commotion, seems he left."

———

Ahmad nursed the bump on his head as he waited in the shadows behind the damaged driver's cab. He had his automatic weapon, an AK-47, in his right hand. There was no way he would have accepted deployment on any mission without his trusted weapon. He had expected visitors to his little hideaway, but none had come. From what he had learned about the U.S., it occurred to him that this might be viewed as a crime scene so everybody was kept away until the proper authorities arrived. That suited his plan perfectly. He glimpsed tanks passing by so knew it was over for him. He should have been in anguish about his imminent capture, but his heart was beating fast in anticipation of what he had in mind. Things had quieted down after the big helicopter departed. It was time to make his move.

He had been thinking about the switch. Should he reset the self-destruct system? What would happen? How would he have designed it?

The vehicle lying on its side should be enough to trigger it. But having been turned off, there would logically be a time delay for maintenance personnel to get clear in case something had been done wrong. He crawled back, reached into the opening, and found the switch with his fingers. After a pause, he switched it on. Nothing happened.

Scrambling forward he worked his way out of the broken windshield into the long grass in the ditch. He crawled to the rear of the vehicle until he was hidden from the group of people by brush. In a stooped position he ran a couple of hundred feet further east. Two dull explosions from inside the vehicle followed by smoke issuing from various openings didn't surprise him.

He took a deep breath and stood. Advancing until he was visible from the waist up he fired a short burst into the air and yelled, "Allah is great! Allah be praised!" All heads instantly turned his way. There were short cries. He saw the looks. He felt the rush. They knew they were about to die.

Greg Daley saw the danger as the others did not. He was in the middle of things and yelled, "Everybody down!" The sharpness of the command had its effect. He turned as he dropped his hand to his gun and drew. As he lifted it his thumb was drawing the hammer back. It centered in front of his face as the left hand rose and clasped the right. The barrel of the automatic weapon he faced began to lower as he squeezed. The report and the recoil only served to heighten his awareness. The mass in front of his sight lurched. The hammer was back again and another report. The barrel of the AK-47 fell and began firing in the ground as the man twisted to the side. A third time the big revolver discharged. The slug hit Ahmad's head above his ear, and parts of his skull flew off as the form disappeared in the tall grass.

"Stay down!" Daley snapped as he limped forward, gun up, hammer back, finger on the trigger. No sign of movement came from the area of the fallen man. Quickly he swept the gun to the left and then right looking for more threats. He looked away from the gun. Crimson splashes on the brown, sun-ripened grass caught his eye first. Advancing, he saw the still form of a man crumpled on the ground, open, lifeless eyes staring at the sky.

The face did not look peaceful. It looked like that of the man on the mountain when Daley had watched him die. He wondered for an instant if a man who spent his life ignoring God and making himself into one, perhaps, at the point where his time ended and eternity began, saw the terrible consequences. And, as the soul left the body it, as a last act, left this look of terrible recognition on the face as a warning to others.

Daley looked around and saw no more movement near the overturned mobile home that still belched smoke. "Okay. You can get up," he said.

Ann was at his side as he holstered his gun. "Oh!" she said in a short gasp. "You killed a man."

"Yes, I did," he said with a catch in his voice. "I know some kids who need a mother to help them grow up."

"And a father," she said putting her arm around his waist.

— 36 —

Martinez sat in an examining room in the hospital with his hands cuffed behind him. No one had said anything to him except to say he was in a lot of trouble. He had asked for a drink of water and was refused. Finally, he was moved to a larger room that looked like an office that was shared by three people. It had three desks, chairs, and the usual file cabinets, bookcases, and associated paraphernalia. The policeman facing him was on the phone. He wore tiny silver bars on his shirt collars indicating he was a lieutenant. The nametag above the left pocket of his shirt said STROM. Periodically he shot Martinez an evil glance.

David Strom had risen rapidly though the ranks, and he intended to rise a lot further. He had top grades in college, and top grades in officer school. He was six feet tall, well built, and good looking. For him the human race was split into three parts, those that could help him, those that could hurt him, and the rest that didn't matter. He also had no intention of spending any longer than necessary in a backwater hick town like Little Falls, Minnesota. If he didn't get promoted to police chief in the next two years, he'd move on and try again.

The business this morning was not in his career plan. True, his plan included the possibility of terrorism. But in his plan the terrorists attacked his town, and he was in charge of stopping them. This was all wrong. A tank had run wild through his town and he couldn't even find out what the score was. The only perpetrator he could come up with was this Hispanic kid wearing a Nomex jumpsuit.

When he had objected to turning over the tank driver, the puke army colonel on the other end of this conversation went into a wild tirade. " . . . and how many dead civilians do you have in your sleepy little town? Huh? Answer. How many?"

"Well none that I know . . . . "

"I have two for sure, and counting! How many injured . . . well?"

Strom cleared his throat, "None have been reported."

"I've got five at least."

"Listen colonel, nobody takes a tank and smashes up my town. There was no battle, there were no bad guys. He came crashing into town and took over."

"Lieutenant, I spoke with one of the doctors. Another five minutes and the tank commander would have died. The gunner wasn't far behind. That driver saw what had to be done and did it. If he had been acting under my direct orders I would have had him do that! Broken things can be repaired or replaced, dead people can't! Now, where is my driver?"

"He's handcuffed sitting here on a chair."

"You creep! Un-cuff him and put him on the phone. Now!"

Martinez was un-cuffed and handed the instrument. "Corporal Martinez, this is Colonel Scranton." Martinez didn't have to be told this was his battalion commander.

"Ye-yes sir."

"Are you wounded?"

"No, sir." He didn't mention his skinned shins and elbow from when the police dragged him off the tank.

"We badly need information from you. Answer with only yes or no. Can you do that? I don't want those people getting in the way and messing with evidence or, God forbid, getting hurt."

"Yes sir."

"Did you find one of those vehicles that look like a mobile home in the gravel pit?"

"Yes sir."

"You fired a training round at close range, and when the breach opened they got small arms fire down the tube. Is that about it?"

"Yes sir."

"Do you know where that vehicle is now?"

"No sir."

"Did your crew disable it?"

"No sir."

"Did it go east from the gravel pit?"

"I don't know, sir."

"Okay. Do you feel up to driving your tank back to post?"

"Oh, yes sir. Absolutely."

"Put the police officer back on the phone."

There followed heated words back and forth, finally Colonel Scranton said. "Lieutenant, my tanks were dispatched by a direct order from the Secretary of Defense in Washington. This is way over your head. In hours there will be Home Land Security, Federal Marshals, Secret Service, FBI, CIA, FTA, and you name it crawling all over your town. Do I tell them you are the man to avoid because you won't cooperate?"

Strom was a good enough politician to know when to hold and when to fold. This was the time to fold. "Sir, I'll do as you say. We will provide him an escort. That machine is too big to go down streets and roads without warning folks it's coming."

"I agree absolutely, but do it now. Get him back here fast. We must insure no evidence walks away. Do you get my meaning?"

"Yes, sir."

Martinez saw Strom visibly struggle to compose himself. As he took his hand off the telephone receiver he looked at Martinez and said, "You. Let's go. You're getting that monstrosity out of my hair."

Walking down the hall toward the emergency entrance Strom became aware of a roar that seemed to be coming from outside. Stepping out the noise became louder to the point of being uncomfortable. He was startled to see a huge flying machine in a camouflage paint scheme settling on the helipad. He could hardly believe what he saw. But, yes, his eyes had not deceived him. It had MARINES painted on the side. How could they react so fast?

Breckon had Harris drop him off at the Har Mar Mall shopping center in Roseville after bumming fifty dollars off him. He went to the men's room on the main mall. To his relief he saw no surveillance cameras in the long corridor leading to it, nor in the room itself. He had been living in his clothes for a week, though he didn't look too bad other than needing a new shirt. Washing up the best he could, he knew what he needed was a shower, but he saw no way that would happen here.

He went out to the mall and bought a golf shirt that covered the bandage on his arm. Then he had to do it. He got the company number out of the phone book, and made the call.

"Yes. Who is this?"

The voice made him tingle. To say he liked her was an understatement. He had been in love with her since shortly after they'd met. Of course, it took him much longer to realize this. Or was that her idea? He never knew for sure when he was around her. Women were so complicated.

"It's Ed," he stammered. He cleared his throat and tried again. "It's Ed Breckon. I need to see you. It's very important. Got back from a trip to the mountains a bit ago. If you haven't seen it on TV yet, you will."

After hesitating she answered. "Oh, I see," she said as she lowered her voice. "Everybody in the place is on the net watching the story on their computer monitors. They're looking for a rogue CIA agent. It's a nationwide man hunt. Could I make a guess here?"

"Yes you can. I need help. I was set up. Wait fifteen minutes or so after we hang up so nobody will be suspicious. Come to Barns and Nobel at Har Mar Mall, used books. Along the way think of a place, you know what I mean, for a few days. Don't say anymore. Okay?"

"Yeah, sure, Meg. I can make it on Saturday. Now, I have to get back to work. Okay, see you, bye."

She's good, Ed thought as he hung up the phone. Now to stay inconspicuous for the next half hour. He went back to the men's room and sat in a stall. It was one place where no body could see him. He kept checking to be sure his shirt sleeve covered the entire bandage. After twenty-five minutes he entered Barnes and Nobel from the mall, and went to the used book section. He worked his way around the stacks to stay in an aisle where he was alone. At last she was there. As always, she looked great as she picked a book off the rack on the opposite side of the aisle.

"Well, you don't look quite as bad as last time. Do you need a doctor?" she asked coolly.

"Sooner or later," he said as he pulled up his sleeve a little. "Right now I have to find a place where I'm out of sight for a few days. It'll sort itself out. But, I need time."

"I know a place. How do we do this?"

"You leave and get your car. I'll leave a few minutes after you. I'll go to the south end of the mall and turn left. Pick me up in the back, less traffic there. That sound okay?"

"Yeah. Guess so."

"Good. I'll be there."

When Ed was in the car he laid the passenger's side seat back so he was out of sight until they were a mile from the mall. As they drove he said, "I thought I had found the most mundane job there was. Now, once again I save the world, and I'm in trouble."

"Can't you go to the police?"

Ed shook his head. "It's the police, FBI, CIA, NSA, you name it, that will be looking for me, and not to say thanks. I've been setup by the Chinese to look like the rogue CIA agent you saw on the news."

"At first they said it was a meteor that hit the plane, now the Chinese are really making a stink saying it wasn't a meteor at all, but that the U.S. tried to shoot it down with a missile?"

"The Chinese had a missile from orbit locked on it, and the plane would have gone down in a ball of fire. Another guy and I managed to trick the system and save the plane. We had the missile headed for the top of a mountain when the plane flew between it and the designated spot and got nicked anyway. I was supposed to try to save the plane, and they must have thought I could never do what I did. One of the CIA guys thinks I tried to shoot it down and failed. We ran into those two local CIA guys on the way out there. We made sort of a joint operation out of it. But, I think they were after me more than any terrorists. So, they were in the vicinity at the time, but didn't see what I did to save the plane. Where are you taking me?"

"The CIA guys wouldn't be Mel and Burl, would they?"

"The same. And, they haven't gotten any nicer since the first time. You still haven't told me where we're going."

Cindy giggled. "I know the perfect place, but I'm not sure you'll agree."

"Try me. It might surprise you how desperate I am."

"Well, there's a Catholic parish in St. Paul that I'm familiar with. They have a large old rectory with plenty of guest rooms. They'll be obliging if you come up with the room and board."

Breckon rolled his eyes up and said, "You just don't give up, do you God?"

— Epilog —

Mel Winger was understandably livid when he awoke to find Ed Breckon had slipped away from him at the hospital. His options were to put out an all-points-bulletin and try to apprehend him, or to wait for him to show up. The APB could be a lot of effort with no results, and it would point out that it was none other than himself that had let the "prisoner" get away. When his anger cooled, and he found that Burl would likely make it, he became more rational. From all the effort he had expended digging into Breckon's life from the last operation, he knew enough about him to know he'd show up sooner rather than later. He could wait. The other disturbing thing was that the medics on the V-22, as well as the doctors in the emergency room, said without Breckon's coat and stocking cap, Carson would have surely died. It could be hard slapping a guy in jail who had saved the life of a federal agent.

Breckon wasn't too worried that events would sort themselves out. He knew Mel Winger had a grudge against him. But, with the testimony of Swensen as to what happened on the mountain, and Daley and his in-laws as to what happened in central Minnesota, it would be hard to make a case that he was a rogue CIA operative, or anything of the sort.

Before picking up Ed, Cindy made a call to St. Isador's and talked to Fr. Aldrich. Cindy parked in the lot between the church and the school and they went to the back door. Two short and a long ring on the door-bell opened the door at once. After introductions, Cindy returned to work. Ed was not at all unhappy with the arrangements. There had been many dark nights as he tried to make sense of the things that had happened in the last several years. Maybe he could get help here. In a strange way, he looked at his present situation as a new beginning.

About the Author

In writing any story the author tends to put some of his life experiences into it, even if distorted and rearranged. That is true of this tale. Having spent many years of his life as an engineer either designing equipment and instruments or managing engineering projects, there was ample opportunity to witness some odd things. It is his belief that nearly everyone has experiences which, if changed a little here and there and put into the appropriate setting, could make a novel. In fact, when some people recount hunting or fishing stories one gets the feeling they embellish the details to the point where it sounds a bit like fiction.

On his one, and only, trip to China in 2001 the author's connecting flight inside China was delayed many hours into the late evening. All through the wait, he observed the people intently watching the monitors at the Beijing airport. Whatever their concern, it was clearly serious business. To his relief the issue was decided to their satisfaction as the people burst into shouts of glee. It was only after boarding the plane to go from Beijing to Nanjing that the man in the adjacent seat spoke to him and he leaned that China had, moments before, been awarded the 2008 summer Olympics.

The setting in the Beartooth wilderness is a compendium of several trips to those parts made by the author with his sons. The book's cover is a composite of several photos we took along the way and the small body of water is the middle tank.

www.ingramcontent.com/pod-product-compliance
Lightning Source LLC
Chambersburg PA
CBHW032227010726
47494CB00002B/379